KATIE THE CATSITTER

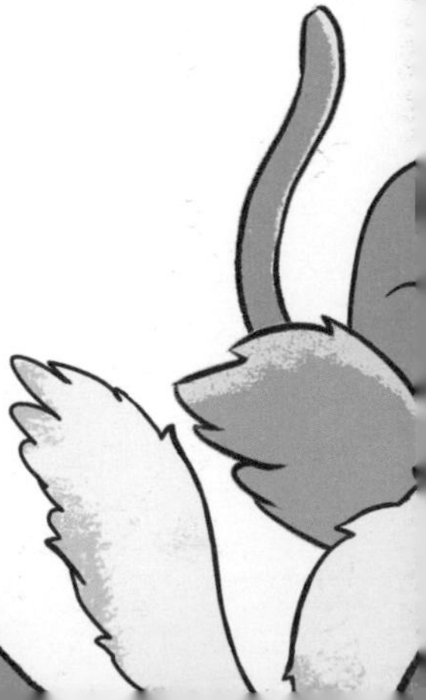

Random House New York

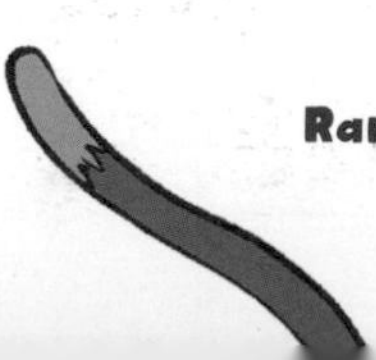

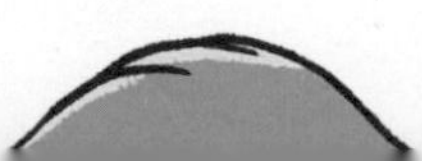

KATIE THE CATSITTER

Colleen AF Venable

ILLUSTRATED BY
Stephanie Yue

WITH COLORS BY
Braden Lamb

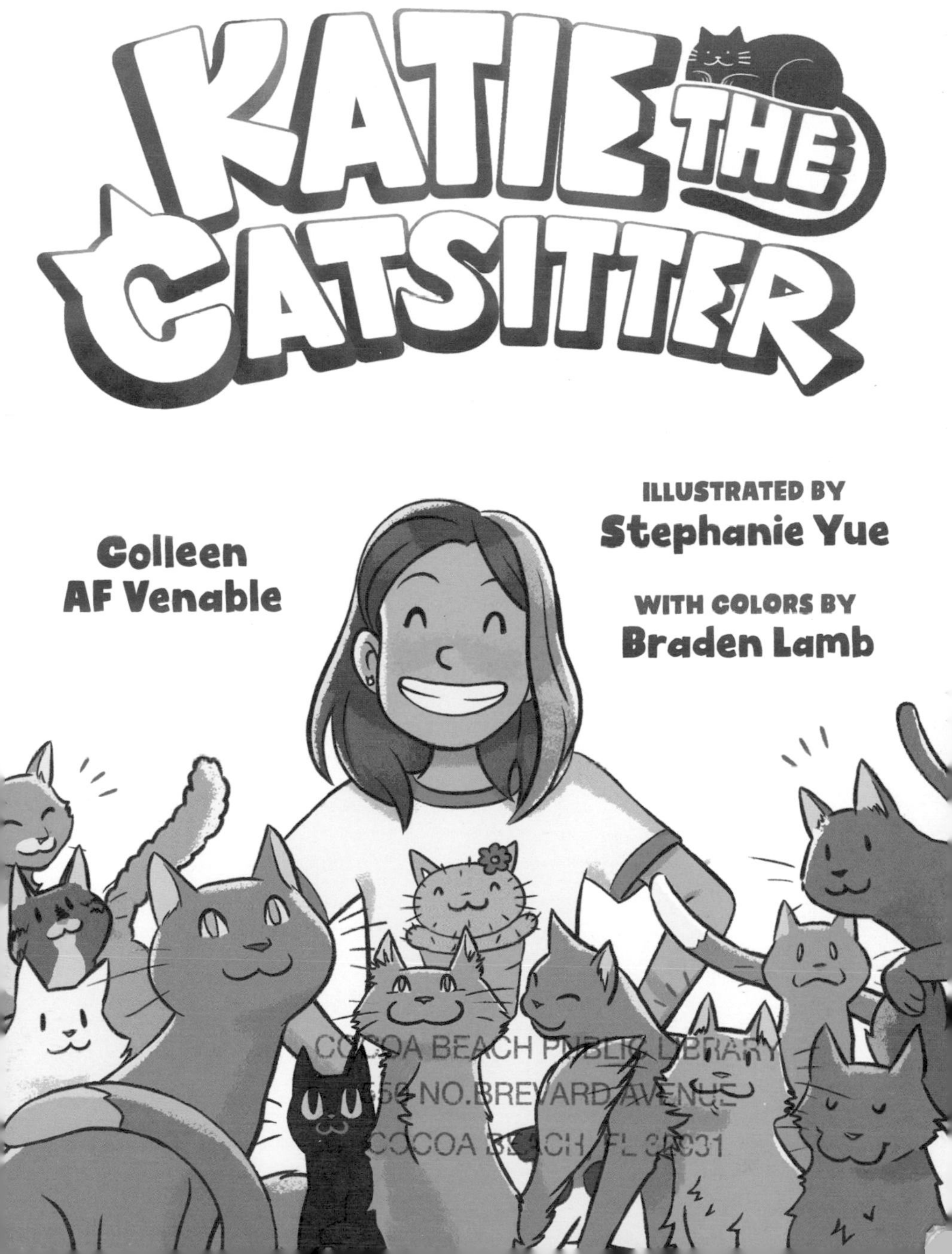

This is a work of fiction. Names, characters, places, and incidents either are the product of the author's imagination or are used fictitiously. Any resemblance to actual persons, living or dead, events, or locales is entirely coincidental.

Special thanks to coloring assistants, Shelli Paroline and Sam Bennett

 Published in the United States by Random House Children's Books, a division of Penguin Random House LLC, New York.

Random House and the colophon are registered trademarks of Penguin Random House LLC.

Visit us on the Web! rhcbooks.com

Educators and librarians, for a variety of teaching tools, visit us at RHTeachersLibrarians.com

Library of Congress Cataloging-in-Publication Data is available upon request.
ISBN 978-0-593-30632-1 (hardcover)
ISBN 978-1-9848-9563-9 (pbk.)
ISBN 978-1-9848-9564-6 (lib. bdg.)
ISBN 978-1-9848-9565-3 (ebook)

Book design by Stephanie Yue and Sylvia Bi

MANUFACTURED IN CHINA
10 9 8 7 6
First Edition

To Teri, Mrs. B, and all the other brave souls who gave me pet-sitting, babysitting, and other odd jobs as a kid. P.S. I'm sorry I killed all your plants.

—C.A.F.V.

To Hotpot, Cho Cho, Cleopatra, Mayhem, and Ginger, mayor of Central Square. To all the cats still with us, all the cats who have left us, and all the cats I have yet to meet.

—S.Y.

CHAPTER ONE

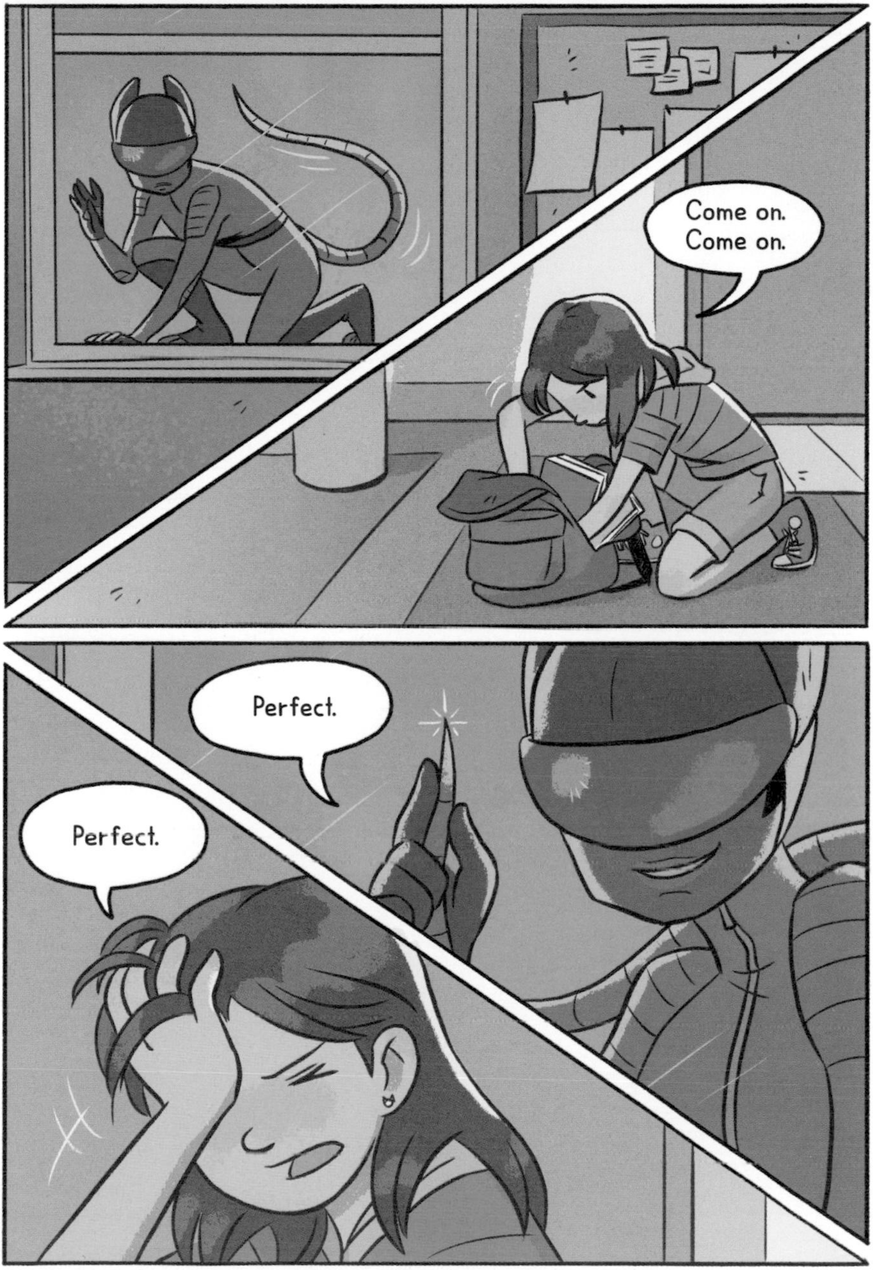
Come on.
Come on.
Perfect.
Perfect.

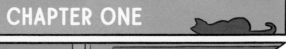

Oh, hello, keys.
I see you decided to
stay home today.

4

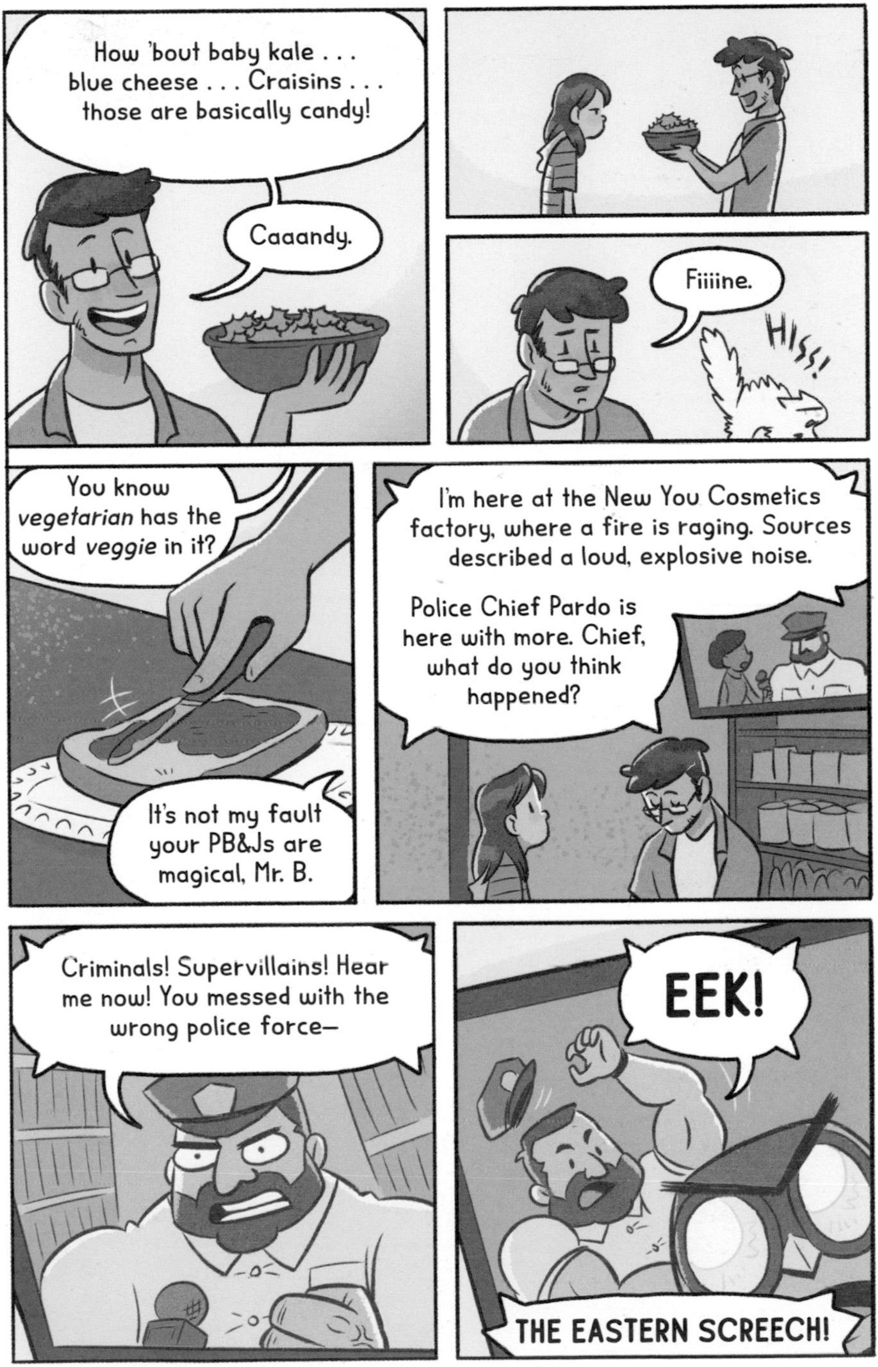
How 'bout baby kale . . . blue cheese . . . Craisins . . . those are basically candy!
Caaandy.
Fiiiine.
HISS!
You know *vegetarian* has the word *veggie* in it?
It's not my fault your PB&Js are magical, Mr. B.
I'm here at the New You Cosmetics factory, where a fire is raging. Sources described a loud, explosive noise.
Police Chief Pardo is here with more. Chief, what do you think happened?
Criminals! Supervillains! Hear me now! You messed with the wrong police force—
EEK!
THE EASTERN SCREECH!

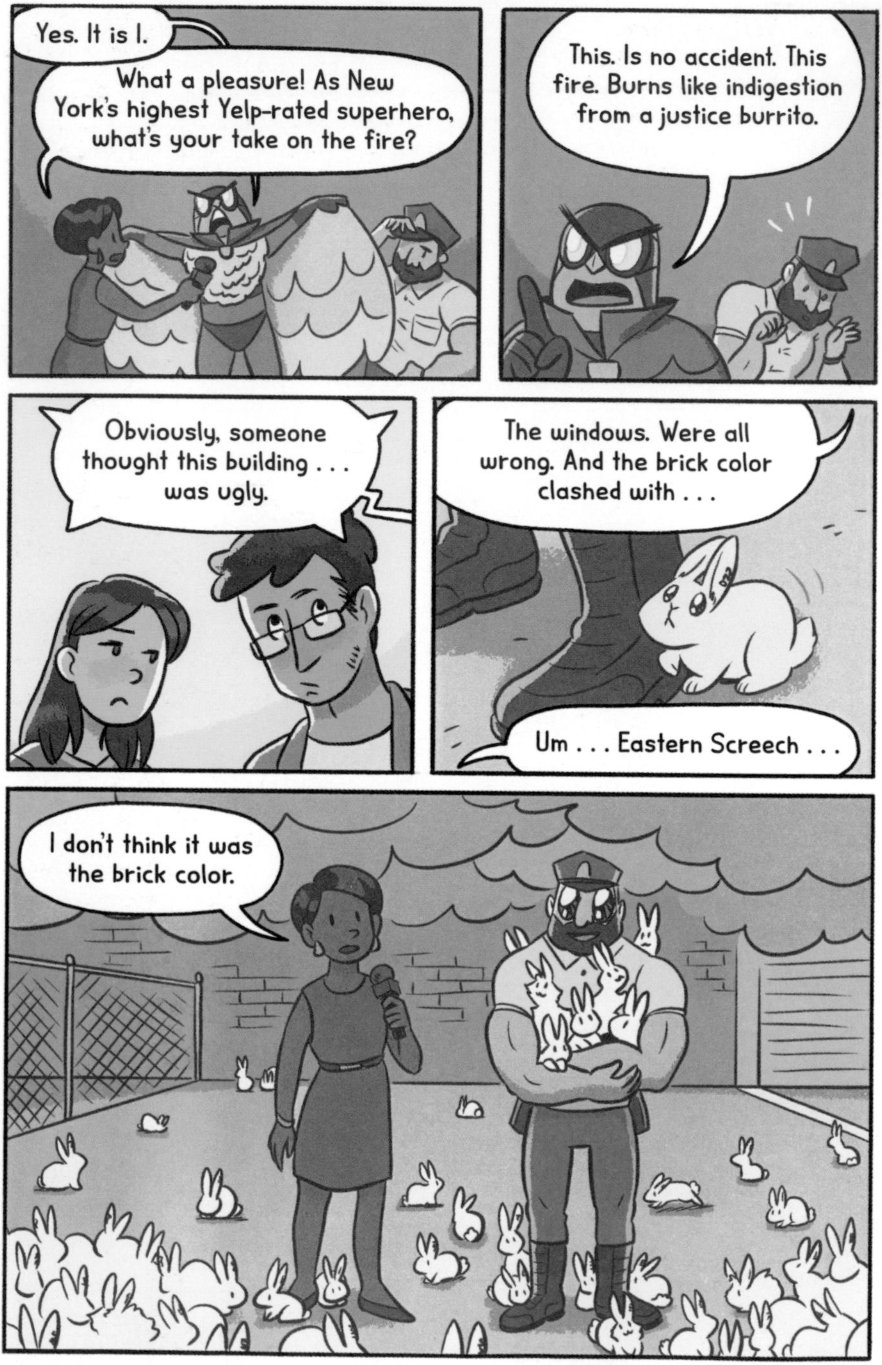
Yes. It is I.
What a pleasure! As New York's highest Yelp-rated superhero, what's your take on the fire?
This. Is no accident. This fire. Burns like indigestion from a justice burrito.
Obviously, someone thought this building . . . was ugly.
The windows. Were all wrong. And the brick color clashed with . . .
Um . . . Eastern Screech . . .
I don't think it was the brick color.

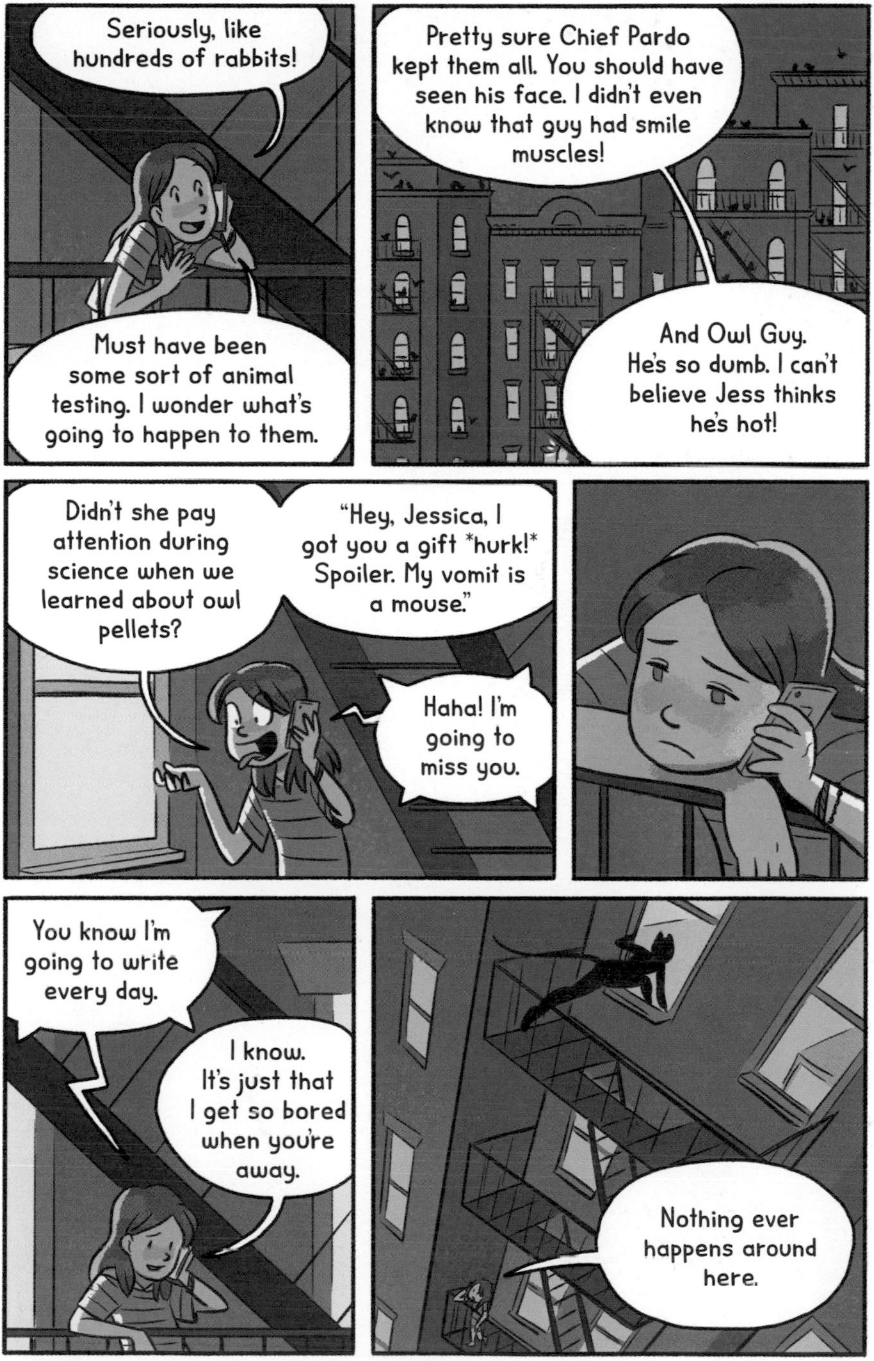
Seriously, like hundreds of rabbits!
Must have been some sort of animal testing. I wonder what's going to happen to them.
Pretty sure Chief Pardo kept them all. You should have seen his face. I didn't even know that guy had smile muscles!
And Owl Guy. He's so dumb. I can't believe Jess thinks he's hot!
Didn't she pay attention during science when we learned about owl pellets?
"Hey, Jessica, I got you a gift *hurk!* Spoiler. My vomit is a mouse."
Haha! I'm going to miss you.
You know I'm going to write every day.
I know. It's just that I get so bored when you're away.
Nothing ever happens around here.

You're still awake?

Thought you might want a hot breakfast to kick off your last week of school.

Marcus made it special at the end of my shift, so when I say hot, I mean HOT.

Too hot.

Too hot? No such thing!

I'm in heaven.

I will never understand your iron stomach.

Eff you can 'eel ya 'ongue, it's 'ot 'ot enough.

Anything exciting happen last night?

GLUG GLUG

Did you see the news? About that factory? There were like A HUNDRED rabbits that got out, and Chief Pardo turned into a mushy pile of muscly goo! And . . .

zzz

zz

CHAPTER TWO

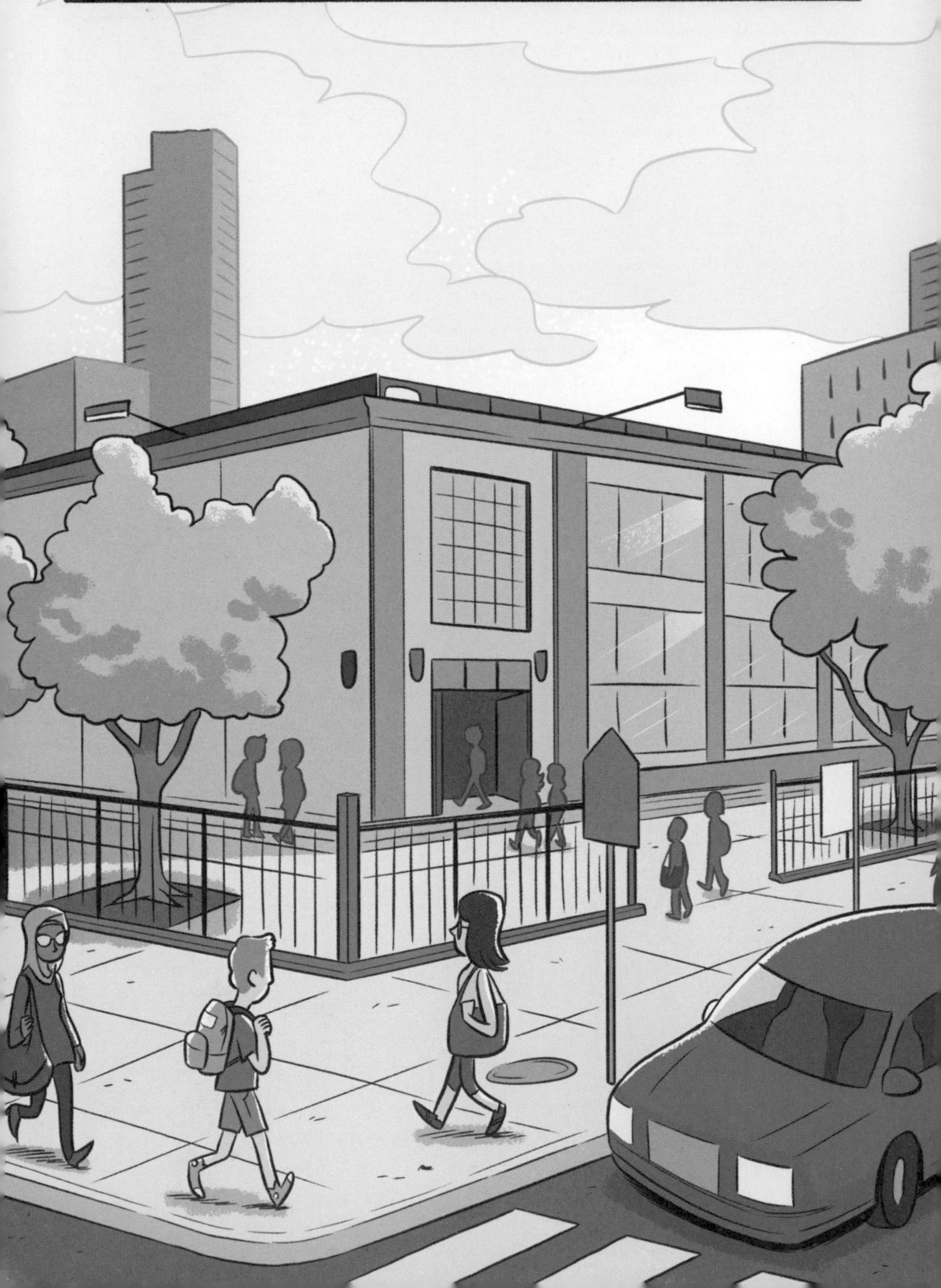

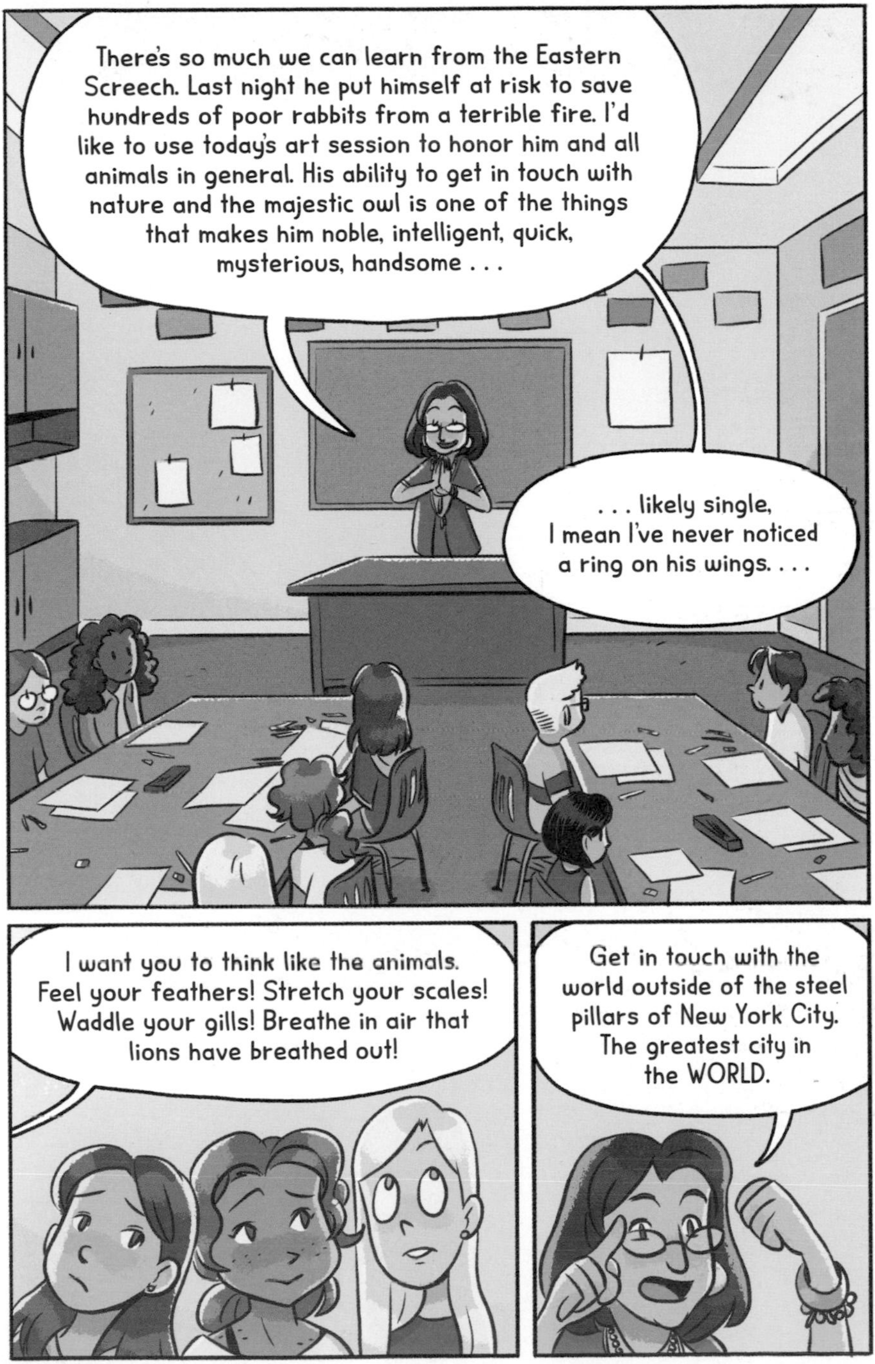
There's so much we can learn from the Eastern Screech. Last night he put himself at risk to save hundreds of poor rabbits from a terrible fire. I'd like to use today's art session to honor him and all animals in general. His ability to get in touch with nature and the majestic owl is one of the things that makes him noble, intelligent, quick, mysterious, handsome . . .
. . . likely single, I mean I've never noticed a ring on his wings. . . .
I want you to think like the animals. Feel your feathers! Stretch your scales! Waddle your gills! Breathe in air that lions have breathed out!
Get in touch with the world outside of the steel pillars of New York City. The greatest city in the WORLD.

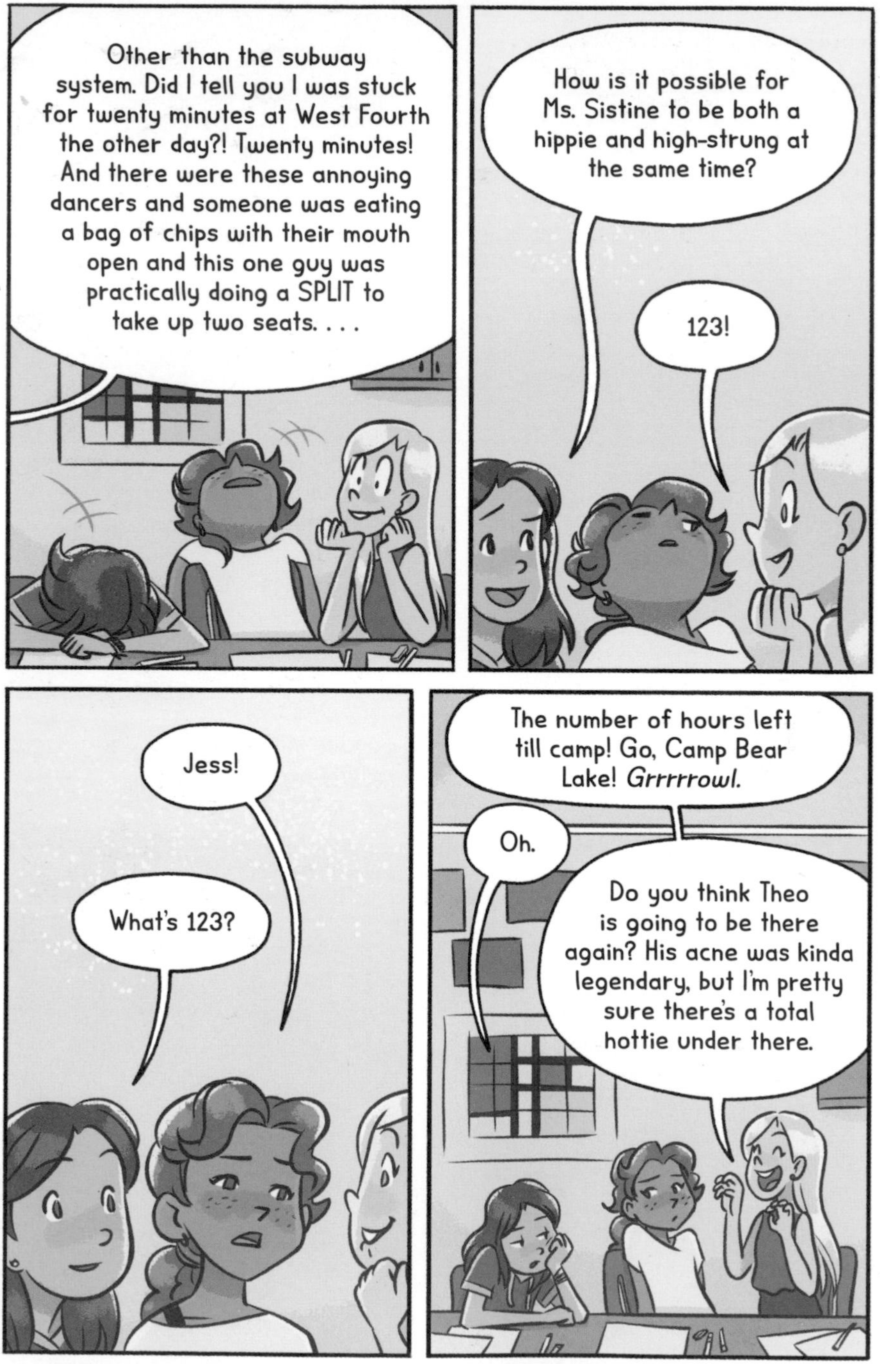
Other than the subway system. Did I tell you I was stuck for twenty minutes at West Fourth the other day?! Twenty minutes! And there were these annoying dancers and someone was eating a bag of chips with their mouth open and this one guy was practically doing a SPLIT to take up two seats. . . .
How is it possible for Ms. Sistine to be both a hippie and high-strung at the same time?
123!
Jess!
What's 123?
The number of hours left till camp! Go, Camp Bear Lake! *Grrrrrowl.*
Oh.
Do you think Theo is going to be there again? His acne was kinda legendary, but I'm pretty sure there's a total hottie under there.

Be one with nature! Embrace the void! Smell the manure!

A cow? Something has to make the manure we're supposed to smell.

What are you gonna draw?

I'm gonna draw that red-tailed hawk we saw last summer. Remember when we were hiking Mount . . .

Jess! Enough about camp!

No, it's okay. I'd be excited too . . . if I was going.

You should totally come! Bethany, don't you think she should come? There's four weeks. I bet you can get into one of them. I'm sure they can find some space for you!

Yeah, it's not really a space issue.

Jess has a point. You don't have to go to ALL the sessions. It would be so much fun to have you there for one! Maybe the week of the canoe races? Or nocturnal week, where we get to stay up crazy late!

It'd be so fun! I can get my mom to spot you for one week. . . .

I should really focus on my cow.

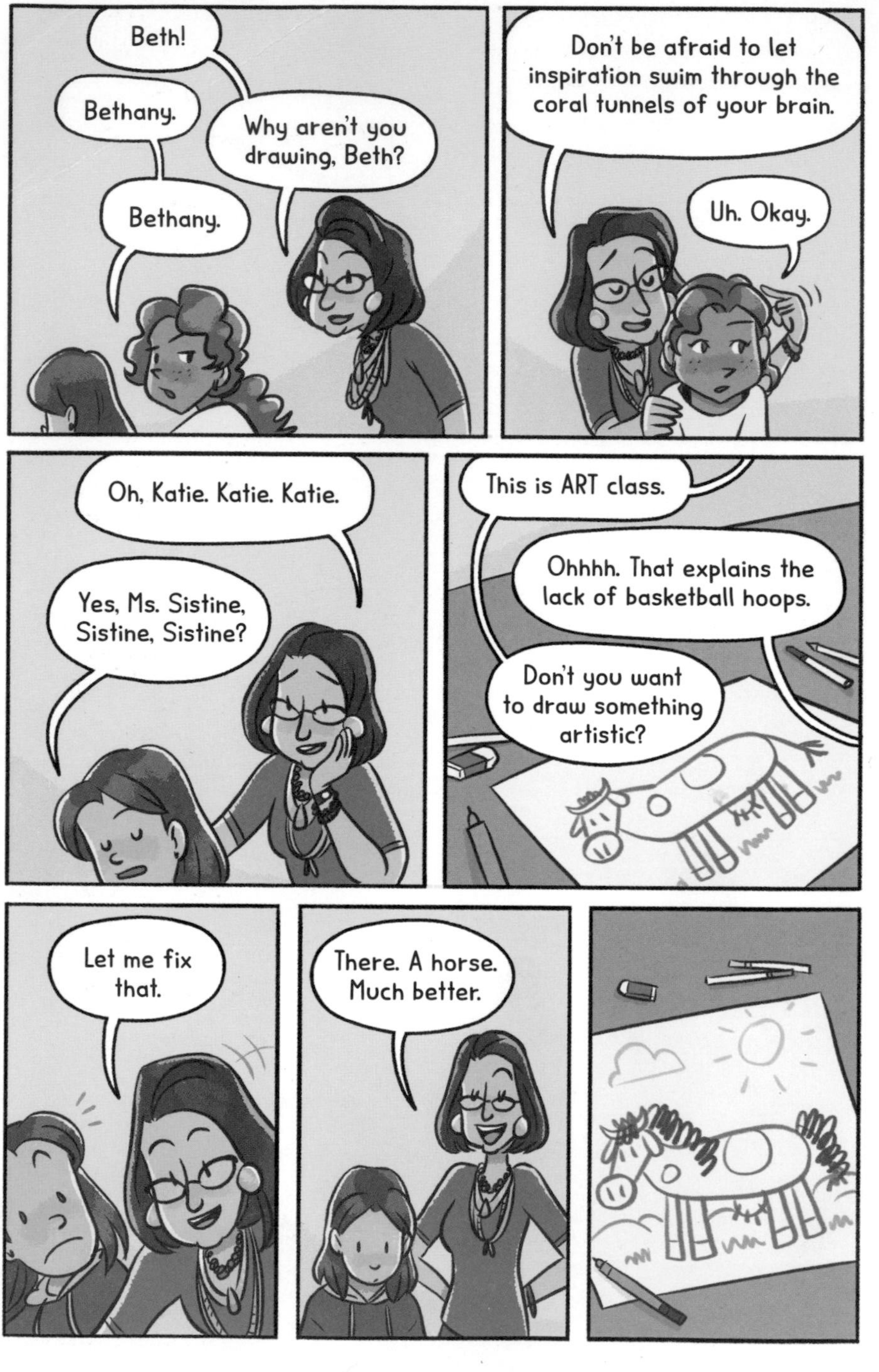
Beth!
Bethany.
Why aren't you drawing, Beth?
Bethany.
Don't be afraid to let inspiration swim through the coral tunnels of your brain.
Uh. Okay.
Oh, Katie. Katie. Katie.
Yes, Ms. Sistine, Sistine, Sistine?
This is ART class.
Ohhhh. That explains the lack of basketball hoops.
Don't you want to draw something artistic?
Let me fix that.
There. A horse. Much better.

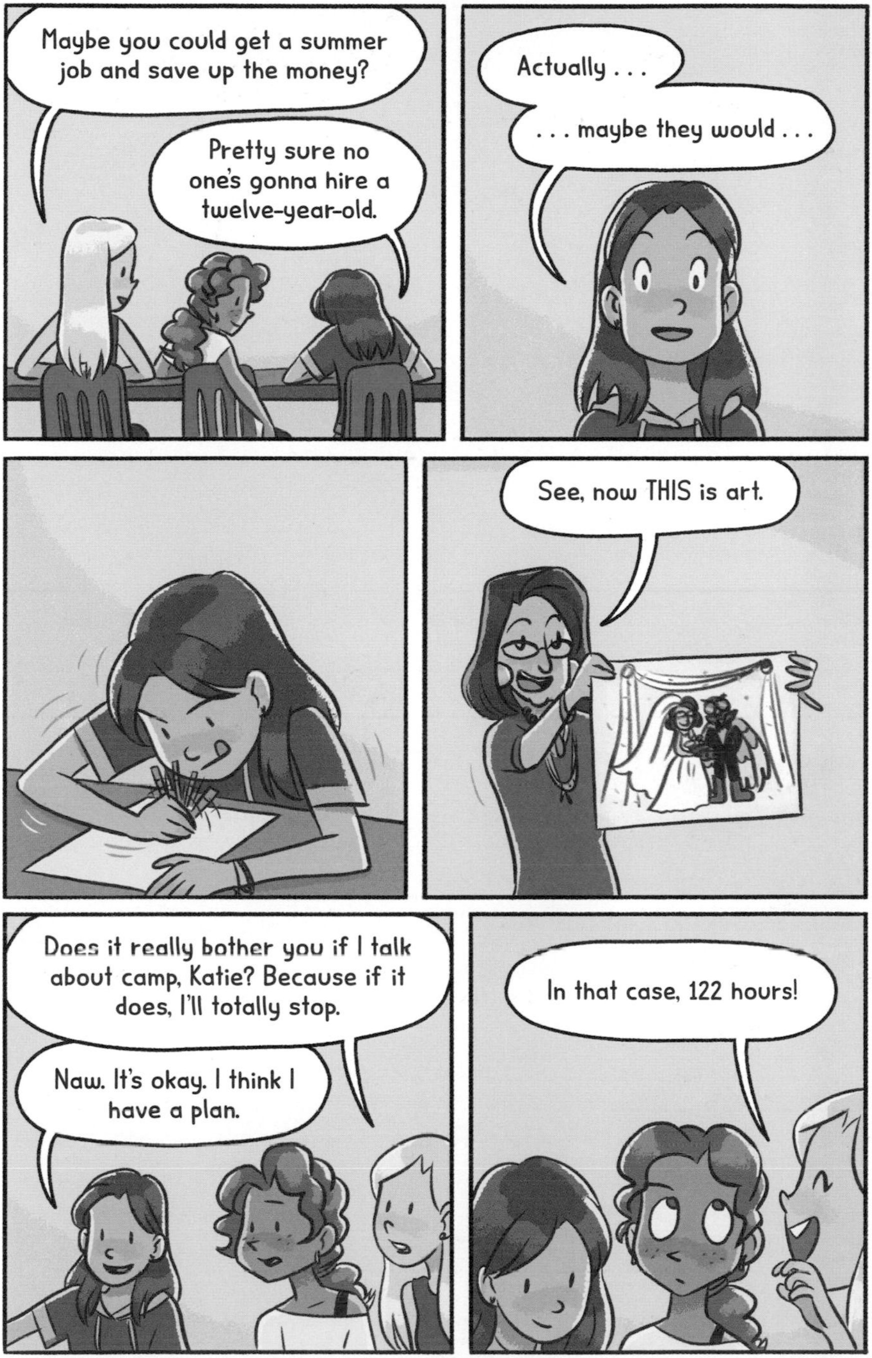
Maybe you could get a summer job and save up the money?
Pretty sure no one's gonna hire a twelve-year-old.
Actually . . .
. . . maybe they would . . .
See, now THIS is art.
Does it really bother you if I talk about camp, Katie? Because if it does, I'll totally stop.
Naw. It's okay. I think I have a plan.
In that case, 122 hours!

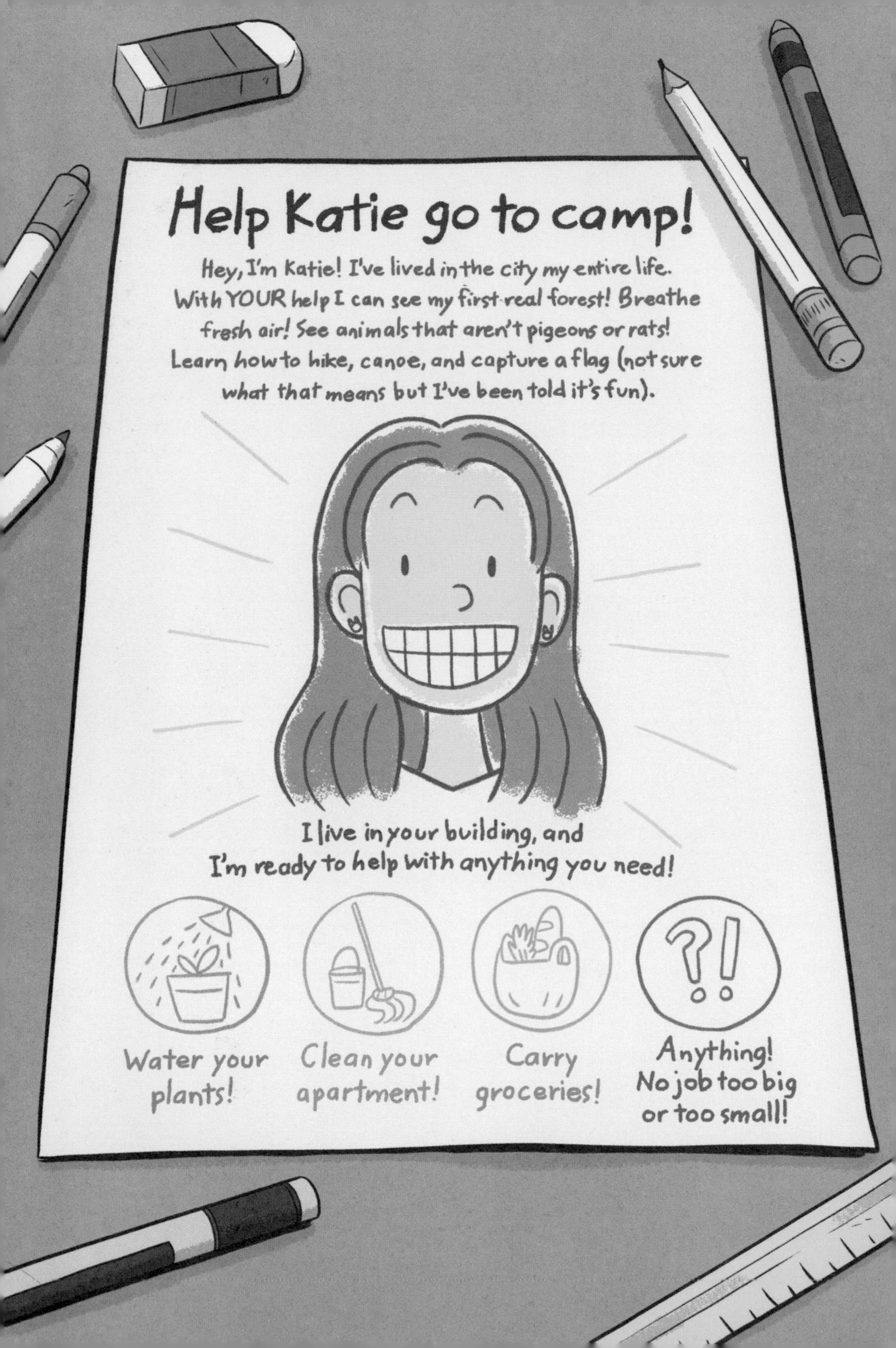
Help Katie go to camp!
Hey, I'm Katie! I've lived in the city my entire life. With YOUR help I can see my first real forest! Breathe the fresh air! See animals that aren't pigeons or rats! Learn how to hike, canoe, and capture a flag (not sure what that means but I've been told it's fun).
I live in your building, and I'm ready to help with anything you need!
Water your plants!
Clean your apartment!
Carry groceries!
?!
Anything! No job too big or too small!

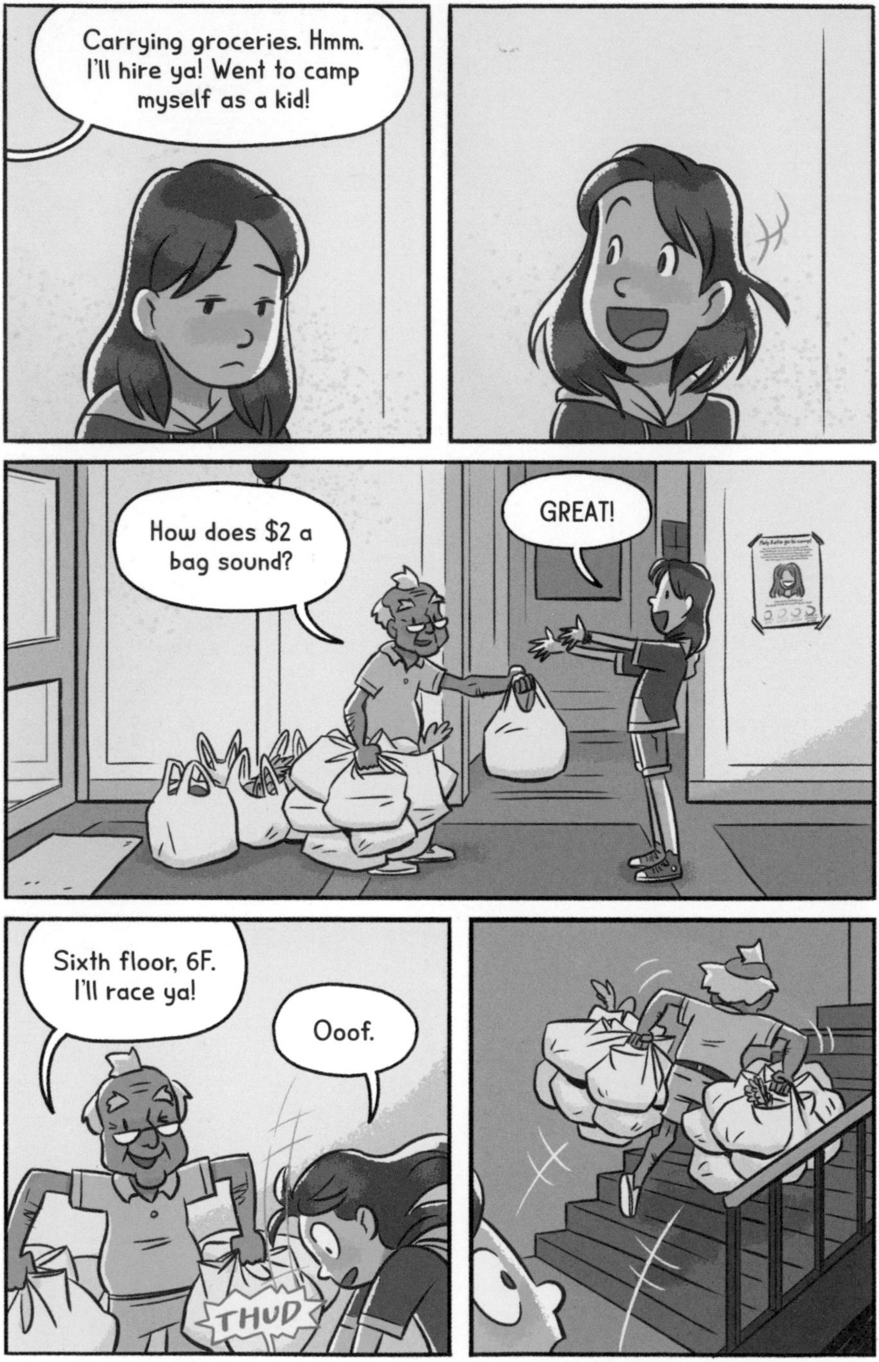
Carrying groceries. Hmm. I'll hire ya! Went to camp myself as a kid!
How does $2 a bag sound?
GREAT!
Sixth floor, 6F. I'll race ya!
Ooof.
THUD

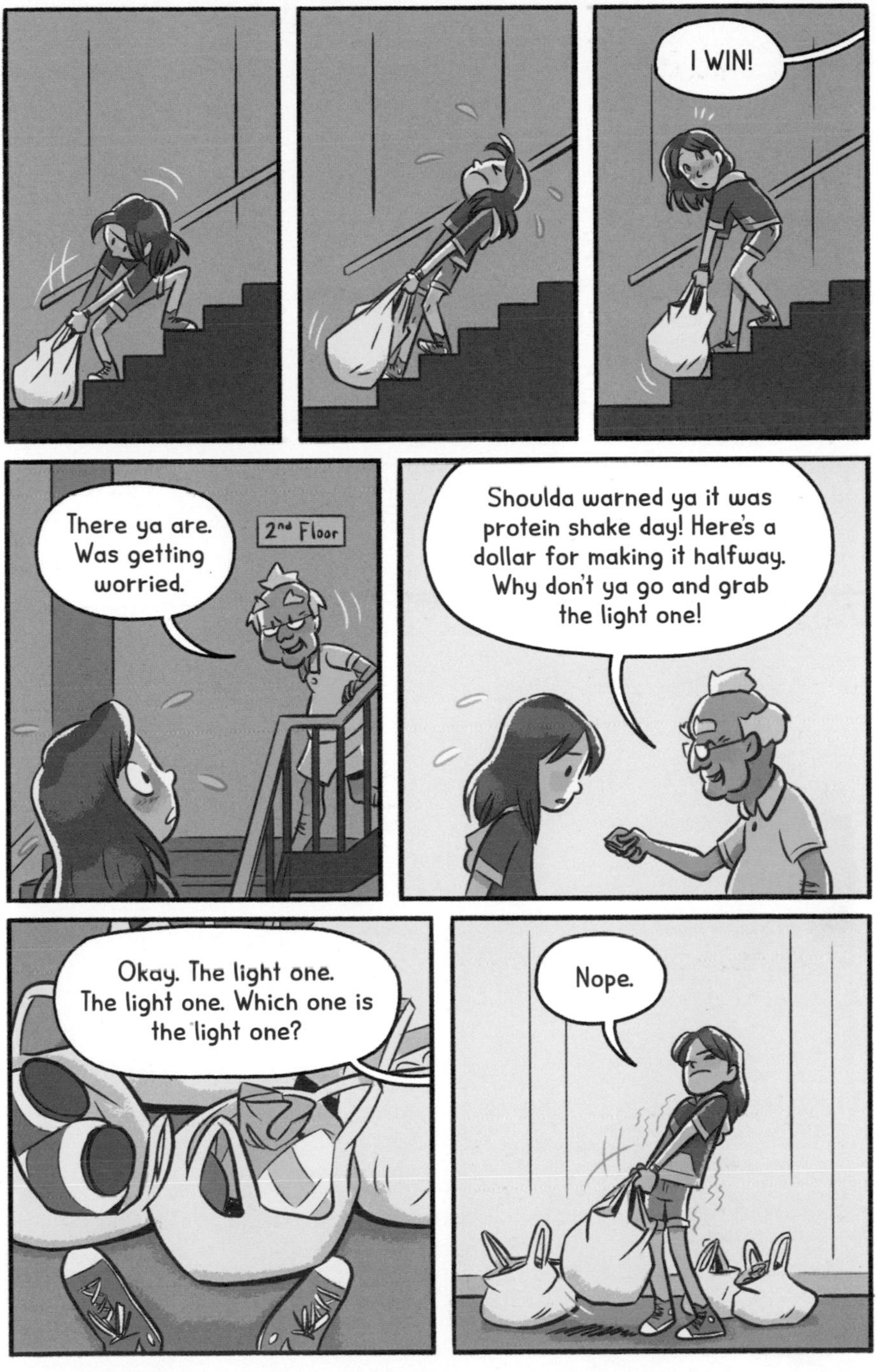
I WIN!
There ya are. Was getting worried.
2nd Floor
Shoulda warned ya it was protein shake day! Here's a dollar for making it halfway. Why don't ya go and grab the light one!
Okay. The light one. The light one. Which one is the light one?
Nope.

KNOCK-KNOCK!

Hello?

3

Oh, good! You're home.

KITTY!

It's KATIE.
Kay-tee.

KITTY!!

Hi, Mrs. Bell.
Hi, Marcie.
Hi, Dink-Dink.

Don't encourage her.

DINK-DINK!

Sorry.
Hi, Dimitri.

I'm leaving for my in-laws' in fifteen and my brain is all over the place. Saw your sign. Would you be willing to water my houseplants till the weekend?

YES!
That would be amazing!

Fantastic. Let's say $10 a day. Here's the spare key. No need to water the succulents. The fern needs some love, and the terrarium just needs two spray bottle spritzes, but fast ones like "spritz spritz." The moss ball needs to be soaked for five minutes, but just the moss part. DON'T wet the top leaves or it gets moldy. Got it?

Yes?

Actually, can you repeat . . .

Phew! You're a lifesaver, Katie.

Bye, KITTY!

Oh, and I almost forgot. Mr. Quinn from 6F asked me to give you this.

See you Friday!

Sorry

YOU EARNED THIS
PLEASE KEEP IT
P.S. DON'T WRITE ON CURRENCY!

CAMP FUN FUND

TUESDAY

98!

Raise your leaves if you're one of the ones I'm not supposed to water.

WEDNESDAY

71!
Groowl!

Ready for your five-minute soak, Mr. Moss Ball? At least this one is easy.

THURSDAY

54! *Grrrrow—*

—oww!

Oh no no no.

FRIDAY

Help Katie go to camp!

Hey, I'm Katie! I've lived in the city my entire life. With YOUR help I can see my first real forest! Breathe fresh air! See animals that aren't pigeons or rats! Learn how to hike, canoe, and capture a flag (not sure what that means but I've been told it's fun).

I live in your building, and I'm ready to help with anything you need!

  Clean your apartment! gr Anything! No job too big or too small!

3 P.M. LAST DAY OF SCHOOL

EACHERS' LOUNGE

26

I'm so jealous of you. There's so many free things in NY in the summer! Movies in the park. Shakespeare in the Park. Renting bikes . . .

In the park?

I wanna see REAL nature. Not just nature planted by old rich dudes.

SHOWTIME! SHOWTIME!

Ugh.

How's the saving REALLY going?

Made a whole dollar.

Hahaha!

Oh. Well, a dollar is a start!

How're your break-dancing skills? Those showtime dancers just made like twenty bucks.

Minus the cost of the lost shoe.

I think most of that was bribery money to make them stop.

Afternoon, Ms. Beth.

Bethany.

There's only ten kids in the building! You'd think he could get my name right.

You're lucky. The oldest kid in my building is a fourth of my age.

Don't.

But how will we know what it does if we don't push it?!

DO NOT PRESS

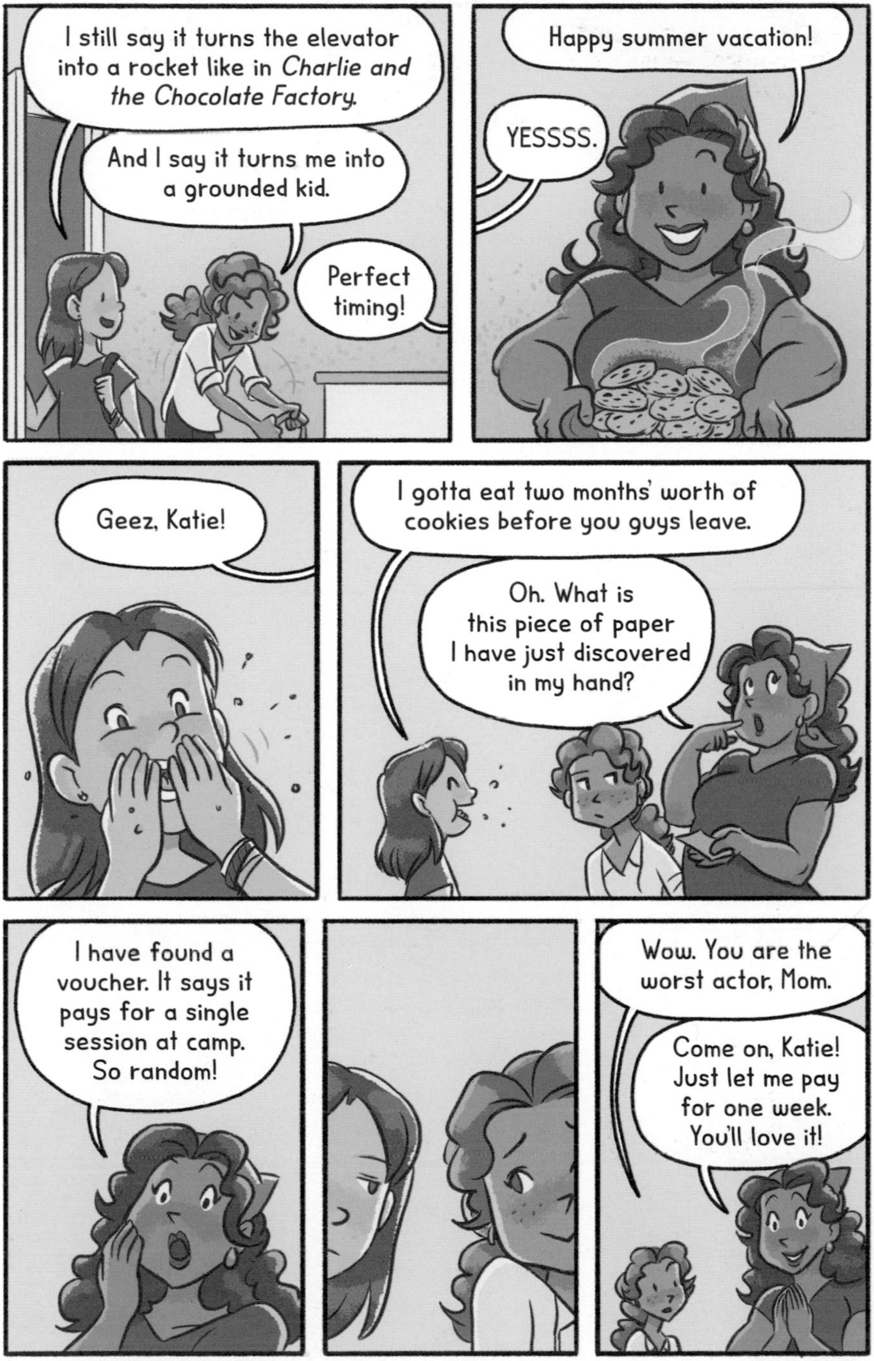
I still say it turns the elevator into a rocket like in *Charlie and the Chocolate Factory.*
And I say it turns me into a grounded kid.
Perfect timing!
Happy summer vacation!
YESSSS.
Geez, Katie!
I gotta eat two months' worth of cookies before you guys leave.
Oh. What is this piece of paper I have just discovered in my hand?
I have found a voucher. It says it pays for a single session at camp. So random!
Wow. You are the worst actor, Mom.
Come on, Katie! Just let me pay for one week. You'll love it!

It's okay, Mrs. Tinoco. I want to raise the money myself.

I HAD to try. We play games all day long, learn these cool crafts, swim in this giant lake . . . but it's never as fun as it could be because you aren't there!

Well, then I guess I have to be there this summer.

I wish you would let me help. But at least I have another surprise for you.

Just got off the phone with your mom.

Wish granted.

DAZZLING HAIR

BRIGHT COLOR

TEAL

YES!!!!

WHOA!

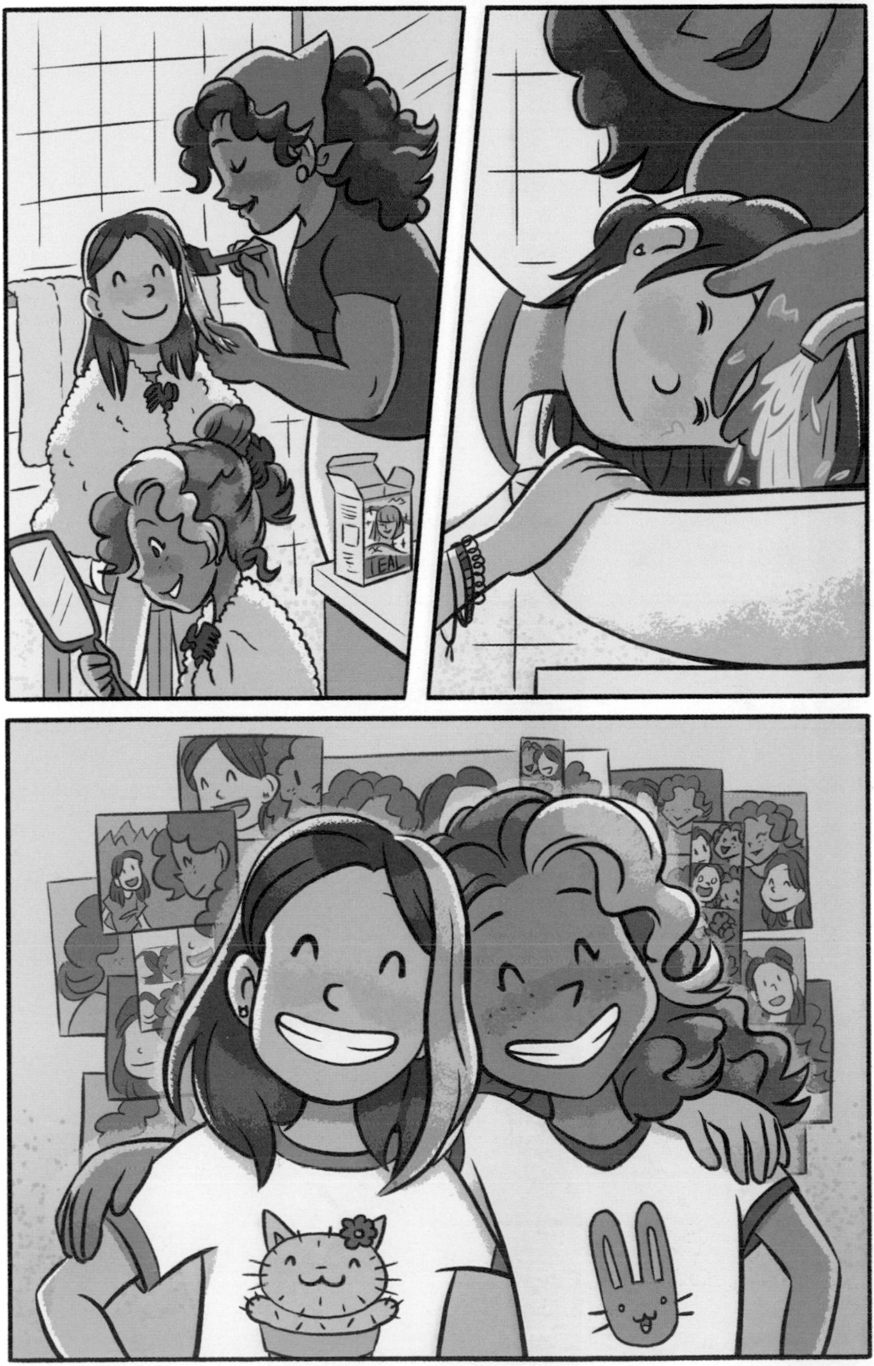
TEAL

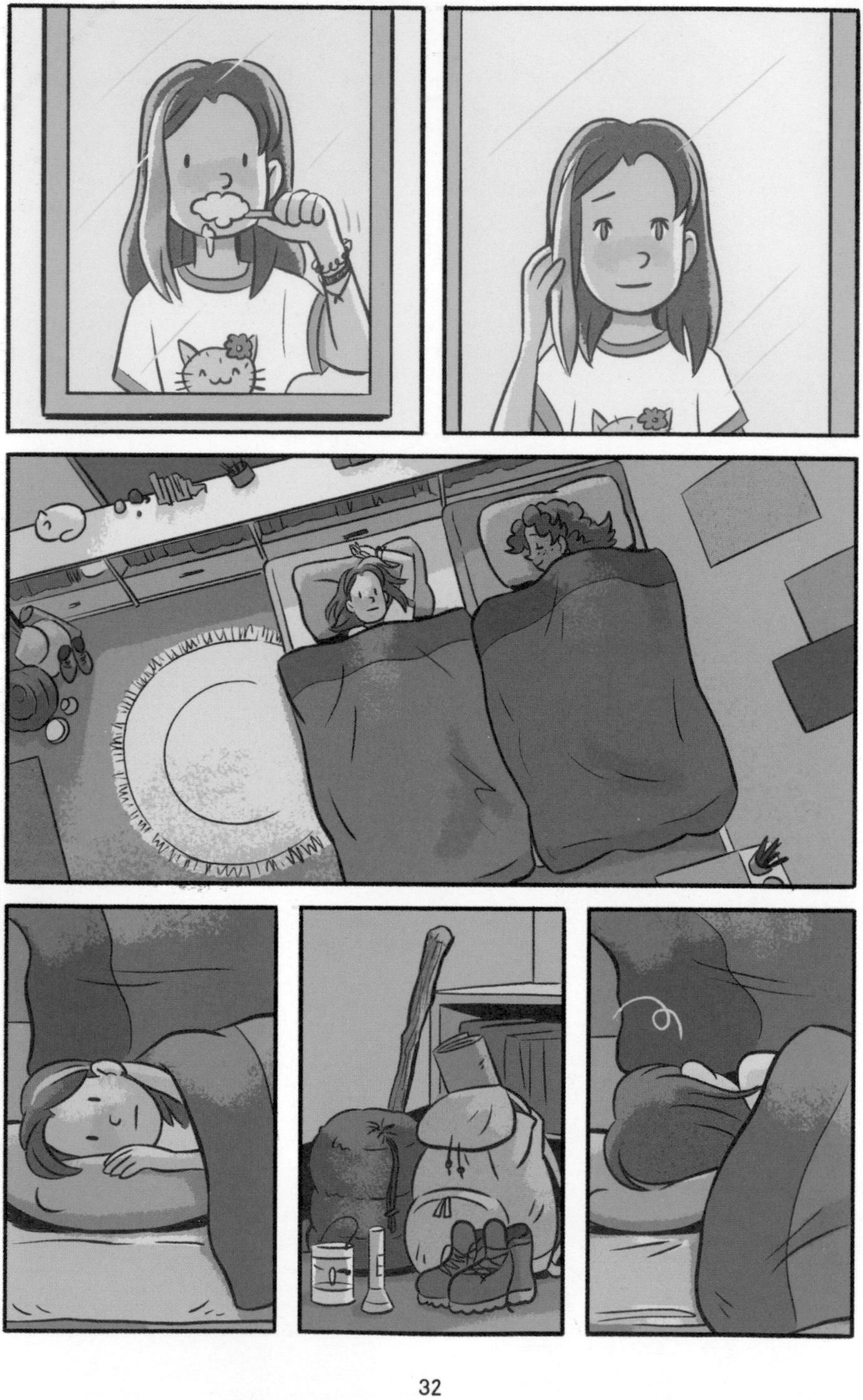

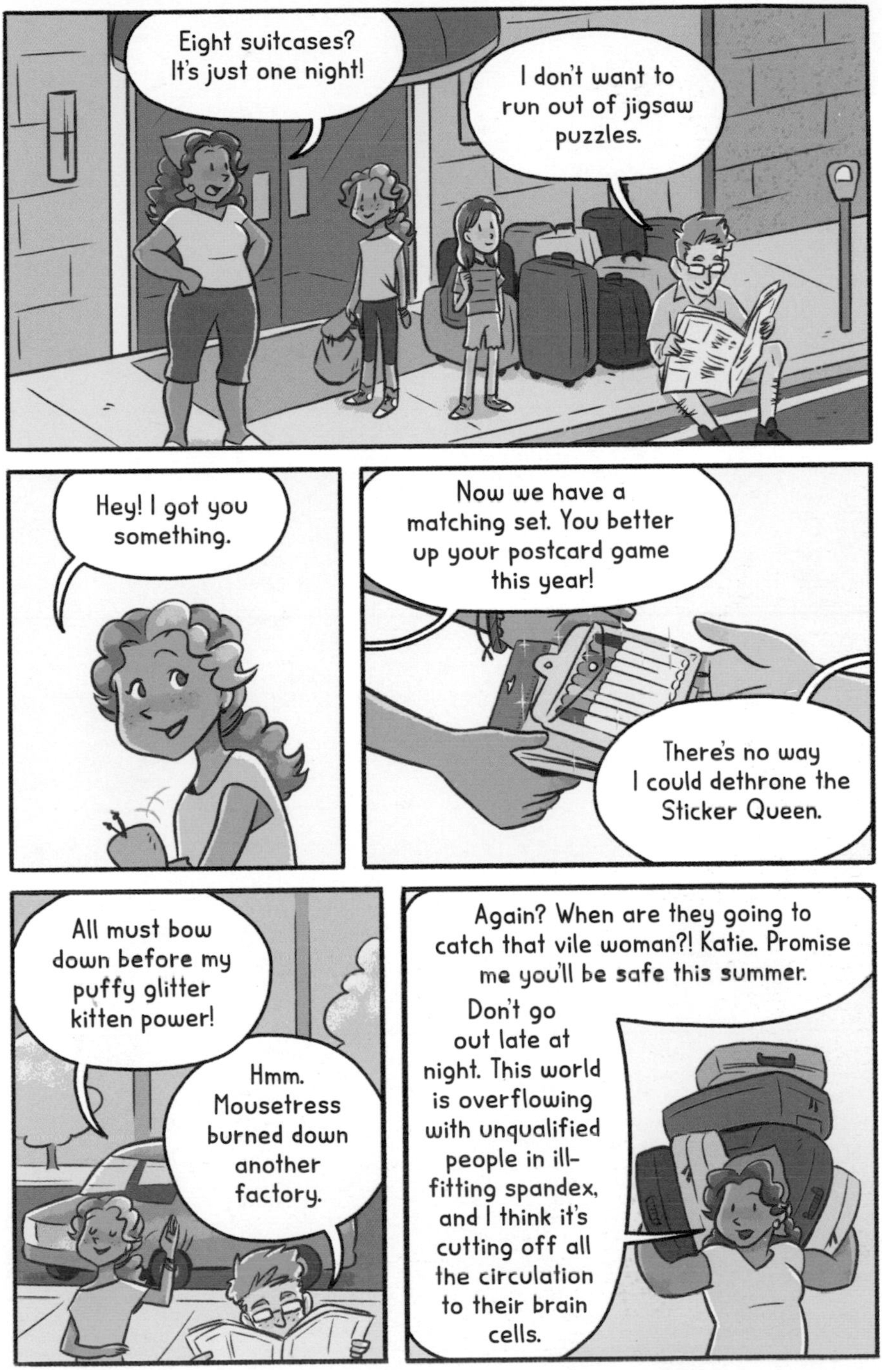

Eight suitcases? It's just one night!
I don't want to run out of jigsaw puzzles.
Hey! I got you something.
Now we have a matching set. You better up your postcard game this year!
There's no way I could dethrone the Sticker Queen.
All must bow down before my puffy glitter kitten power!
Hmm. Mousetress burned down another factory.
Again? When are they going to catch that vile woman?! Katie. Promise me you'll be safe this summer.
Don't go out late at night. This world is overflowing with unqualified people in ill-fitting spandex, and I think it's cutting off all the circulation to their brain cells.

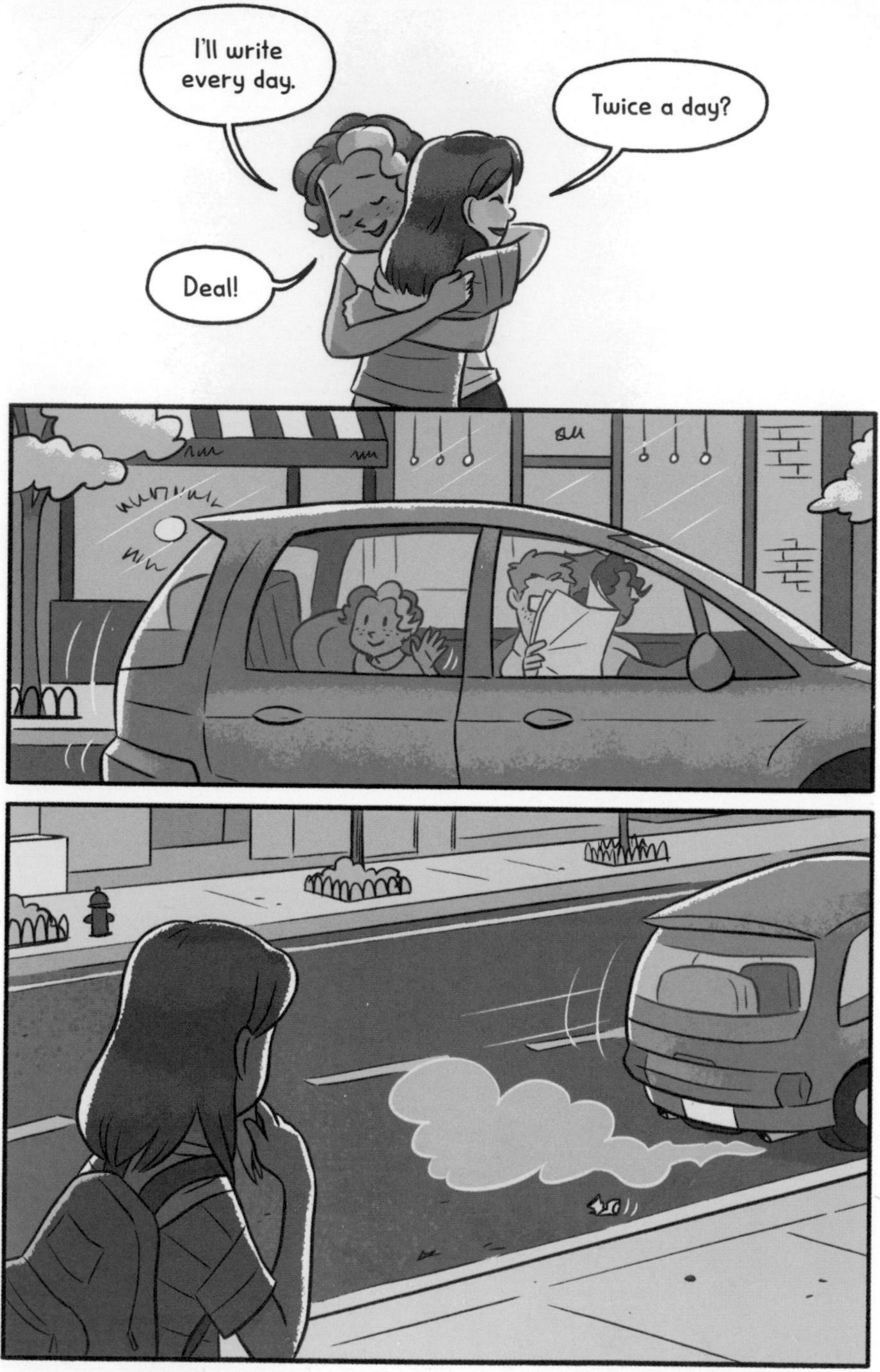
I'll write every day.
Twice a day?
Deal!

I can do this.

CHAPTER THREE

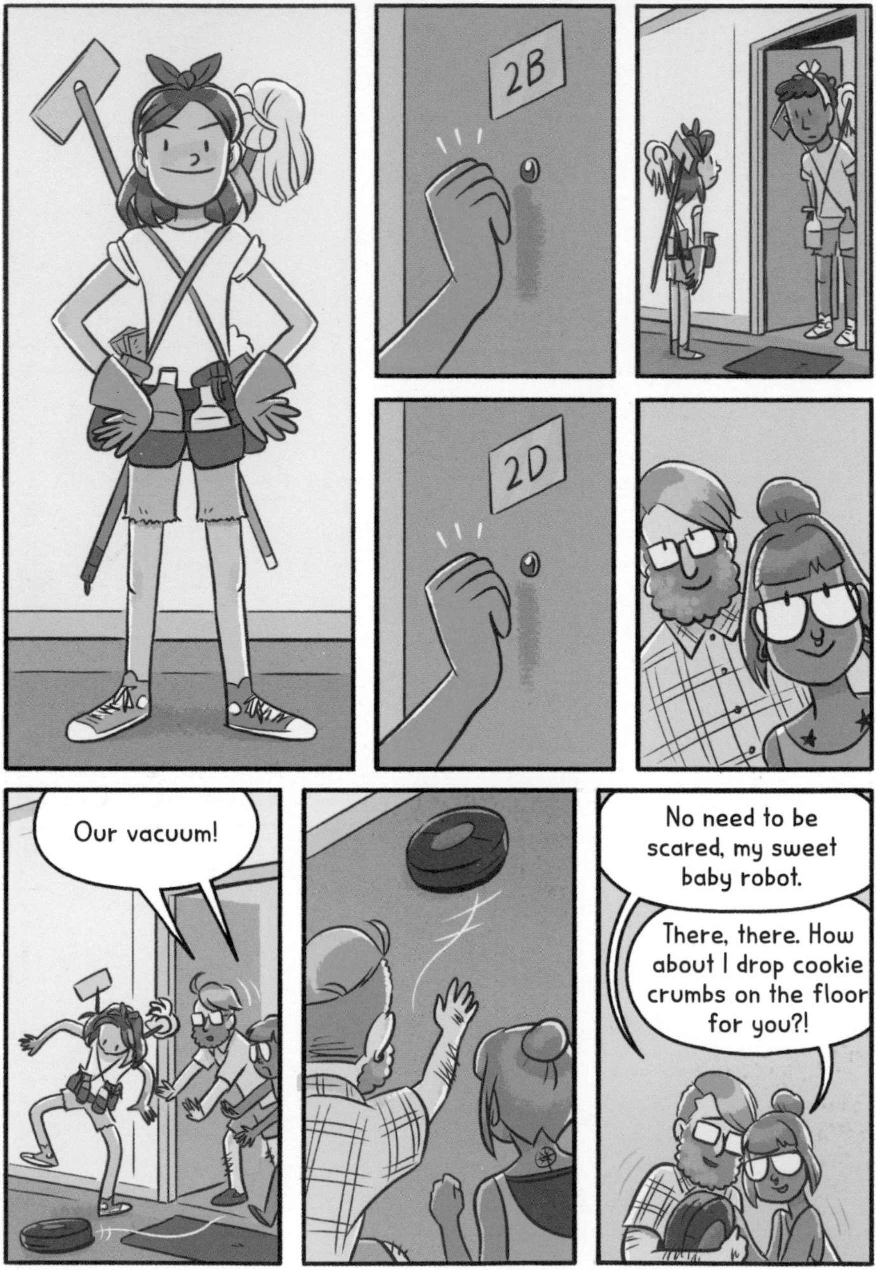
2B
2D
Our vacuum!
No need to be scared, my sweet baby robot.
There, there. How about I drop cookie crumbs on the floor for you?!

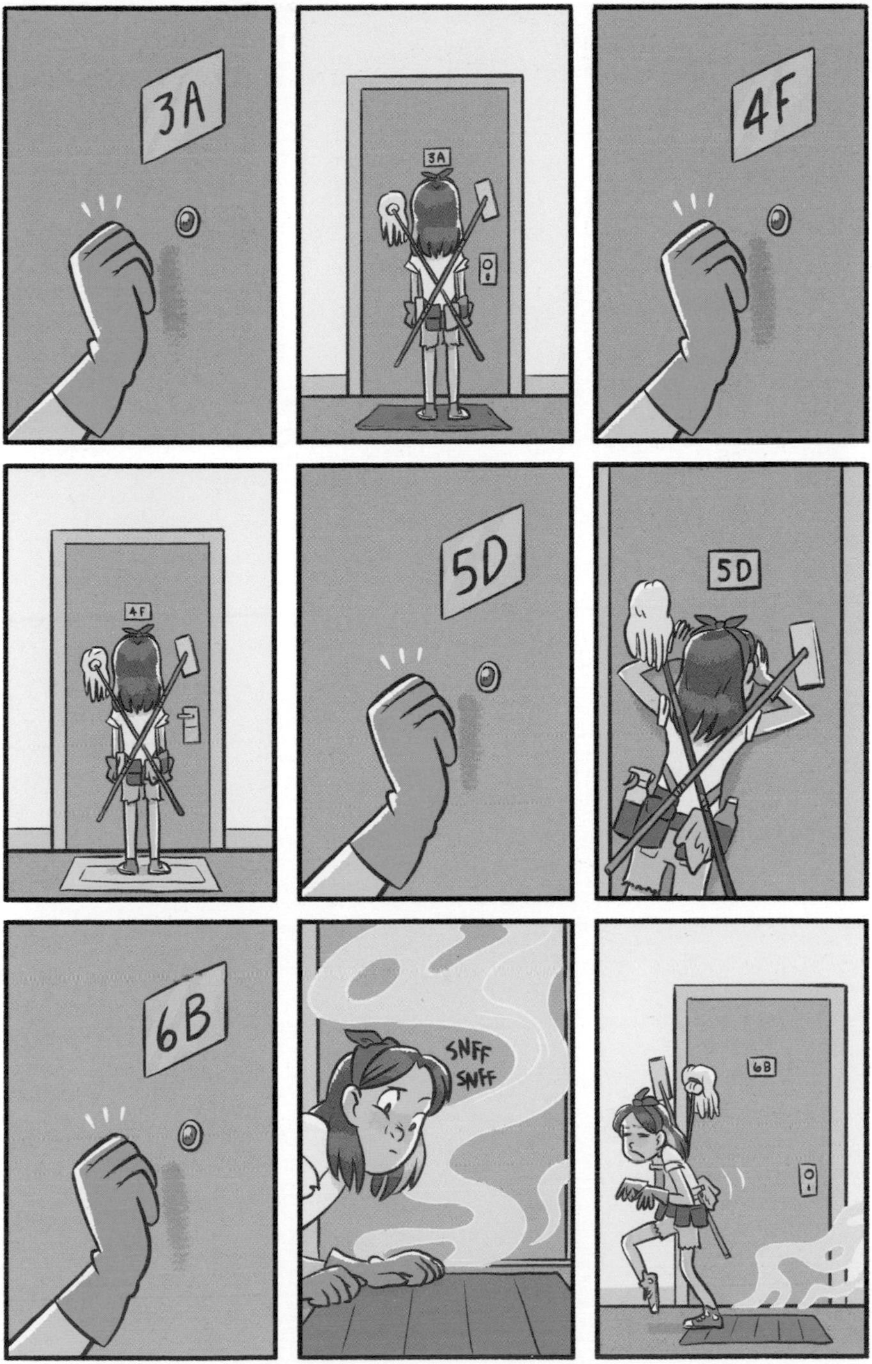
3A
3A
4F
4F
5D
5D
6B
SNFF
SNFF
6B

Help Katie go to camp!

Nature is overrated.

38

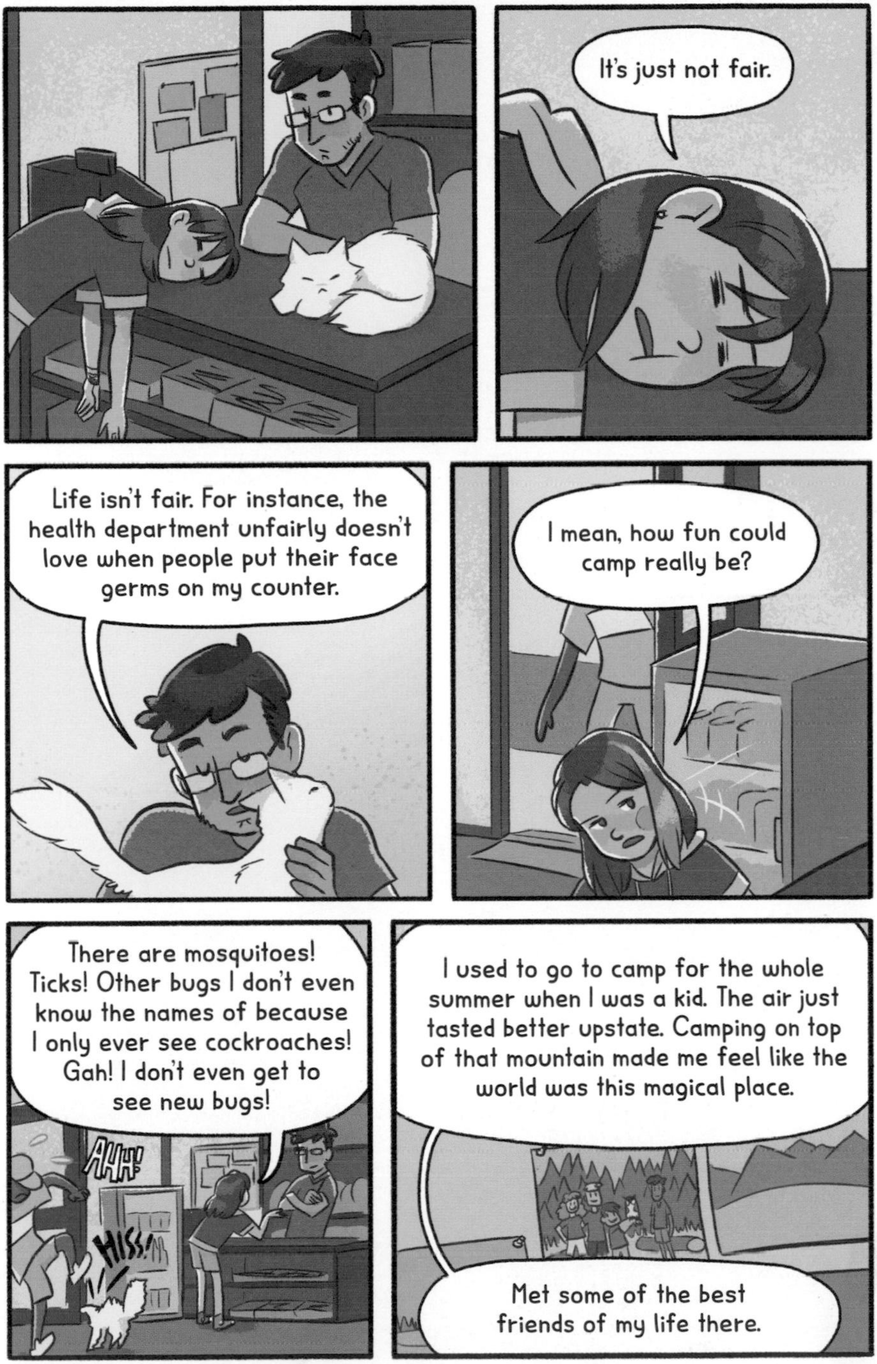

It's just not fair.
Life isn't fair. For instance, the health department unfairly doesn't love when people put their face germs on my counter.
I mean, how fun could camp really be?
There are mosquitoes! Ticks! Other bugs I don't even know the names of because I only ever see cockroaches! Gah! I don't even get to see new bugs!
AHH!
HISS!
I used to go to camp for the whole summer when I was a kid. The air just tasted better upstate. Camping on top of that mountain made me feel like the world was this magical place.
Met some of the best friends of my life there.

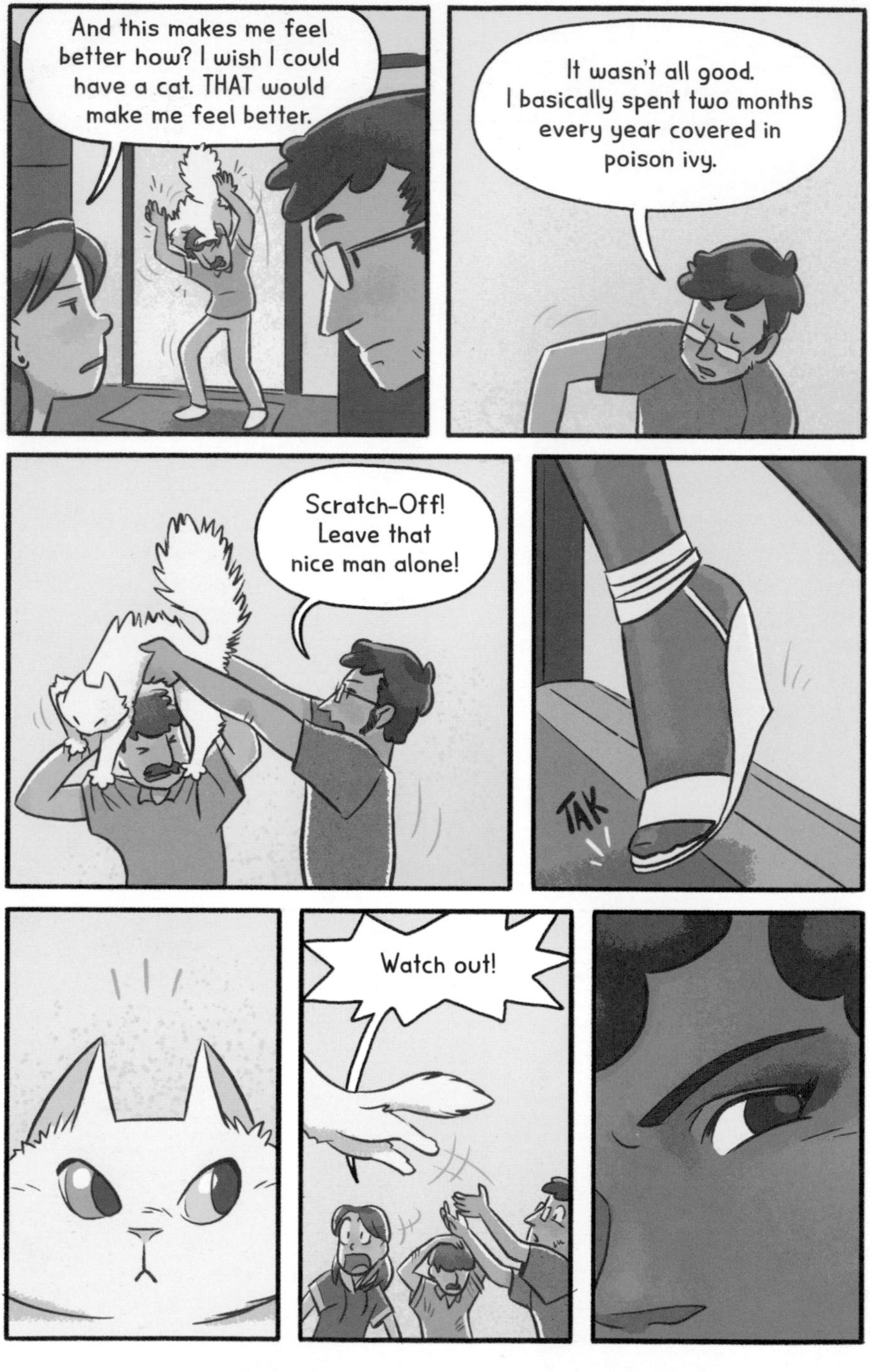
And this makes me feel better how? I wish I could have a cat. THAT would make me feel better.
It wasn't all good. I basically spent two months every year covered in poison ivy.
Scratch-Off! Leave that nice man alone!
TAK
Watch out!

Hello, Vincent.

Five p.m.? Isn't it a bit early for you, Madeline?

I wouldn't do that, dear. He's not the friendliest of ca–

Interesting.

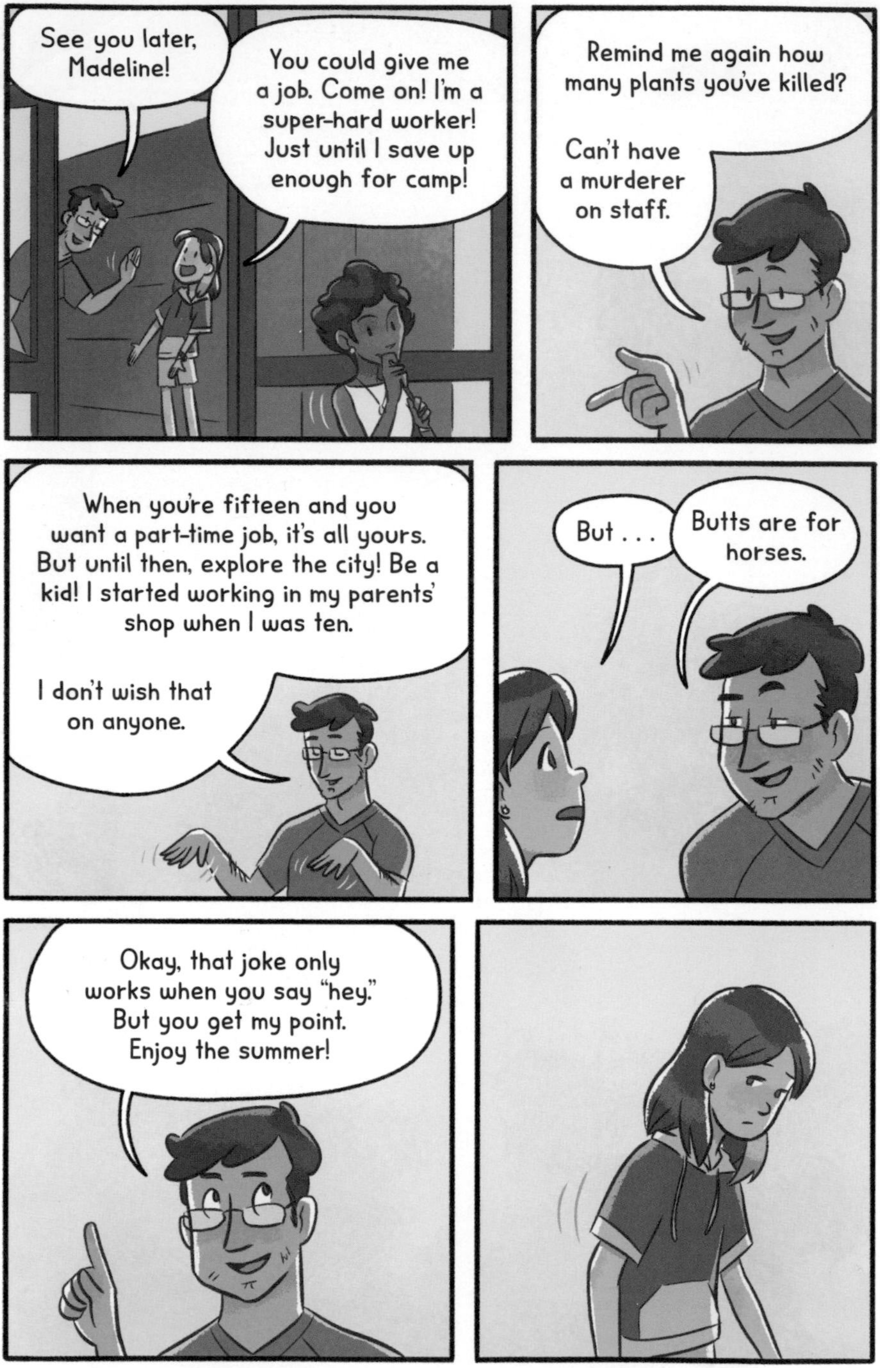
See you later, Madeline!
You could give me a job. Come on! I'm a super-hard worker! Just until I save up enough for camp!
Remind me again how many plants you've killed?
Can't have a murderer on staff.
When you're fifteen and you want a part-time job, it's all yours. But until then, explore the city! Be a kid! I started working in my parents' shop when I was ten.
I don't wish that on anyone.
But . . .
Butts are for horses.
Okay, that joke only works when you say "hey." But you get my point. Enjoy the summer!

CHAPTER FOUR

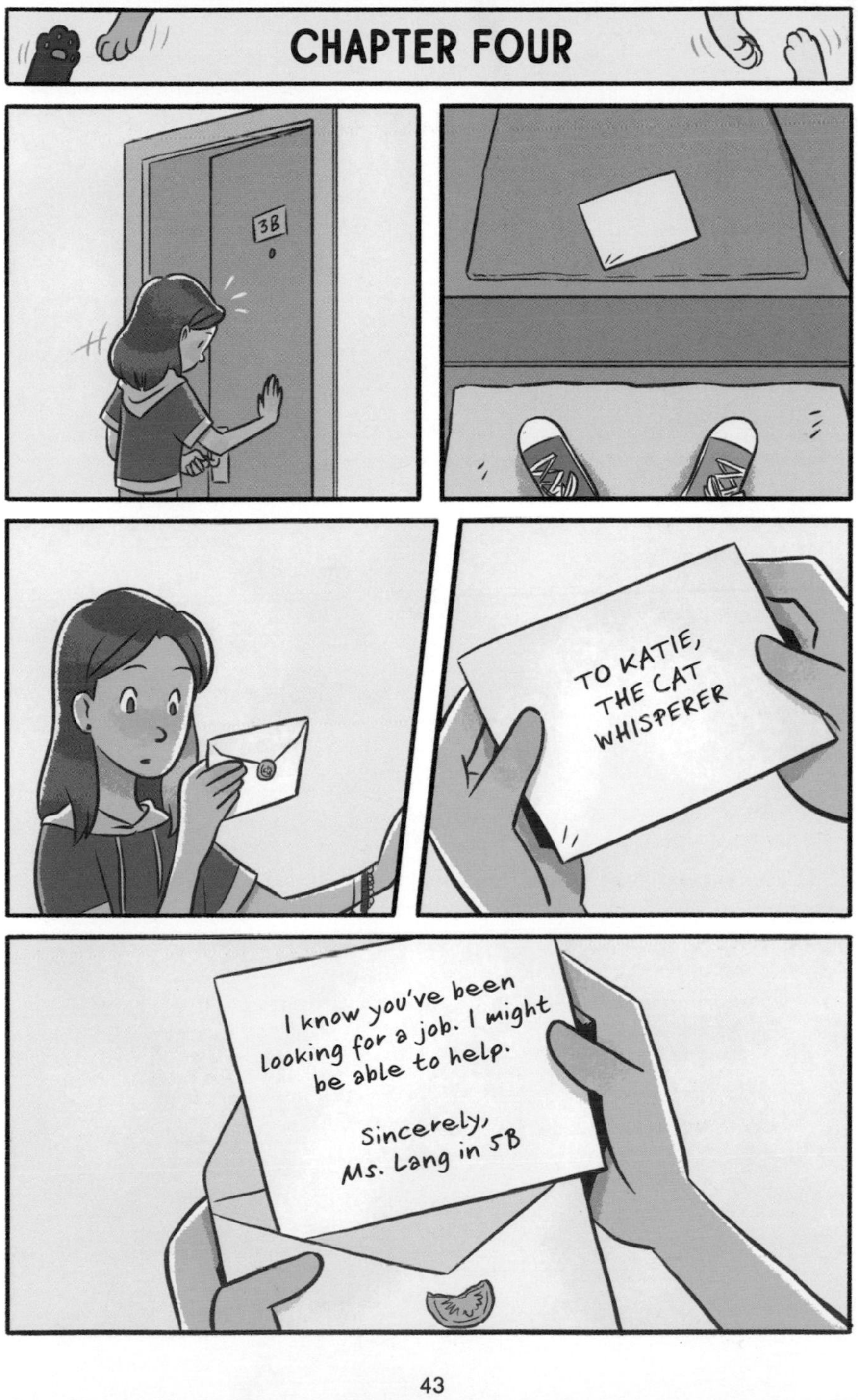
3B
TO KATIE, THE CAT WHISPERER
I know you've been looking for a job. I might be able to help.
Sincerely, Ms. Lang in 5B

I said no pets!

Huh?

You sound like you live with elephants! Walk quieter!

Sorry, Mrs. Piper.

Elephants!!!

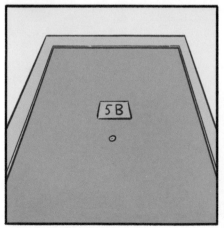

5B

Ah. There you are. I'm so glad.

AH!

Tonight I'll be working till midnight. I'm actually running a bit late already.

How does $25 an hour sound?

Um . . .

Okay, okay. $30?

For . . . what?

Goodness! Got ahead of myself.

I need a cat sitter.

GASP

Mrs. Piper let you have . . .

. . . two cats?!

Wrong and wrong. Mrs. Piper doesn't know.

And . . .

45

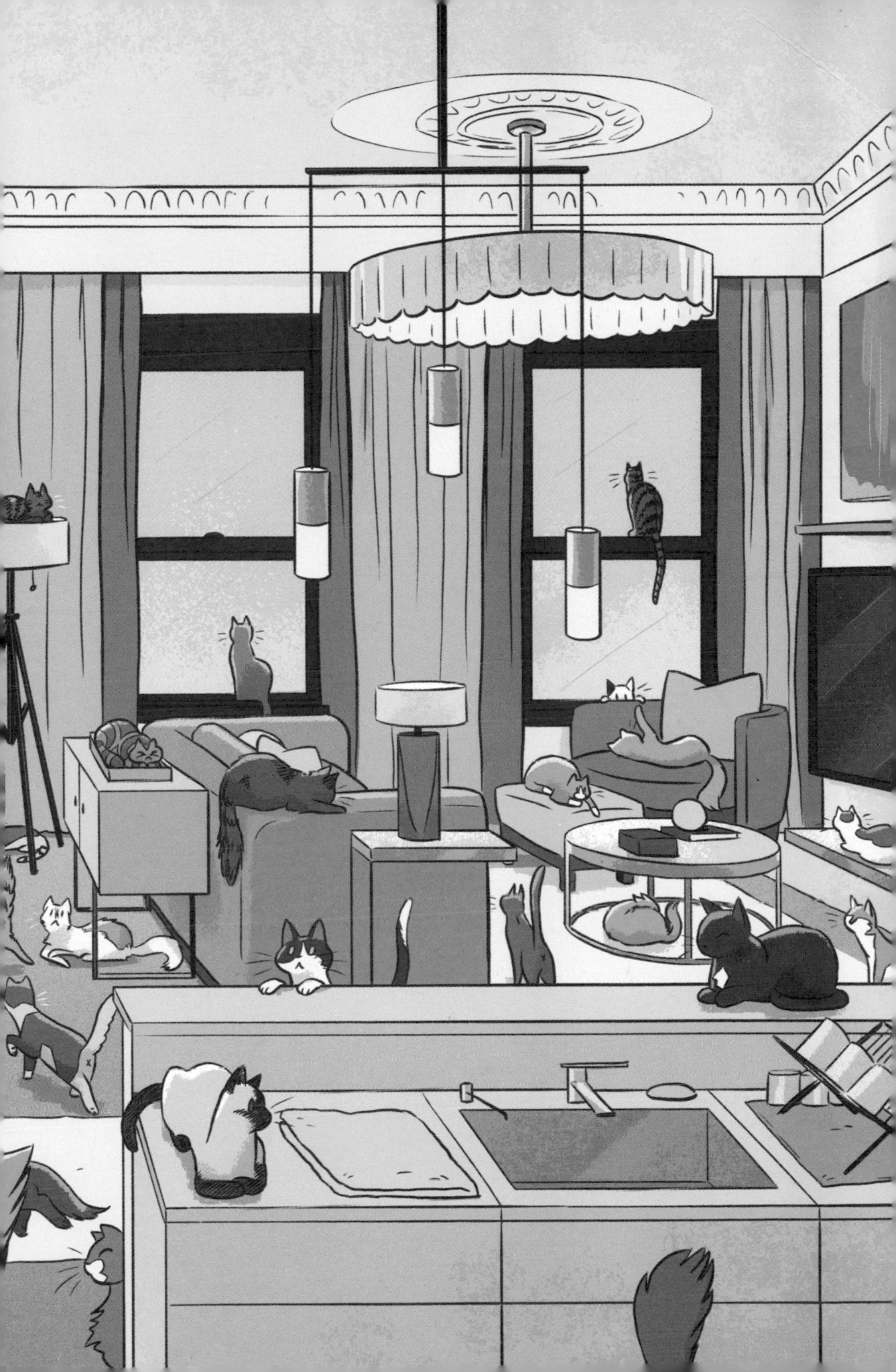

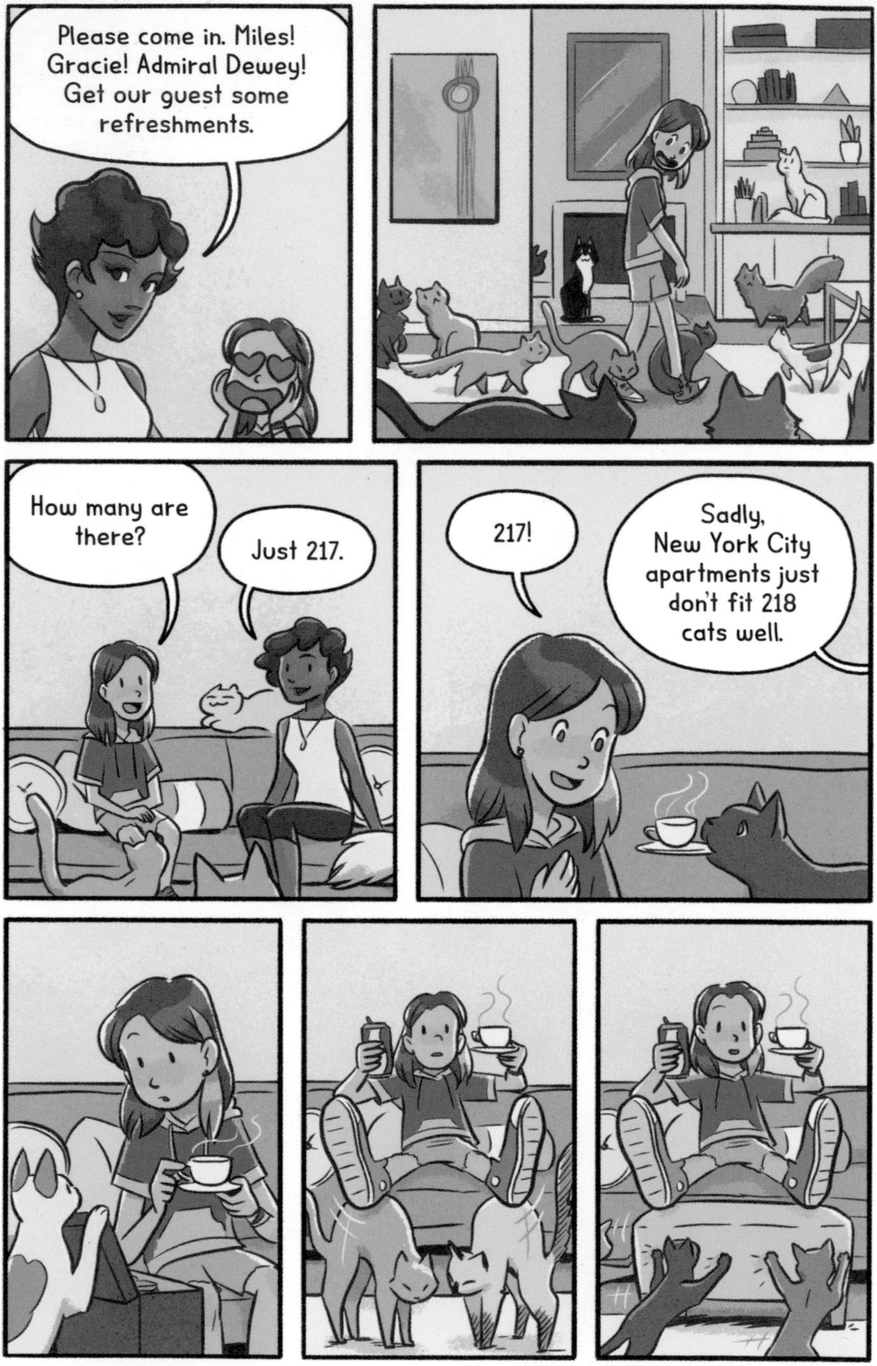
Please come in. Miles! Gracie! Admiral Dewey! Get our guest some refreshments.
How many are there?
Just 217.
217!
Sadly, New York City apartments just don't fit 218 cats well.

49

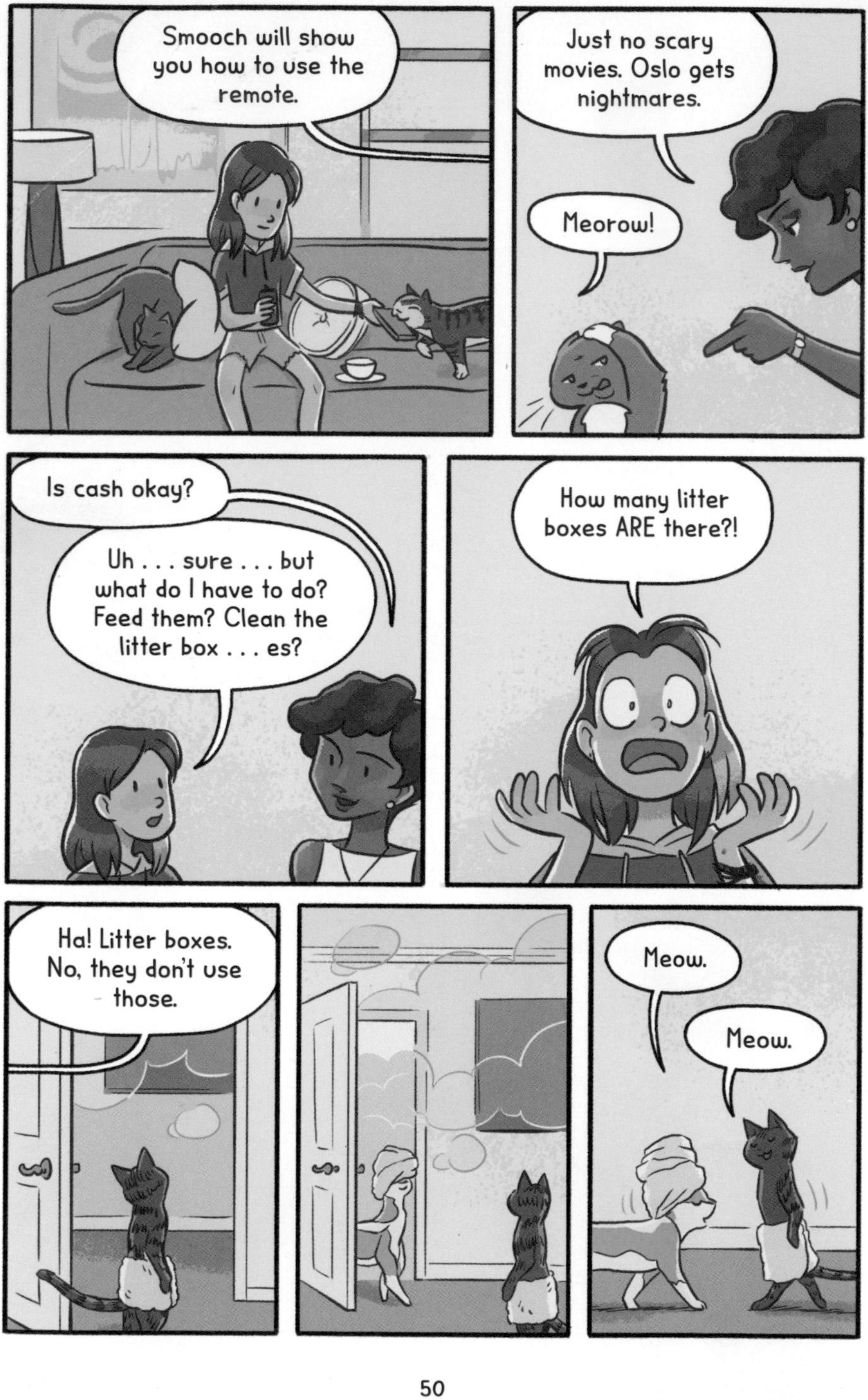
Smooch will show you how to use the remote.
Just no scary movies. Oslo gets nightmares.
Meorow!
Is cash okay?
Uh . . . sure . . . but what do I have to do? Feed them? Clean the litter box . . . es?
How many litter boxes ARE there?!
Ha! Litter boxes. No, they don't use those.
Meow.
Meow.

Oh, good. It's done.

Everything in my apartment locks and unlocks by fingerprint scanner, so here's your key.

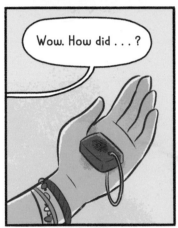

Wow. How did . . . ?

Teaching a cat to create a 3-D model, render and print a mold, then cast and cure a silicone fingerprint is easy.

I'm off! There's a list on the fridge with emergency contact information and all their names. I'll be home at midnight.

Be good, kitties.

Wait . . . I . . .

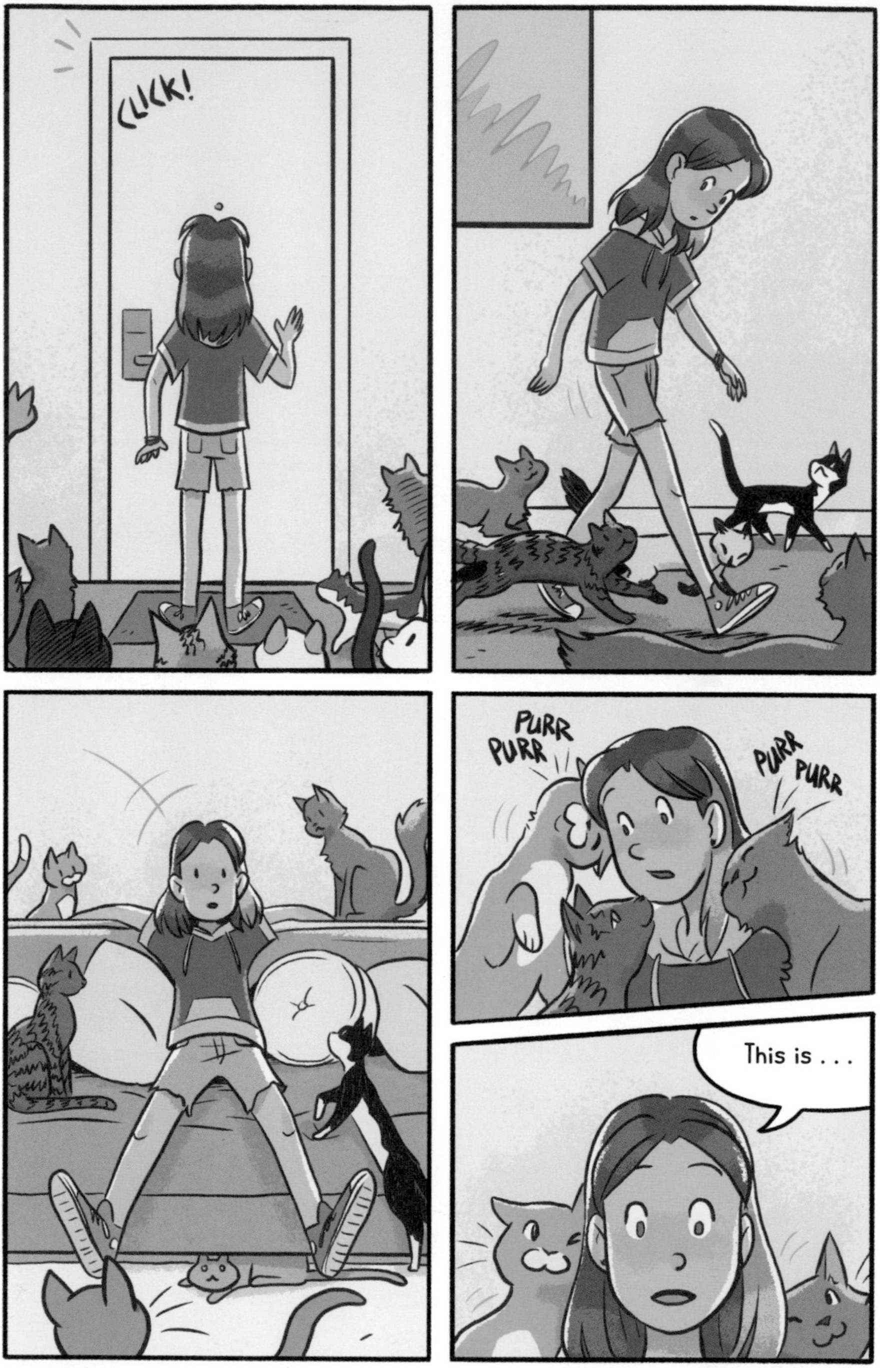
CLICK!
PURR
PURR
PURR
PURR
This is . . .

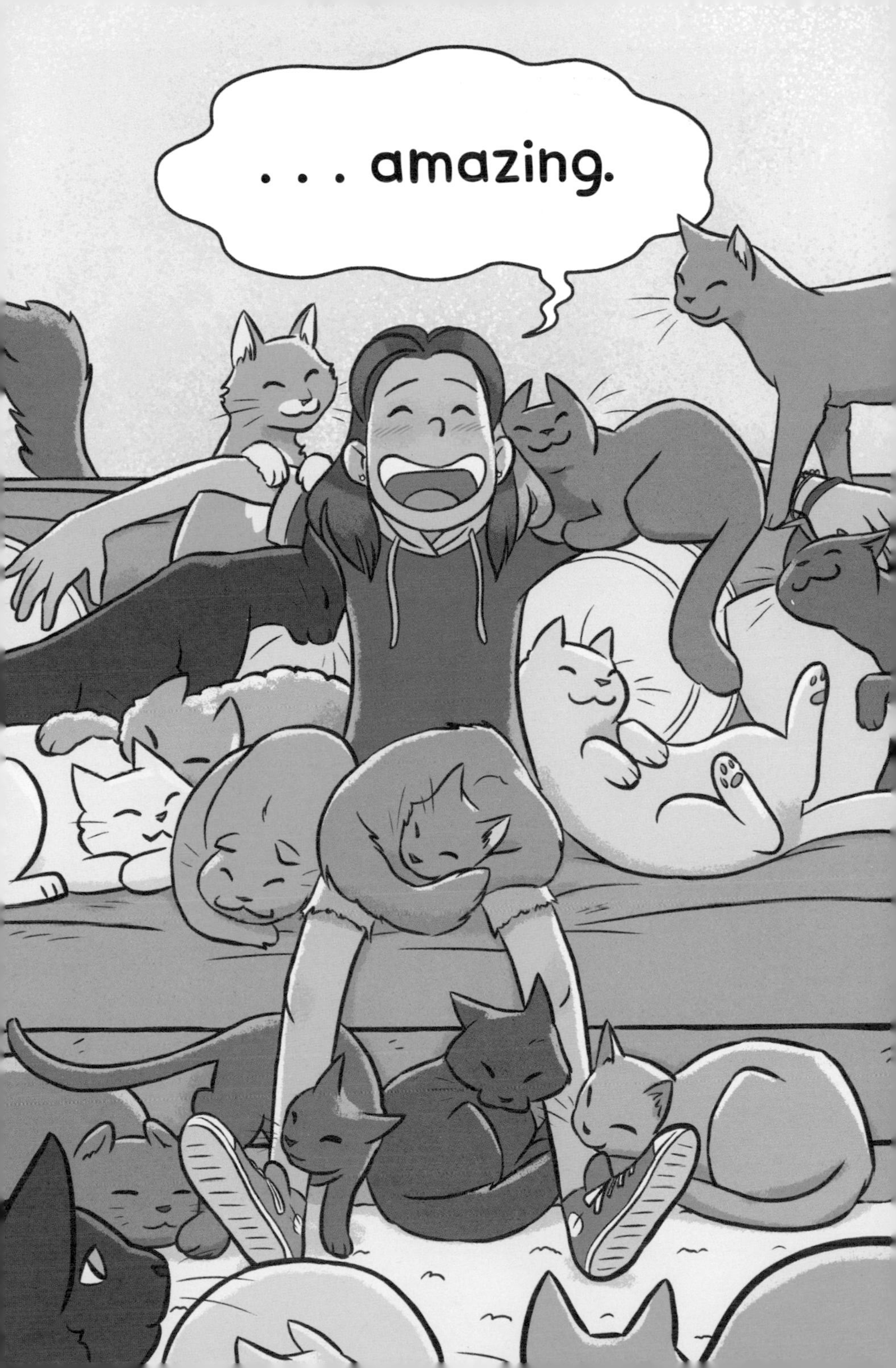
. . . amazing.

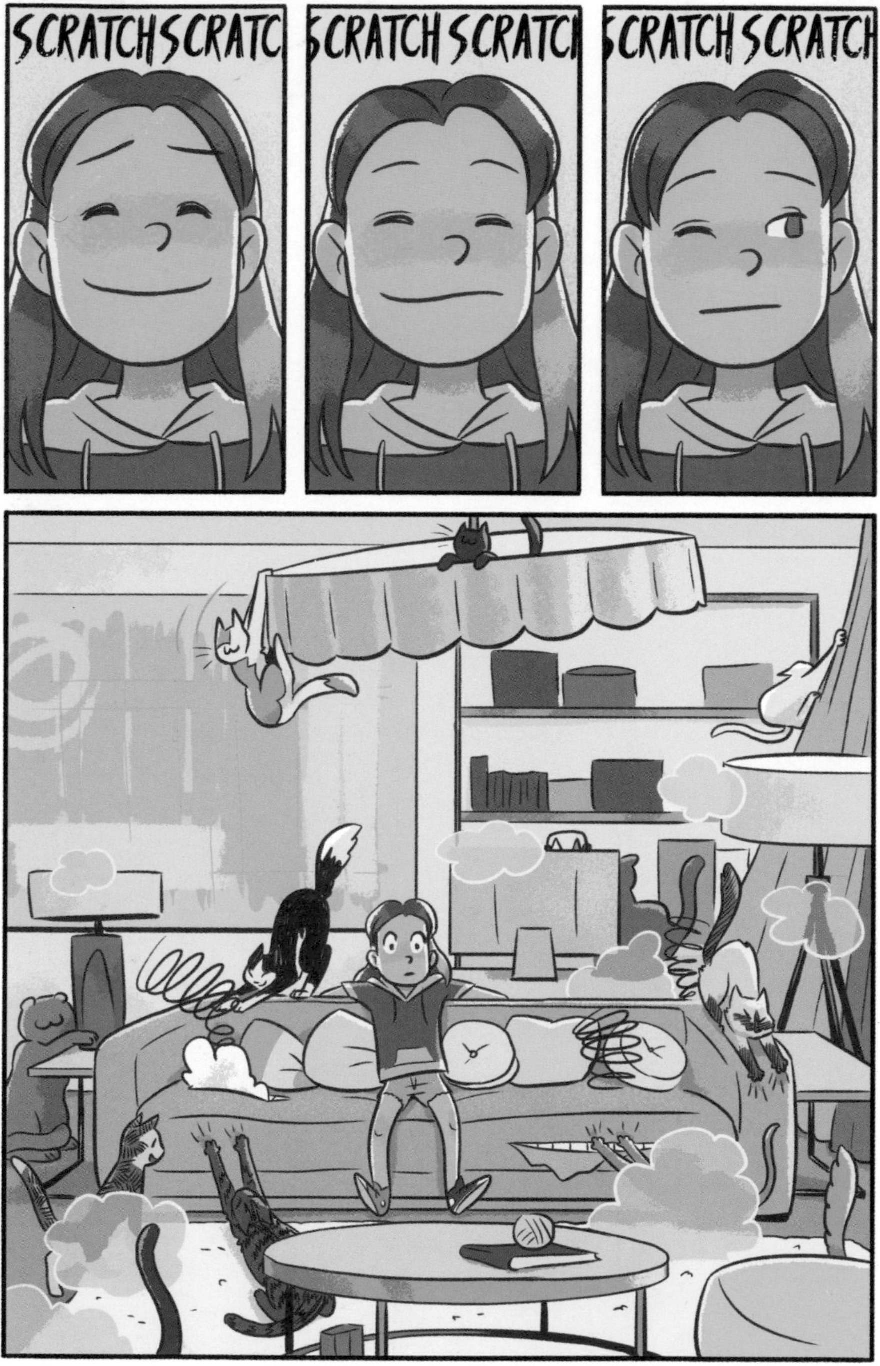
SCRATCH SCRATC
SCRATCH SCRATCH
SCRATCH SCRATCH

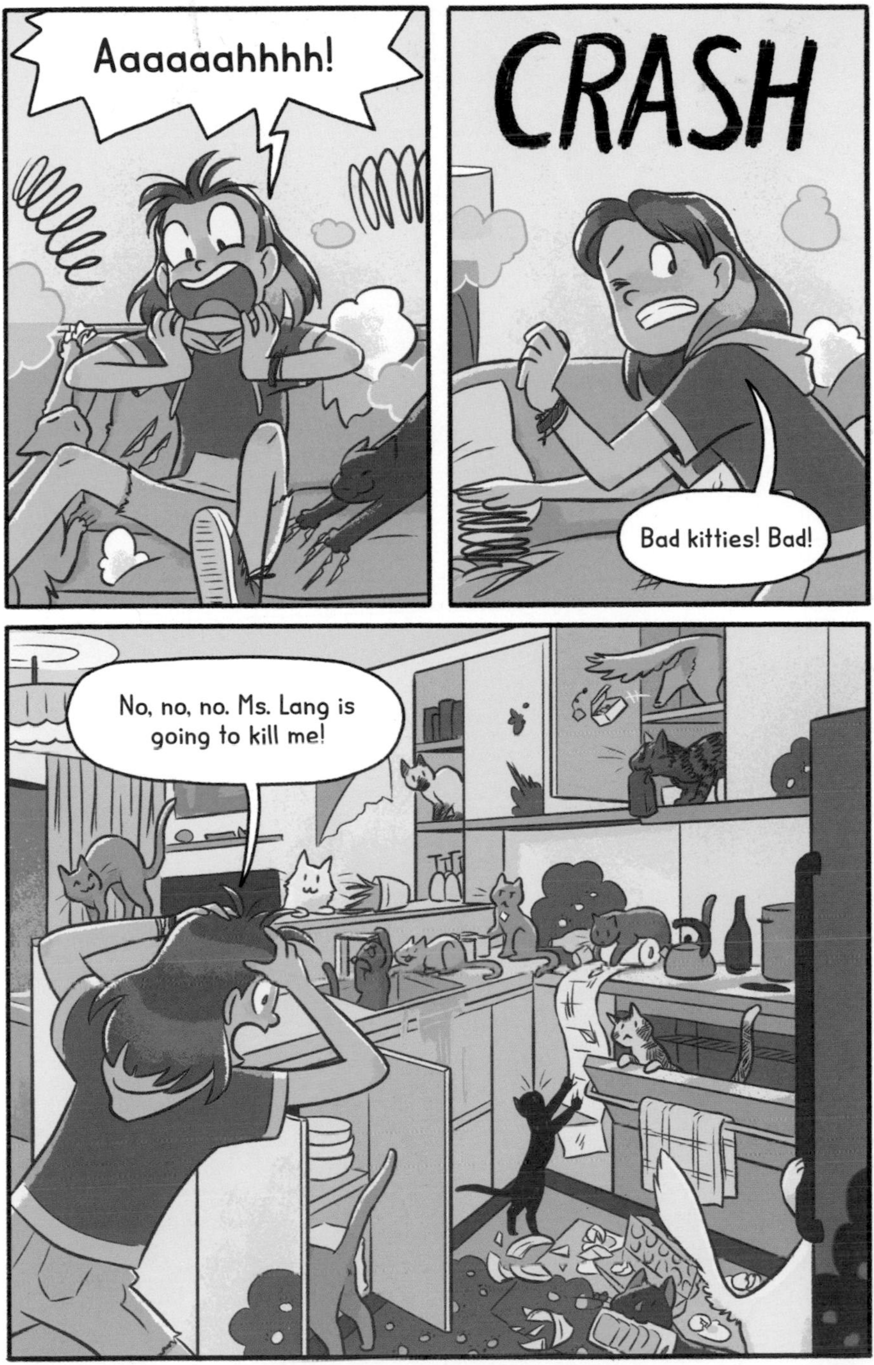
Aaaaaahhhh!
CRASH
Bad kitties! Bad!
No, no, no. Ms. Lang is going to kill me!

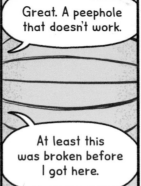
Great. A peephole that doesn't work.

At least this was broken before I got here.

Pizza delivery.

I didn't order any . . .

e-buy
Jet Engine Like New!
BUY!

HEY! NO BUYING JET ENGINES!

DING DING♪
BZZZZZT!

CLICK

KNOCK KNOCK

Mom
Hey, Katie-Cat! How's Operation Camp Fund going? Any jobs?

I told you I didn't order these pizzas.

WHAT IS GOING ON HERE?

They aren't my cats!

CATS?!

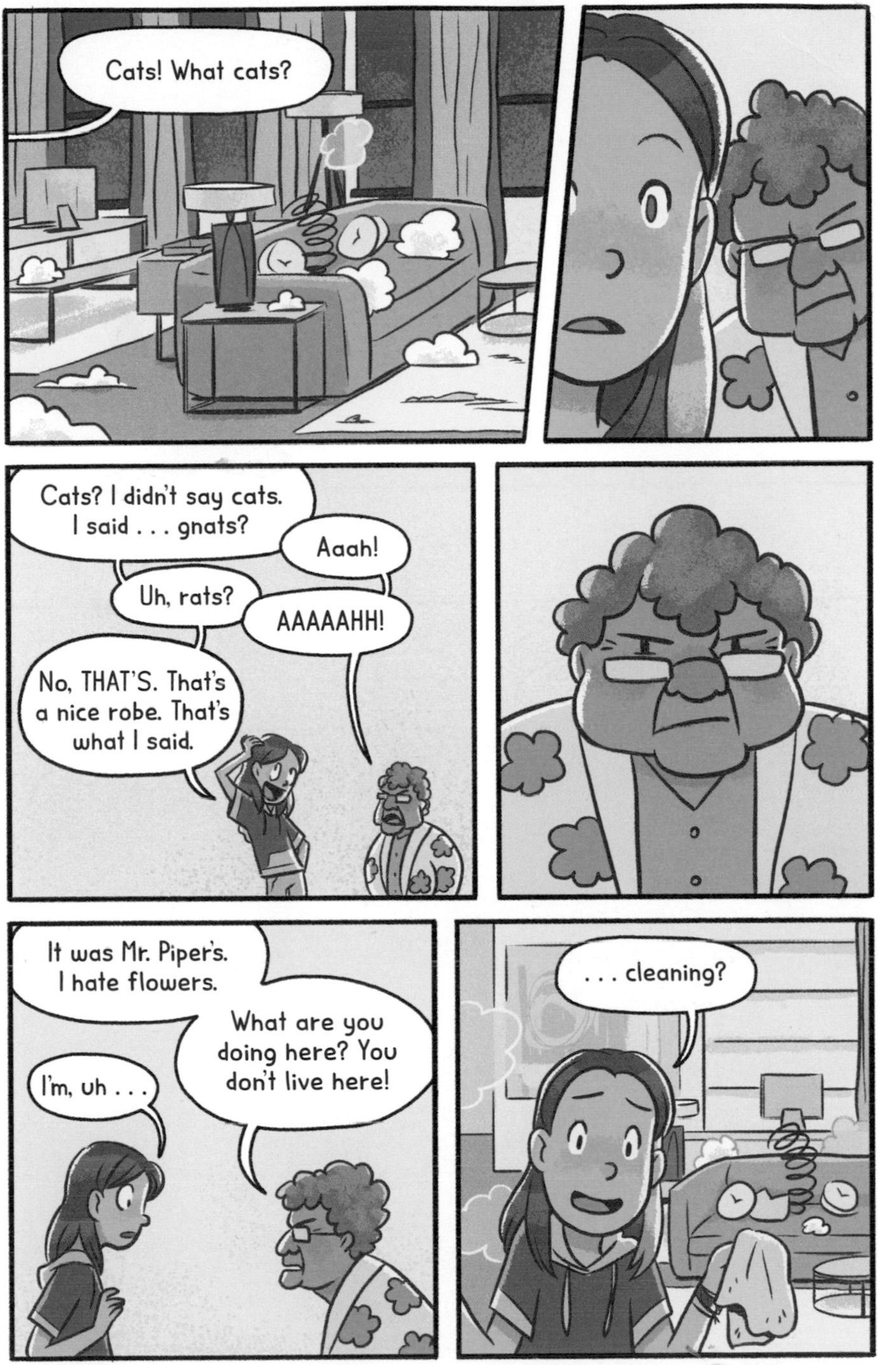
Cats! What cats?
Cats? I didn't say cats.
I said . . . gnats?
Aaah!
Uh, rats?
AAAAAHH!
No, THAT'S. That's
a nice robe. That's
what I said.
It was Mr. Piper's.
I hate flowers.
What are you
doing here? You
don't live here!
I'm, uh . . .
. . . cleaning?

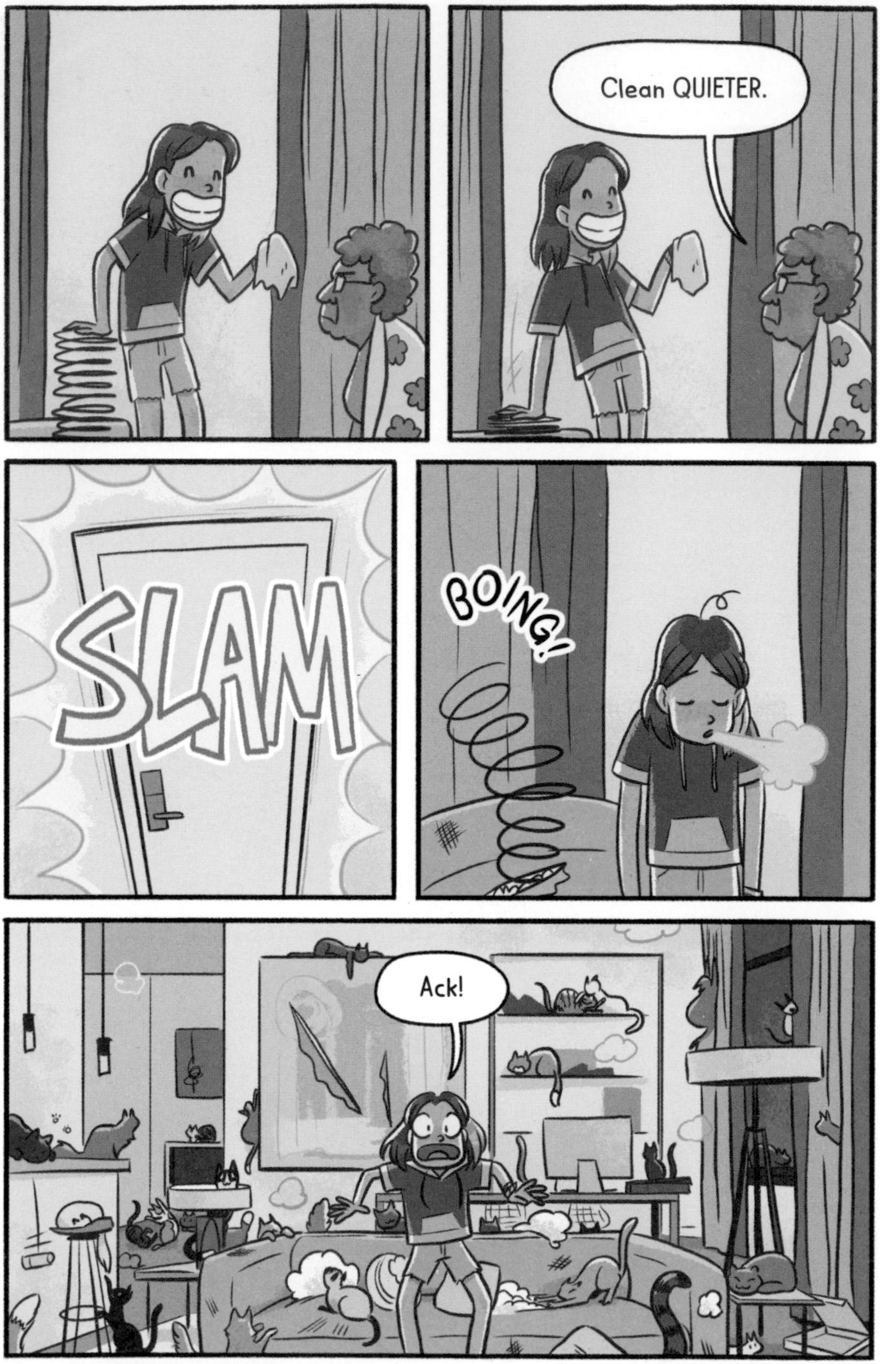
Clean QUIETER.
SLAM
BOING!
Ack!

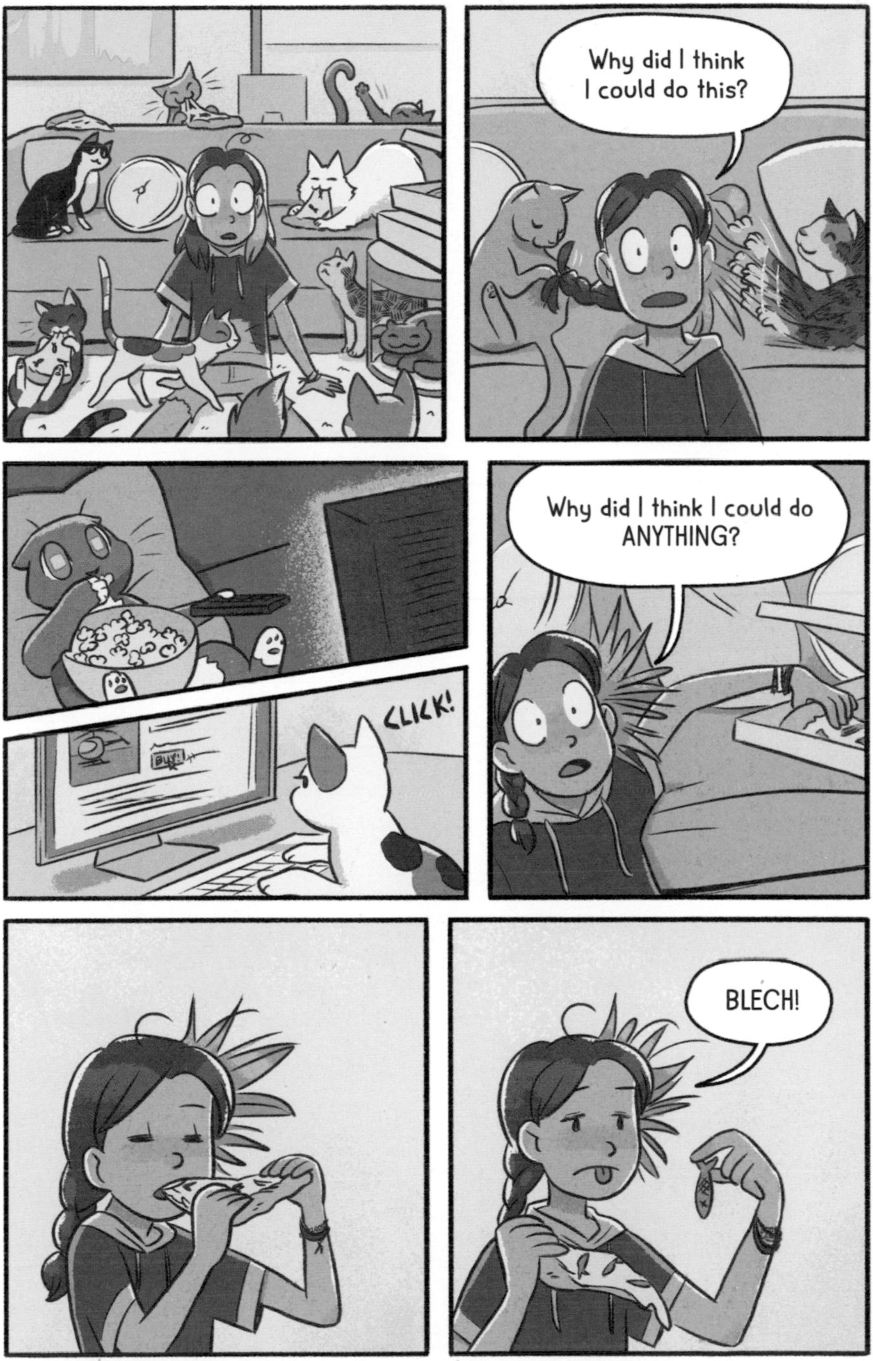
Why did I think
I could do this?
Why did I think I could do
ANYTHING?
CLICK!
BUY!
BLECH!

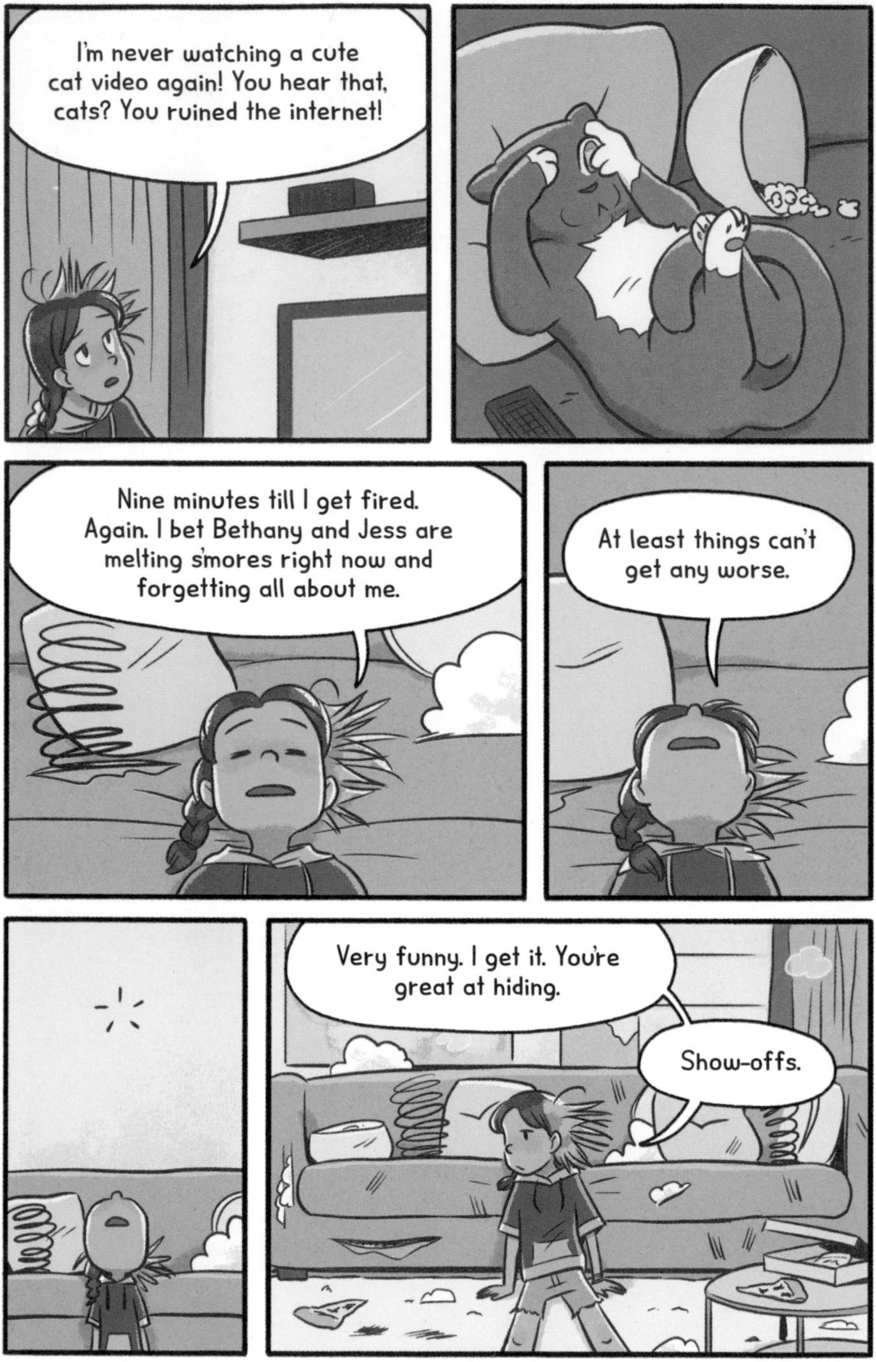
I'm never watching a cute cat video again! You hear that, cats? You ruined the internet!
Nine minutes till I get fired. Again. I bet Bethany and Jess are melting s'mores right now and forgetting all about me.
At least things can't get any worse.
Very funny. I get it. You're great at hiding.
Show-offs.

Guys?

GUYS?!
Oh no, no, no, no.

How do you lose 217 cats?!

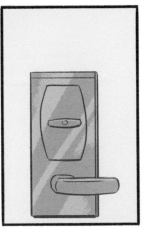

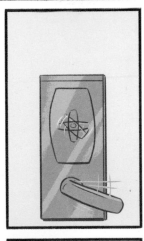

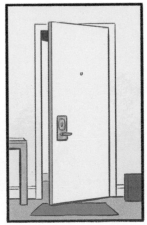

Are those . . . couch pillows?

Where did you . . . ?

TWO MINUTES EARLIER

Weird kid.

I thought I had a couch here.

64

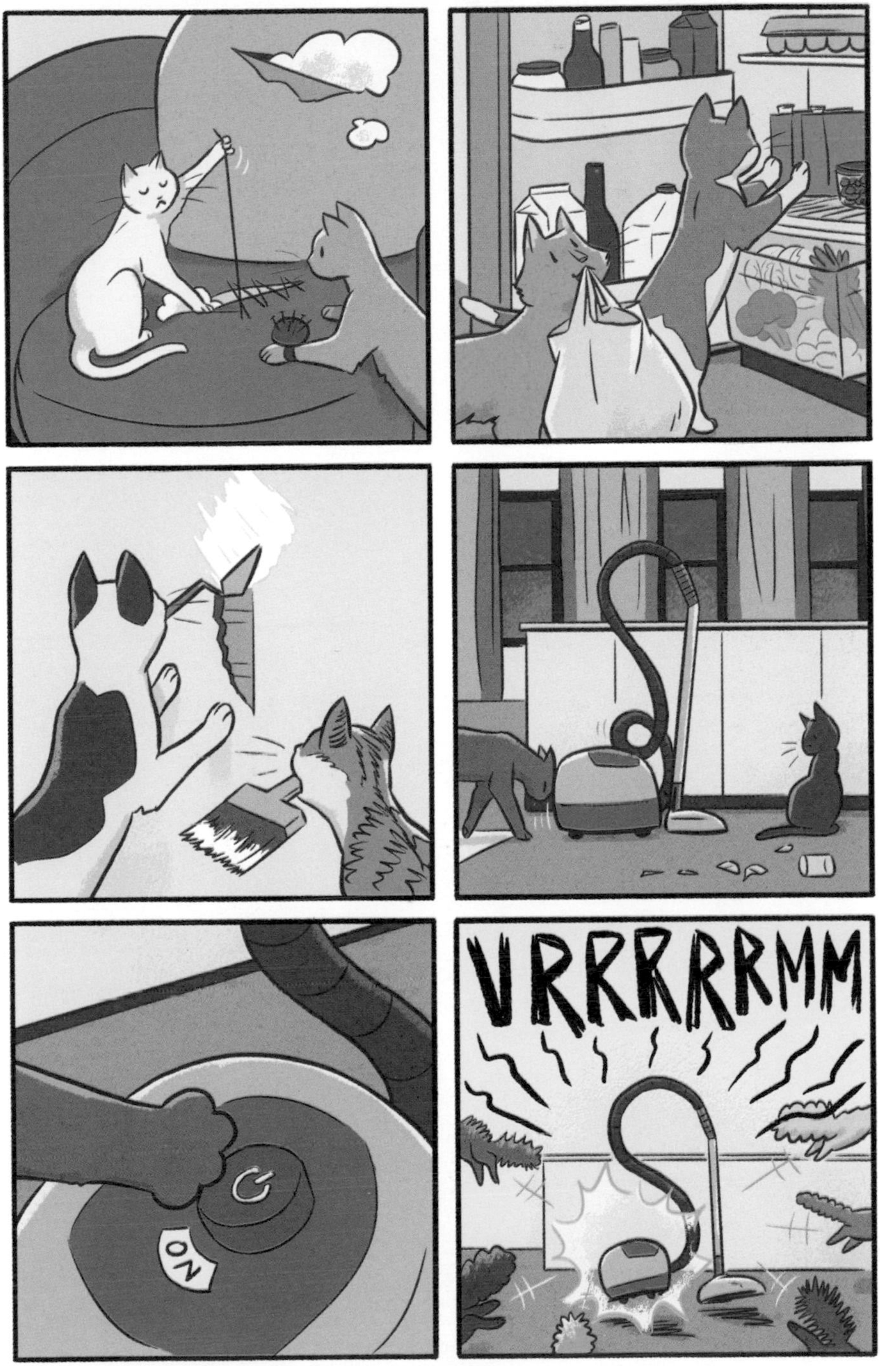
ON
VRRRRRMM

Interesting.

AH!

I'm so sorry! I didn't know what to do! There are just so many of them and . . .

I've never seen the apartment so clean!

As promised.

Same time tomorrow night?

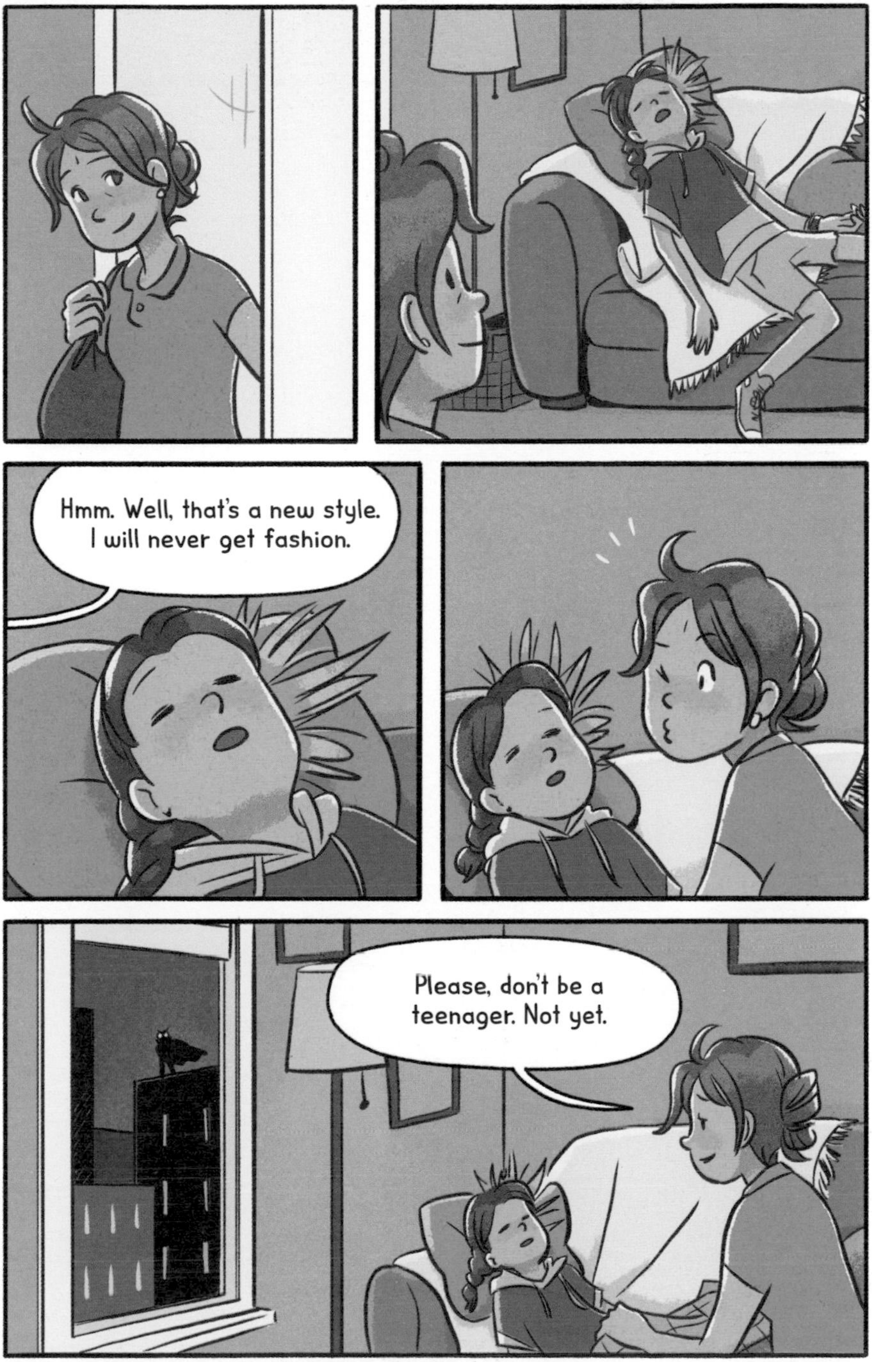
Hmm. Well, that's a new style. I will never get fashion.
Please, don't be a teenager. Not yet.

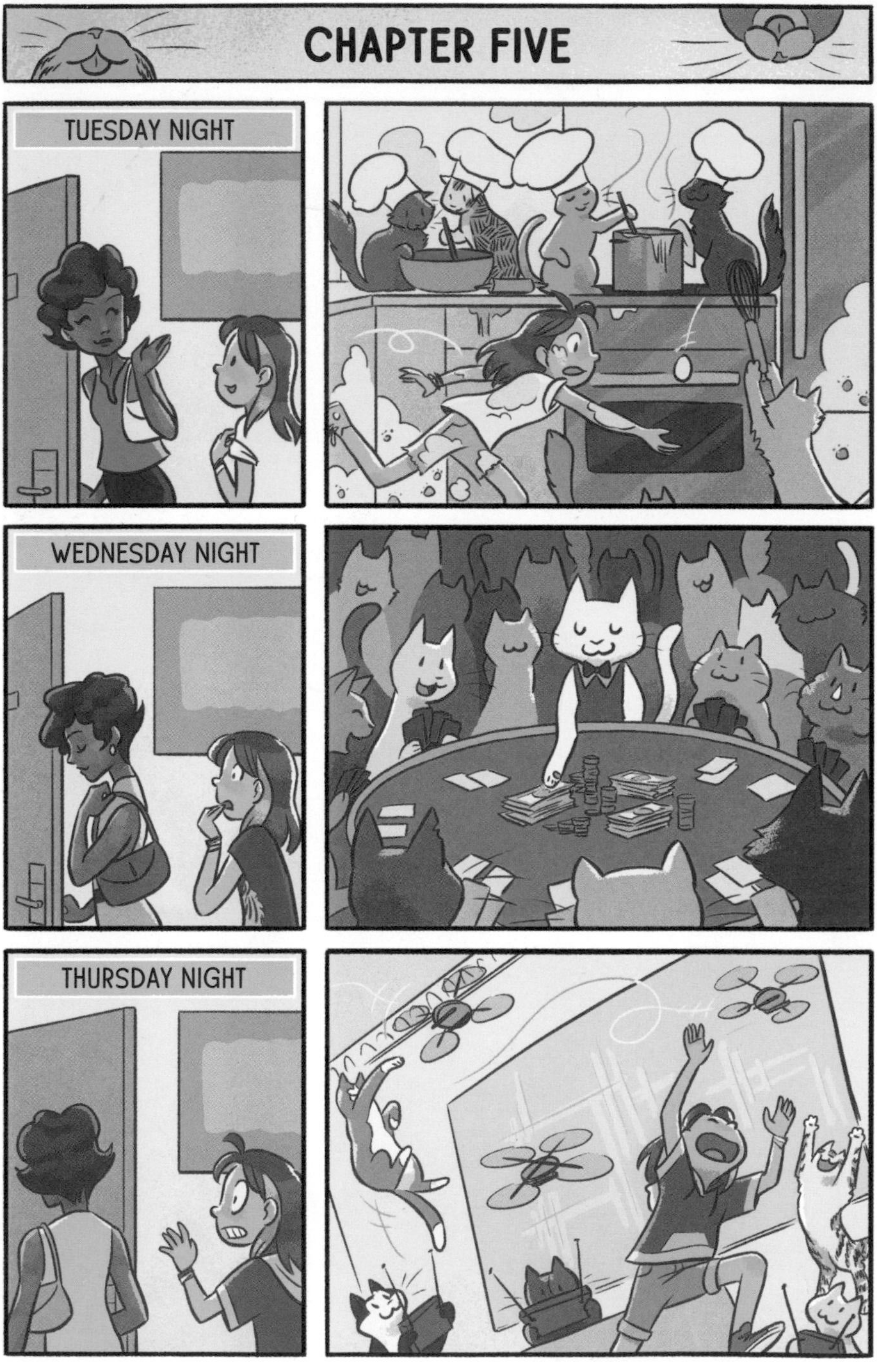
CHAPTER FIVE
TUESDAY NIGHT
WEDNESDAY NIGHT
THURSDAY NIGHT

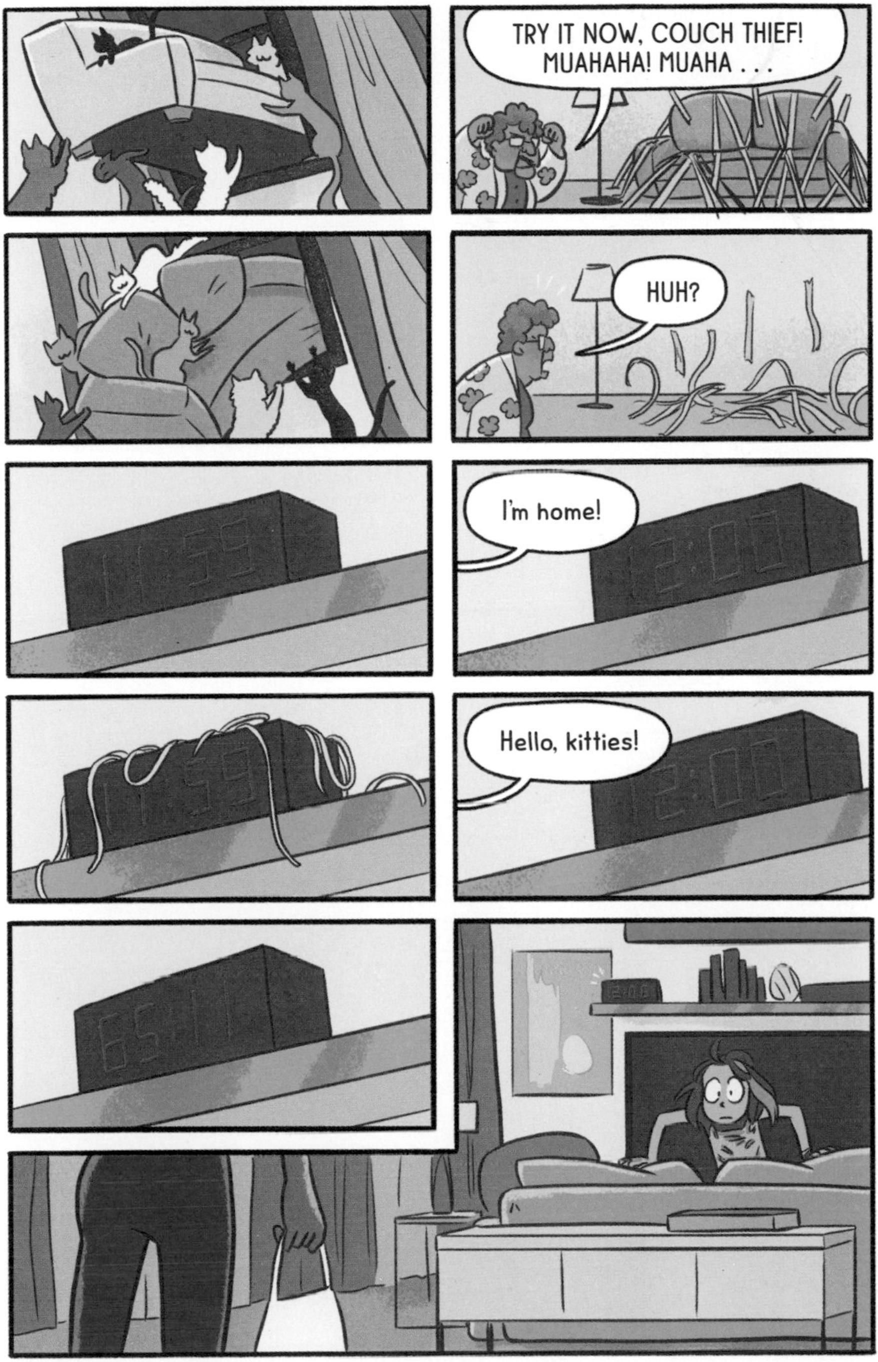
TRY IT NOW, COUCH THIEF! MUAHAHA! MUAHA . . .
HUH?
I'm home!
Hello, kitties!

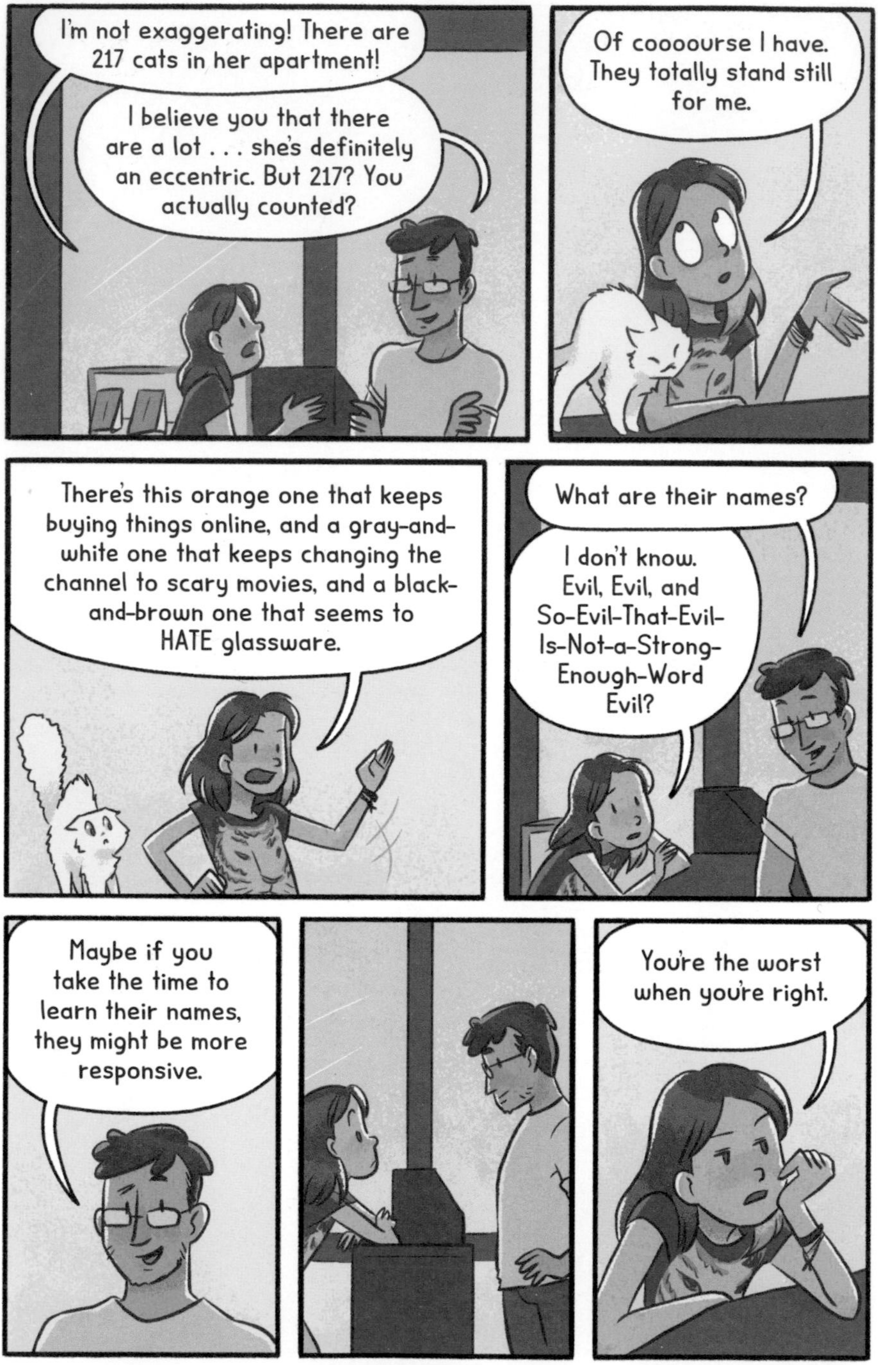
I'm not exaggerating! There are 217 cats in her apartment!
I believe you that there are a lot . . . she's definitely an eccentric. But 217? You actually counted?
Of cooooourse I have. They totally stand still for me.
There's this orange one that keeps buying things online, and a gray-and-white one that keeps changing the channel to scary movies, and a black-and-brown one that seems to HATE glassware.
What are their names?
I don't know. Evil, Evil, and So-Evil-That-Evil-Is-Not-a-Strong-Enough-Word Evil?
Maybe if you take the time to learn their names, they might be more responsive.
You're the worst when you're right.

THAT EVENING . . .

All right, let's see. . . .

Jolie. White with black and brown spots.

Jolie
Fashion designer
White with black and brown spots. Likes: hacking, 3-D modeling, online gaming

Gracie

Likes: hacking, 3-D modeling, online gaming.

Jolie: Computer Hacking

TAP TAP TAP

Why are you raiding our village?! We're on the same team!

Okaaaay.

Hmm . . . I think you're Gracie? Says here you can understand and interpret eighty-two languages.

Hola, Gracie. Uh . . . ¿Dónde está el baño?

Gracie: Language Expert

MIAU

Lyapa

Master of various martial arts and weapons

Mackerel

Semaphore expert

Lyapa: Master of various martial arts and weapons?

Lyapa: Weapons Expert

Jujitsu? Lock-picking? Helicopter repair? Counterattacks?

Camouflage? Smoke bombs? Bath bombs? Getaway driver?! What is this list?!

At least THIS one is normal. Miles: Long black cat, bright green eyes, loves lasers.

Yoga instructor

Miles

Long black cat, bright green eyes, loves lasers.

Minnie

Which one of you is Miles?

There you are! Do you want to play? Let's play!

CLICK

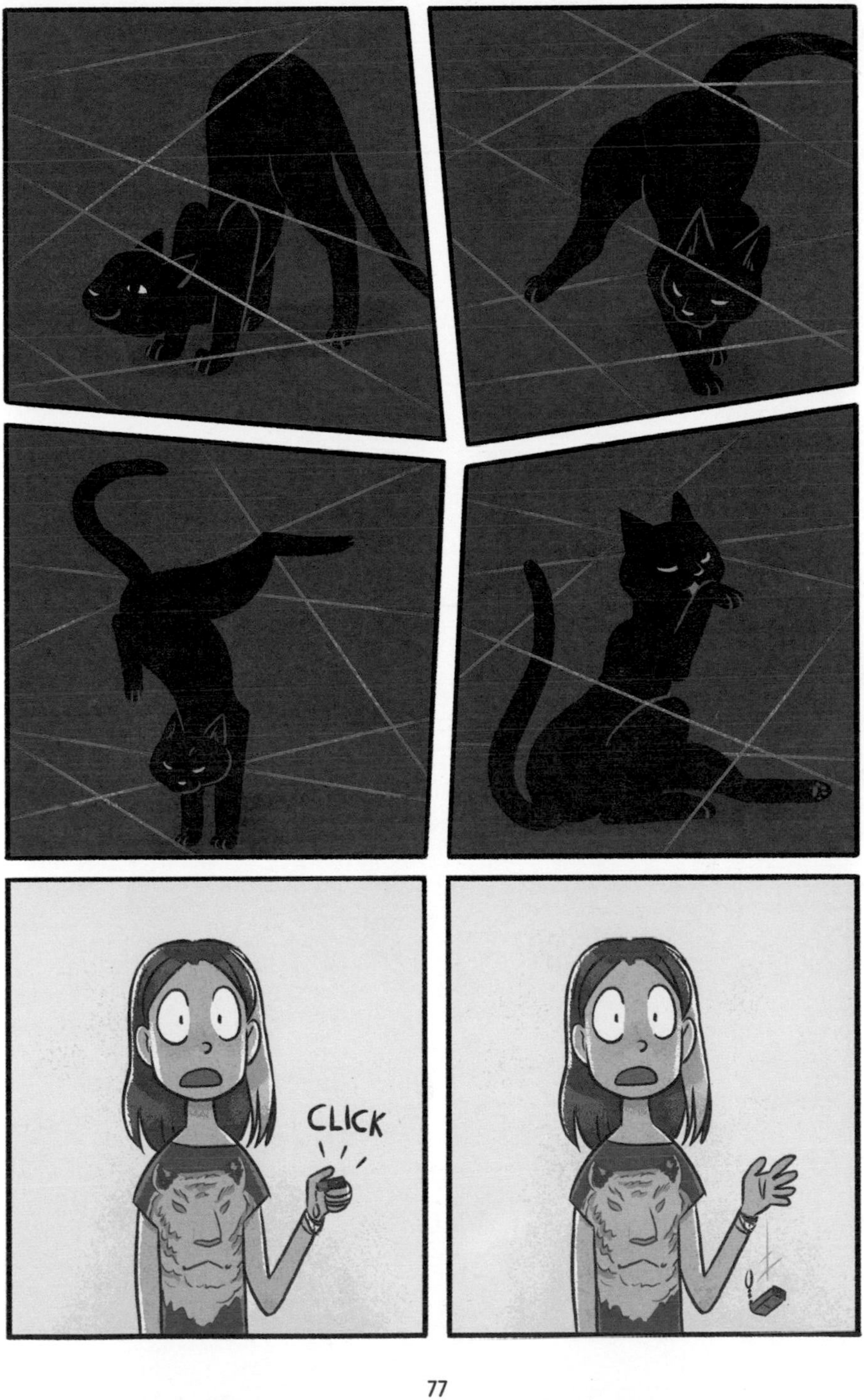
CLICK

CHAPTER SIX

I'm telling you! The cats are evil.

All cats are a little evil. That's what makes them cats.

But these are like SUPERVILLAIN-level! GASP! Maybe they are supervillains! I should warn Ms. Lang!

Have you checked the database?

Good idea!

Come on! Load! When are we going to upgrade this thing?!

Yeah, two hundred years ago. Our router is older than Mrs. Piper!

We're locked into a really great rate!

That reminds me. Have you seen anyone walking out of the building carrying a couch?

Mrs. Piper is CONVINCED there's a couch thief on the loose. Haha.

Huh. Yeah. Weird.

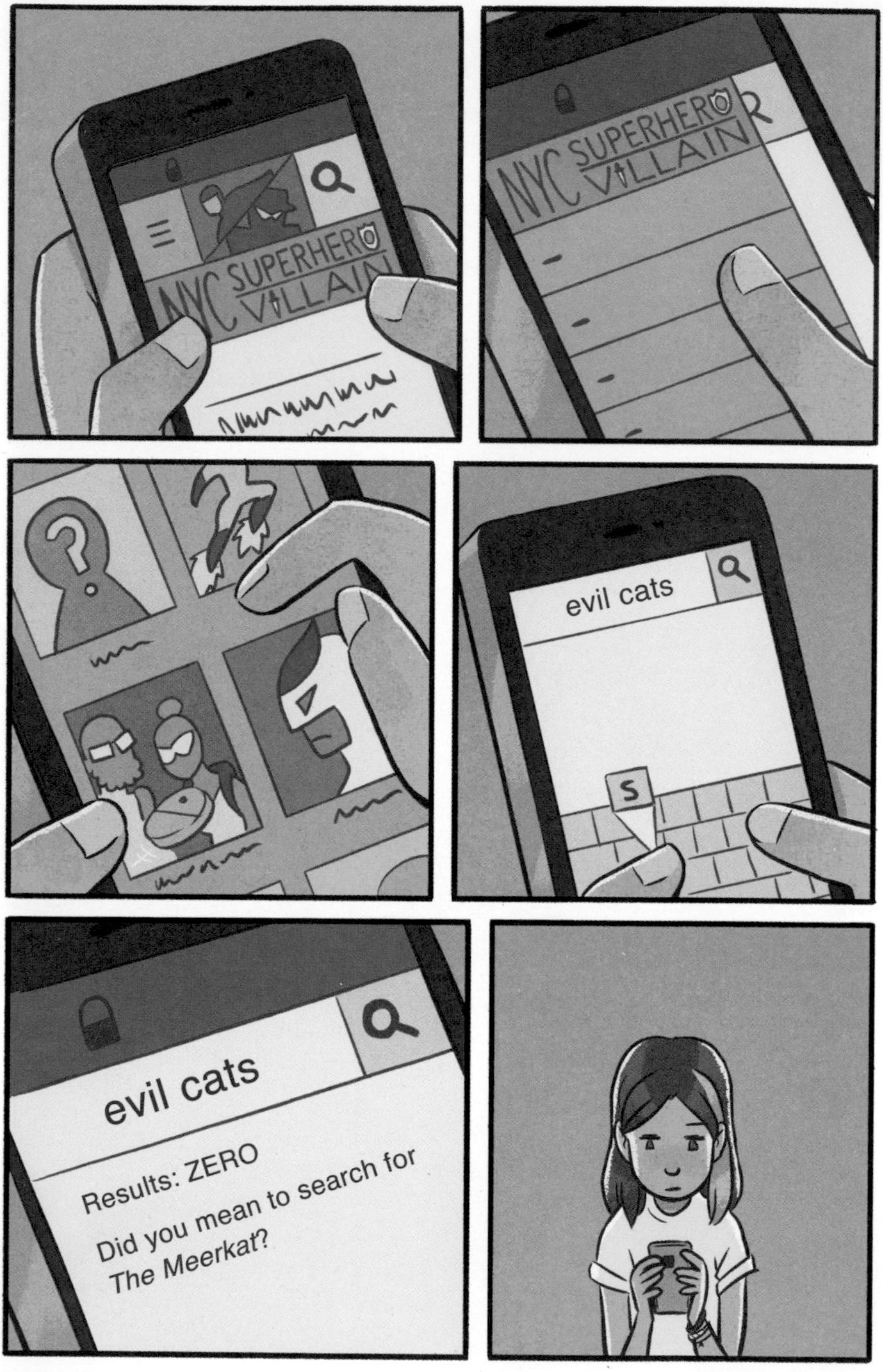
NYC SUPERHERO VILLAIN
NYC SUPERHERO VILLAIN
evil cats
evil cats
Results: ZERO
Did you mean to search for
The Meerkat?

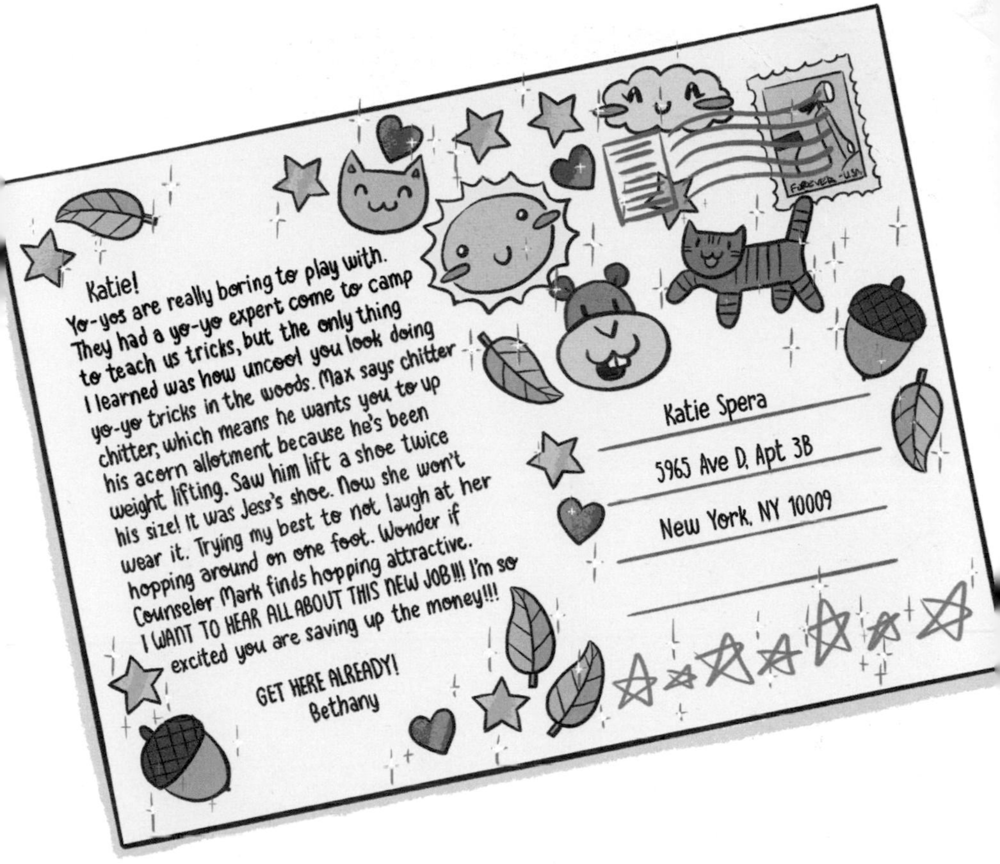
Katie!
Yo-yos are really boring to play with.
They had a yo-yo expert come to camp
to teach us tricks, but the only thing
I learned was how uncool you look doing
yo-yo tricks in the woods. Max says chitter
chitter, which means he wants you to up
his acorn allotment because he's been
weight lifting. Saw him lift a shoe twice
his size! It was Jess's shoe. Now she won't
wear it. Trying my best to not laugh at her
hopping around on one foot. Wonder if
Counselor Mark finds hopping attractive.
I WANT TO HEAR ALL ABOUT THIS NEW JOB!!! I'm so
excited you are saving up the money!!!
GET HERE ALREADY!
Bethany
FOREVER USA
Katie Spera
5965 Ave D, Apt 3B
New York, NY 10009

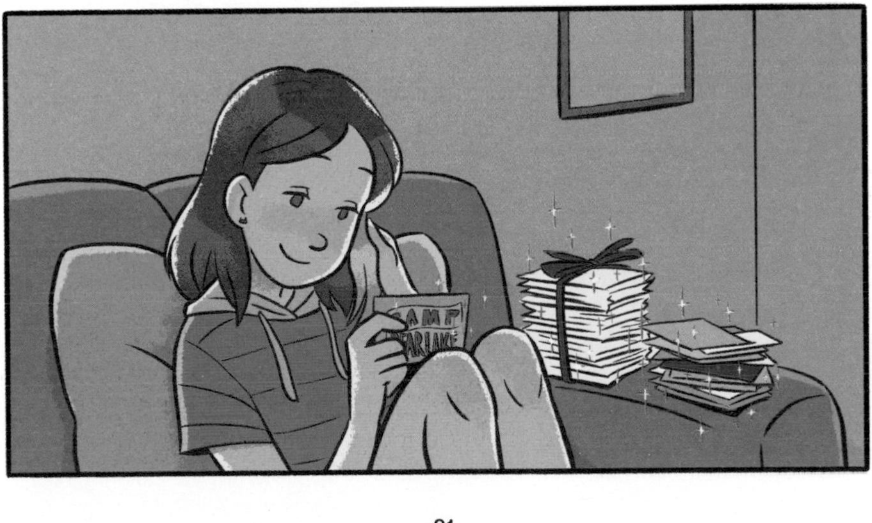

Nox: Robotics Expert

DJ Bootie Butler: Mad Beats

Pierogi: Textiles Expert

CLICK CLICK CLICK

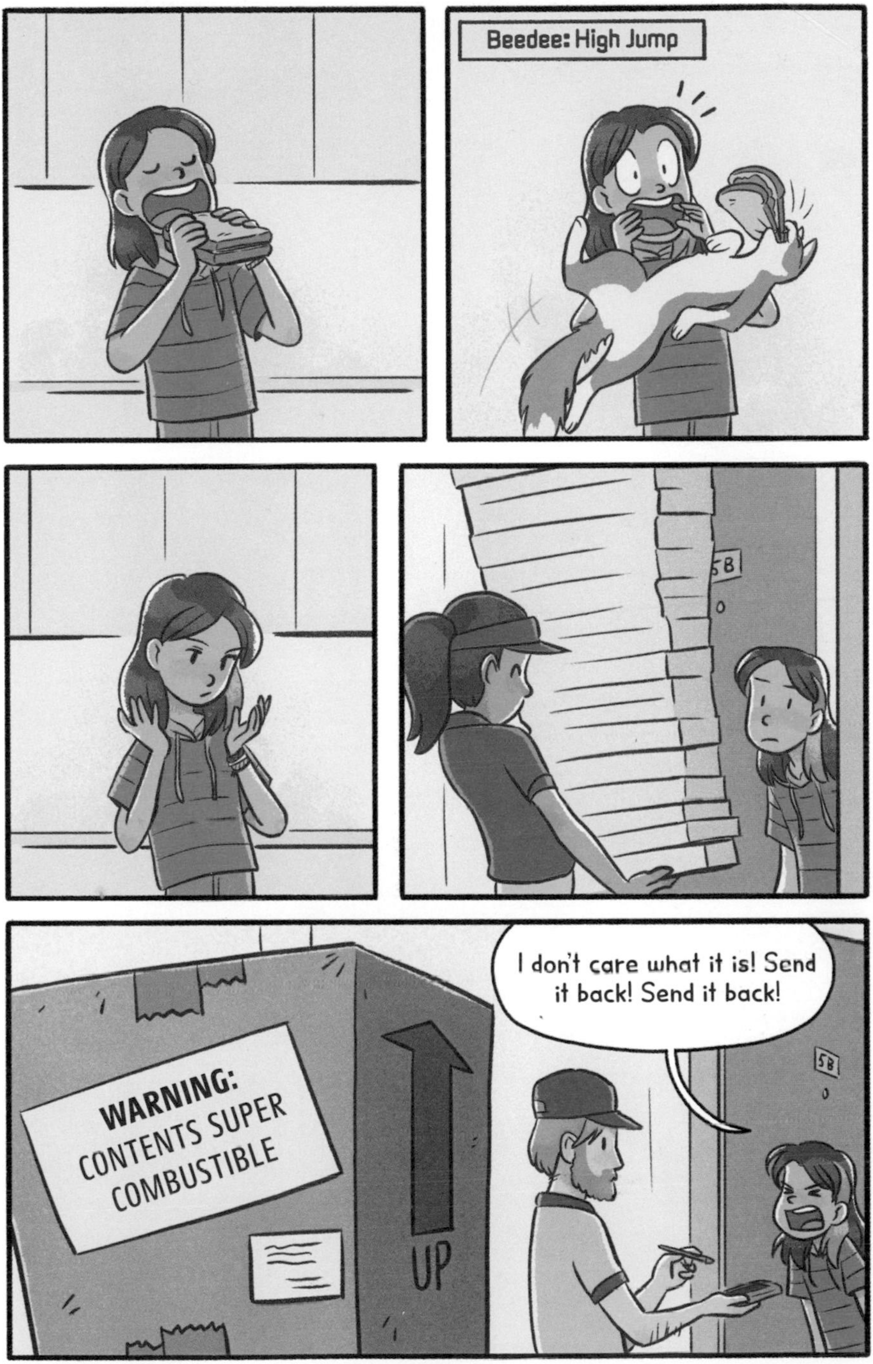
Beedee: High Jump
5B
I don't care what it is! Send it back! Send it back!
WARNING:
CONTENTS SUPER COMBUSTIBLE
UP
5B

THE NEXT WEEK

You should take a night off. Surely Ms. Lang doesn't need you to work EVERY night.

But I need the money! The more I work, the faster I get to camp!

How about tonight I help out. I've got the night off. It's been a while since I changed a litter box, but I think it'll come back to me.

You do NOT want to meet these cats. Also, they don't use litter boxes.

They aren't litter-box trained? No wonder you're so stressed!

Oh, and I almost forgot— two postcards today.

Got my Benadryl, some treats, and I bought a few cat toys. I'm ready!

Trust me. You are NOT ready.

Awwww. Look at all these cuties!

I know it's a lot of them, but they couldn't be sweeter!

Maybe you've just been hanging out with Scratch-Off too much and forgot what a nice cat is like!

86

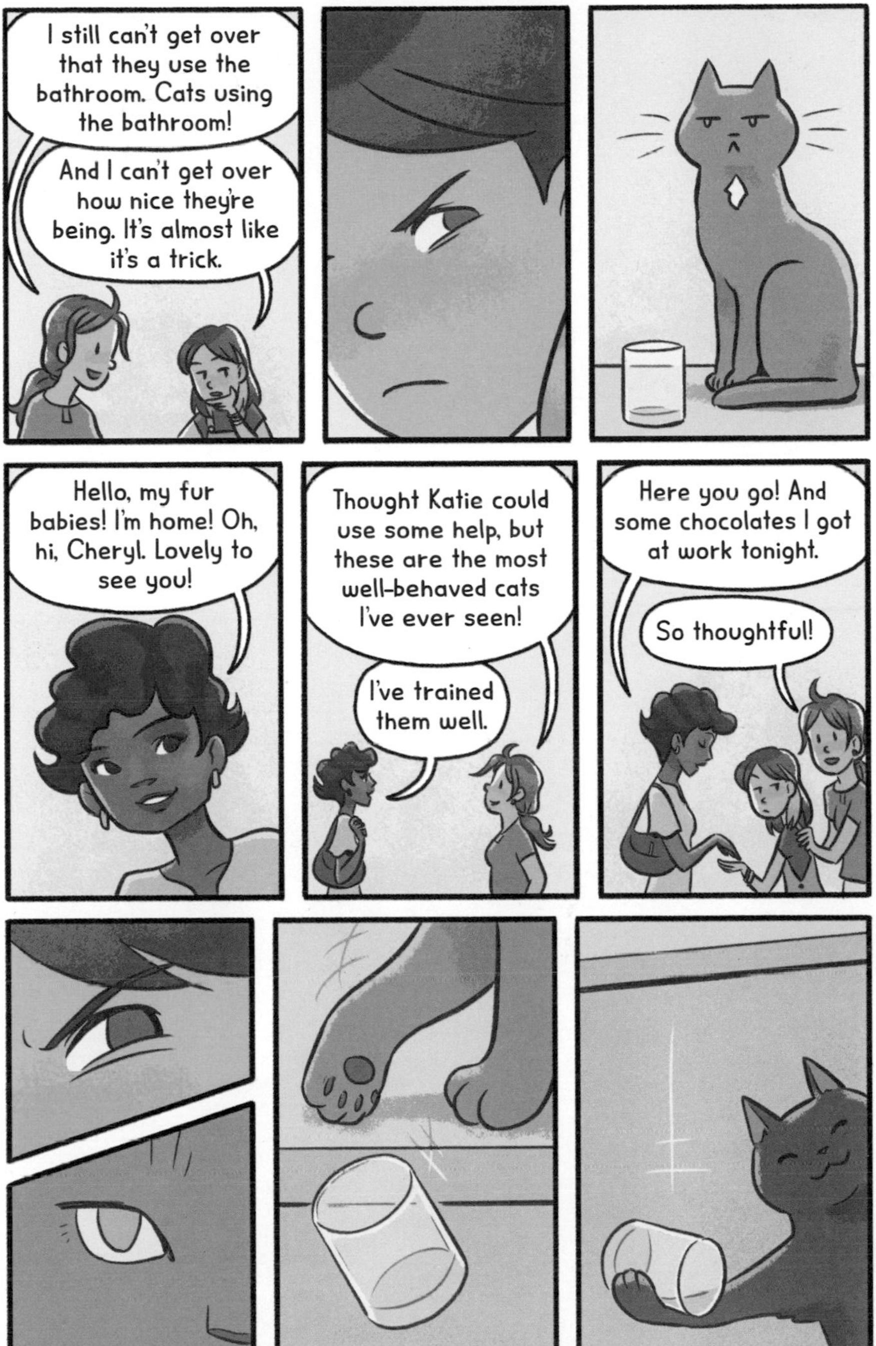
I still can't get over that they use the bathroom. Cats using the bathroom!
And I can't get over how nice they're being. It's almost like it's a trick.
Hello, my fur babies! I'm home! Oh, hi, Cheryl. Lovely to see you!
Thought Katie could use some help, but these are the most well-behaved cats I've ever seen!
I've trained them well.
Here you go! And some chocolates I got at work tonight.
So thoughtful!

Bethany!!!!

Okay, so good news is I'm only six nights of cat sitting away from my camp money goal! I can't wait to see you (and Max, of course—please tell him chitter chitter chitter, he'll understand).

I don't know how it's possible, but I swear the cats are EVEN MORE evil than usual. I feel like they're plotting something. Something big. I can't figure out how to outsmart them! They've stolen at least 9 couches from Mrs. Piper, and she's bound to figure it out eventually. What should I dooooooo?

Not a couch thief, just an accessory to couch thief-ery,

Katie

Katie the Cat Conqueror—

You're smart! You're fast! You're tall . . . well, maybe not that last one. You can play some tricks on THEM before they get a chance to play a trick on you. Remember that fifteen-minute trick we used to do to the clock in Ms. Sistine's room?

Max says you should try bribery first. Also, he says there's a boy named Ben who's not the worst. He's got these crazy dark brown eyes that are like melty. I think I might have a crush. On Ben. Not Max. Because that would be weird.

Cannot WAIT for you to meet everyone. Conquer the kitties, then come join me!!! I've perfected my s'more game. The trick is heating up the graham cracker TOO so the chocolate melts on both sides. I'll make you a Bethany Original!

—Bethany

CHAPTER SEVEN

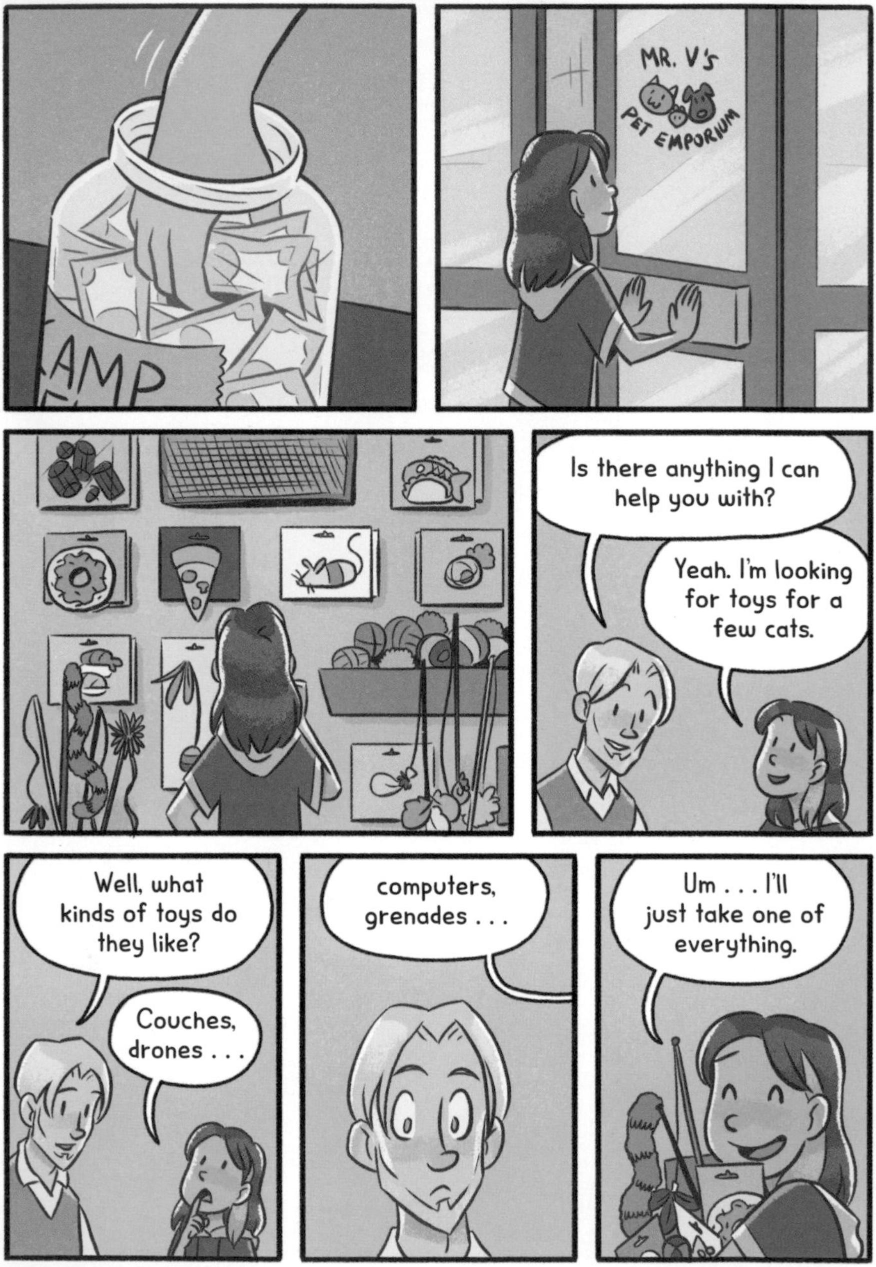
AMP
MR. V's PET EMPORIUM
Is there anything I can help you with?
Yeah. I'm looking for toys for a few cats.
Well, what kinds of toys do they like?
Couches, drones . . .
computers, grenades . . .
Um . . . I'll just take one of everything.

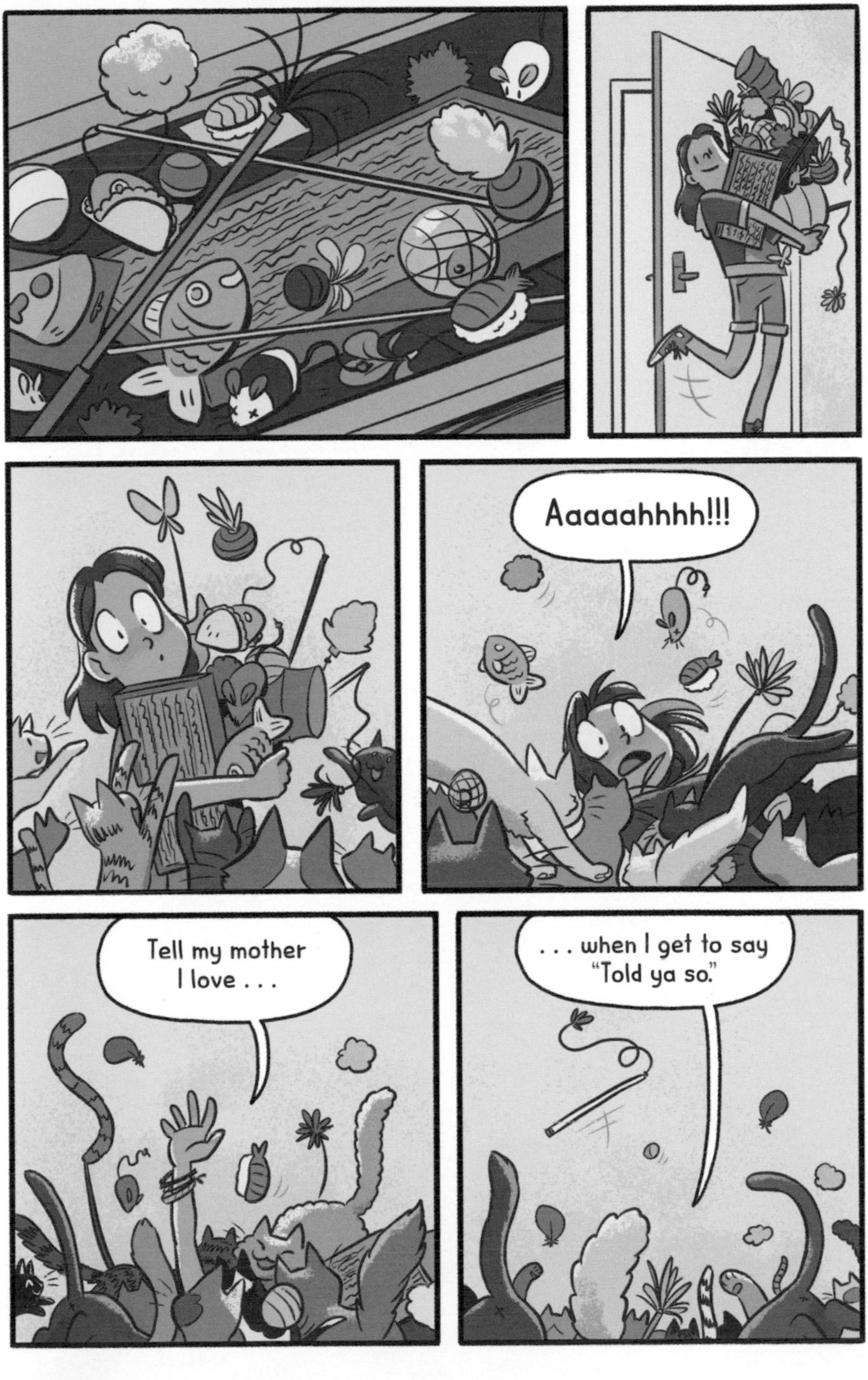
Aaaaahhhh!!!
Tell my mother I love . . .
. . . when I get to say "Told ya so."

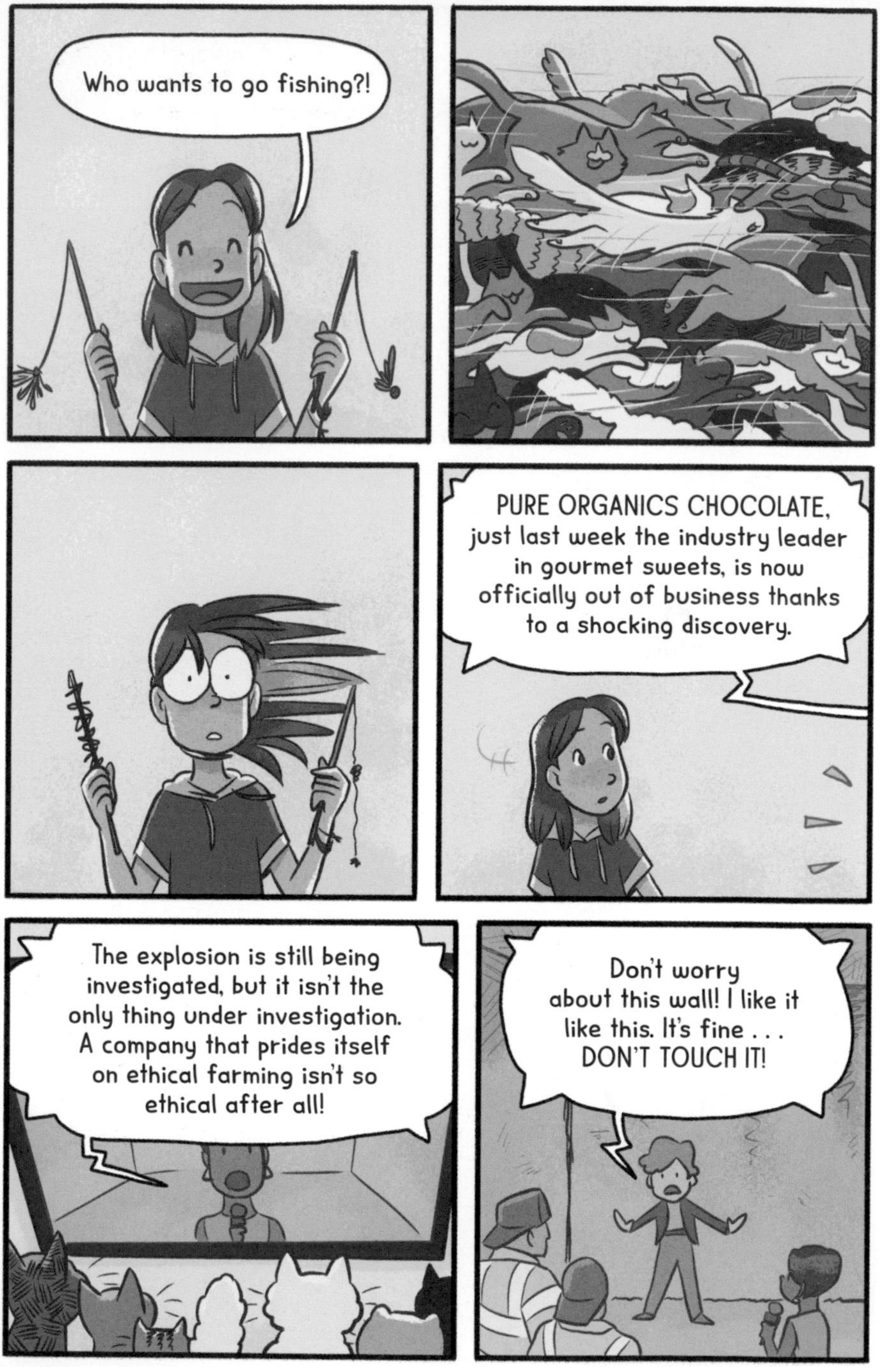
Who wants to go fishing?!
PURE ORGANICS CHOCOLATE, just last week the industry leader in gourmet sweets, is now officially out of business thanks to a shocking discovery.
The explosion is still being investigated, but it isn't the only thing under investigation. A company that prides itself on ethical farming isn't so ethical after all!
Don't worry about this wall! I like it like this. It's fine . . . DON'T TOUCH IT!

While searching for clues, it was discovered that PURE ORGANICS owner Lydia Staples has not been using her frequent trips to Africa to "pay living wages to migrant farmers" . . .

. . . but instead was using the trips to illegally hunt animals. Endangered animals. Animals she THEN put on display in a secret office.

We've got animal expert Thea Robbins here with us. Can you tell us what we're looking at?

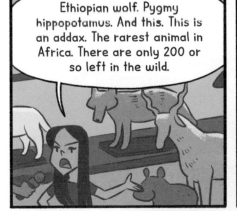

Ethiopian wolf. Pygmy hippopotamus. And this. This is an addax. The rarest animal in Africa. There are only 200 or so left in the wild.

IN THE WORLD, LYDIA STAPLES! YOU BETTER HOPE YOU GET A LONG JAIL SENTENCE BECAUSE YOU MESSED WITH THE WRONG BIOLOGIST, LADY! LET ME AT HER!

If it wasn't for that explosion, who knows how long Lydia Staples would have kept poaching.

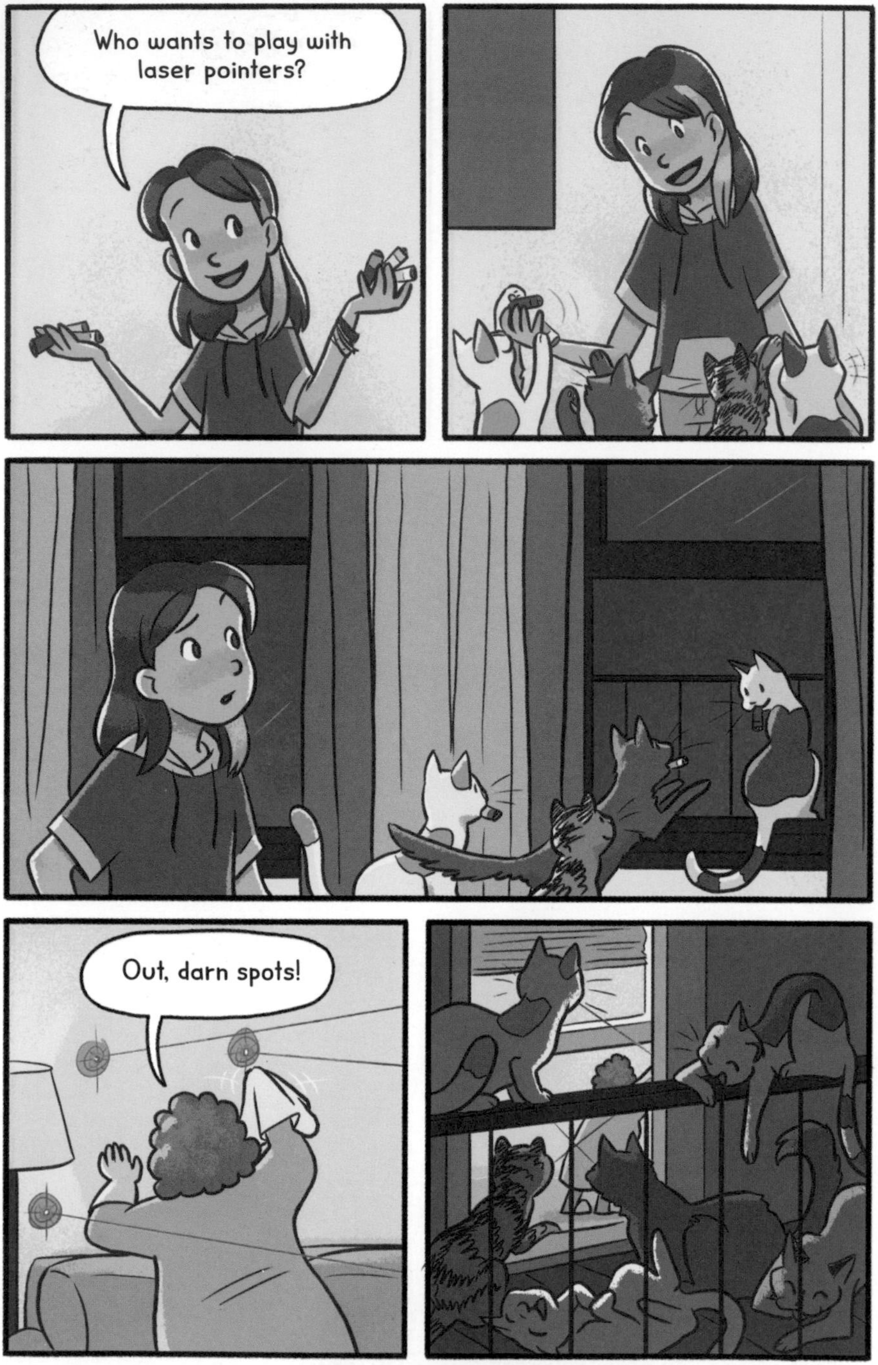
Who wants to play with laser pointers?
Out, darn spots!

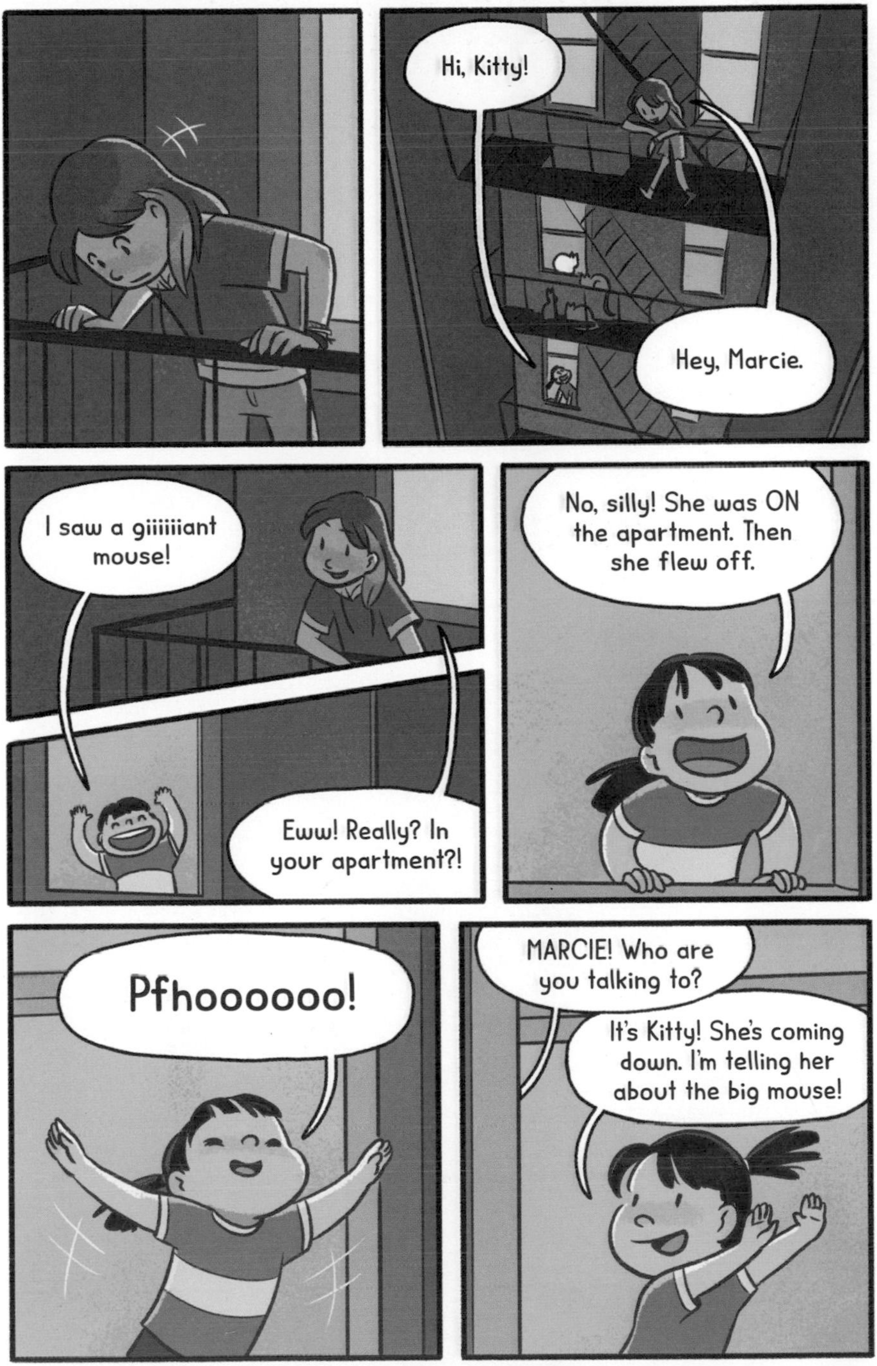
Hi, Kitty!
Hey, Marcie.
I saw a giiiiiiant mouse!
Eww! Really? In your apartment?!
No, silly! She was ON the apartment. Then she flew off.
Pfhoooooo!
MARCIE! Who are you talking to?
It's Kitty! She's coming down. I'm telling her about the big mouse!

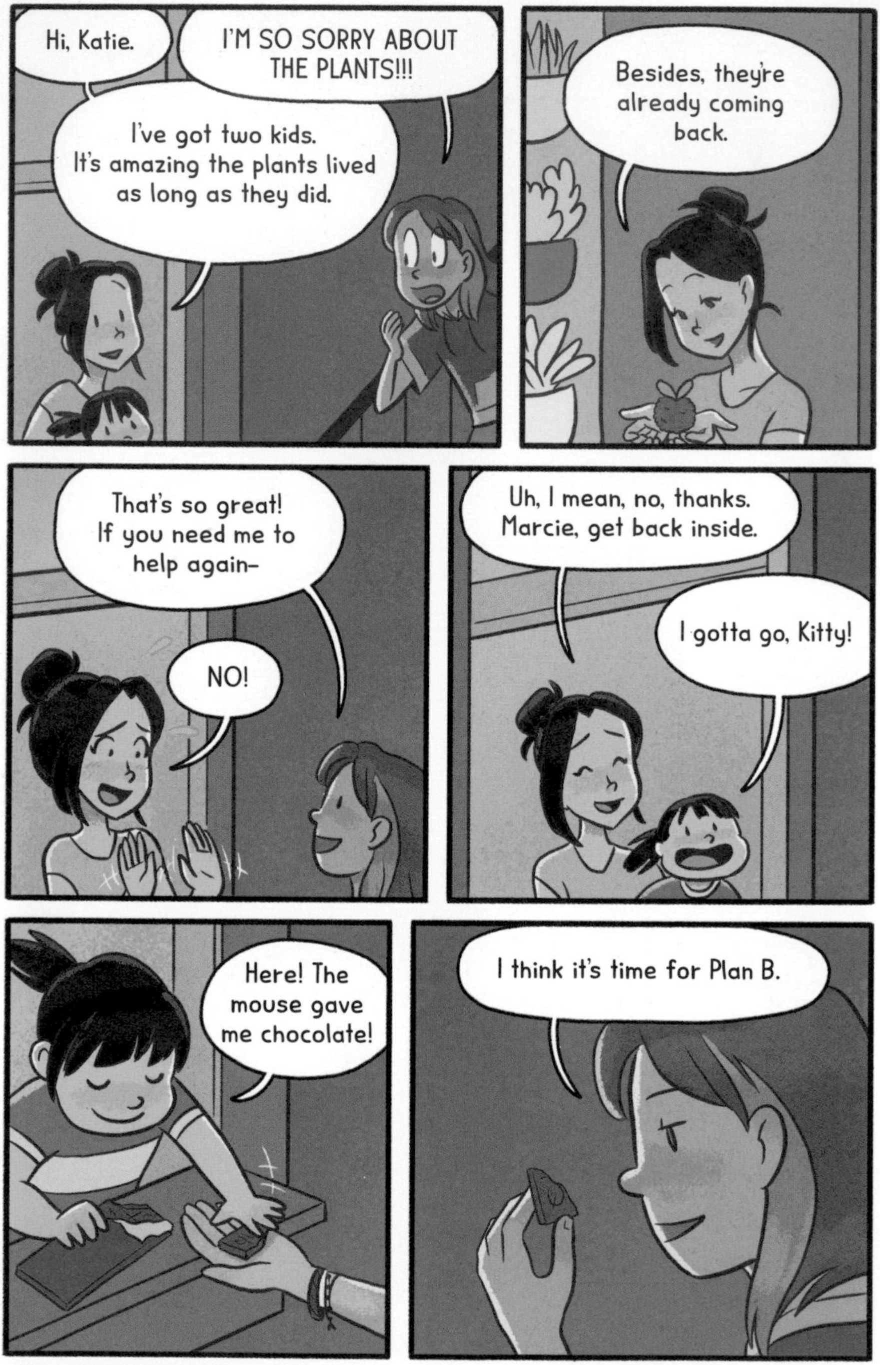

Hi, Katie.
I'M SO SORRY ABOUT THE PLANTS!!!
I've got two kids. It's amazing the plants lived as long as they did.
Besides, they're already coming back.
That's so great! If you need me to help again–
NO!
Uh, I mean, no, thanks. Marcie, get back inside.
I gotta go, Kitty!
Here! The mouse gave me chocolate!
I think it's time for Plan B.

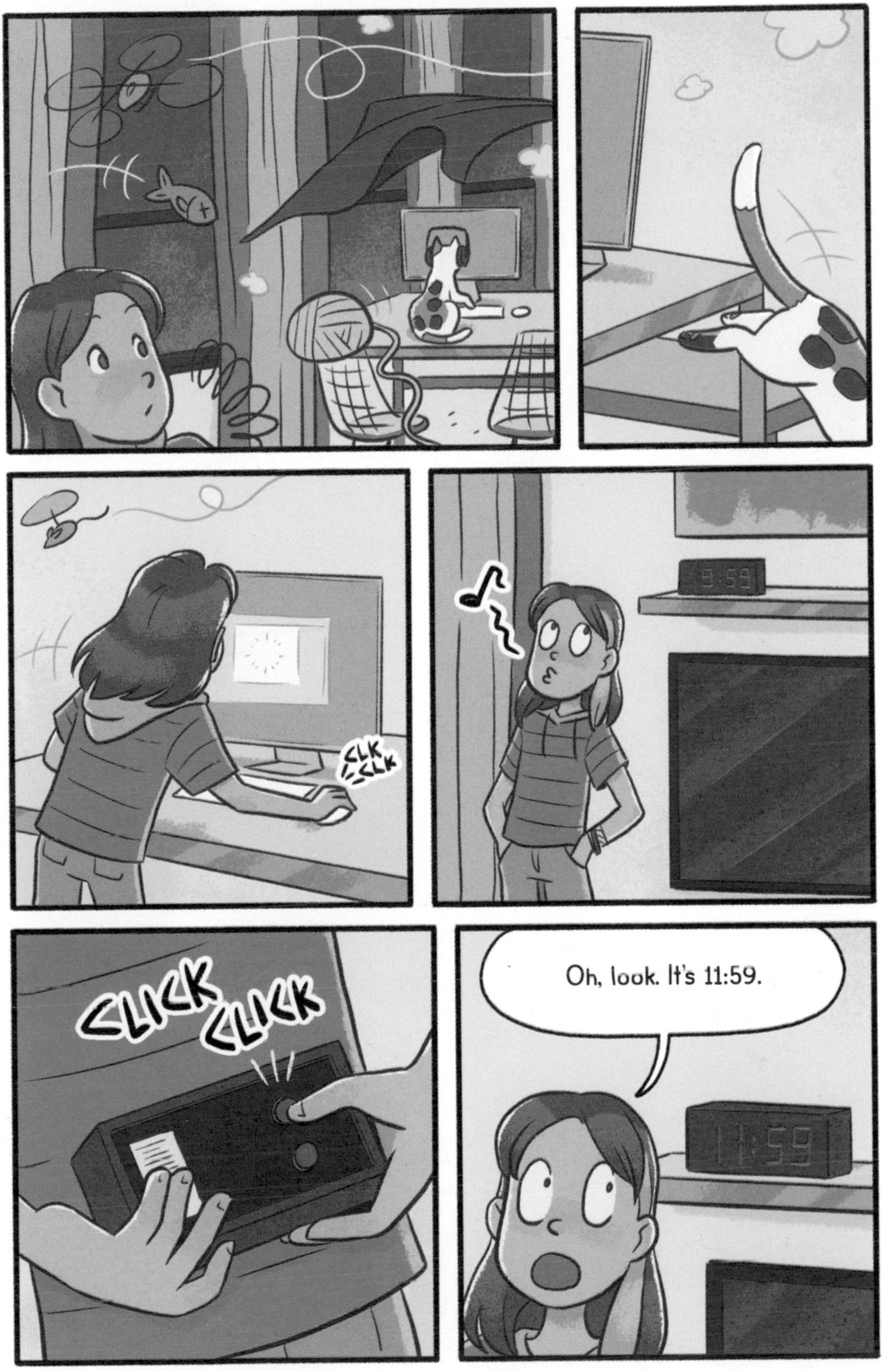
CLK
CLK
CLICK
CLICK
Oh, look. It's 11:59.

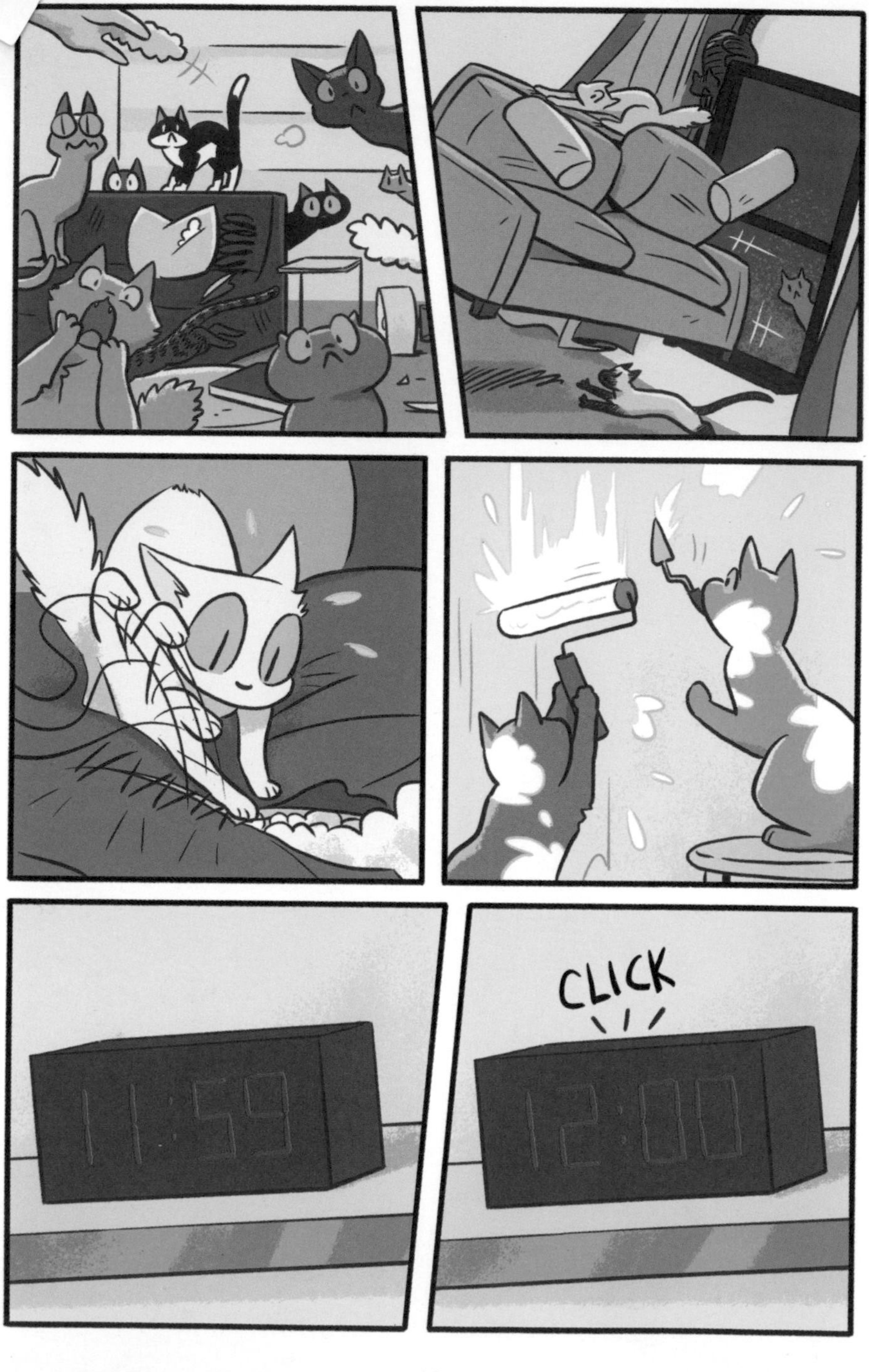
11:59
CLICK
12:00

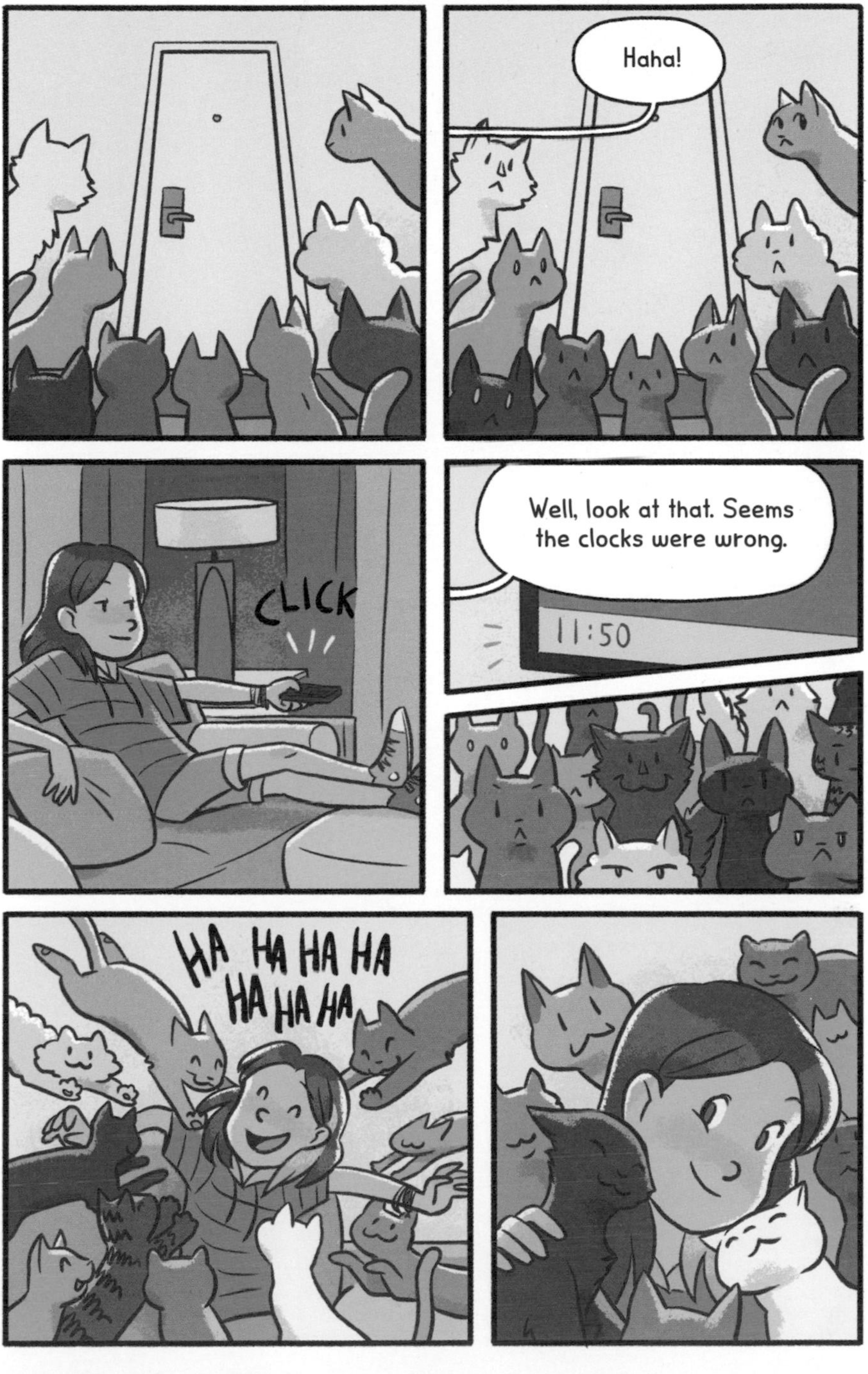
Haha!
CLICK
Well, look at that. Seems the clocks were wrong.
11:50
HA HA HA HA
HA HA HA

CHAPTER EIGHT

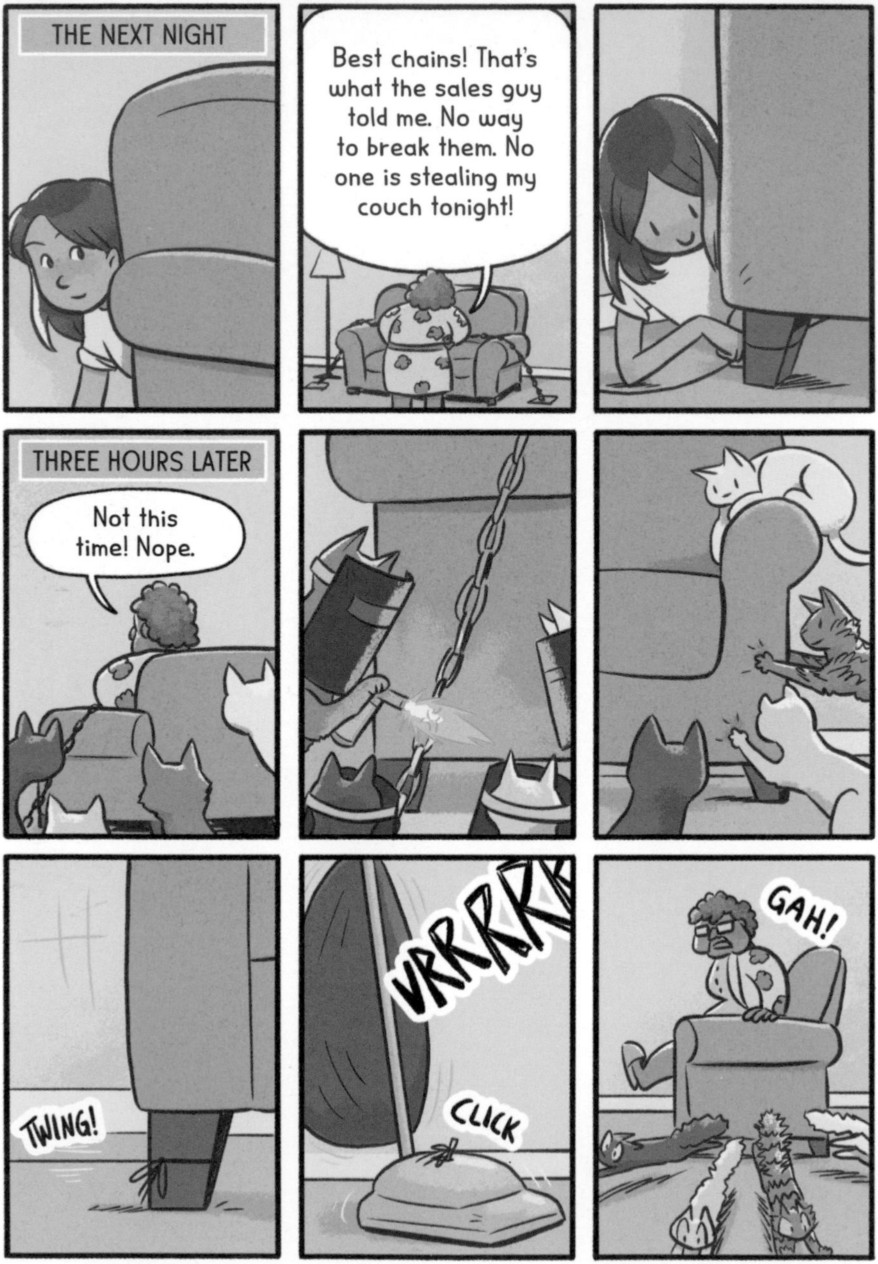
THE NEXT NIGHT
Best chains! That's what the sales guy told me. No way to break them. No one is stealing my couch tonight!
THREE HOURS LATER
Not this time! Nope.
TWING!
VRRRRR
CLICK
GAH!

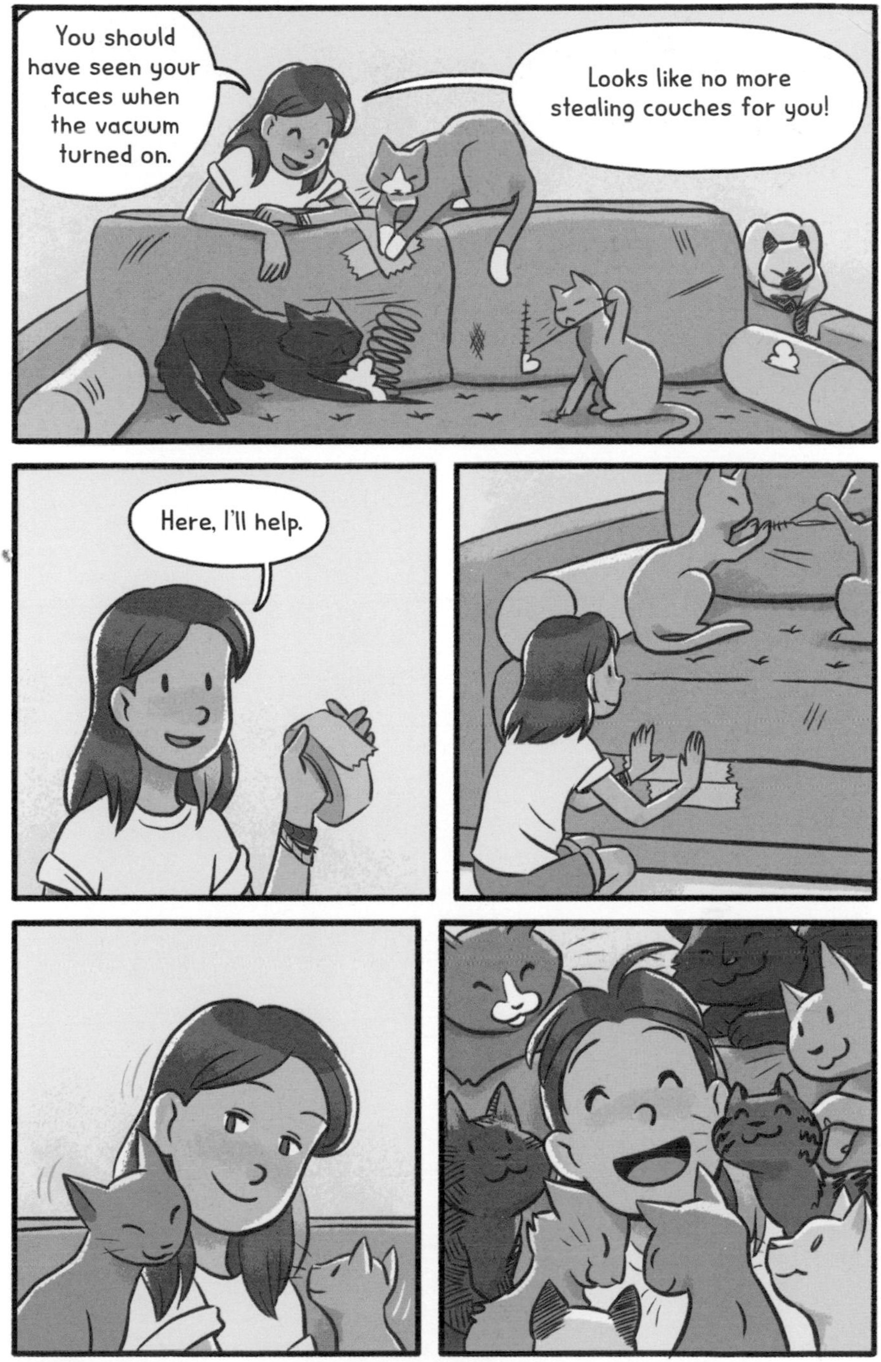
You should have seen your faces when the vacuum turned on.
Looks like no more stealing couches for you!
Here, I'll help.

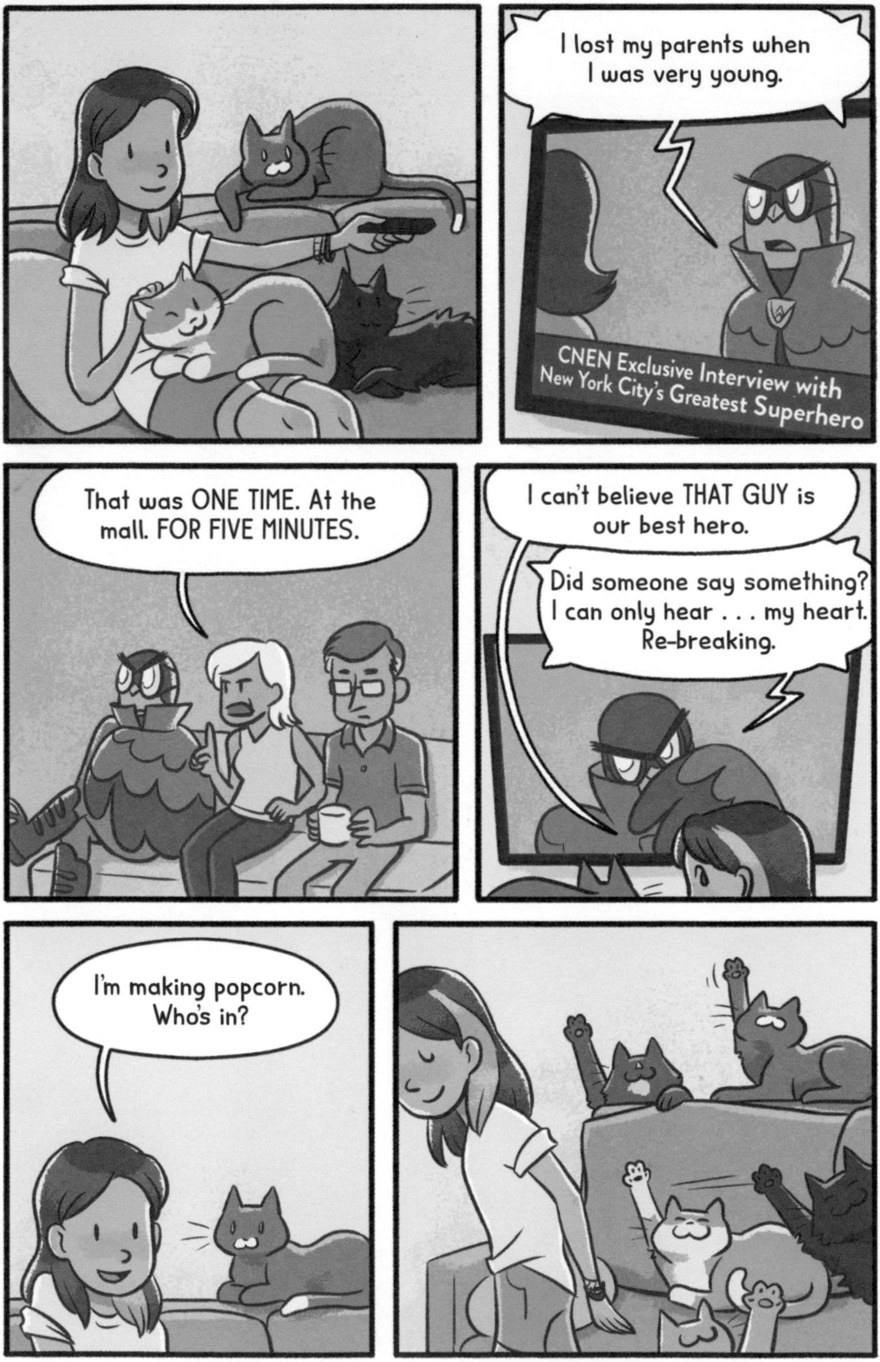
I lost my parents when I was very young.
CNEN Exclusive Interview with New York City's Greatest Superhero
That was ONE TIME. At the mall. FOR FIVE MINUTES.
I can't believe THAT GUY is our best hero.
Did someone say something? I can only hear . . . my heart. Re-breaking.
I'm making popcorn. Who's in?

We interrupt this interview for a special report.

Last night a robbery took place. The victim? Hunter Q. Prescott—musician, actor, philanthropist, and sorta slam poet.

Yeah, Girl-Bro. They took my TV, my rad audio setup, even my fave sunglahs right off my eyeballs.

The sunglasses are Hunter's custom-made Gocheez, a vital and EXPENSIVE part of his signature look.

I've got a poem for you, thief! Roses are red, violets are blue. Gimme my glasses back, because . . . something something goo?

A witness—who identified as "TOTALLY NOT A STALKER HIDING IN THE BUSH BY HUNTER'S WESTERN WINDOW"—claims they saw a mouse-shaped silhouette on the roof. Could this be the work of New York's most dangerous supervillain?!

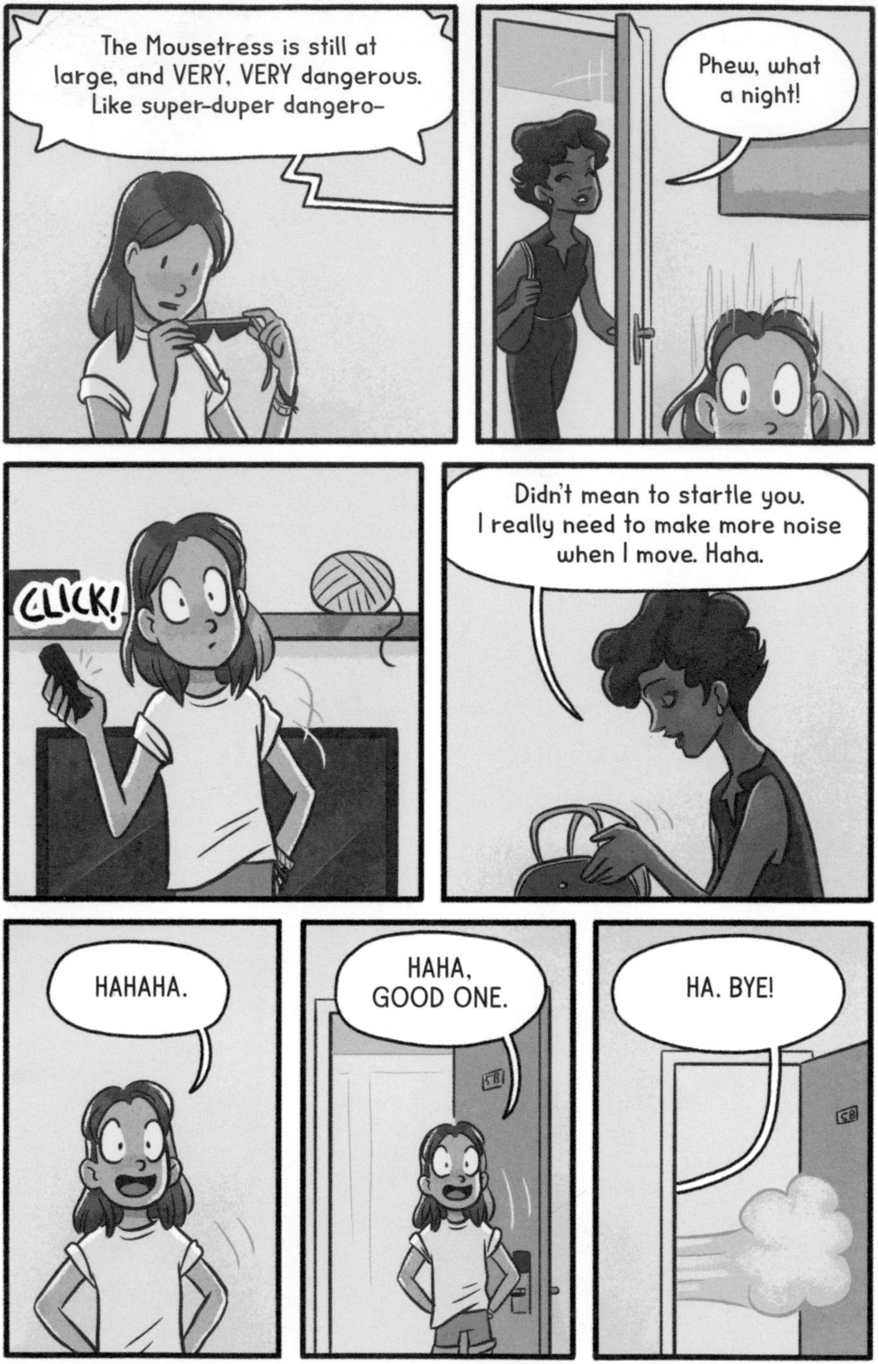
The Mousetress is still at large, and VERY, VERY dangerous. Like super-duper dangero–
Phew, what a night!
CLICK!
Didn't mean to startle you. I really need to make more noise when I move. Haha.
HAHAHA.
HAHA, GOOD ONE.
HA. BYE!

I'm telling you! Ms. Lang is the . . .

. . . Mousetress.

I see these every day. Knockoffs for the fans.

And you *really* think she's a FAN of his music?

I don't judge. When I was a kid, I went to a Twisted Sister concert wearing one of my mom's wigs as chest hair.

If you're trying to make me scared of you, too, it's working.

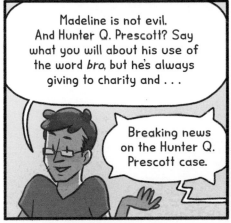

Madeline is not evil. And Hunter Q. Prescott? Say what you will about his use of the word *bro*, but he's always giving to charity and . . .

Breaking news on the Hunter Q. Prescott case.

While searching for clues, the police uncovered a secret trap door in the living room.

BREAKING NEWS:
Hunter "Questionable" Prescott?

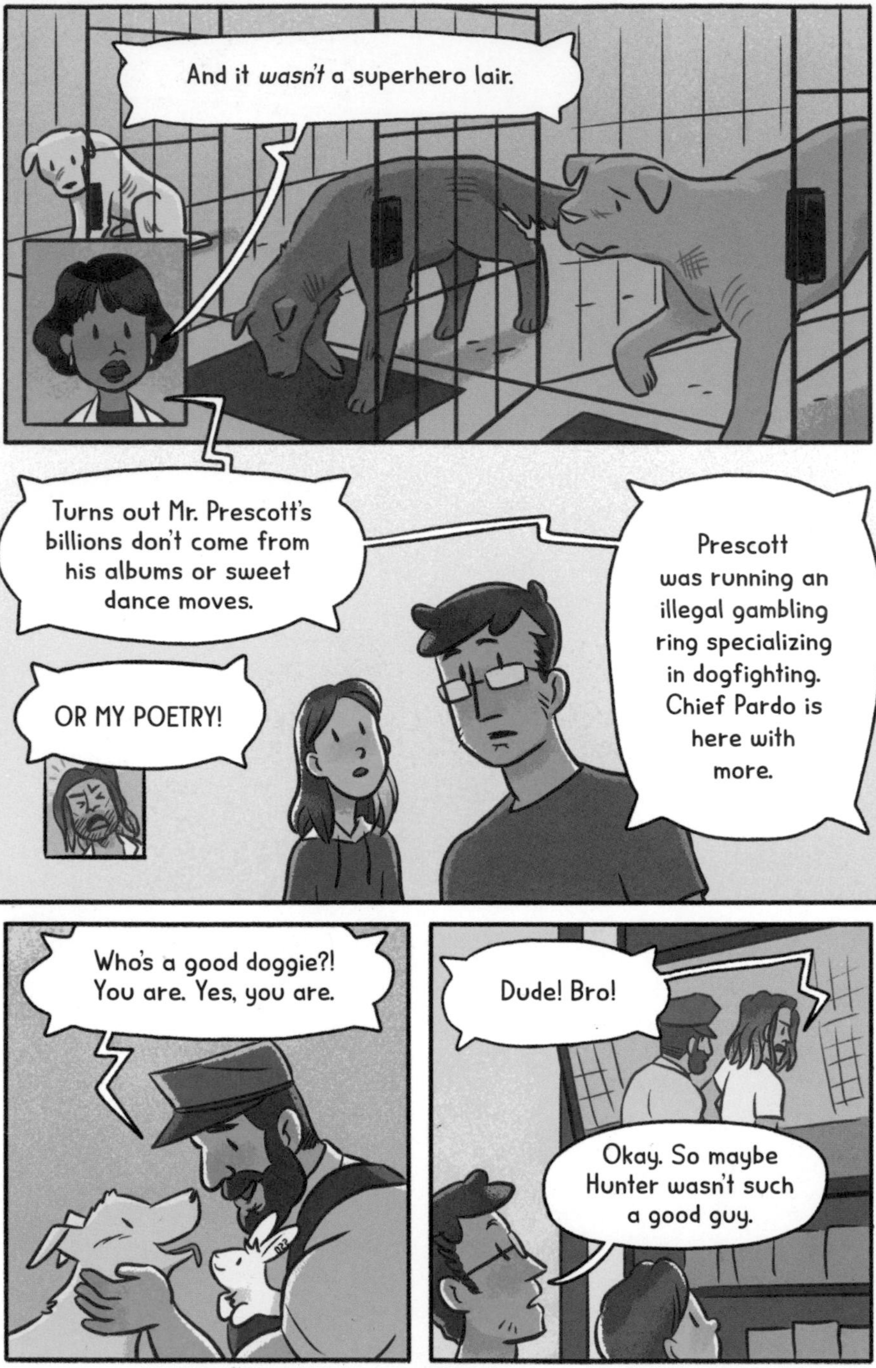

And it *wasn't* a superhero lair.
Turns out Mr. Prescott's billions don't come from his albums or sweet dance moves.
OR MY POETRY!
Prescott was running an illegal gambling ring specializing in dogfighting. Chief Pardo is here with more.
Who's a good doggie?! You are. Yes, you are.
Dude! Bro!
Okay. So maybe Hunter wasn't such a good guy.

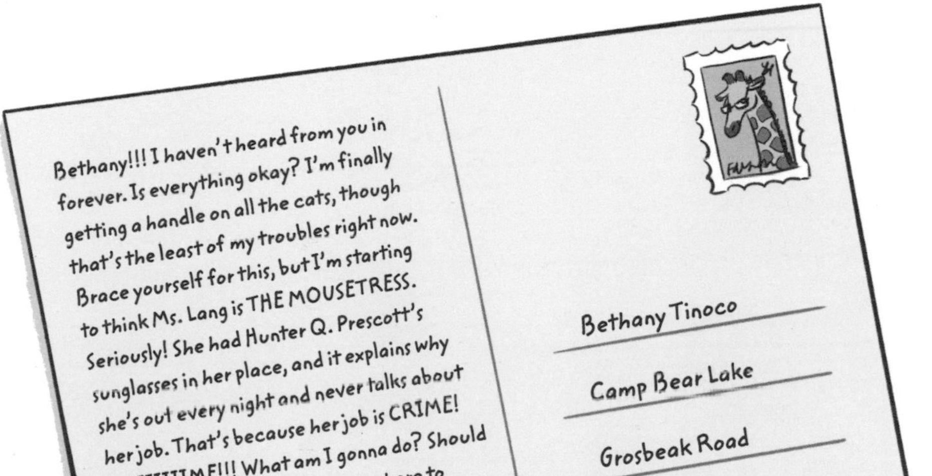

Bethany!!! I haven't heard from you in forever. Is everything okay? I'm finally getting a handle on all the cats, though that's the least of my troubles right now. Brace yourself for this, but I'm starting to think Ms. Lang is THE MOUSETRESS. Seriously! She had Hunter Q. Prescott's sunglasses in her place, and it explains why she's out every night and never talks about her job. That's because her job is CRIME! CRIIIIIIME!!! What am I gonna do? Should I confront her? I wish you were here to help me figure out what to do!!! I miss you. Please write back as soon as possible!!!!

Hearts and Cats and Eeeeeeee,
Katie

Bethany Tinoco

Camp Bear Lake

Grosbeak Road

Bear Lake Valley, NY

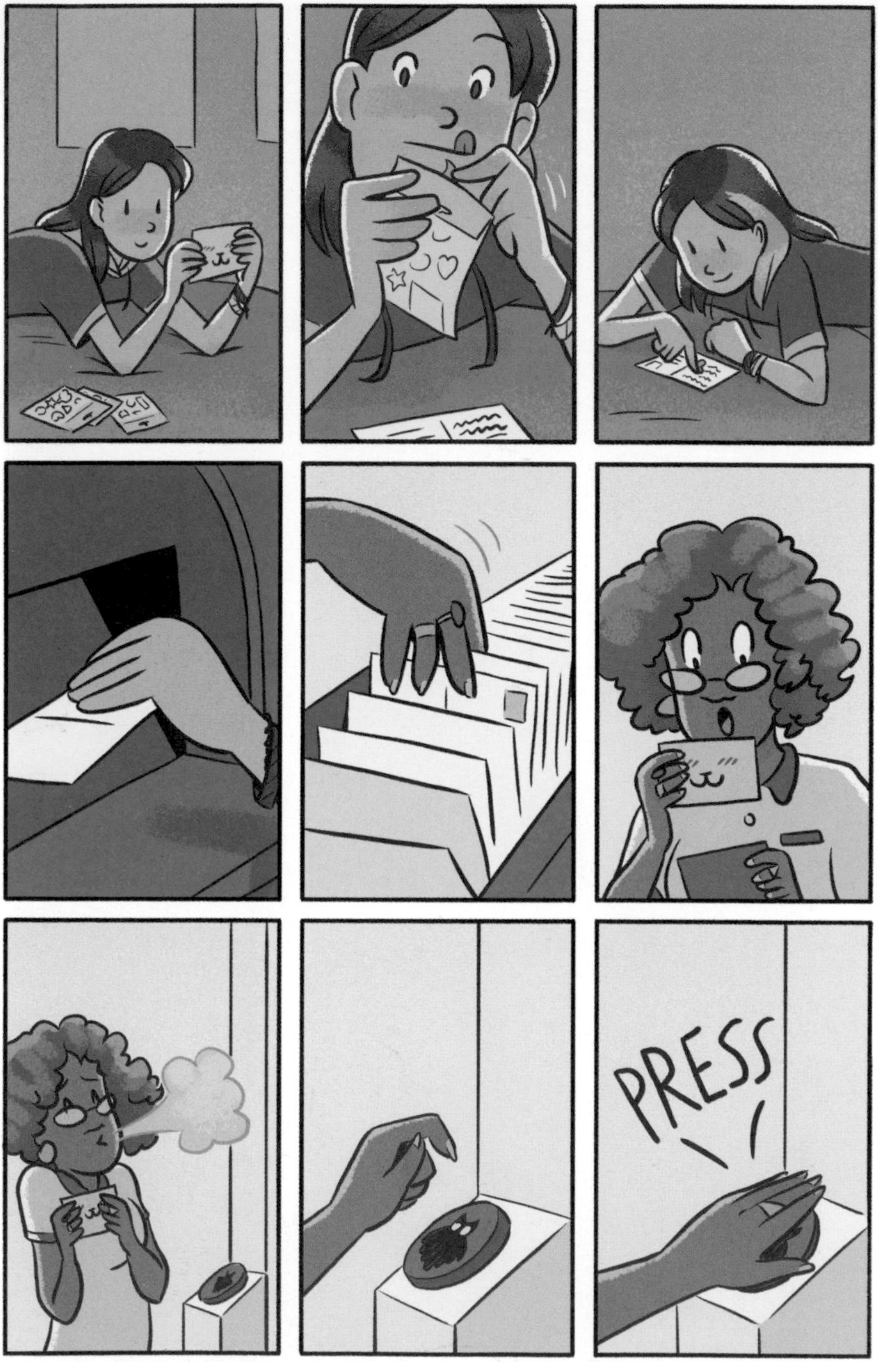
PRESS

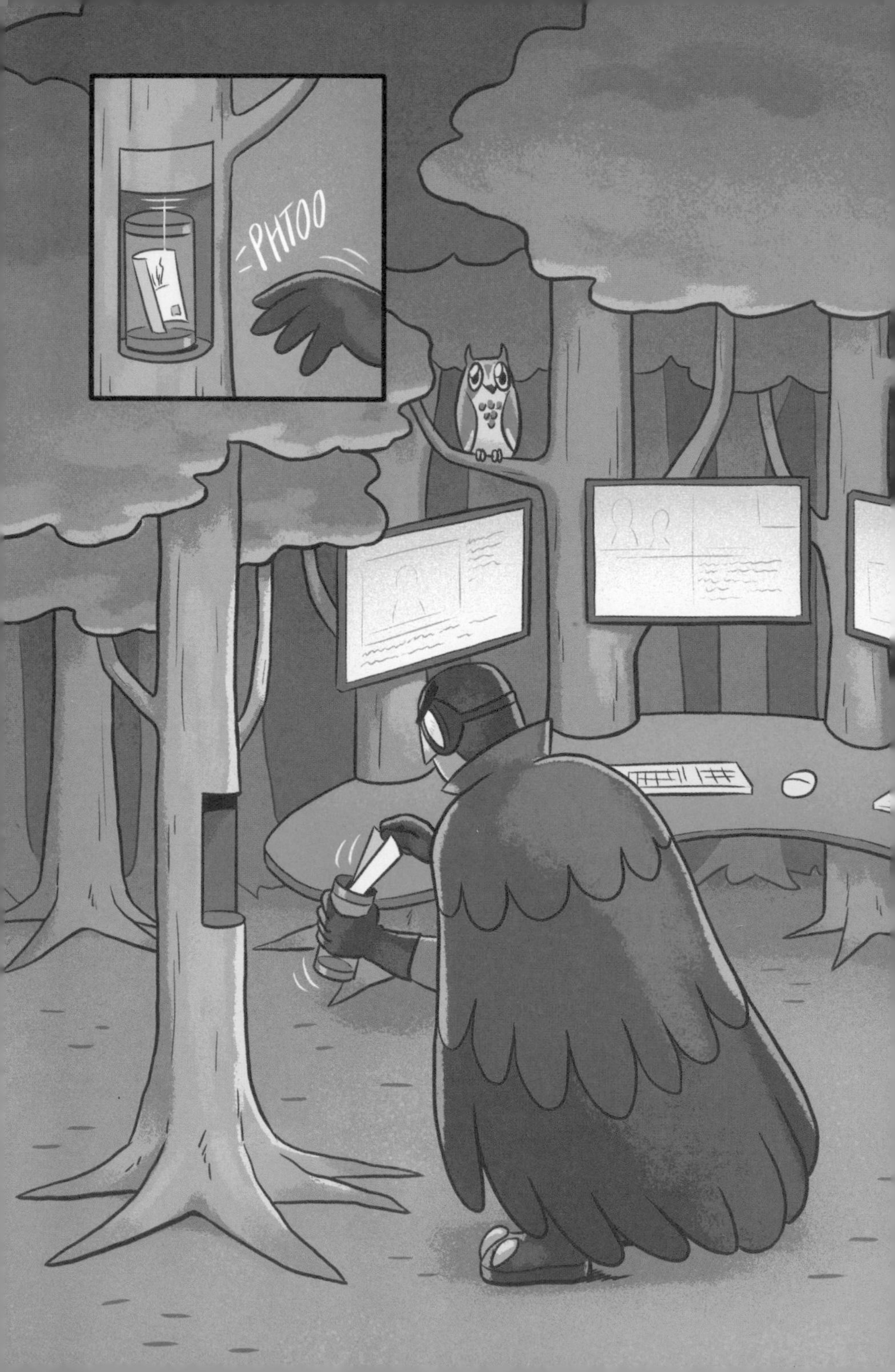
PHTOO

CHAPTER NINE

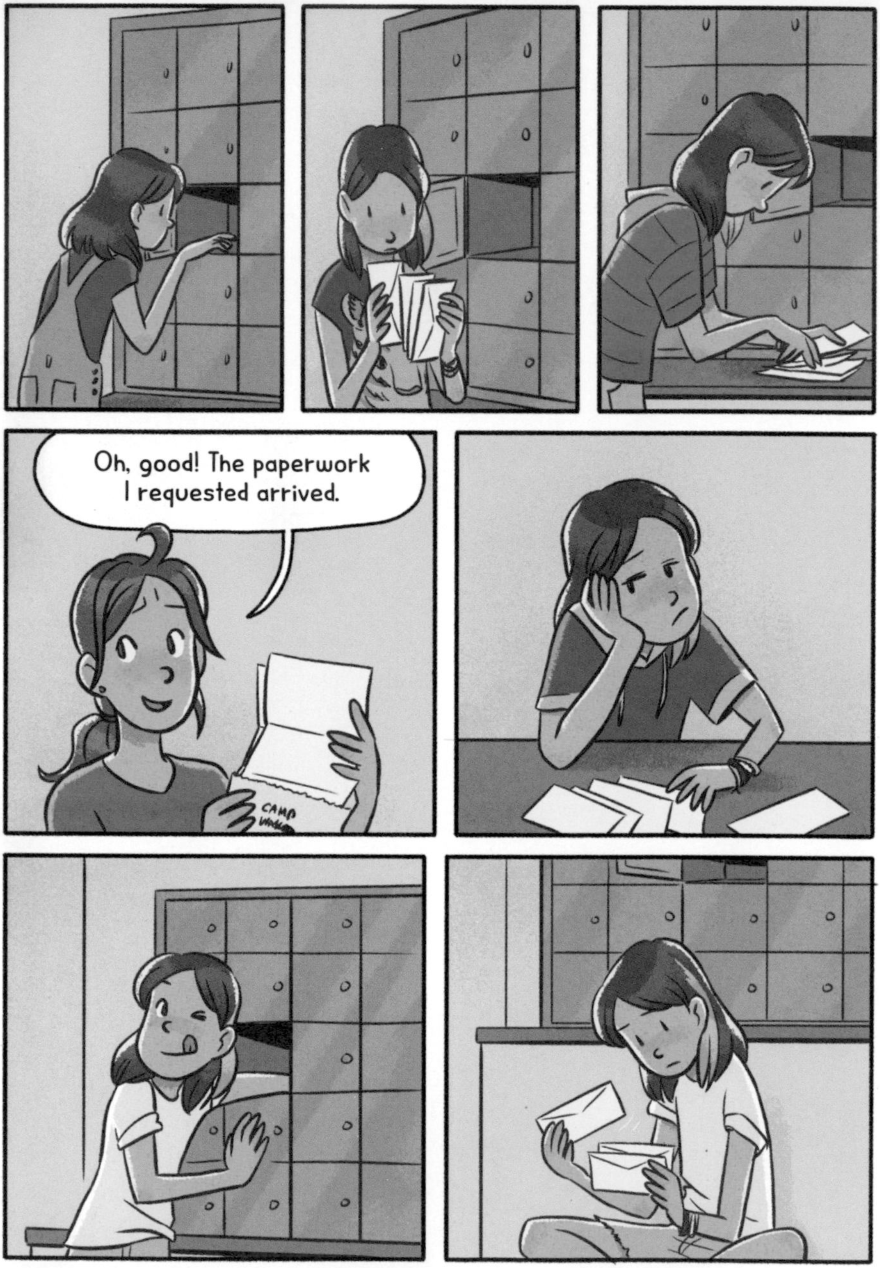
Oh, good! The paperwork I requested arrived.
CAMP

Hey, has the mail dude been by yet today?

He has a name.

What's his name?

Well, I'm pretty sure it's not "mail dude." Expecting something?

I haven't gotten a postcard from Bethany in a week.

She's probably just been busy.

She's never gone this long without writing! And the last postcard I sent was really important.

113

No sulking! I've got a few days off! What'll it be? Concert in the park? Bike ride? Movie?! There's a new nature doc about lemurs, isn't there?

The Wax Museum of Justice.

You *hate* superheroes.

But it'll be . . . educational.

And you know I *haaaate* wax museums.

I saw a TV show that said it's good for you to confront your fears.

Sigh. Fine.

114

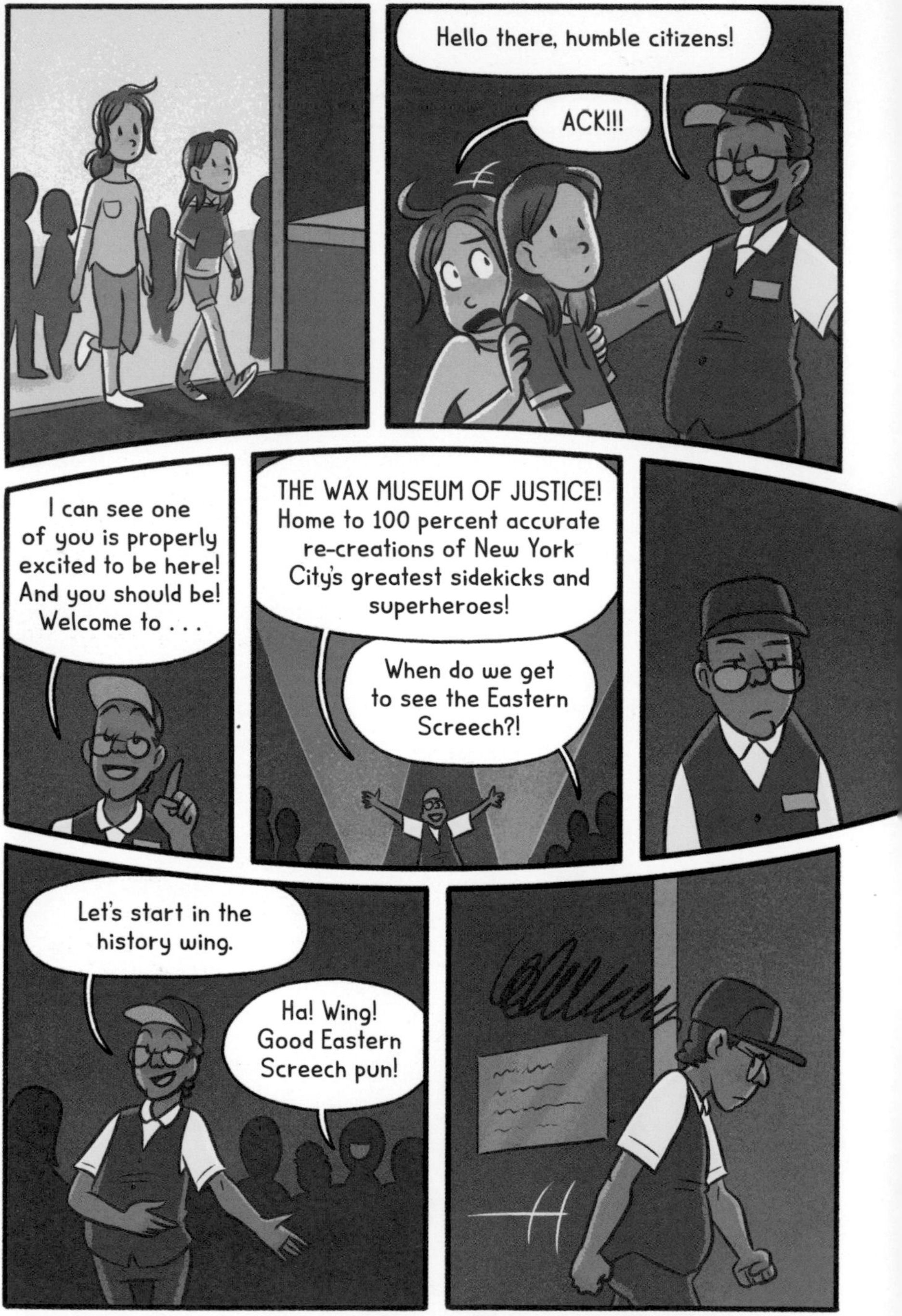

Hello there, humble citizens!
ACK!!!
I can see one of you is properly excited to be here! And you should be! Welcome to . . .
THE WAX MUSEUM OF JUSTICE! Home to 100 percent accurate re-creations of New York City's greatest sidekicks and superheroes!
When do we get to see the Eastern Screech?!
Let's start in the history wing.
Ha! Wing! Good Eastern Screech pun!

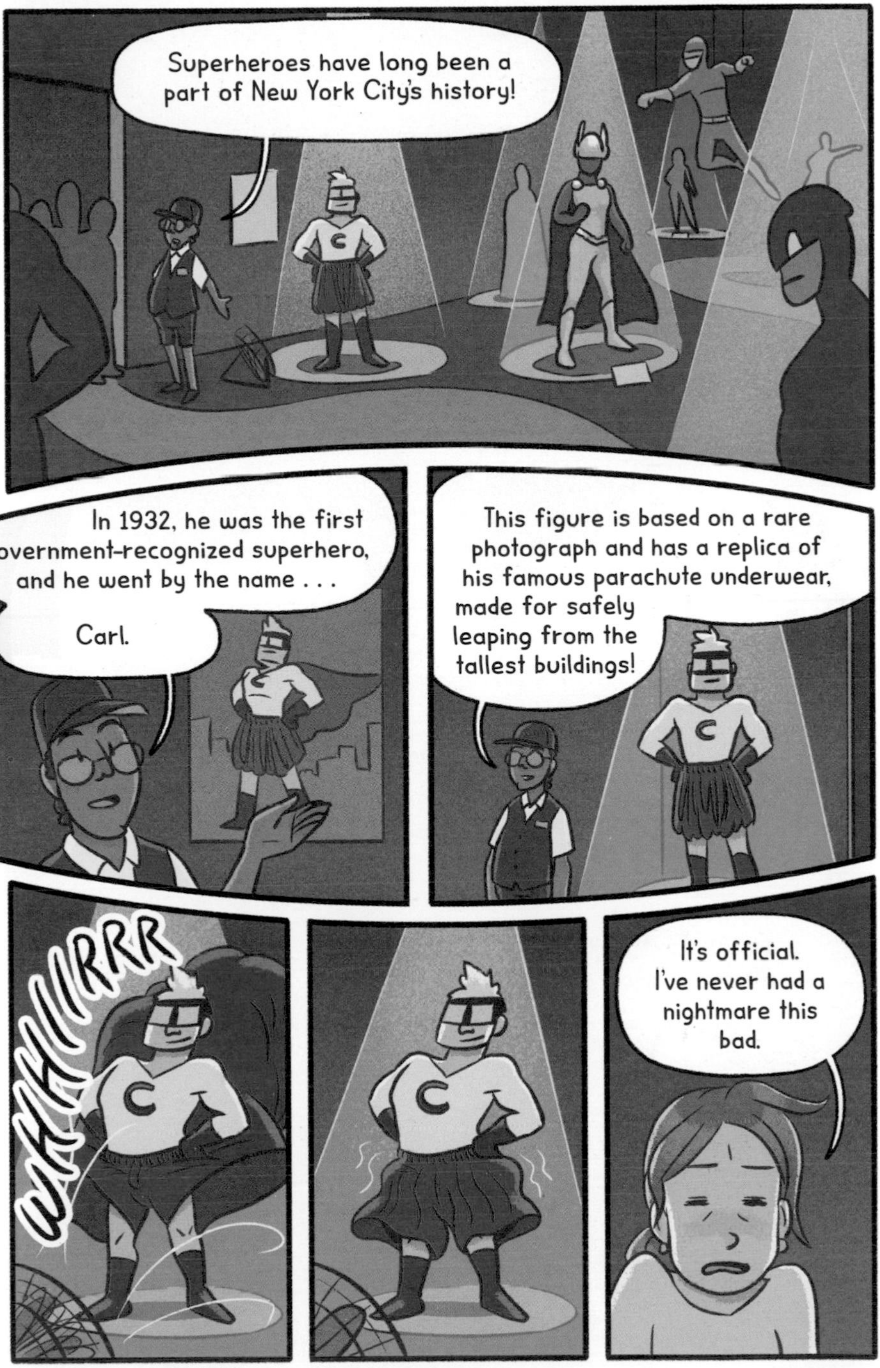
Superheroes have long been a part of New York City's history!
In 1932, he was the first government-recognized superhero, and he went by the name . . .
Carl.
This figure is based on a rare photograph and has a replica of his famous parachute underwear, made for safely leaping from the tallest buildings!
WHHHIRRR
It's official. I've never had a nightmare this bad.

And *this* is one of the biggest milestones. Get your cameras ready, folks!

Ready for . . .

THE MEERKAT.

CLICK

You know The Meerkat! The first super-sidekick? Had the coolest superpowers. Like being able to sit upright for hours, excellent 20/20 vision, and . . .

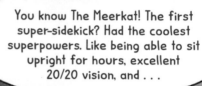

Is that the Eastern Screech's statue?!

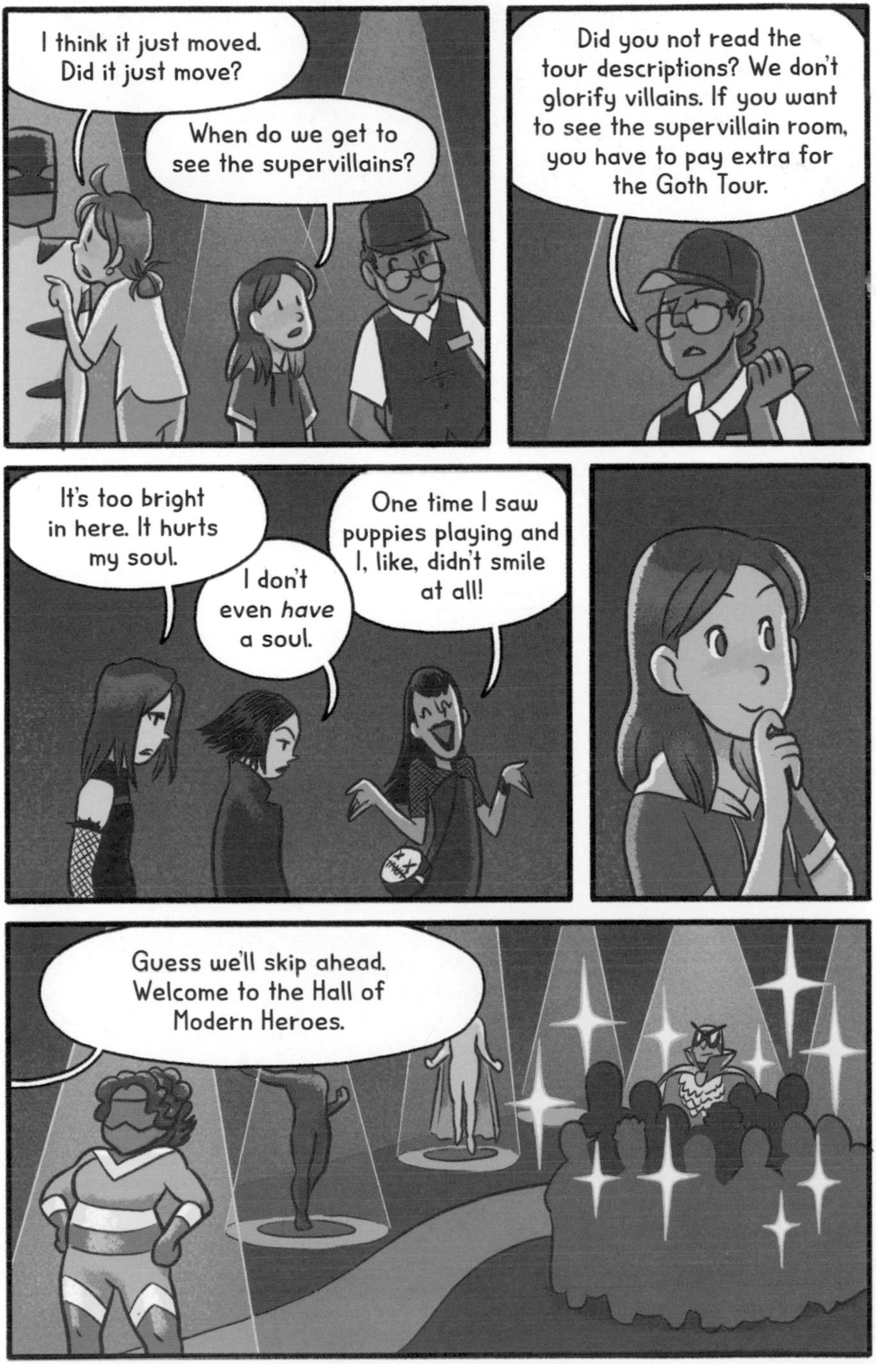
I think it just moved. Did it just move?
When do we get to see the supervillains?
Did you not read the tour descriptions? We don't glorify villains. If you want to see the supervillain room, you have to pay extra for the Goth Tour.
It's too bright in here. It hurts my soul.
I don't even *have* a soul.
One time I saw puppies playing and I, like, didn't smile at all!
Guess we'll skip ahead. Welcome to the Hall of Modern Heroes.

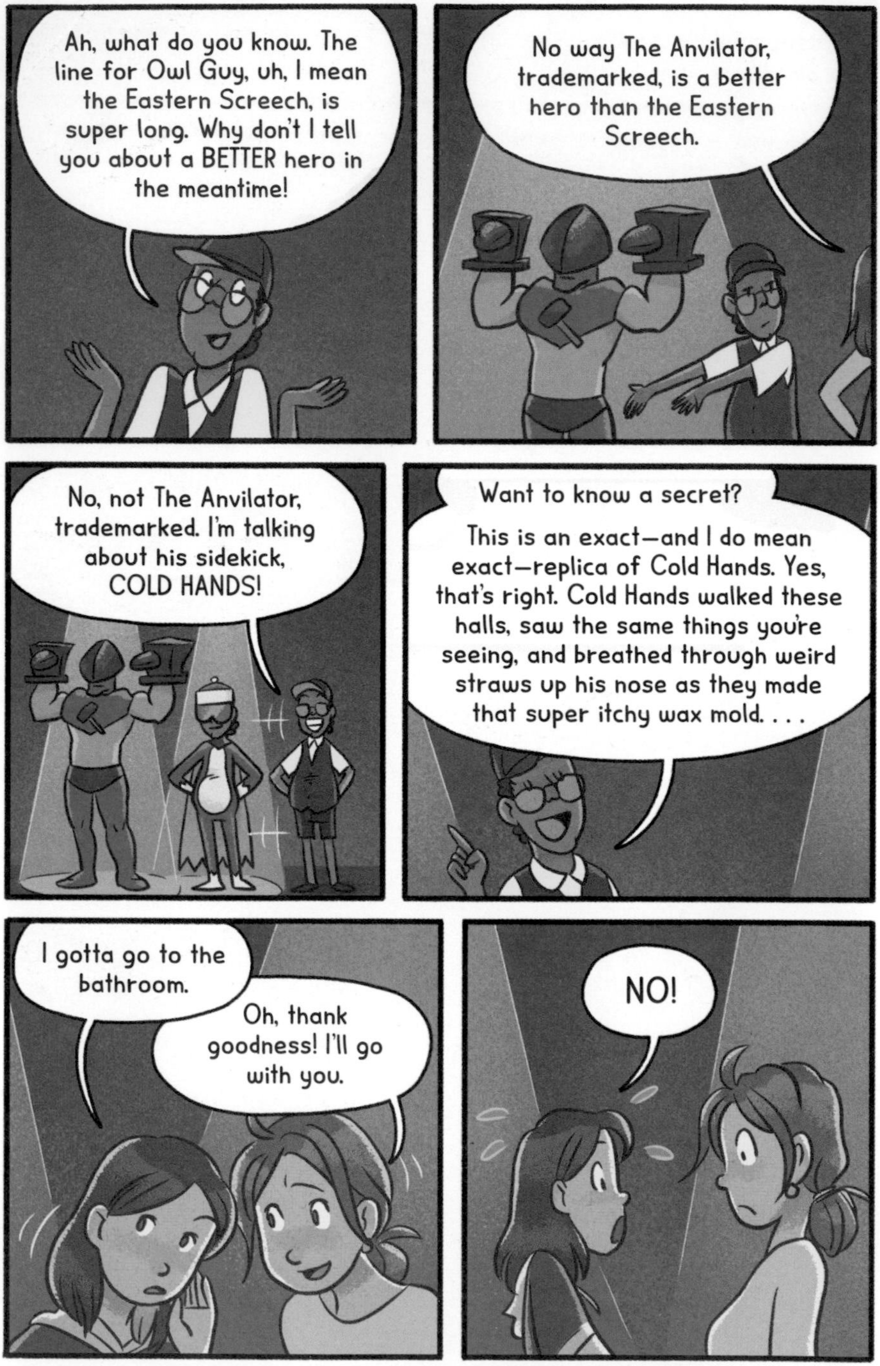
Ah, what do you know. The line for Owl Guy, uh, I mean the Eastern Screech, is super long. Why don't I tell you about a BETTER hero in the meantime!
No way The Anvilator, trademarked, is a better hero than the Eastern Screech.
No, not The Anvilator, trademarked. I'm talking about his sidekick, COLD HANDS!
Want to know a secret?
This is an exact—and I do mean exact—replica of Cold Hands. Yes, that's right. Cold Hands walked these halls, saw the same things you're seeing, and breathed through weird straws up his nose as they made that super itchy wax mold. . . .
I gotta go to the bathroom.
Oh, thank goodness! I'll go with you.
NO!

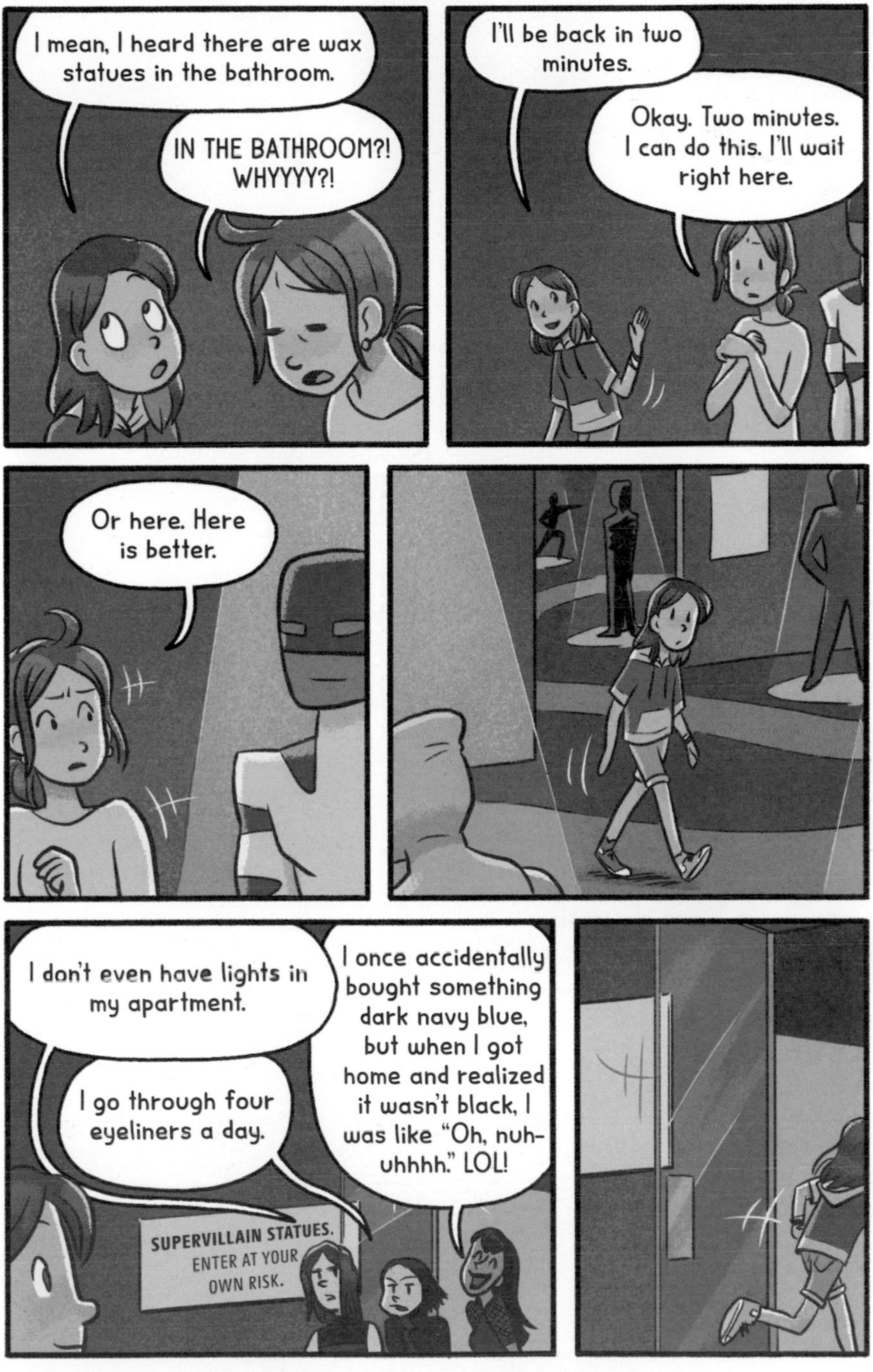
I mean, I heard there are wax statues in the bathroom.
IN THE BATHROOM?! WHYYYY?!
I'll be back in two minutes.
Okay. Two minutes. I can do this. I'll wait right here.
Or here. Here is better.
I don't even have lights in my apartment.
I go through four eyeliners a day.
I once accidentally bought something dark navy blue, but when I got home and realized it wasn't black, I was like "Oh, nuh-uhhhh." LOL!
SUPERVILLAIN STATUES. ENTER AT YOUR OWN RISK.

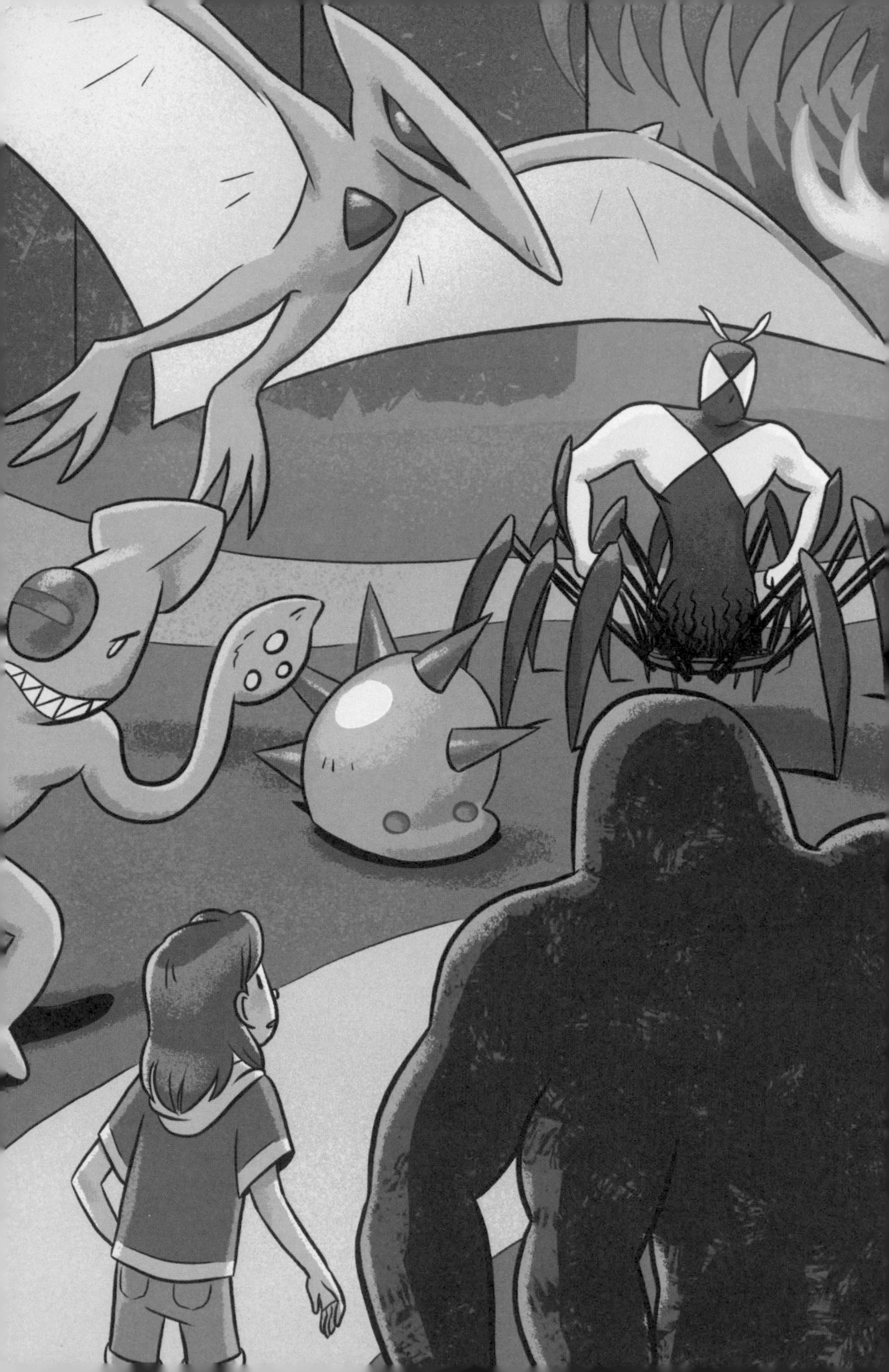

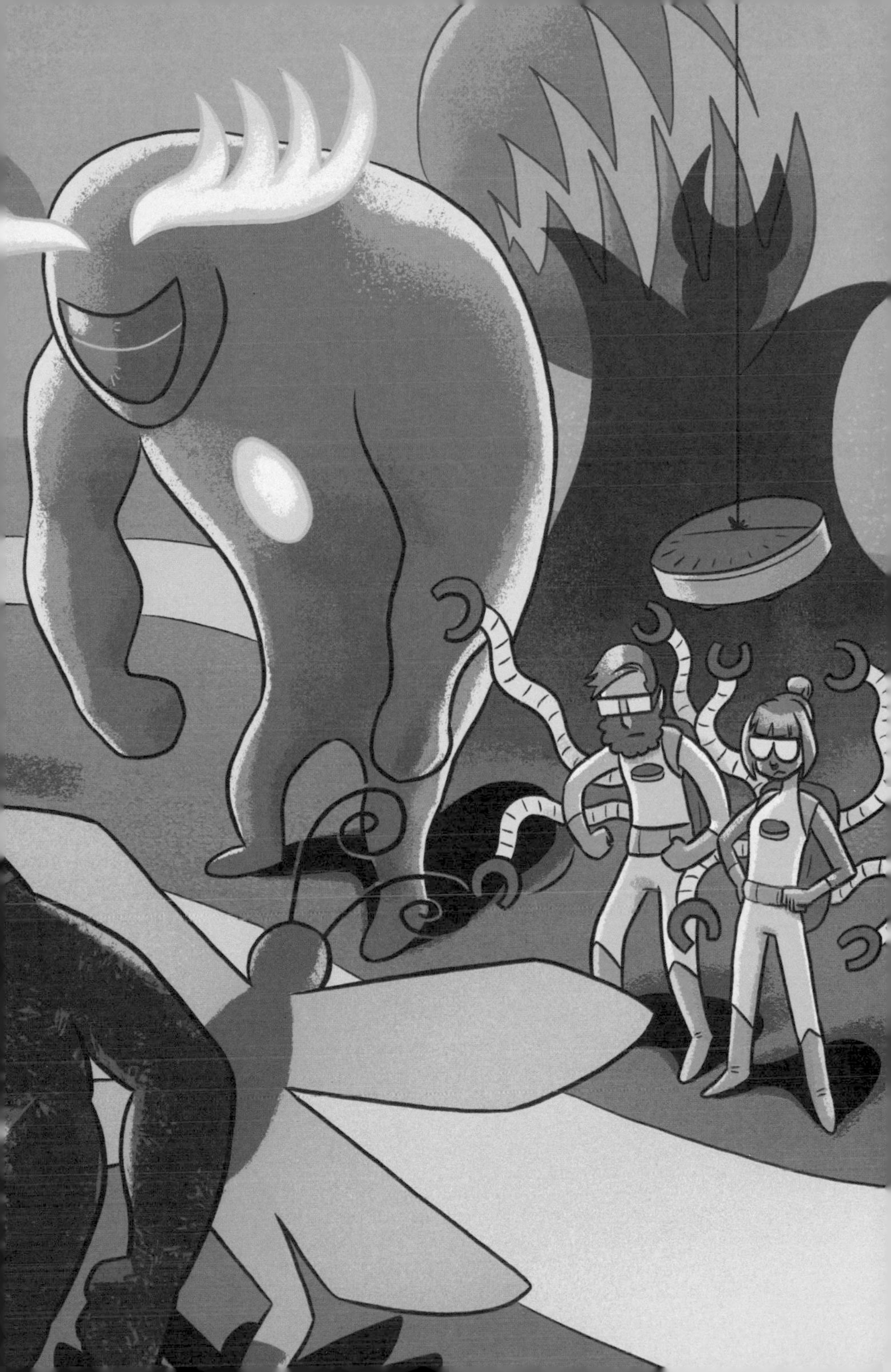

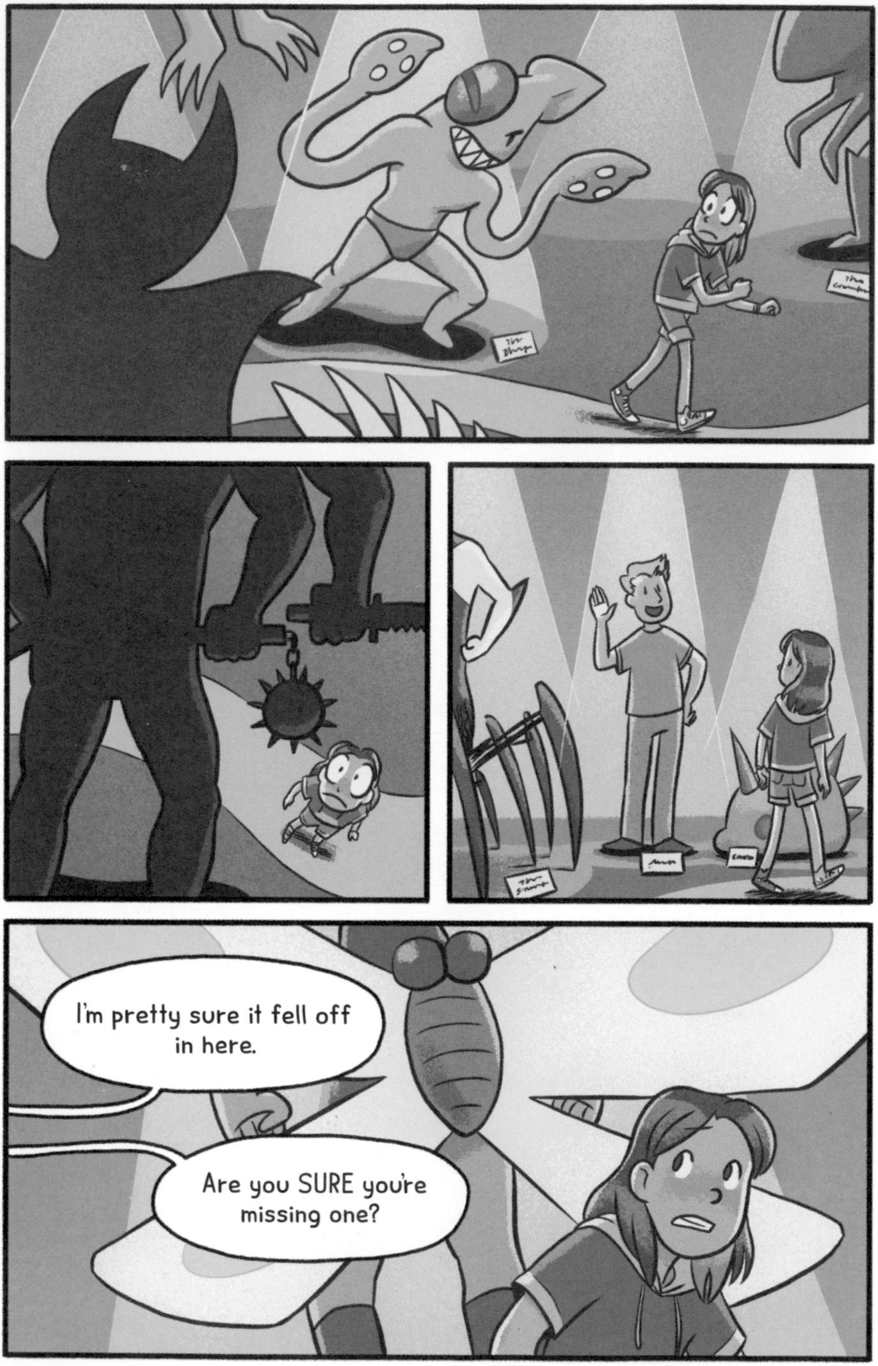
I'm pretty sure it fell off in here.
Are you SURE you're missing one?

. . . fourteen, fifteen. See? It's gone.

Got it. Phew. It woulda been so embarrassing walking around with only fifteen earrings.

PHEW!

KICK

MOU

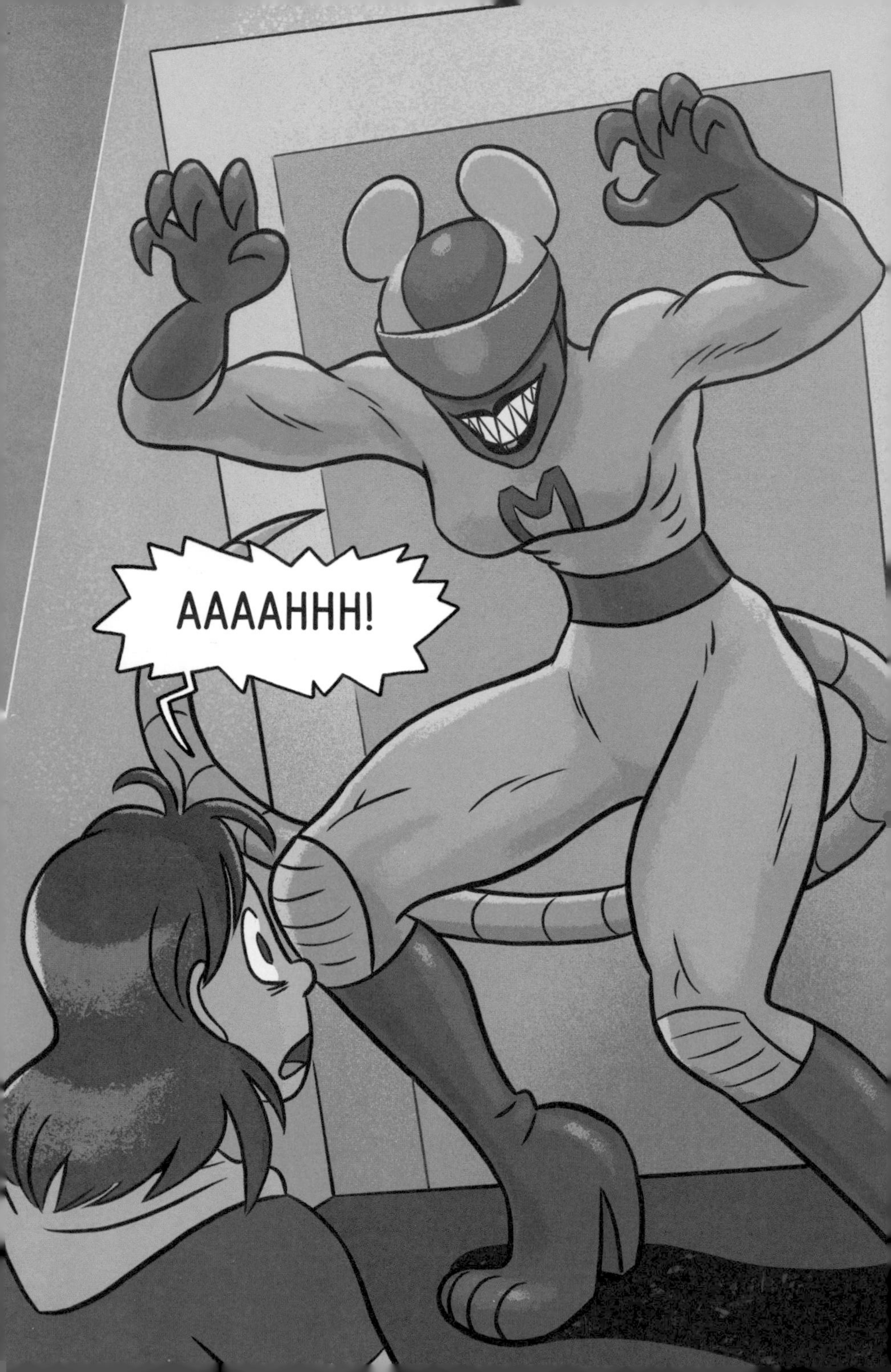
AAAAHHH!

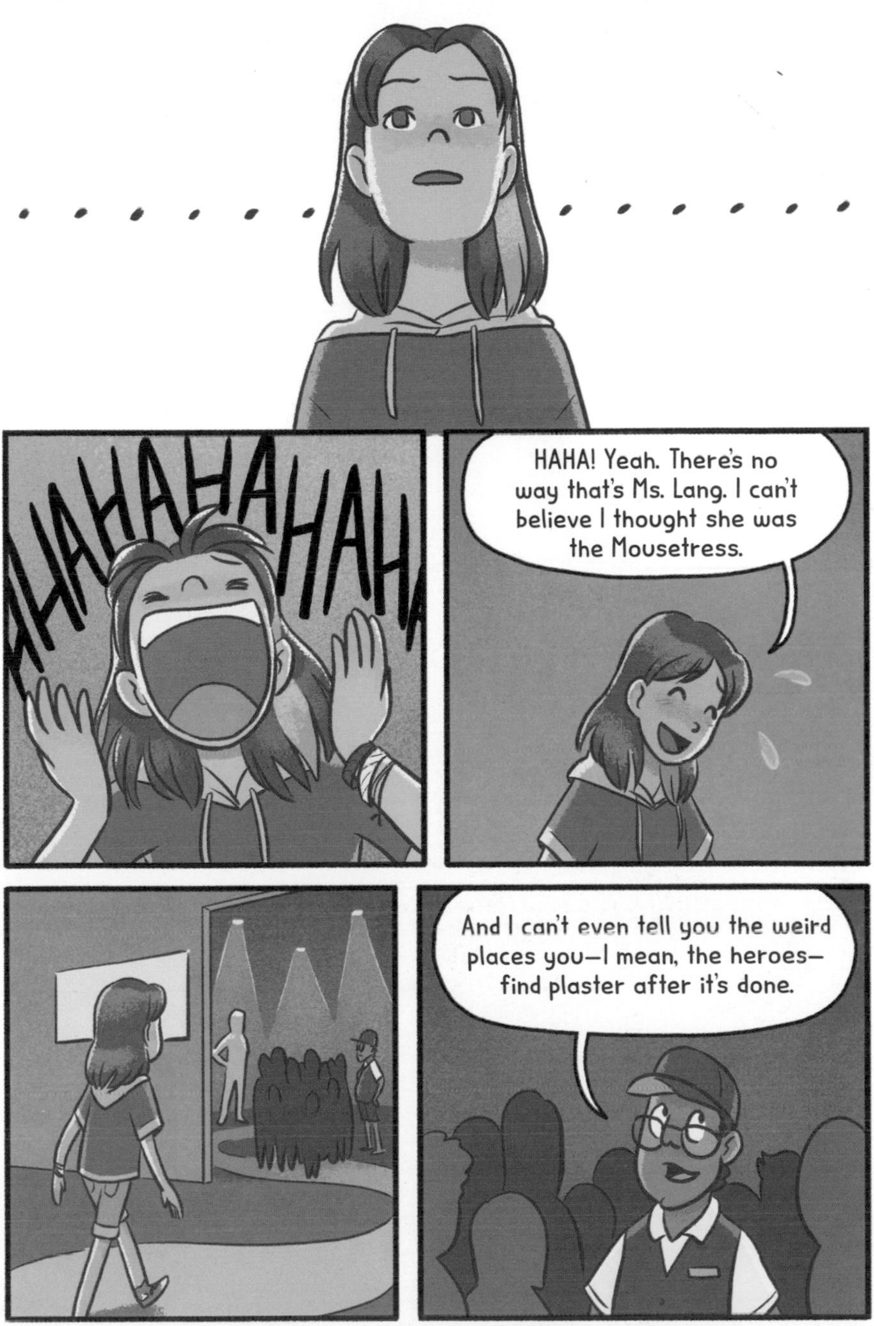
HAHAHAHAHAHAHA
HAHA! Yeah. There's no way that's Ms. Lang. I can't believe I thought she was the Mousetress.
And I can't even tell you the weird places you—I mean, the heroes—find plaster after it's done.

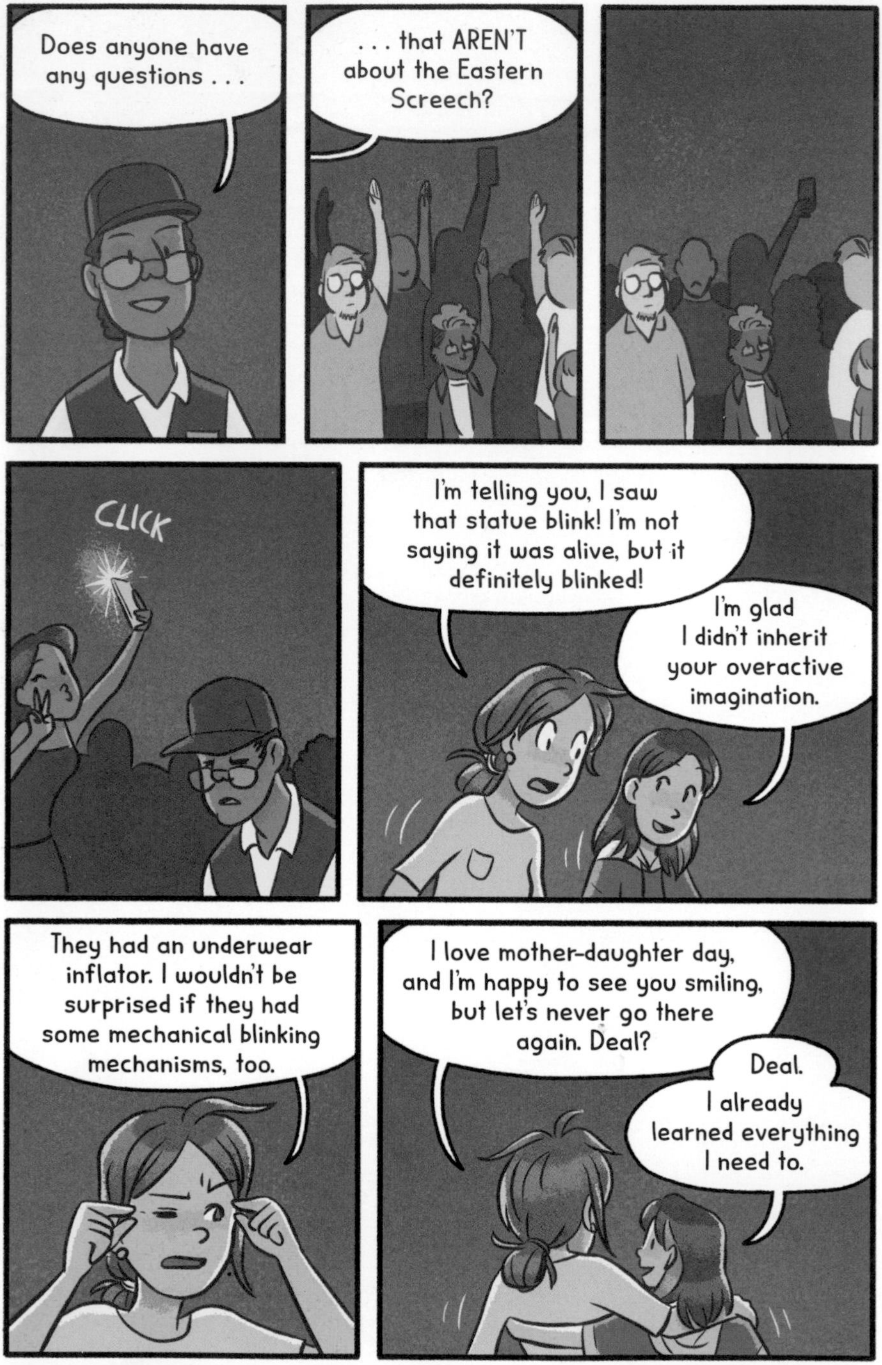
Does anyone have any questions . . .
. . . that AREN'T about the Eastern Screech?
CLICK
I'm telling you, I saw that statue blink! I'm not saying it was alive, but it definitely blinked!
I'm glad I didn't inherit your overactive imagination.
They had an underwear inflator. I wouldn't be surprised if they had some mechanical blinking mechanisms, too.
I love mother-daughter day, and I'm happy to see you smiling, but let's never go there again. Deal?
Deal.
I already learned everything I need to.

CHAPTER TEN

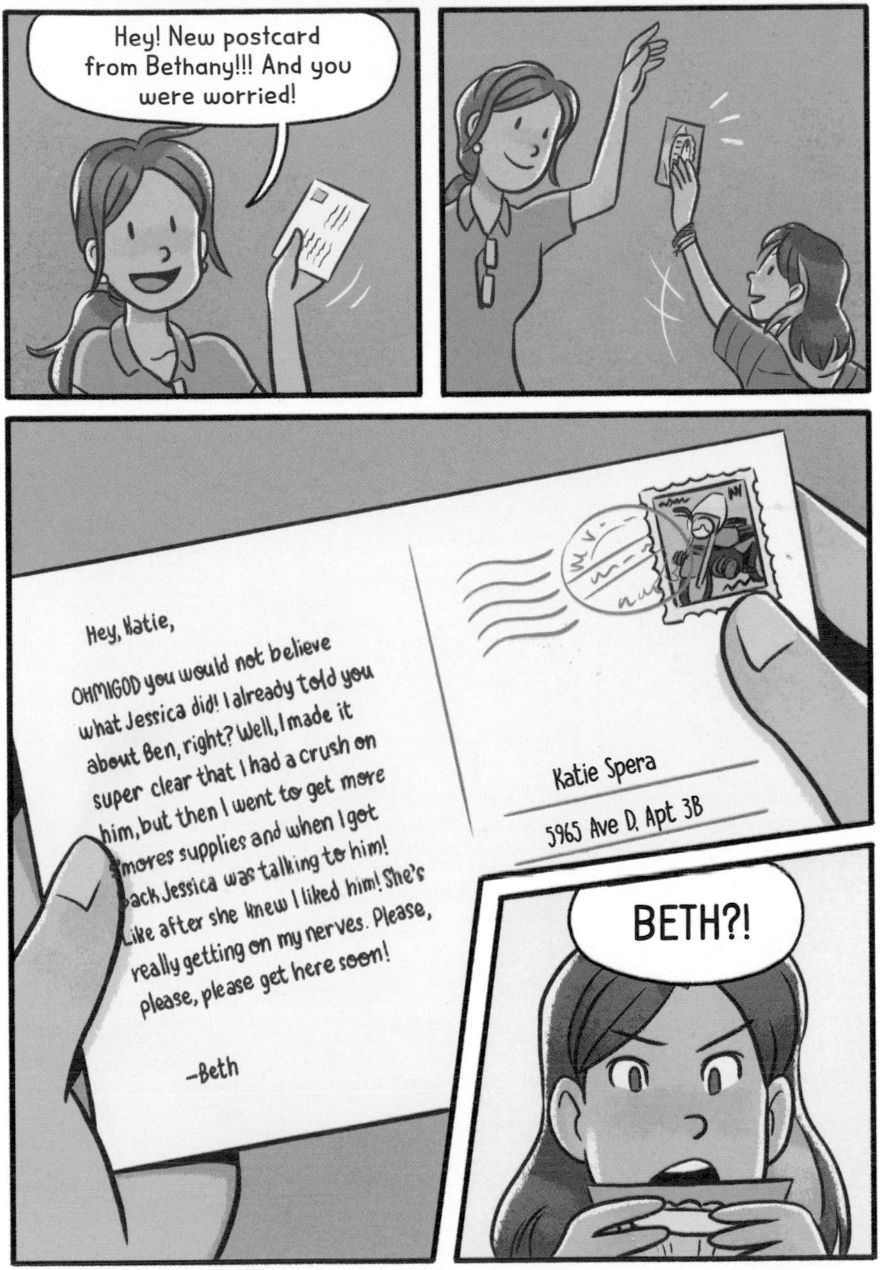
Hey! New postcard from Bethany!!! And you were worried!
Hey, Katie,
OHMIGOD you would not believe what Jessica did! I already told you about Ben, right? Well, I made it super clear that I had a crush on him, but then I went to get more s'mores supplies and when I got back Jessica was talking to him! Like after she knew I liked him! She's really getting on my nerves. Please, please, please get here soon!
-Beth
Katie Spera
5965 Ave D, Apt 3B
BETH?!

FWUMP

Hey, Pouty McPoutface.

I got you something.

You've been doing such a good job saving for camp. I wanted to help.

Camp bear bucks

Mom! How . . . ?

Just a few bucks here and there. Let's put down that deposit!

Isn't that Bethany?

No . . . it's BETH.

CAMP BEARLAKE

It's $3,500 a week now?! Why did it go up? How can sleeping in the woods be this expensive?!

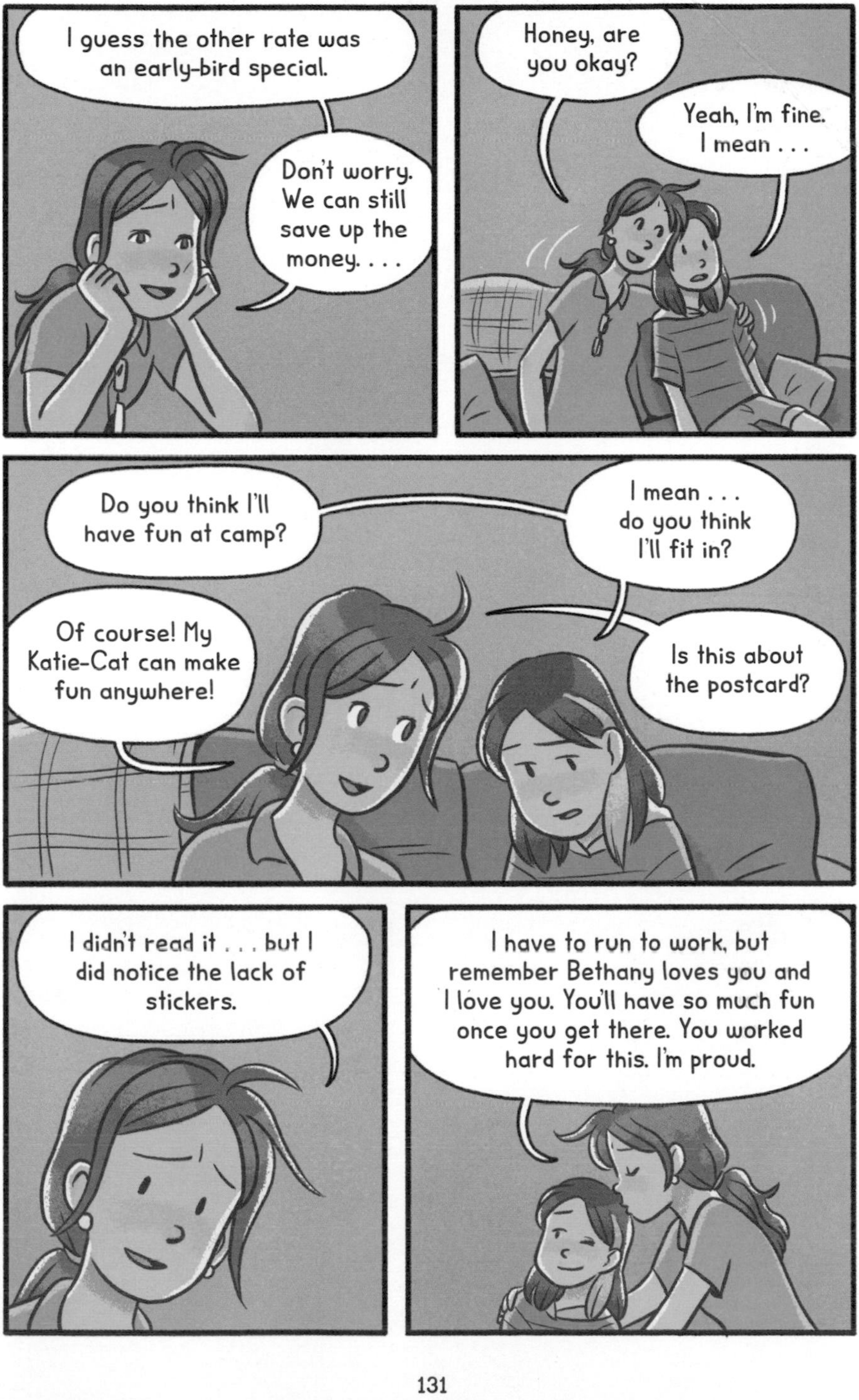
I guess the other rate was an early-bird special.
Don't worry. We can still save up the money. . . .
Honey, are you okay?
Yeah, I'm fine. I mean . . .
Do you think I'll have fun at camp?
I mean . . . do you think I'll fit in?
Of course! My Katie-Cat can make fun anywhere!
Is this about the postcard?
I didn't read it . . . but I did notice the lack of stickers.
I have to run to work, but remember Bethany loves you and I love you. You'll have so much fun once you get there. You worked hard for this. I'm proud.

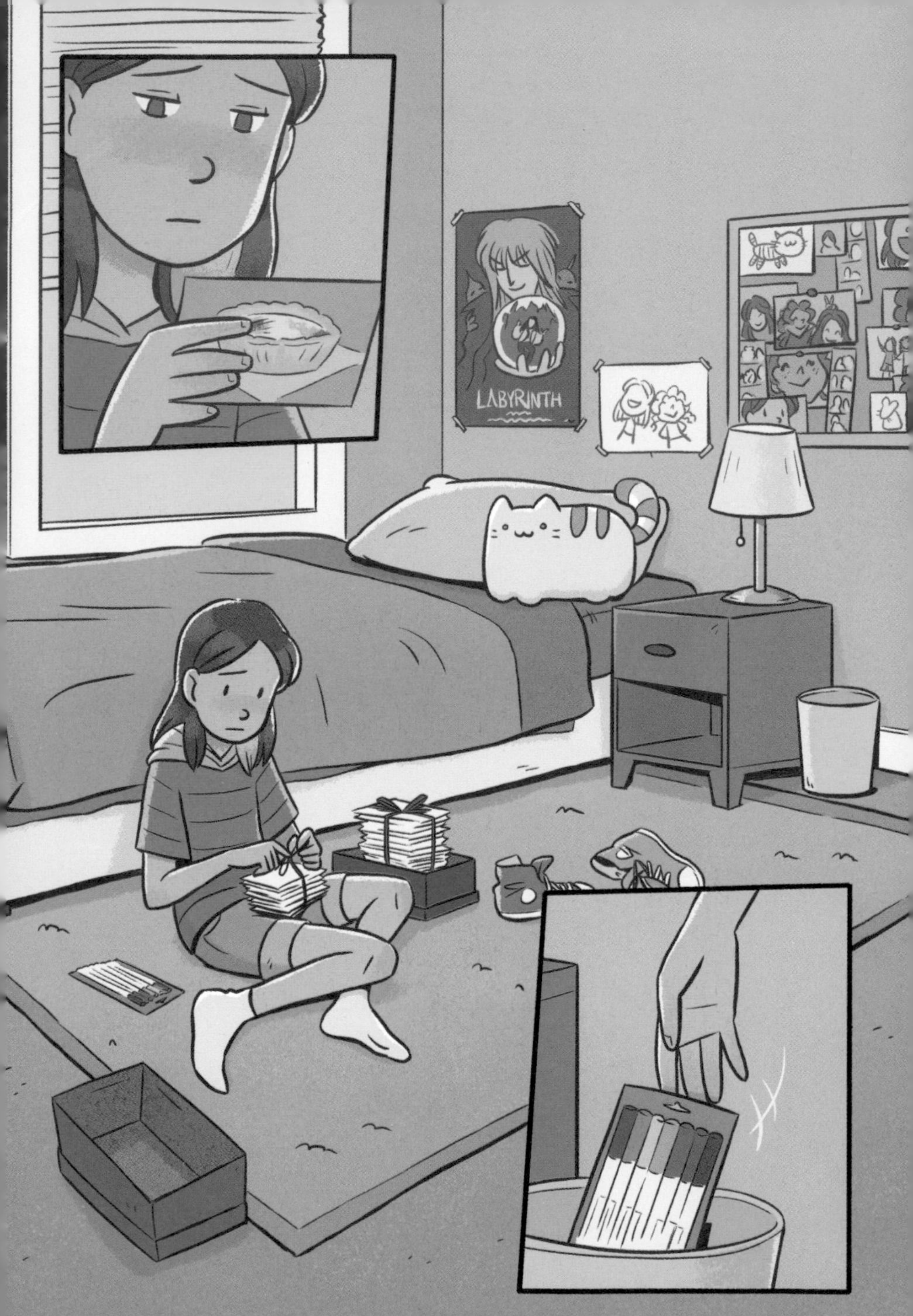
LABYRINTH

You're early!

Thank goodness! Save me from eating this entire chocolate cake before it eats me!

Hmm, not my best material, but I think it warranted a bit more than that. You okay?

I'm just having a bad day. Thought the cats could distract me.

Do you want to talk about it?

No.

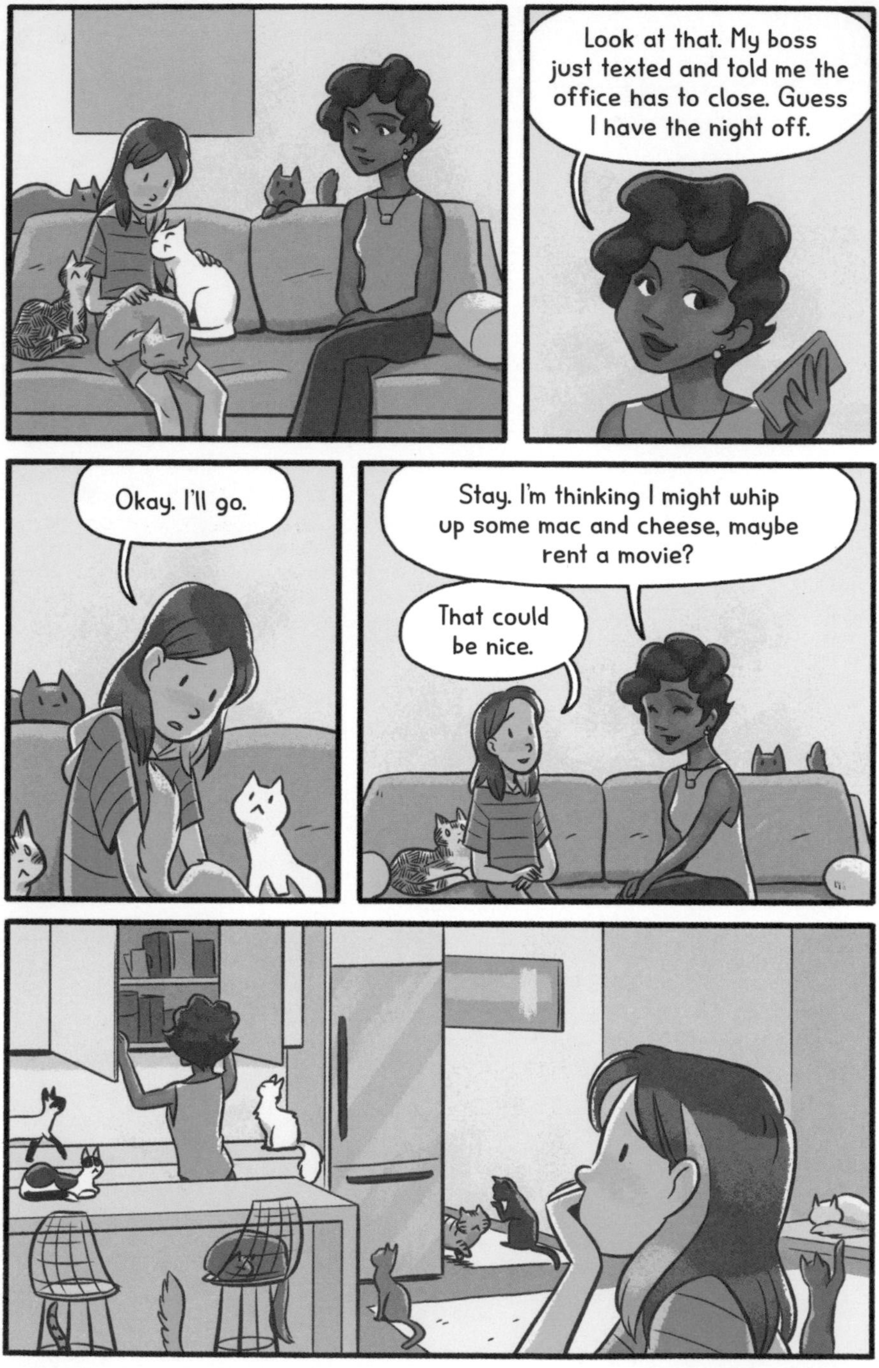
Look at that. My boss just texted and told me the office has to close. Guess I have the night off.
Okay. I'll go.
Stay. I'm thinking I might whip up some mac and cheese, maybe rent a movie?
That could be nice.

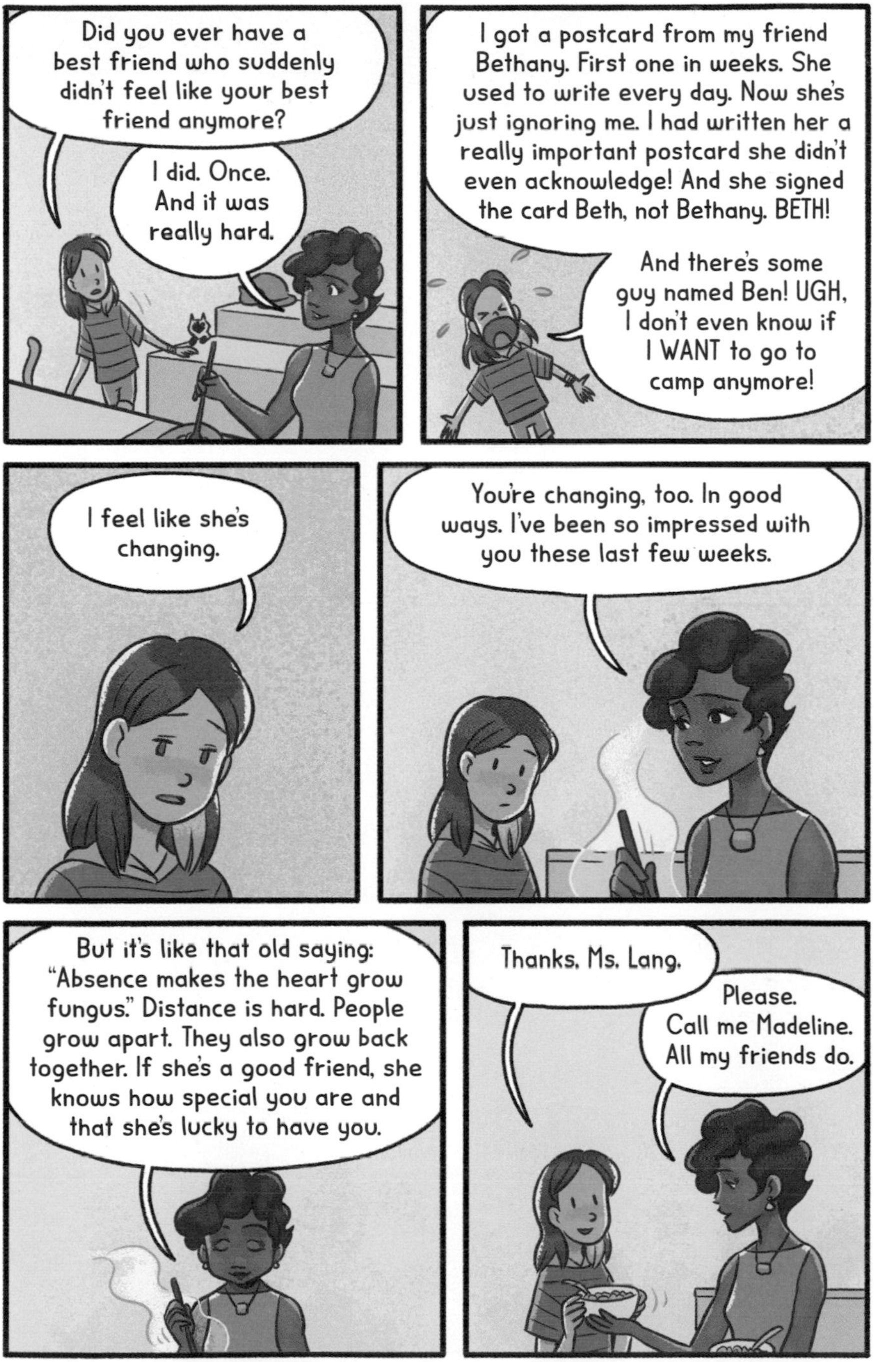
Did you ever have a best friend who suddenly didn't feel like your best friend anymore?
I did. Once. And it was really hard.
I got a postcard from my friend Bethany. First one in weeks. She used to write every day. Now she's just ignoring me. I had written her a really important postcard she didn't even acknowledge! And she signed the card Beth, not Bethany. BETH!
And there's some guy named Ben! UGH, I don't even know if I WANT to go to camp anymore!
I feel like she's changing.
You're changing, too. In good ways. I've been so impressed with you these last few weeks.
But it's like that old saying: "Absence makes the heart grow fungus." Distance is hard. People grow apart. They also grow back together. If she's a good friend, she knows how special you are and that she's lucky to have you.
Thanks, Ms. Lang.
Please. Call me Madeline. All my friends do.

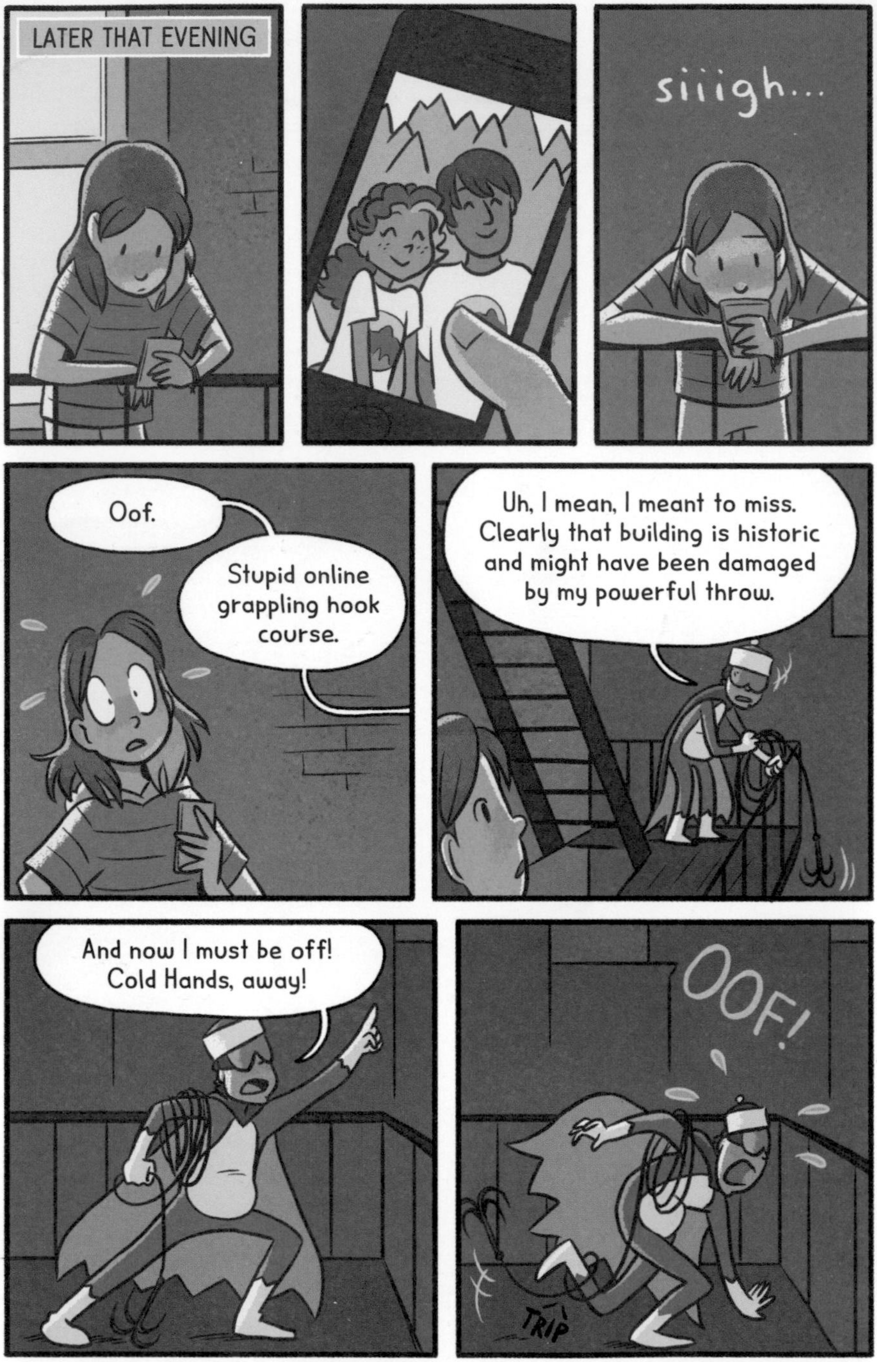
LATER THAT EVENING
siiigh...
Oof.
Stupid online grappling hook course.
Uh, I mean, I meant to miss. Clearly that building is historic and might have been damaged by my powerful throw.
And now I must be off! Cold Hands, away!
OOF!
TRIP

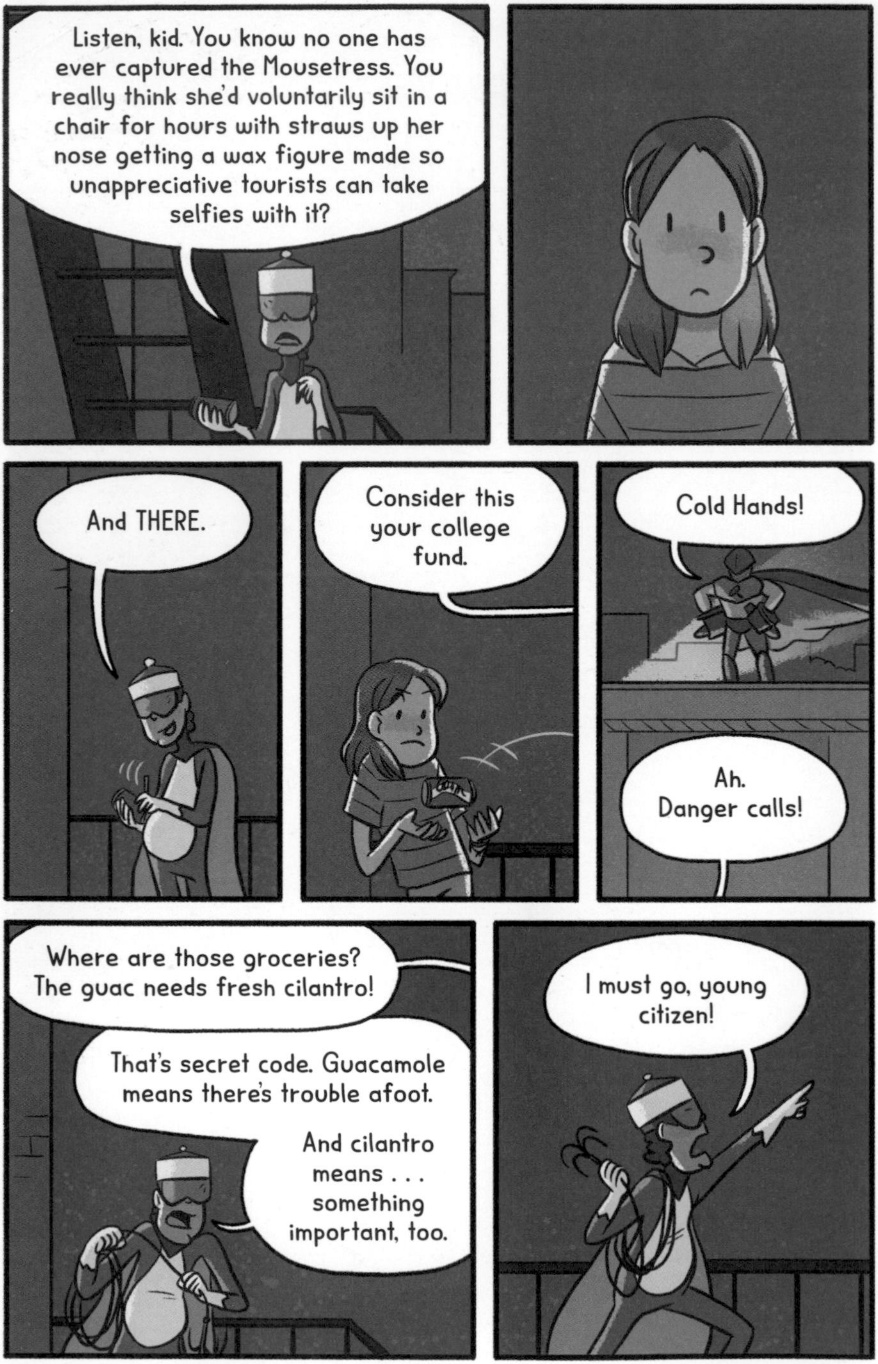
Listen, kid. You know no one has ever captured the Mousetress. You really think she'd voluntarily sit in a chair for hours with straws up her nose getting a wax figure made so unappreciative tourists can take selfies with it?
And THERE.
Consider this your college fund.
Cold Hands!
Ah. Danger calls!
Where are those groceries? The guac needs fresh cilantro!
That's secret code. Guacamole means there's trouble afoot.
And cilantro means . . . something important, too.
I must go, young citizen!

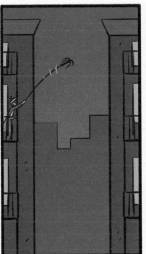
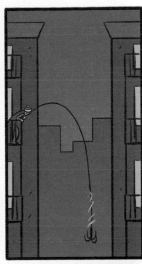

Uh. Keep it.

College fund.

Mousetress sightings

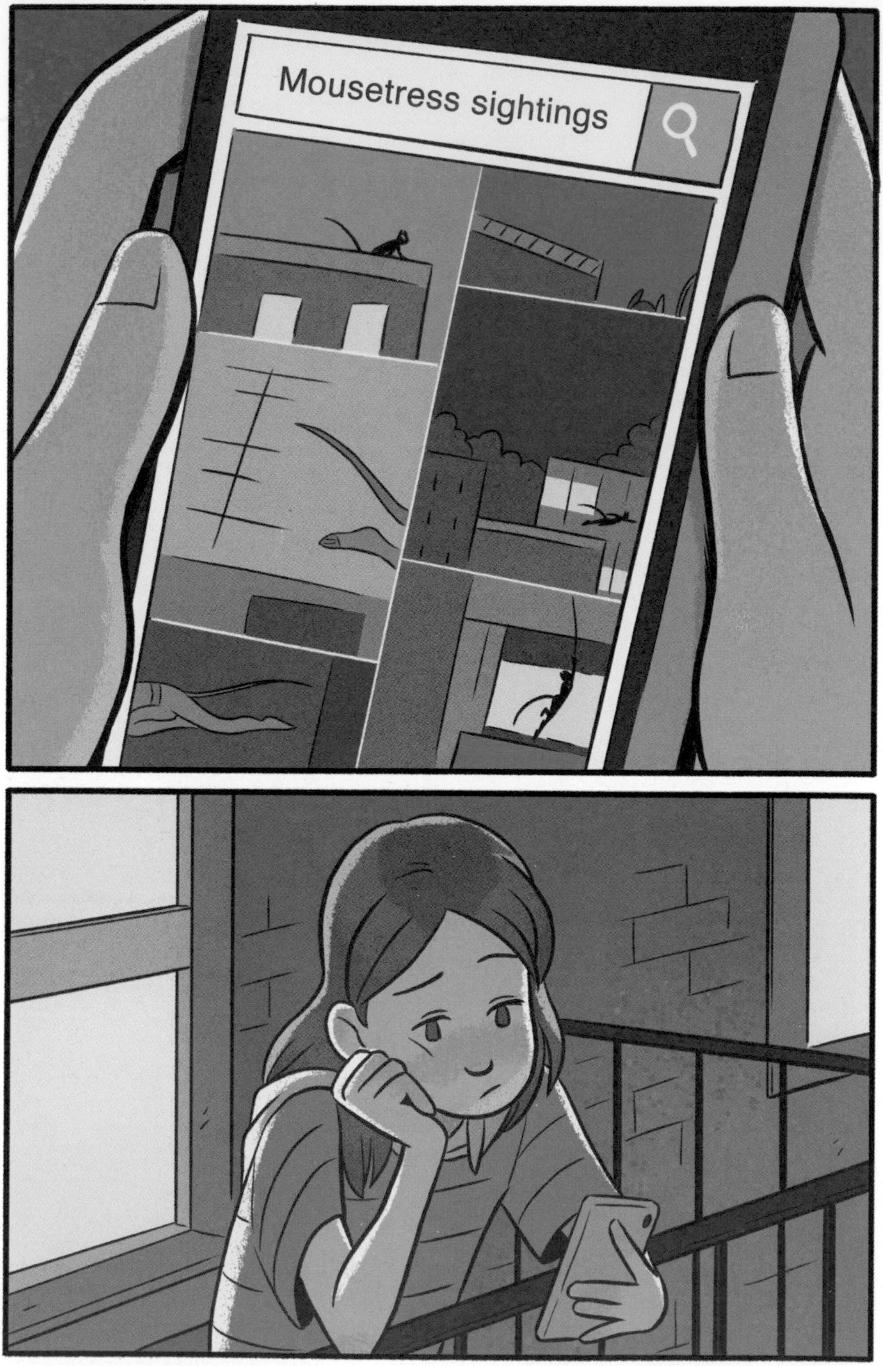
Mousetress sightings

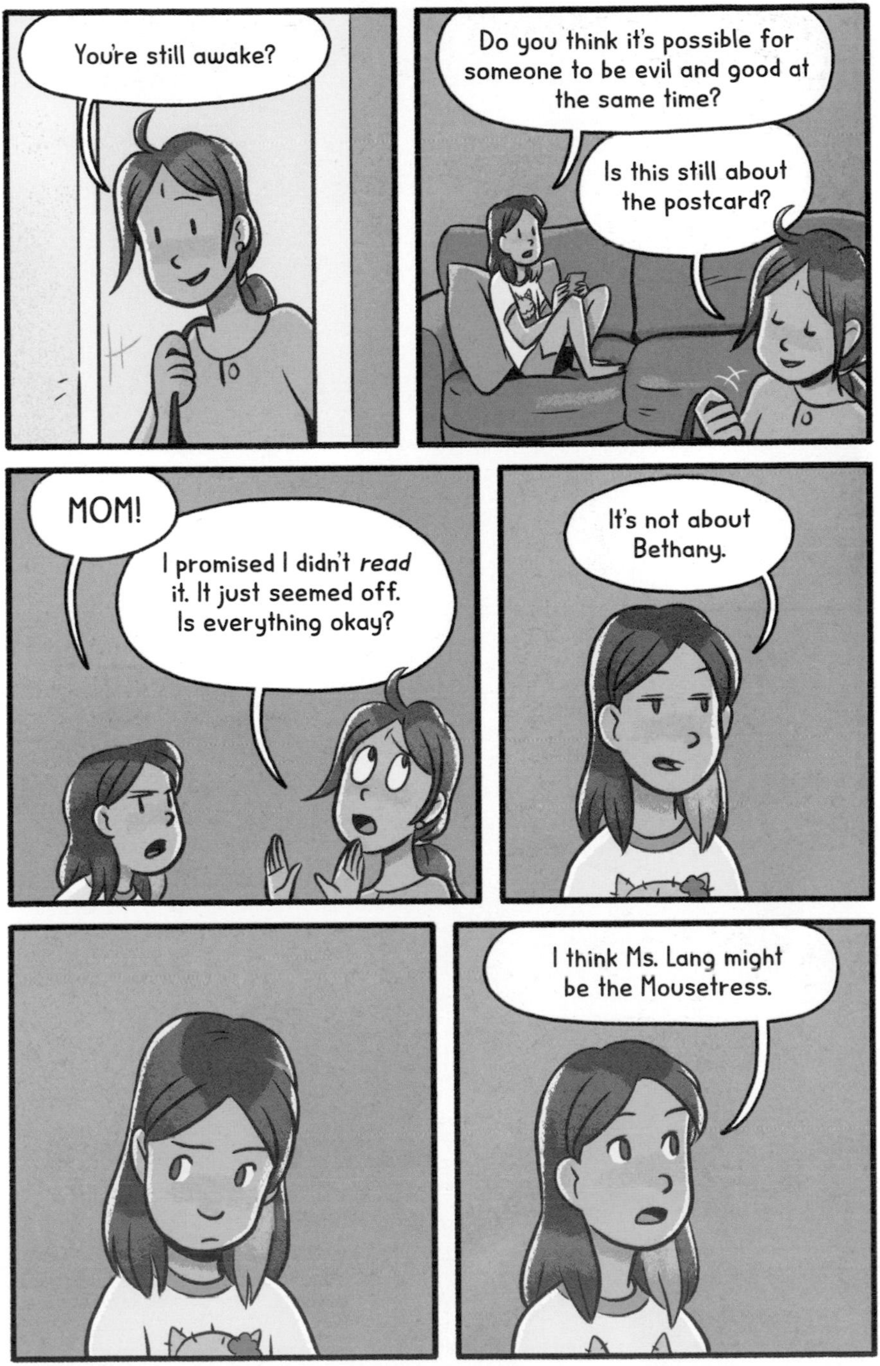
You're still awake?
Do you think it's possible for someone to be evil and good at the same time?
Is this still about the postcard?
MOM!
I promised I didn't *read* it. It just seemed off. Is everything okay?
It's not about Bethany.
I think Ms. Lang might be the Mousetress.

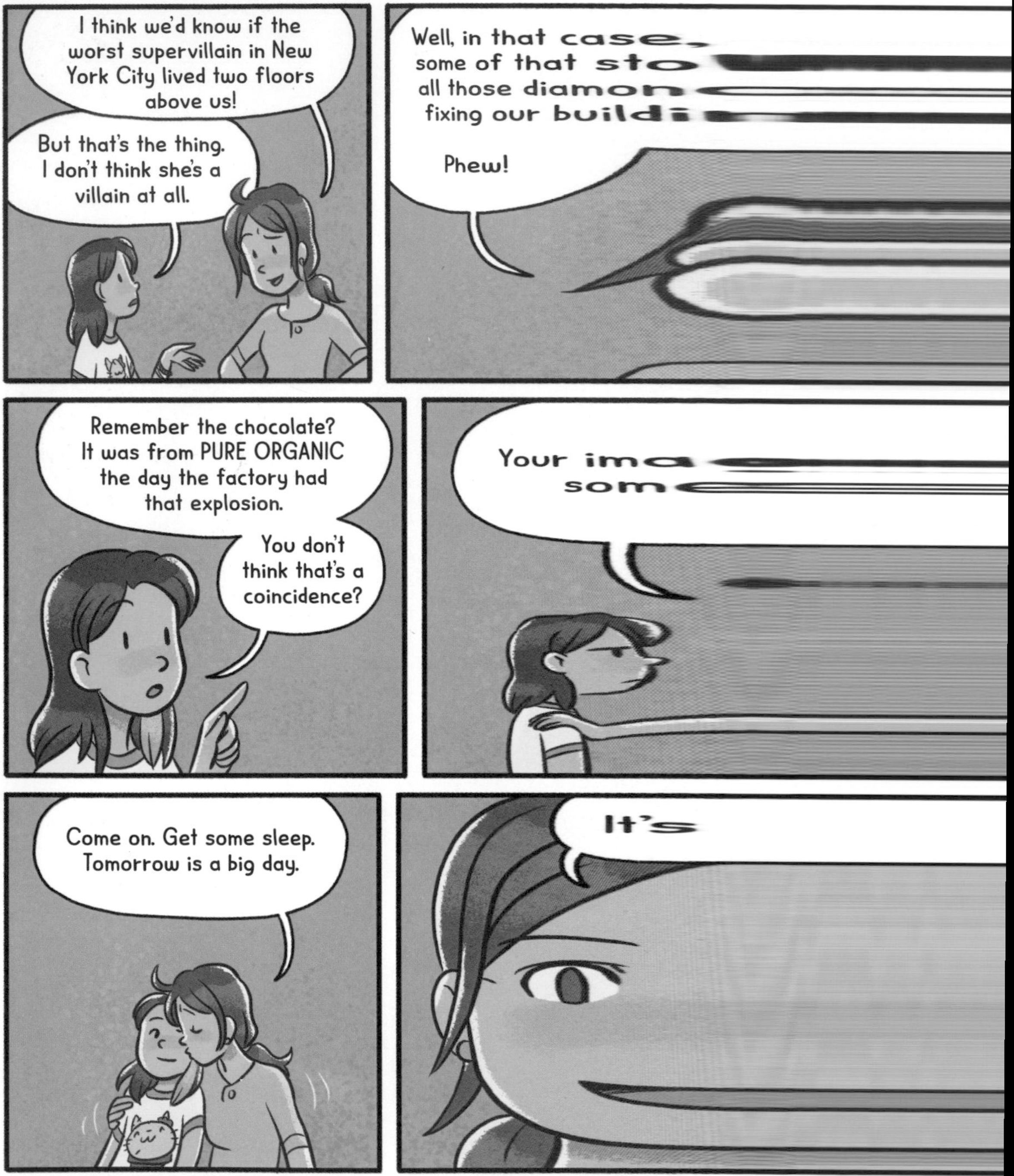

I think we'd know if the worst supervillain in New York City lived two floors above us!
But that's the thing. I don't think she's a villain at all.
Well, in that case, some of that sto
all those diamon
fixing our buildi
Phew!
Remember the chocolate? It was from PURE ORGANIC the day the factory had that explosion.
You don't think that's a coincidence?
Your ima
som
Come on. Get some sleep. Tomorrow is a big day.
It's

CHAPTER ELEVEN

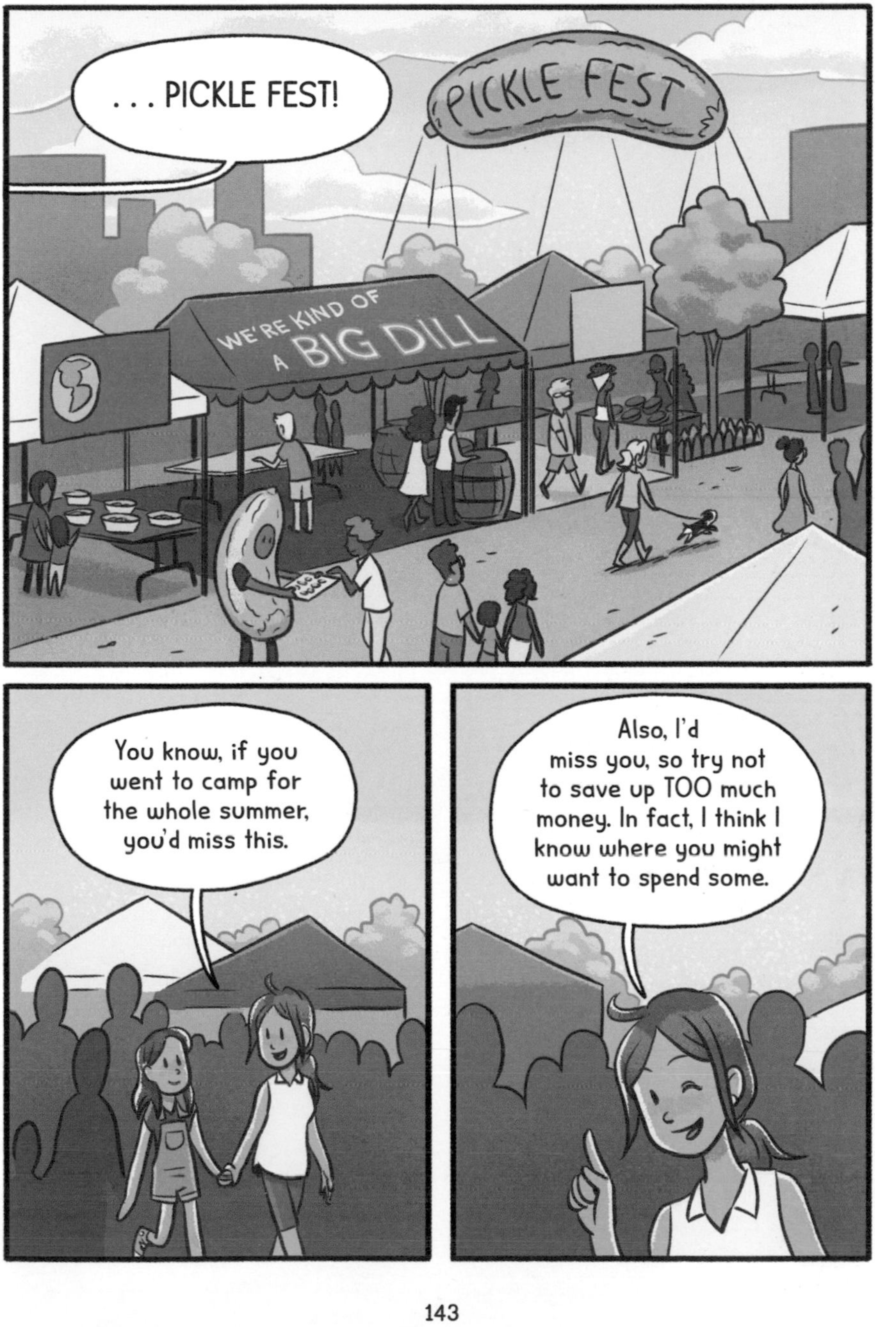
. . . PICKLE FEST!
PICKLE FEST
WE'RE KIND OF A BIG DILL
You know, if you went to camp for the whole summer, you'd miss this.
Also, I'd miss you, so try not to save up TOO much money. In fact, I think I know where you might want to spend some.

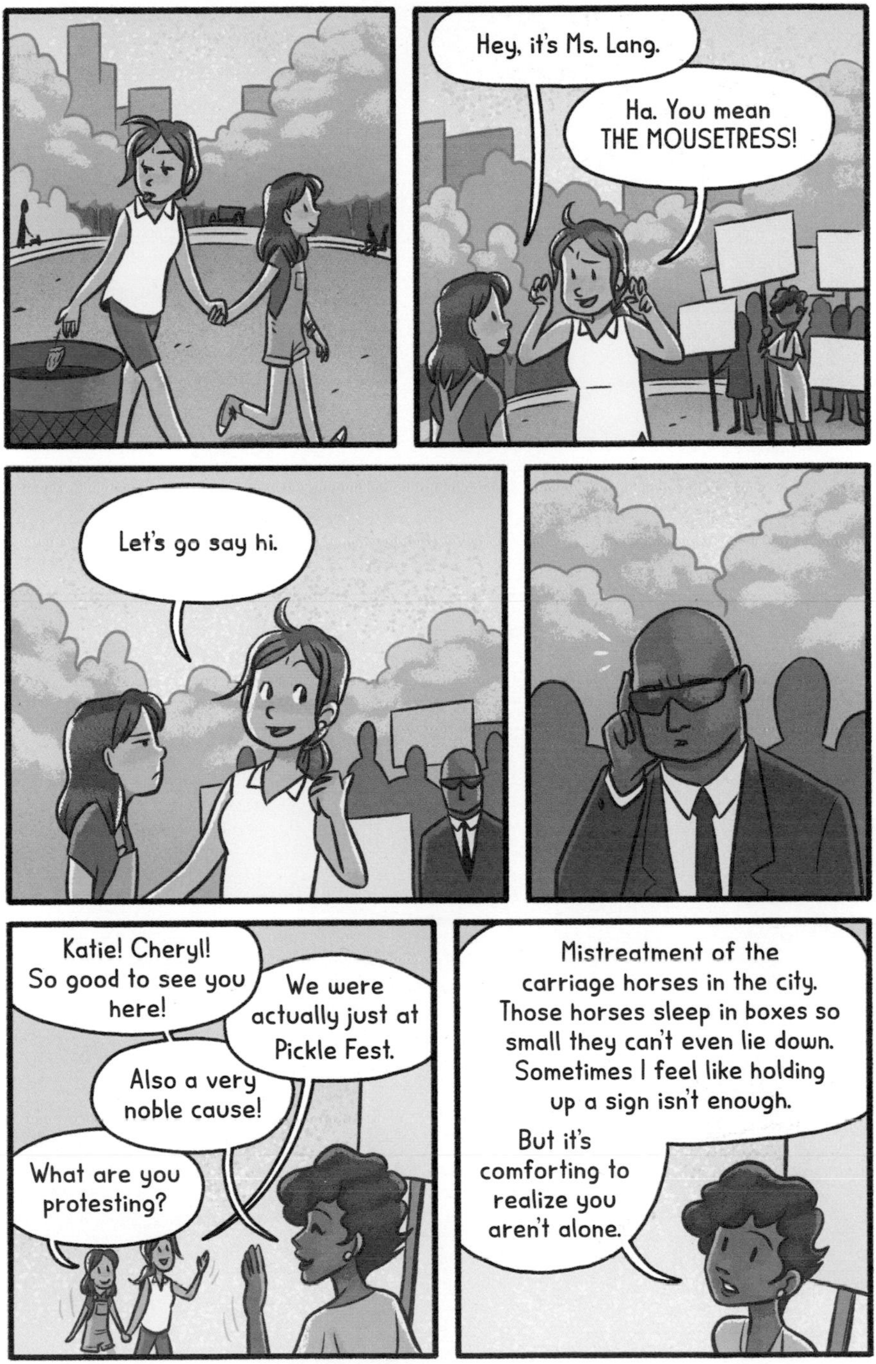
Hey, it's Ms. Lang.
Ha. You mean THE MOUSETRESS!
Let's go say hi.
Katie! Cheryl! So good to see you here!
We were actually just at Pickle Fest.
Also a very noble cause!
What are you protesting?
Mistreatment of the carriage horses in the city. Those horses sleep in boxes so small they can't even lie down. Sometimes I feel like holding up a sign isn't enough.
But it's comforting to realize you aren't alone.

I basically landed it!

BUMP

You totally didn't land it.

Sorry about that! I'm normally really good at ollies.

No, you aren't.

She doesn't know that, Nicole!

Cool to see another kid at the protest! I feel like we're always the only ones.

I was just passing by and ran into my friend Ms. Lang.

You know Ms. Lang?! She's the coolest. Do you want to know a secret about her? I think she's secretly . . .

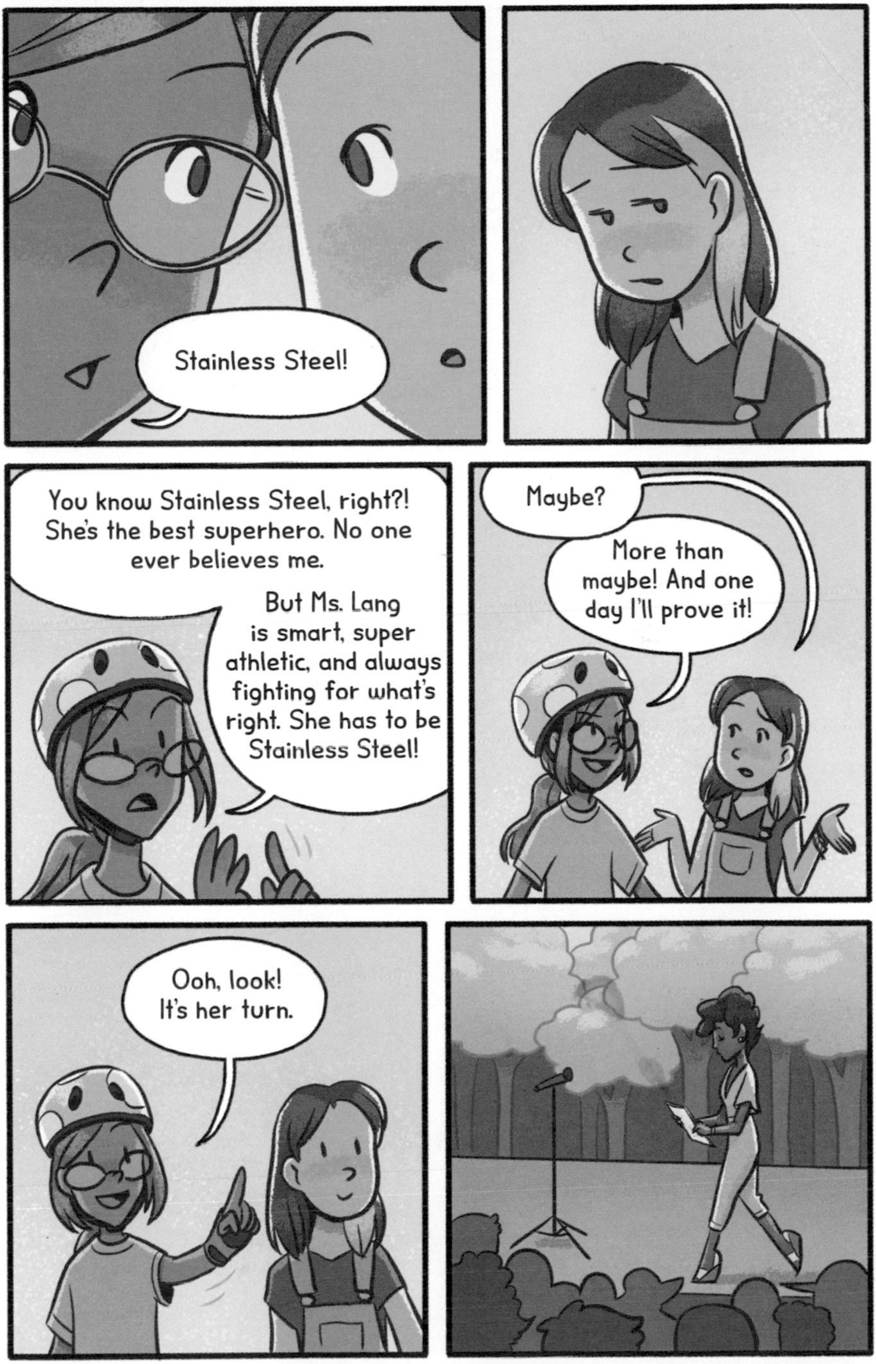
Stainless Steel!
You know Stainless Steel, right?! She's the best superhero. No one ever believes me.
But Ms. Lang is smart, super athletic, and always fighting for what's right. She has to be Stainless Steel!
Maybe?
More than maybe! And one day I'll prove it!
Ooh, look! It's her turn.

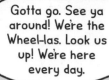 
Gotta go. See ya around! We're the Wheel-las. Look us up! We're here every day.

KLAK

I'm Marie, by the waaaaaay.

OOF

I was hoping you'd meet Marie. She's a great kid.

She seems cool.

Meant to do that!

It's getting late. I've got a big night at the office. See you at six o'clock, Katie?

I'll be there!

CHAPTER TWELVE

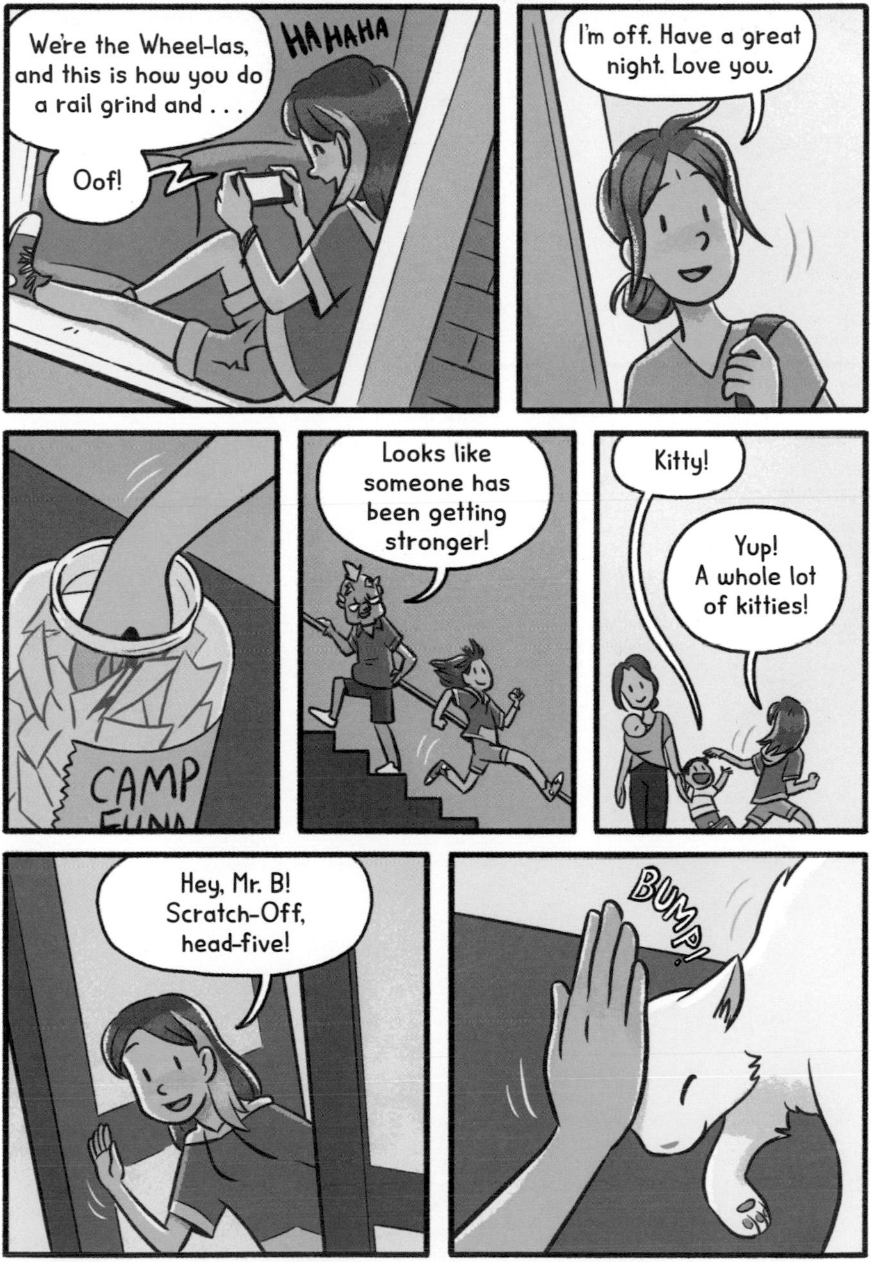
We're the Wheel-las, and this is how you do a rail grind and . . .
HAHAHA
Oof!
I'm off. Have a great night. Love you.
CAMP
Looks like someone has been getting stronger!
Kitty!
Yup! A whole lot of kitties!
Hey, Mr. B! Scratch-Off, head-five!
BUMP!

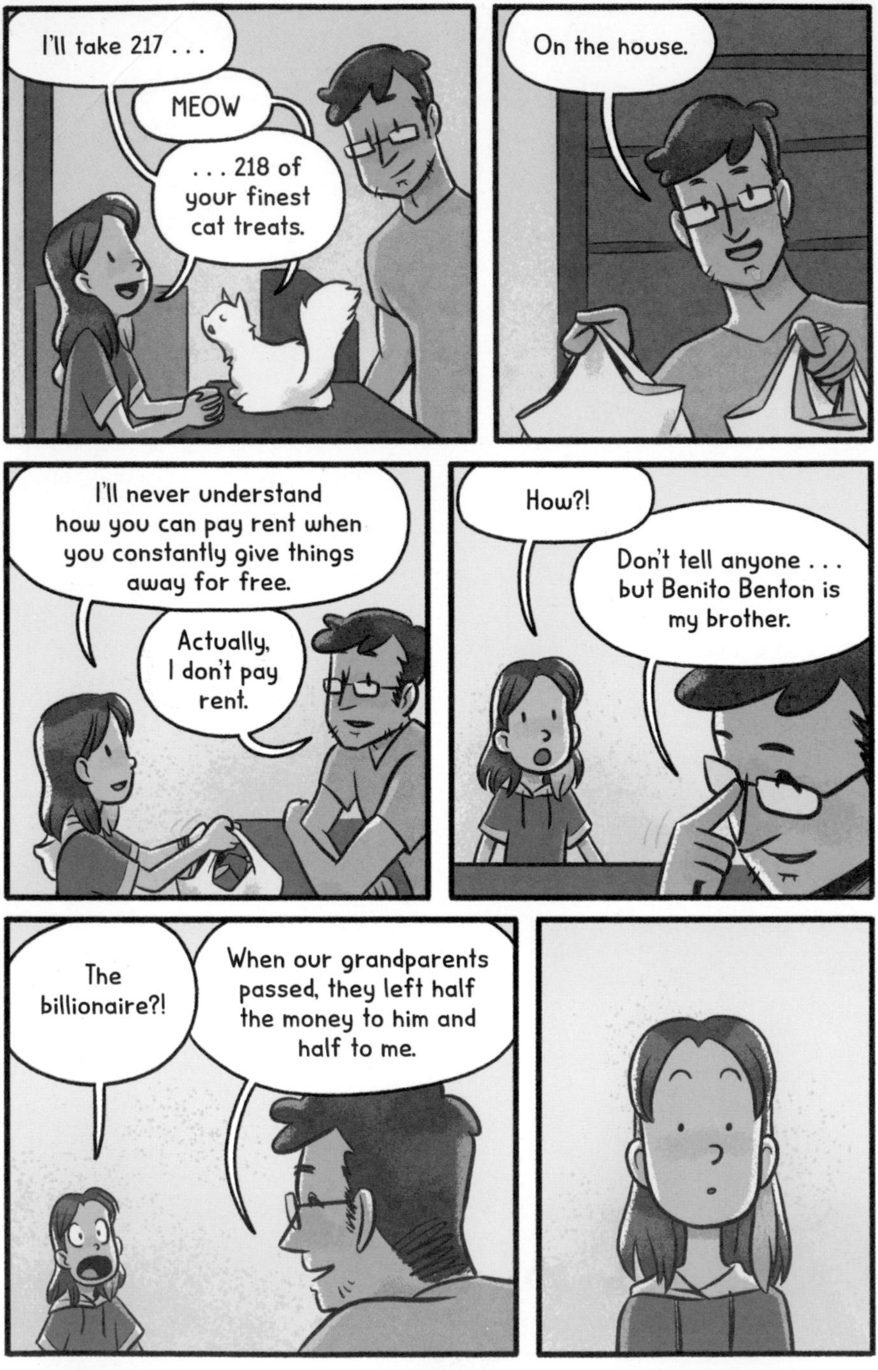
I'll take 217 . . .
MEOW
. . . 218 of your finest cat treats.
On the house.
I'll never understand how you can pay rent when you constantly give things away for free.
Actually, I don't pay rent.
How?!
Don't tell anyone . . . but Benito Benton is my brother.
The billionaire?!
When our grandparents passed, they left half the money to him and half to me.

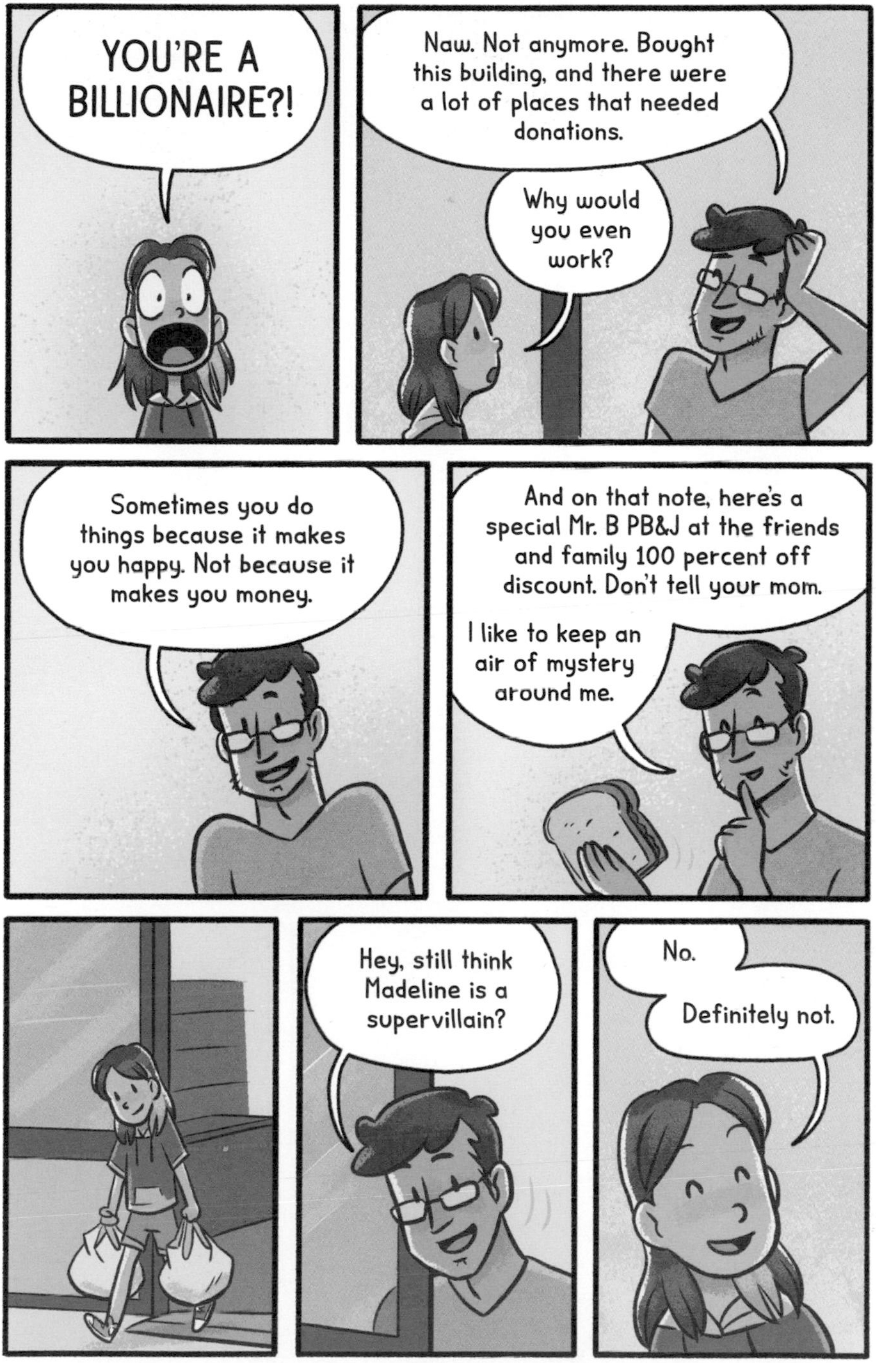
YOU'RE A BILLIONAIRE?!
Naw. Not anymore. Bought this building, and there were a lot of places that needed donations.
Why would you even work?
Sometimes you do things because it makes you happy. Not because it makes you money.
And on that note, here's a special Mr. B PB&J at the friends and family 100 percent off discount. Don't tell your mom.
I like to keep an air of mystery around me.
Hey, still think Madeline is a supervillain?
No.
Definitely not.

This time . . . I'm gonna win.

Who's in for board game night?

5 HOURS AND 59 MINUTES LATER

You're just lucky Madeline will be home in a minute or I'd TOTALLY win the rematch.

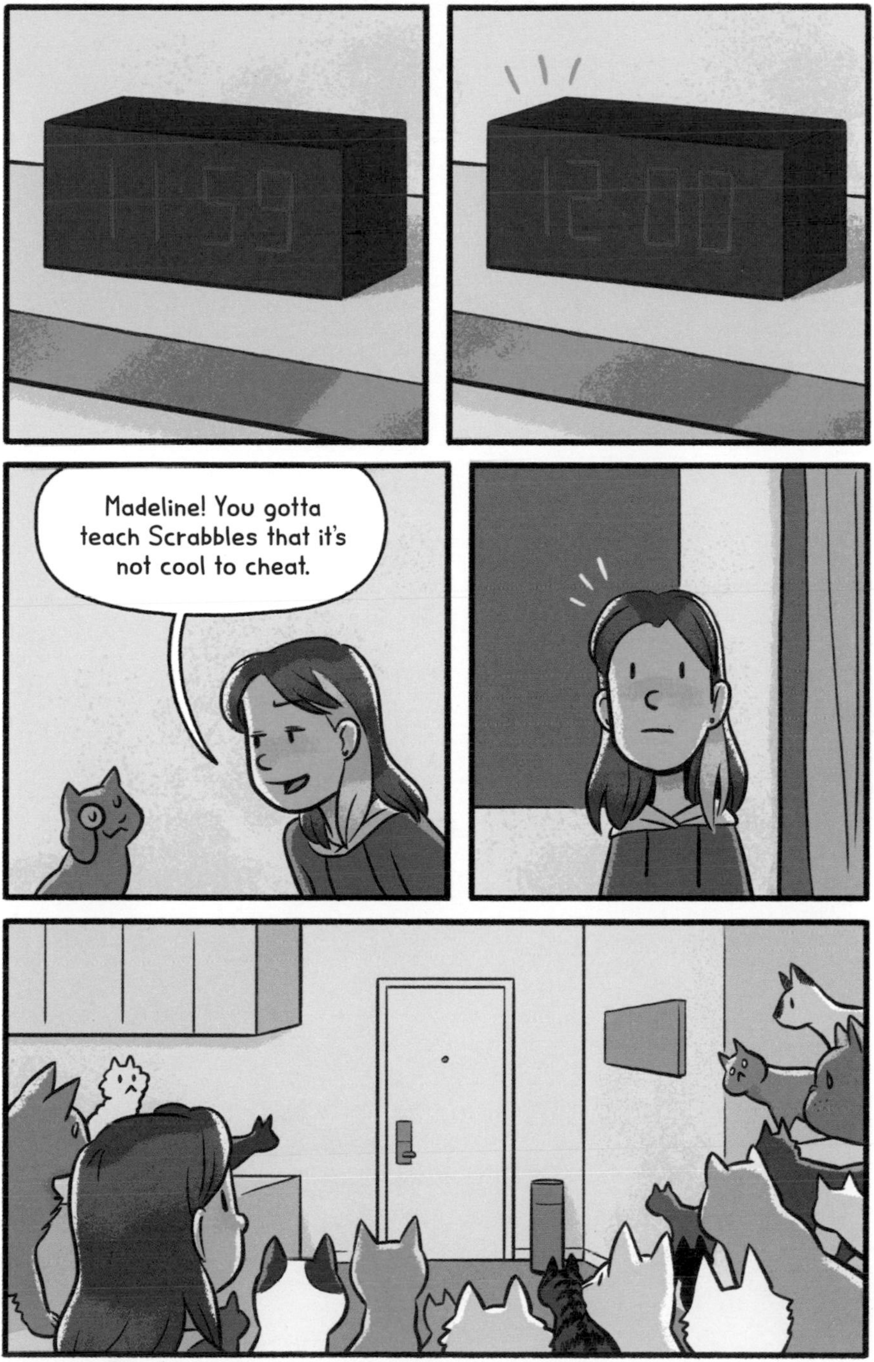
Madeline! You gotta teach Scrabbles that it's not cool to cheat.

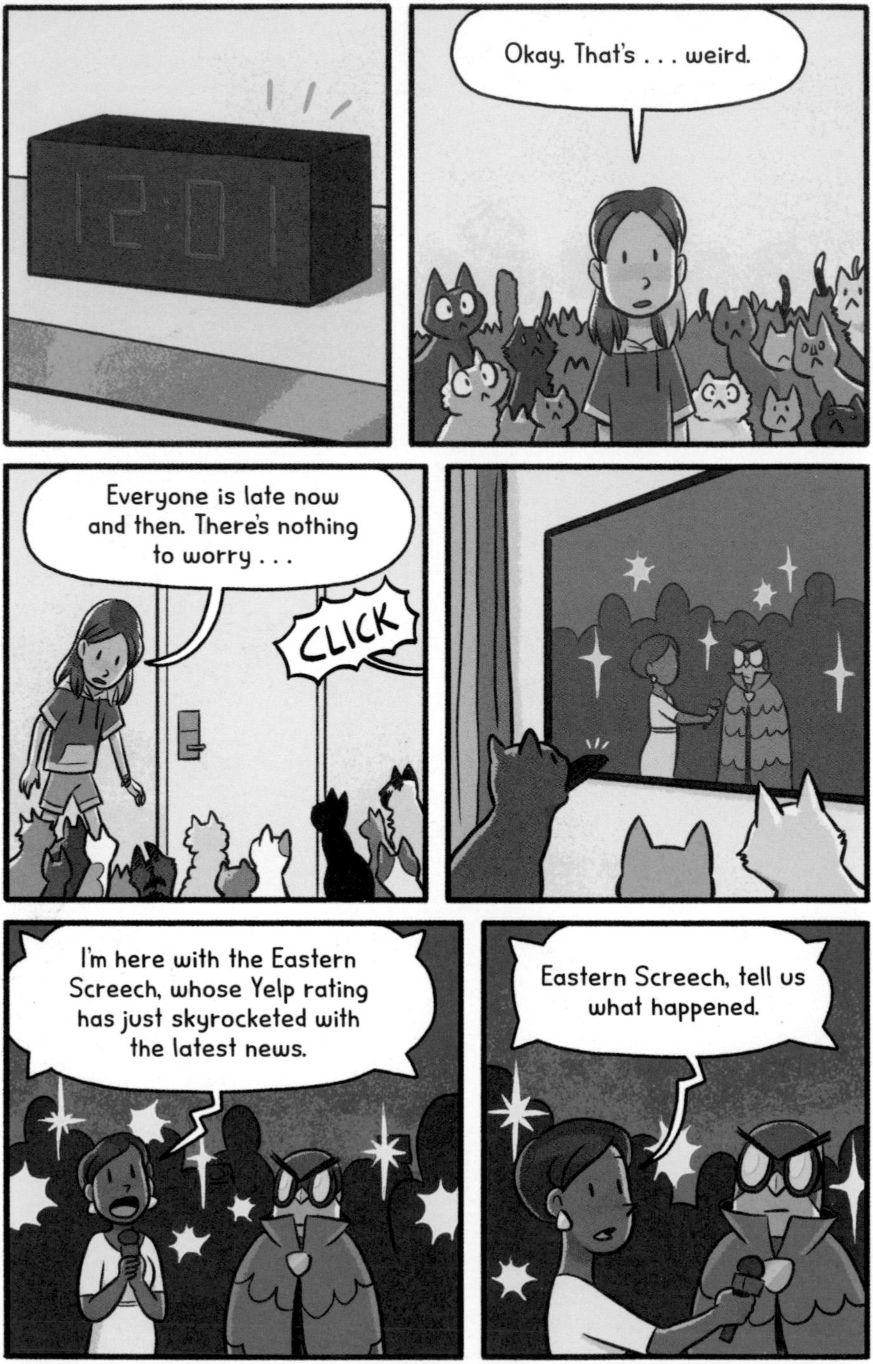
12:01
Okay. That's . . . weird.
Everyone is late now and then. There's nothing to worry . . .
CLICK
I'm here with the Eastern Screech, whose Yelp rating has just skyrocketed with the latest news.
Eastern Screech, tell us what happened.

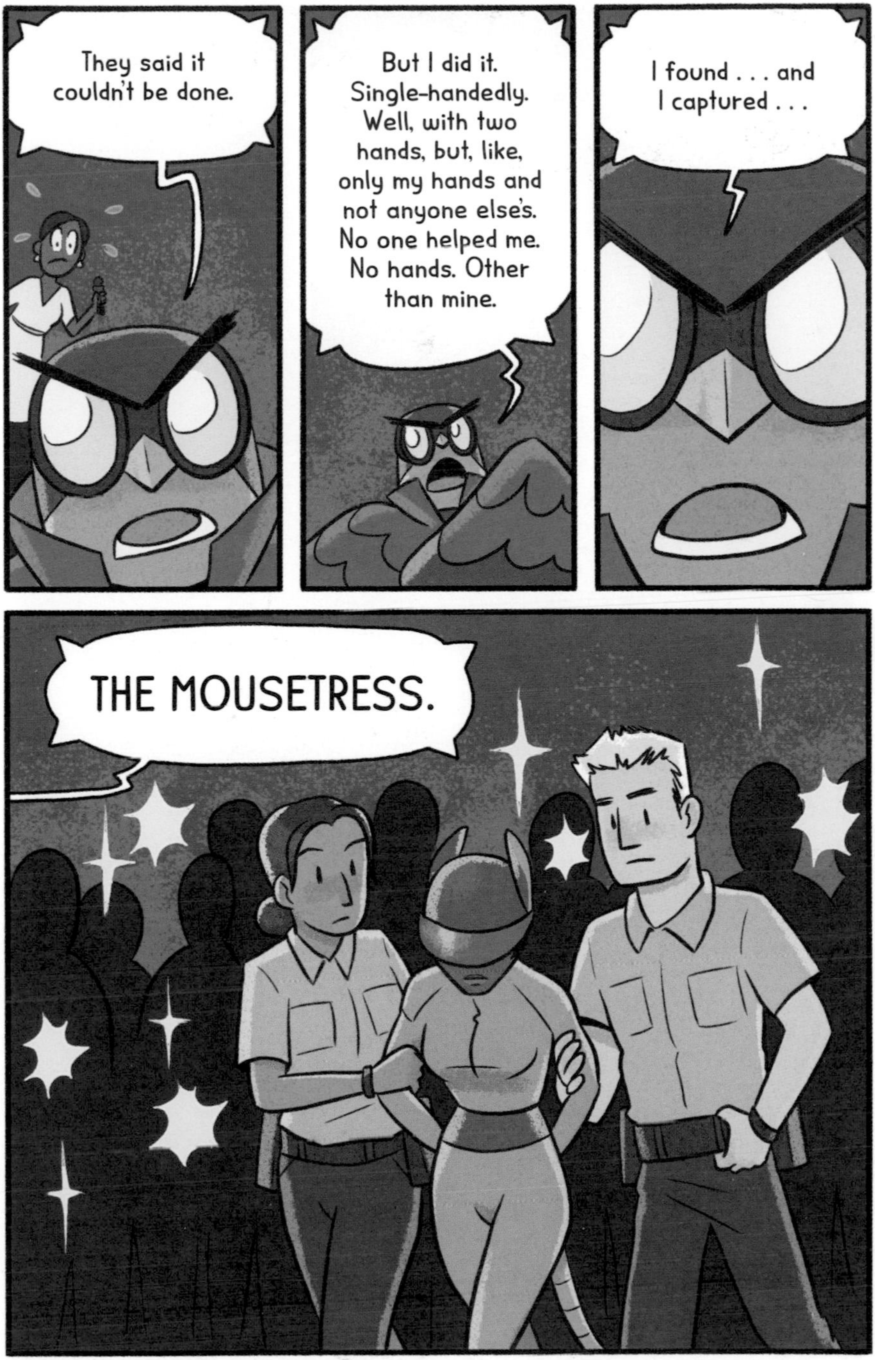
They said it couldn't be done.
But I did it. Single-handedly. Well, with two hands, but, like, only my hands and not anyone else's. No one helped me. No hands. Other than mine.
I found . . . and I captured . . .
THE MOUSETRESS.

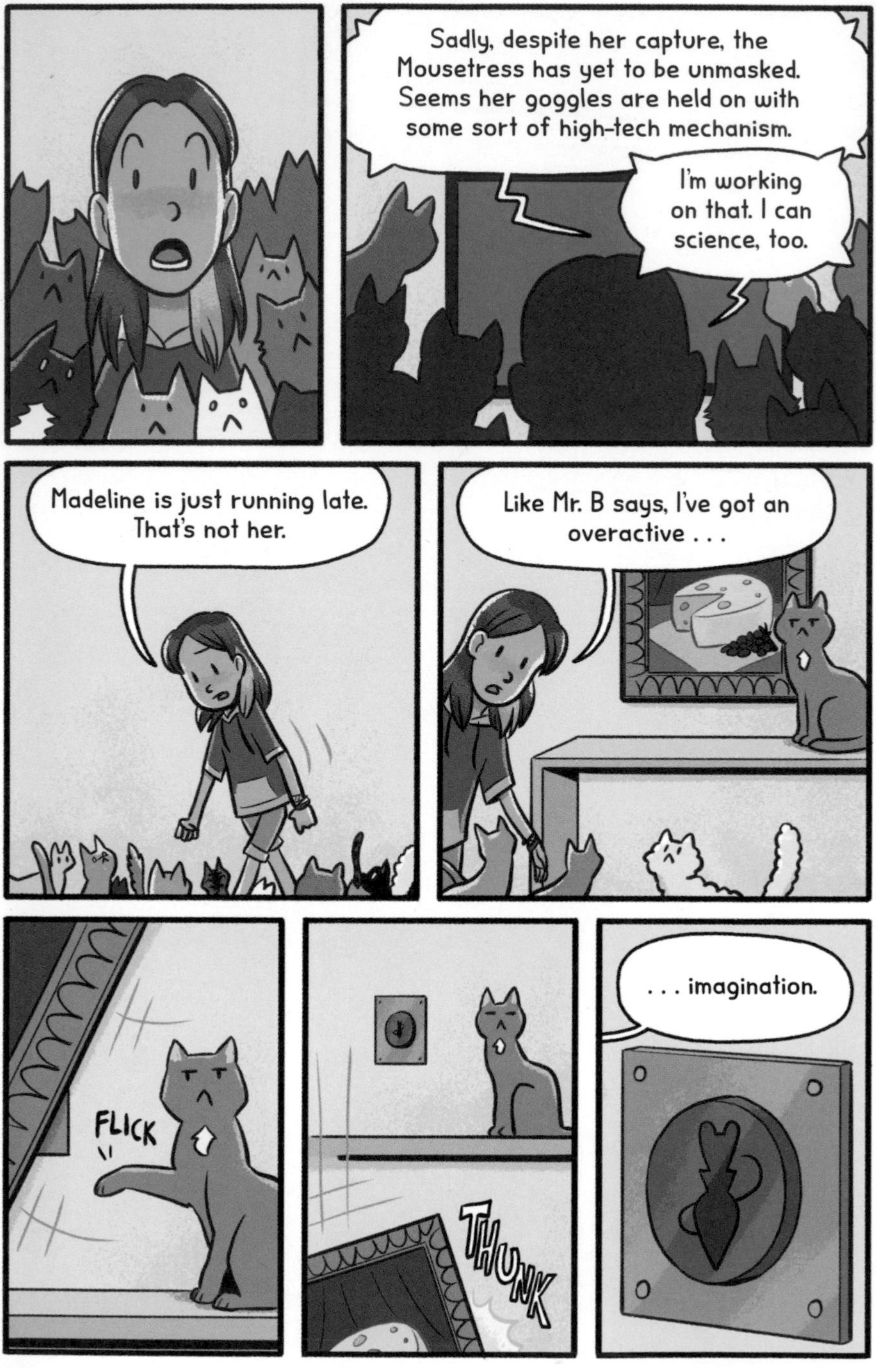
Sadly, despite her capture, the Mousetress has yet to be unmasked. Seems her goggles are held on with some sort of high-tech mechanism.
I'm working on that. I can science, too.
Madeline is just running late. That's not her.
Like Mr. B says, I've got an overactive . . .
FLICK
THUNK
. . . imagination.

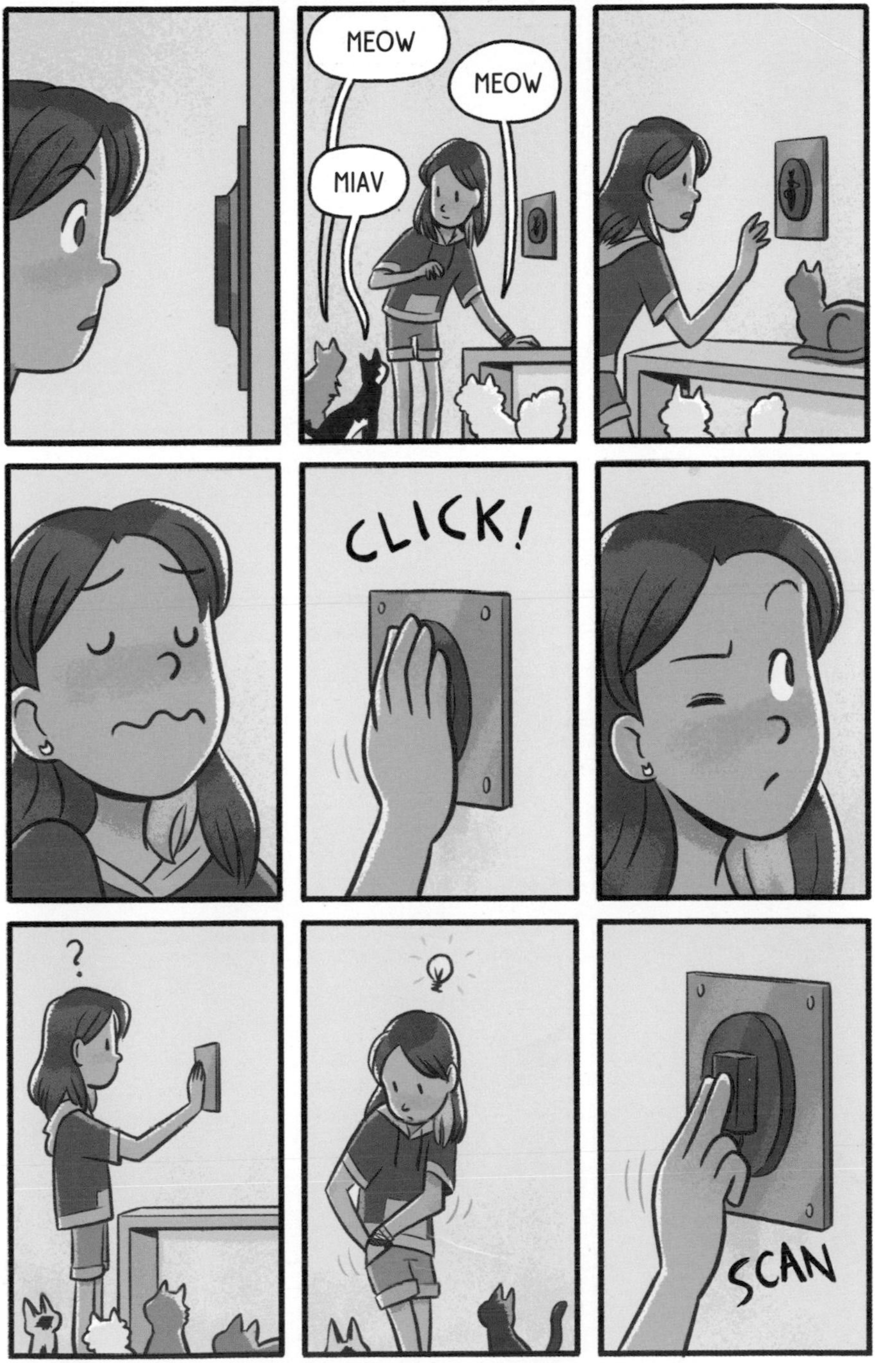
MEOW
MEOW
MIAV
CLICK!
?
SCAN

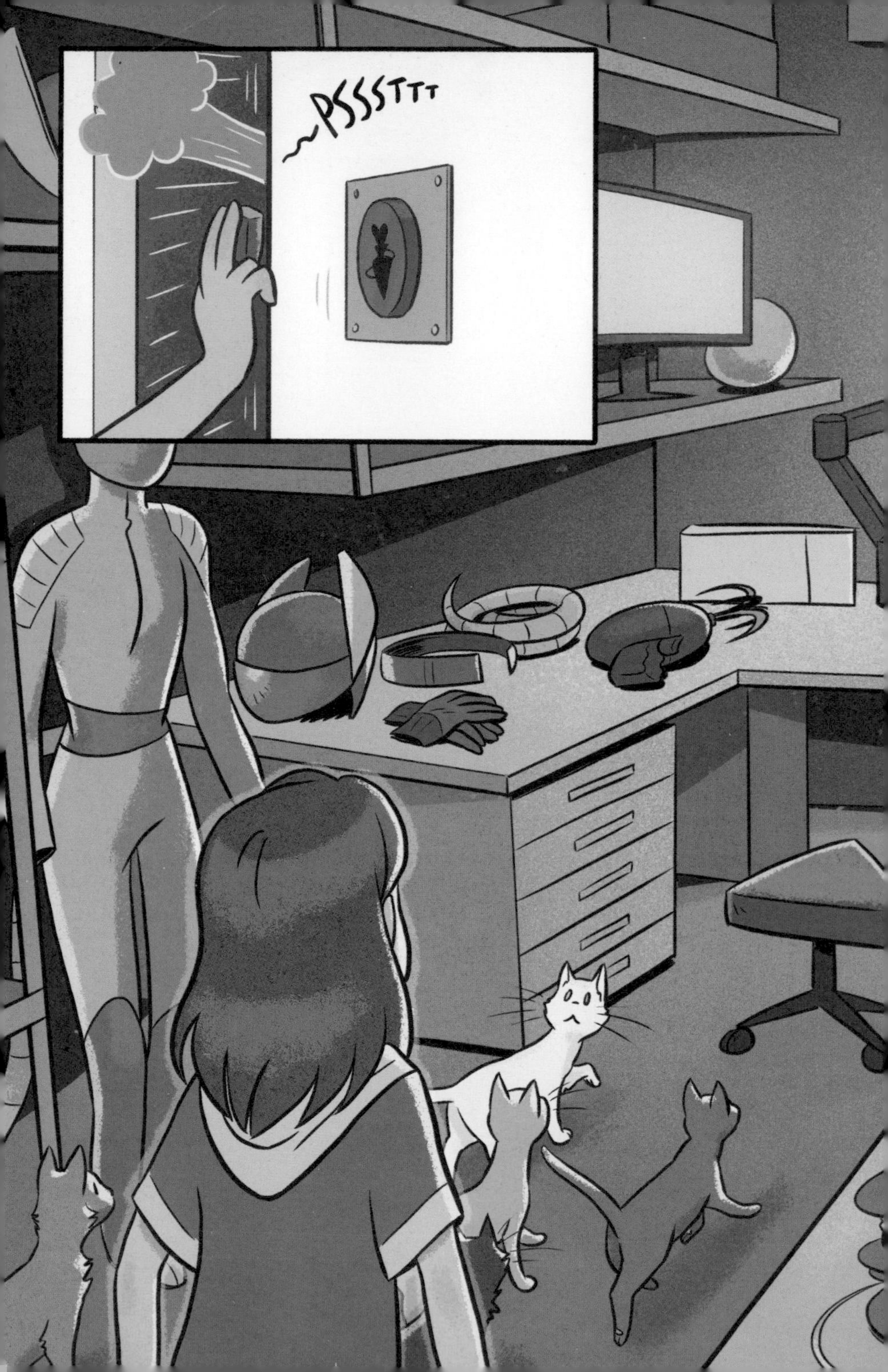
~PSSSTTT

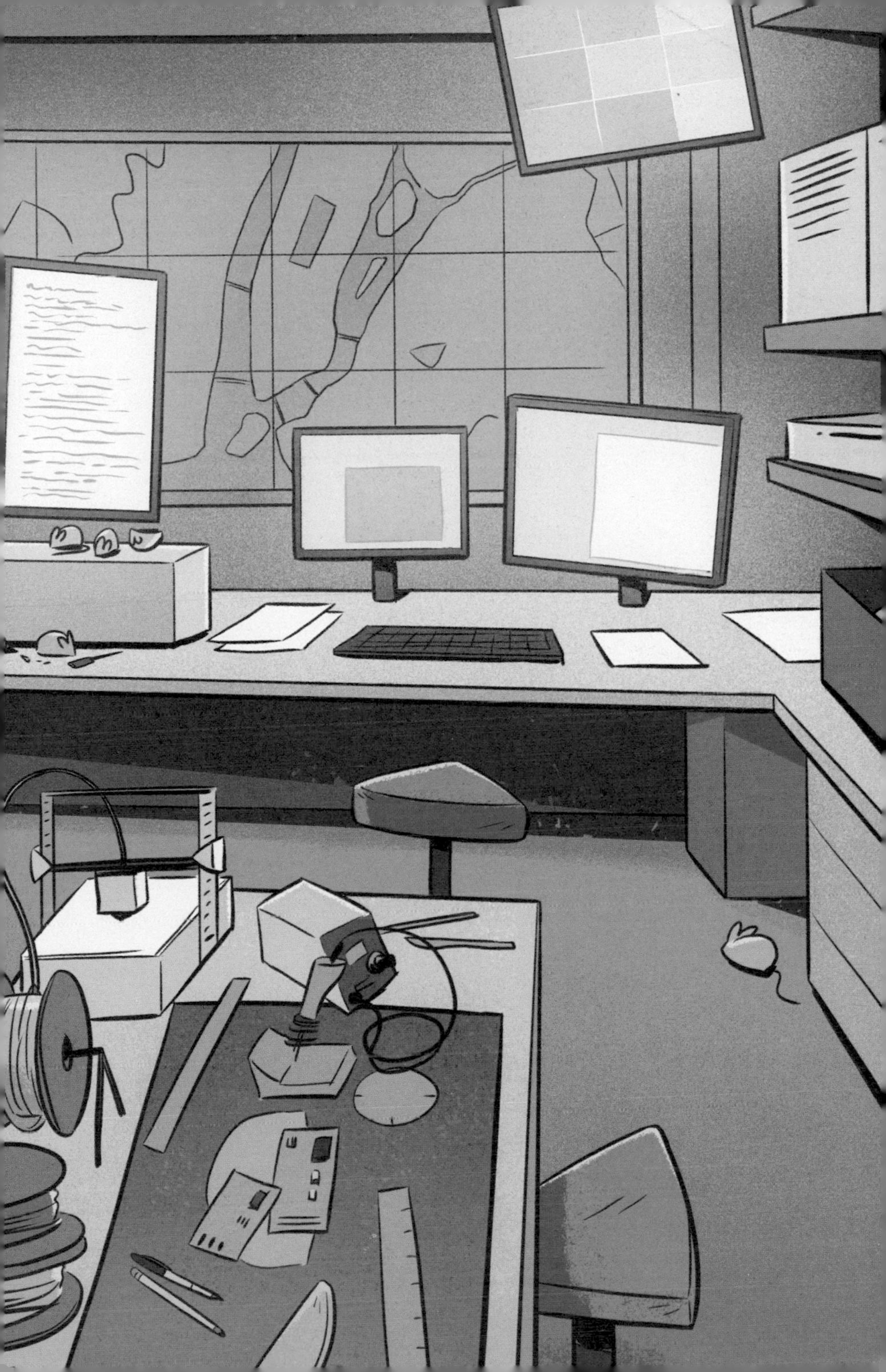

Whoa.

What are you doing?

I'm not a superhero! Or villain or whatever! I'm just a kid! There's nothing I can do.

PRISON FLOOR PLAN

TAP TAP
TAPPITY
TAPPITY
TAP
TAP

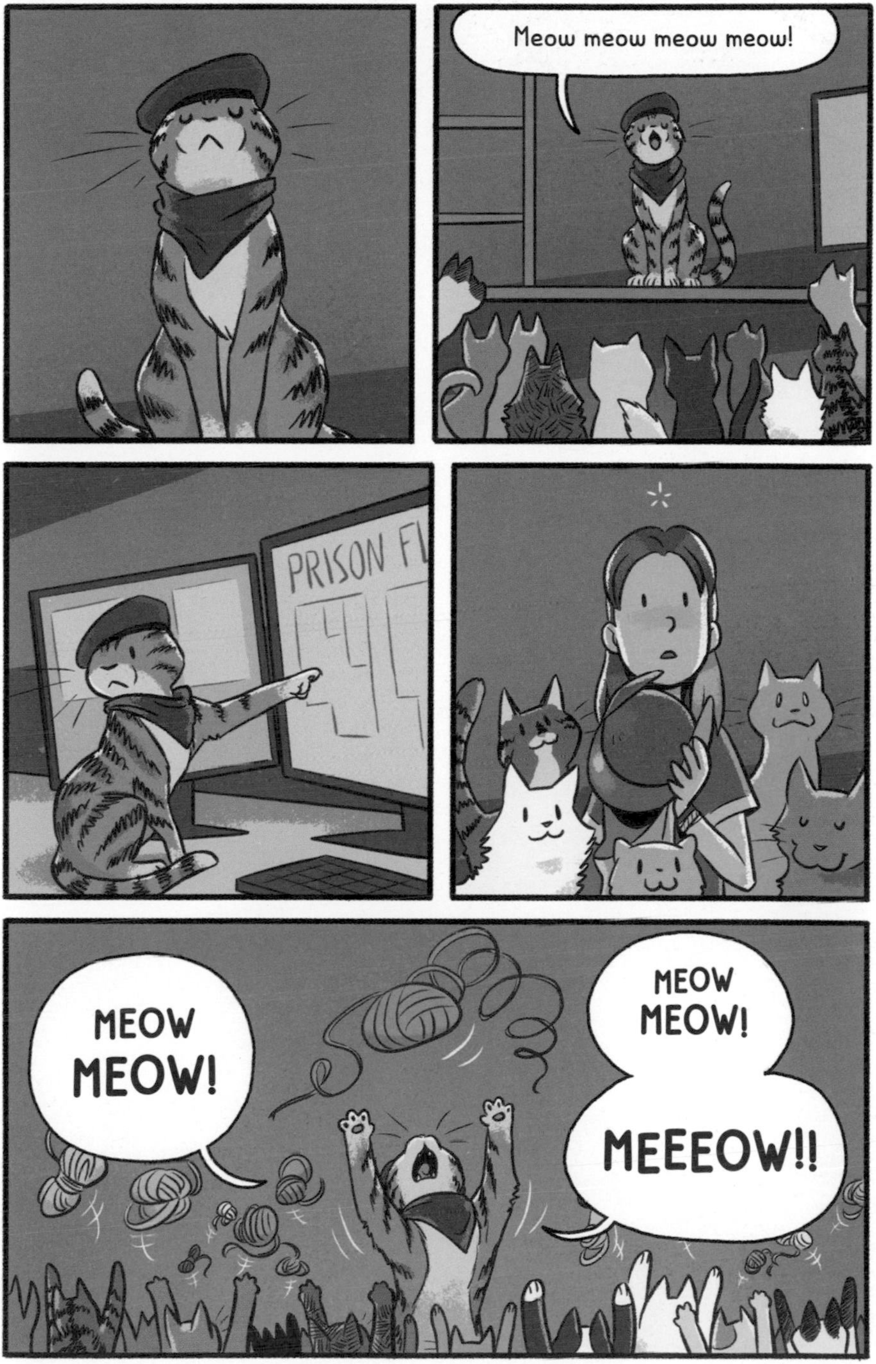
Meow meow meow meow!
PRISON F
MEOW
MEOW!
MEOW
MEOW!
MEEEOW!!

Yeah. I still don't speak cat.

Wow, Frida, you are a GREAT artist. Is this the prison . . . and all of you . . . and me?

Only six guards?

And a window near Madeline's cell?

I can actually understand this!

You're right. Let's save Madeline.

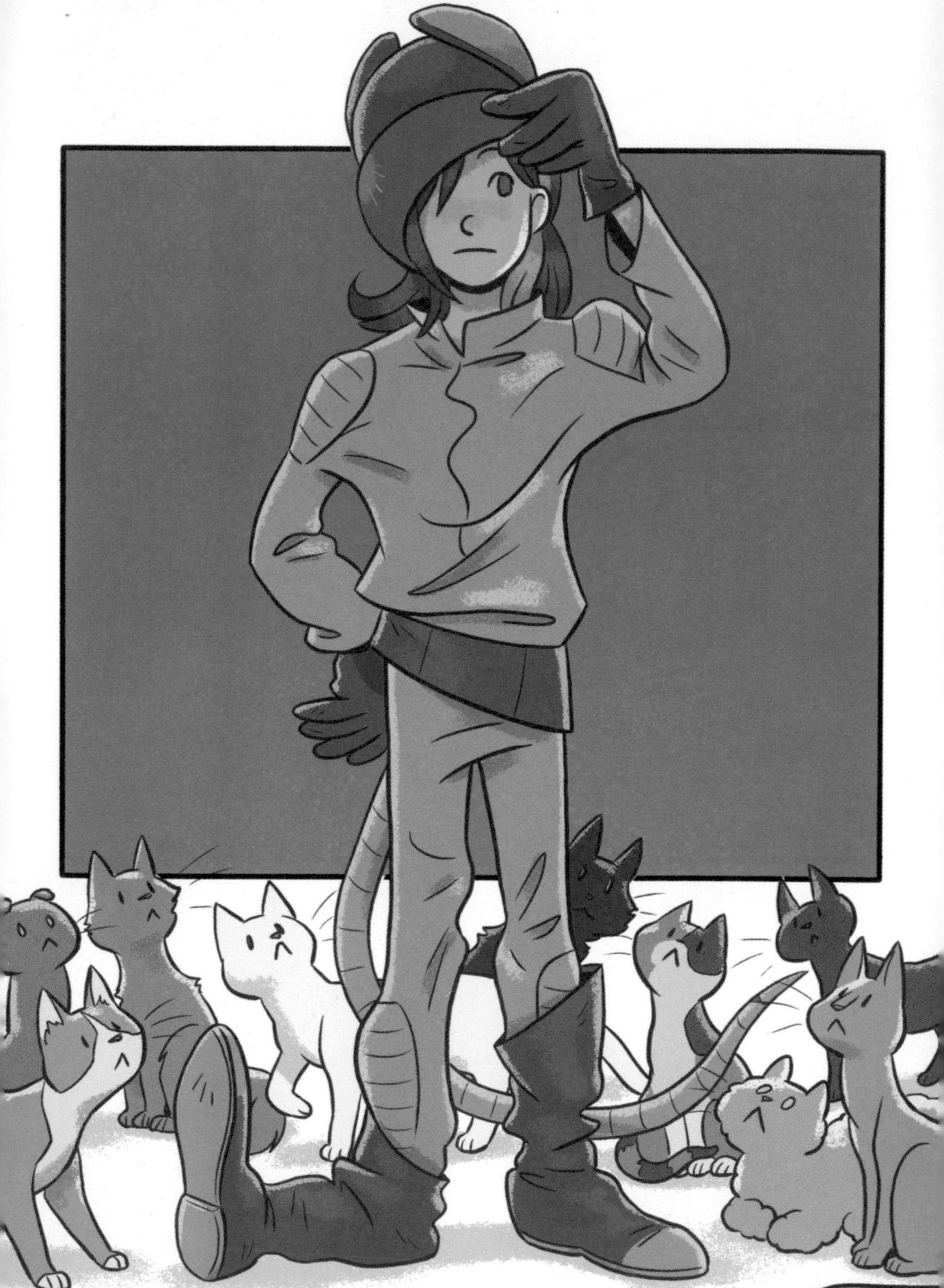

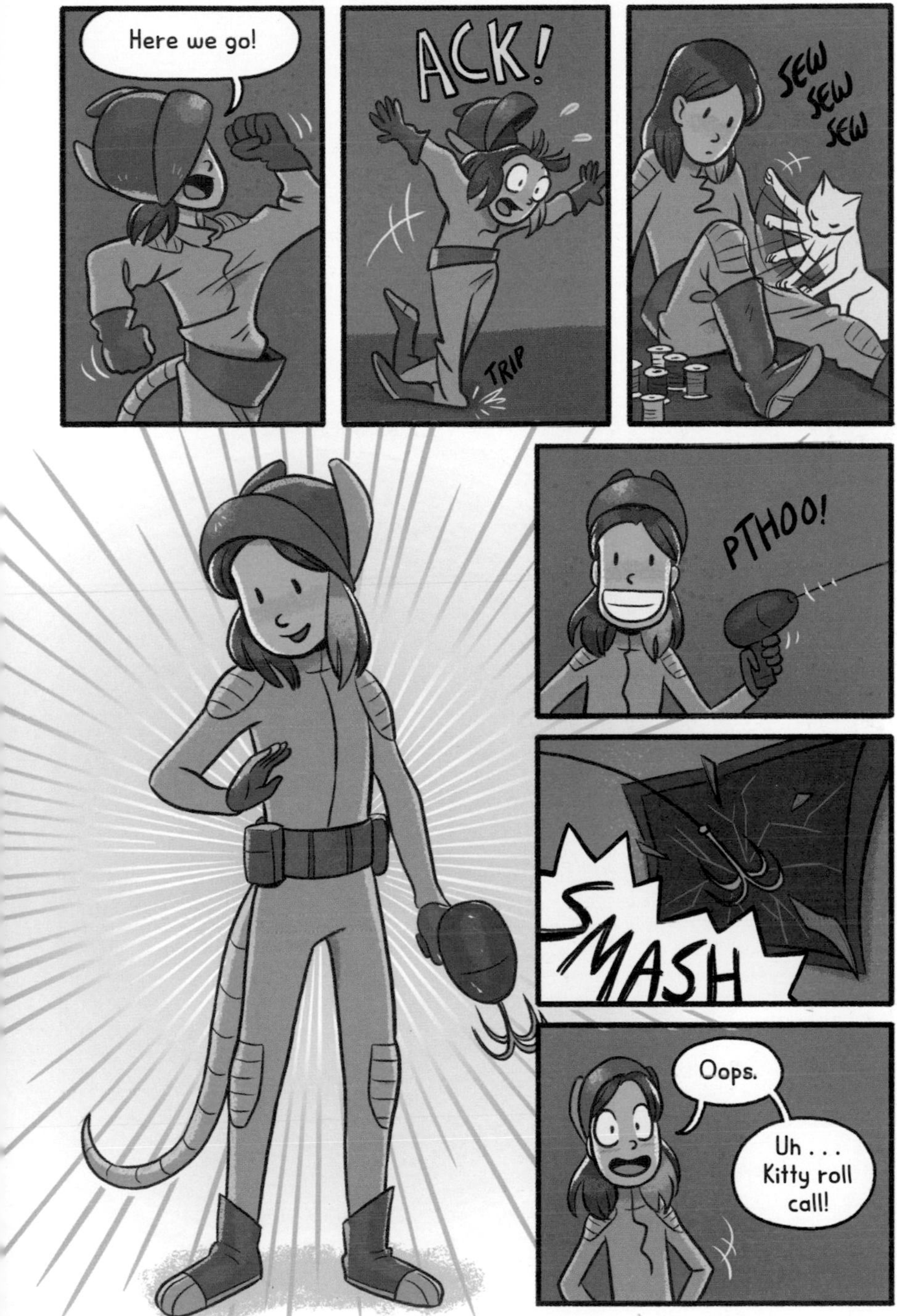
Here we go!
ACK!
TRIP
SEW
SEW
SEW
PTHOO!
SMASH
Oops.
Uh . . .
Kitty roll call!

Jolie: Computer Hacking

Gracie: Language Expert

Myau.

Moritz: Counterattacks

Miles: Laser Expert

Hildy: Super-Speed Reflexes

Chaz: YouTube Tutorials

General Titus: Super Strength

Frida: Master Artist

Peeve: Military Strategist

Captain Von Smooch: Audiovisual Expert

Curly: Expert Seamstress

Jack Slayer: Getaway Driver

168

Paw Simon: Splitting Up Teams

Pierogi: Textiles Expert

Nox: Robotics Expert

Puff: Smoke Bombs

Dr. Claw: Bath Bombs

Lyapa: Weapons Expert

Smushy: Mixed Martial Arts

Bentley: Sonic Purr

Seamus: Math Genius

Lasagna: Camouflage Expert

DJ Bootie Butler: Mad Beats

Ahhh! We don't have time for this! We need to go save Madeline!

CHAPTER THIRTEEN

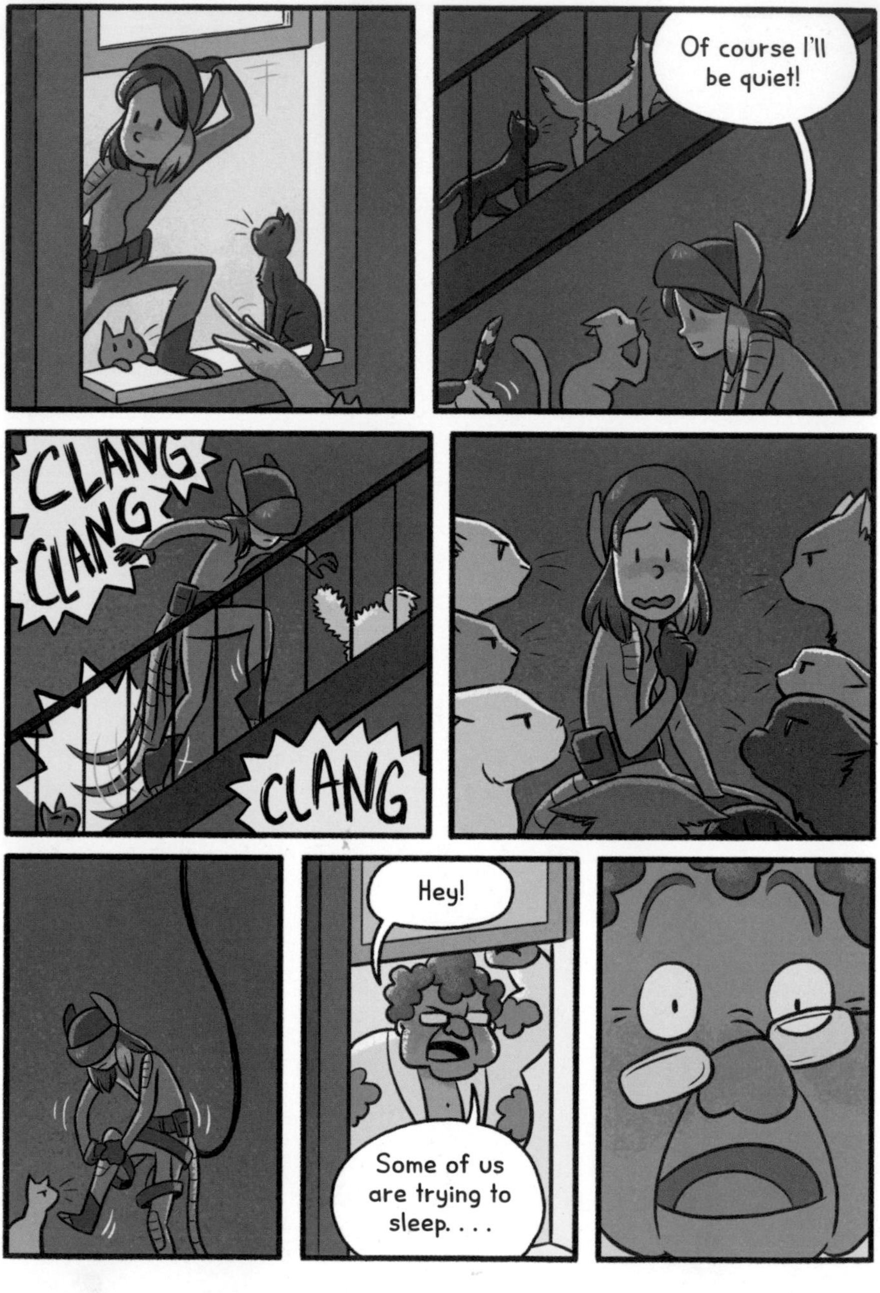
Of course I'll be quiet!
CLANG
CLANG
CLANG
Hey!
Some of us are trying to sleep. . . .

Aaaaahhh! It's the Mousetress!!!!

How do you get this . . .

SWIPE!

Scratch-Off! You're one of Madeline's, too?!

CLIK

WHOA.

WHHIIIIIIRRRR

BZZZ!!

Hi, Mom.

I just got the strangest call from Mrs. Piper.

Stranger than usual? Is that even possible? Heh. Heh.

She's convinced she saw the Mousetress climbing the building—going on and on about giant claws, glowing red eyes . . .

Didn't Owl Guy just catch her?

All I know is she seemed really scared . . . almost concerned, which is definitely not like her.

Just promise me you'll stay with the cats. They'll keep you safe.

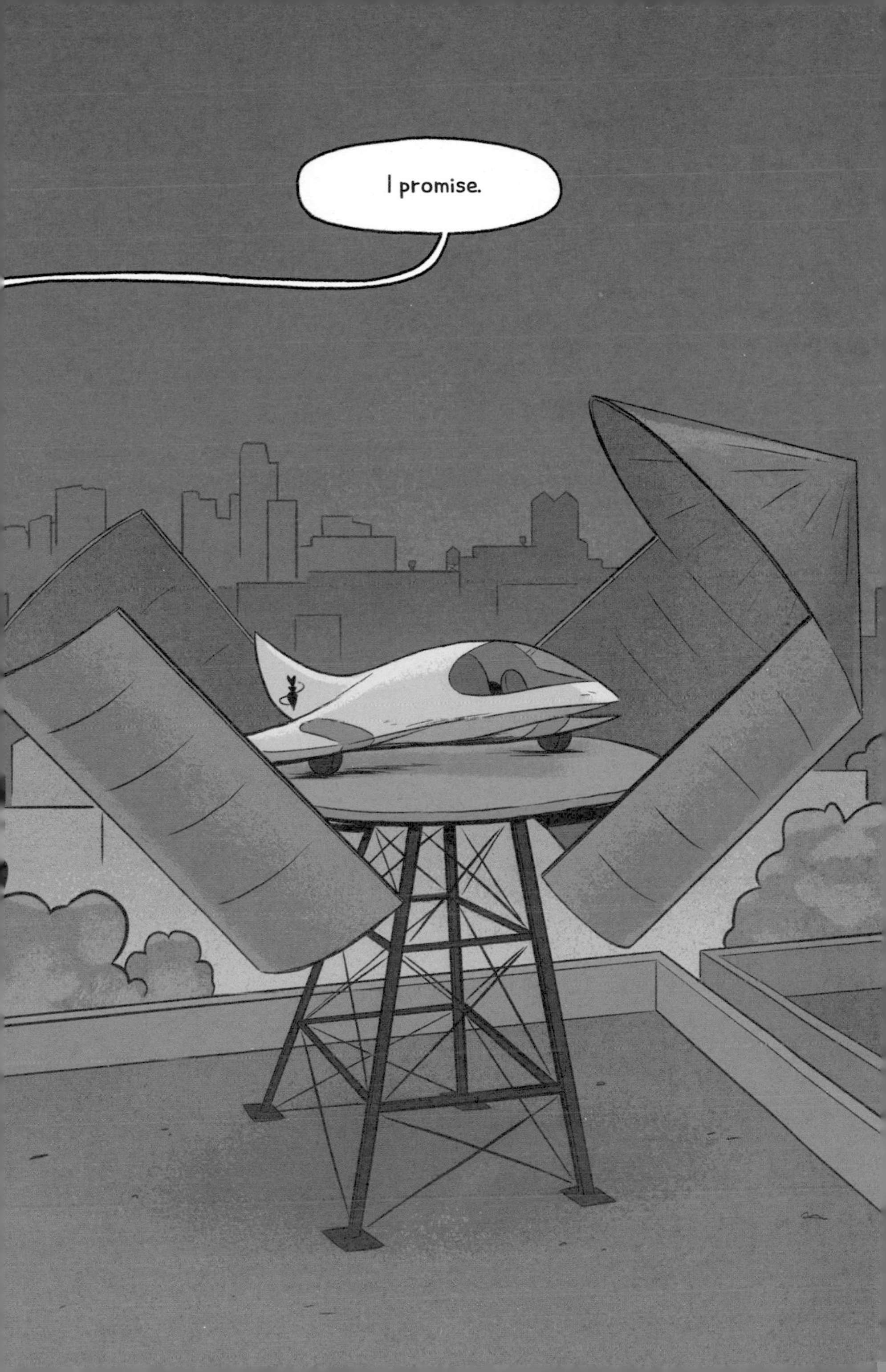
I promise.

I can do this. I can totally do this. I've played video games like this.

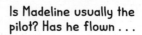

Is Madeline usually the pilot? Has he flown . . .

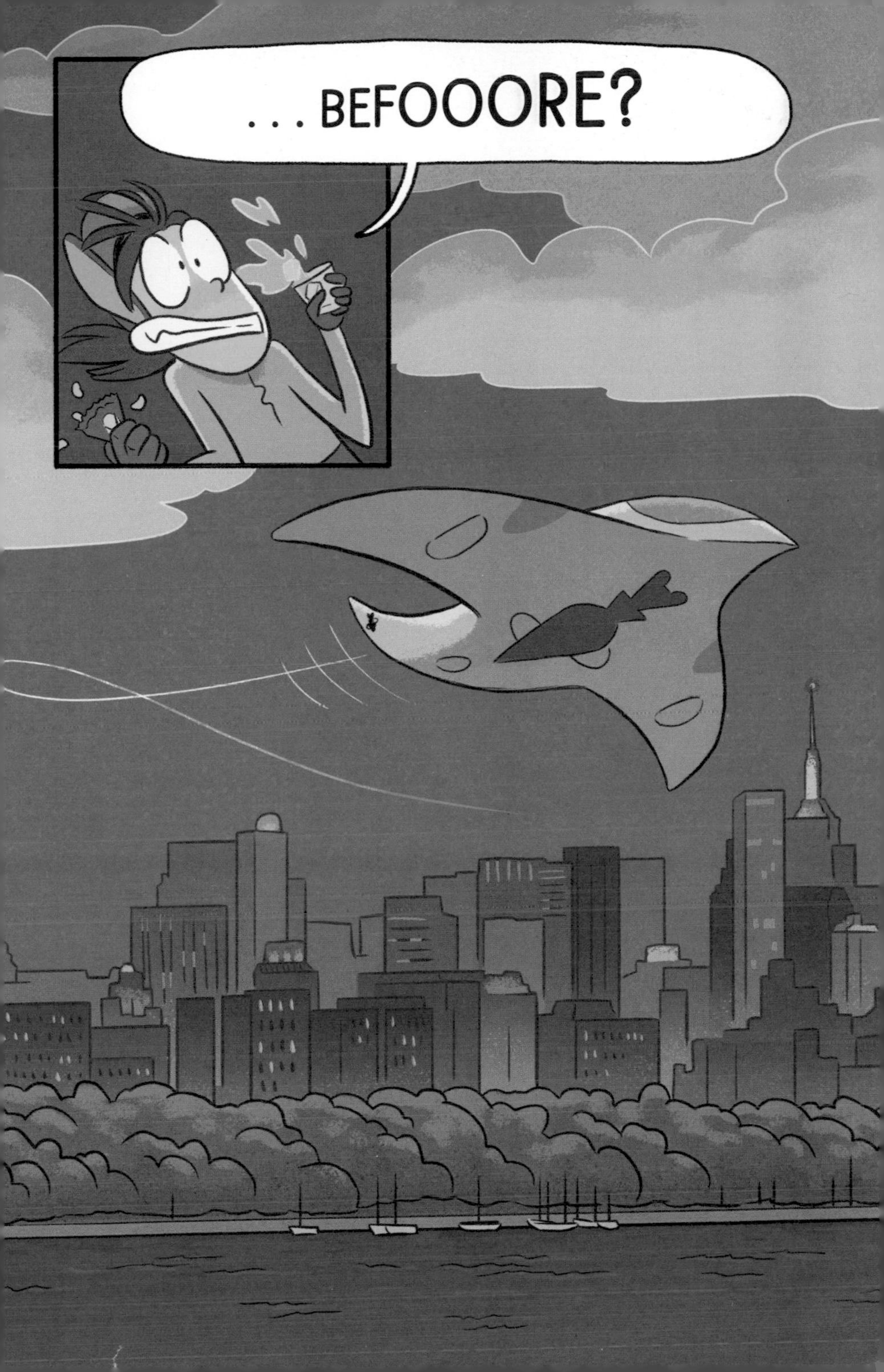
. . . BEFOOORE?

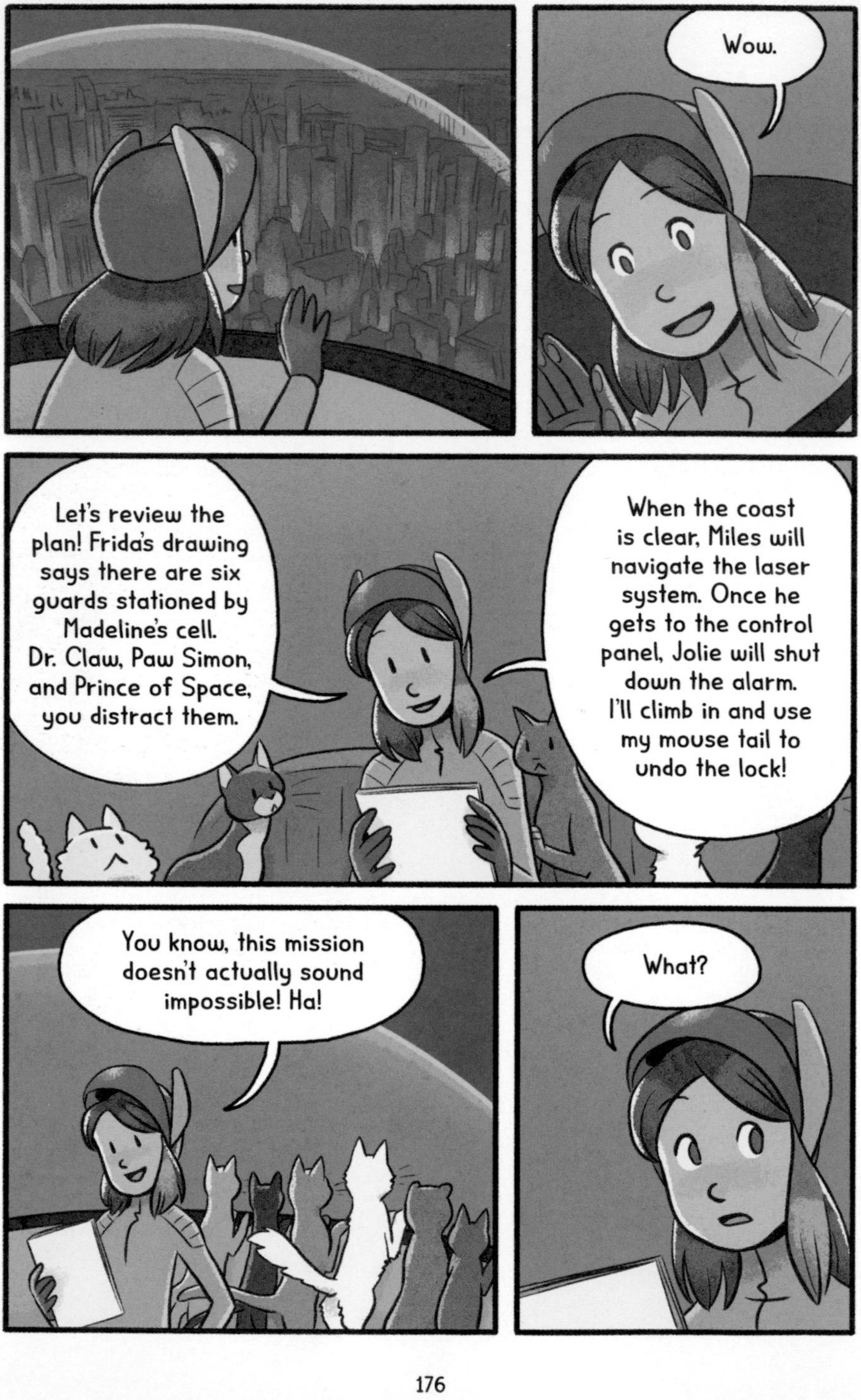

Wow.
Let's review the plan! Frida's drawing says there are six guards stationed by Madeline's cell. Dr. Claw, Paw Simon, and Prince of Space, you distract them.
When the coast is clear, Miles will navigate the laser system. Once he gets to the control panel, Jolie will shut down the alarm. I'll climb in and use my mouse tail to undo the lock!
You know, this mission doesn't actually sound impossible! Ha!
What?

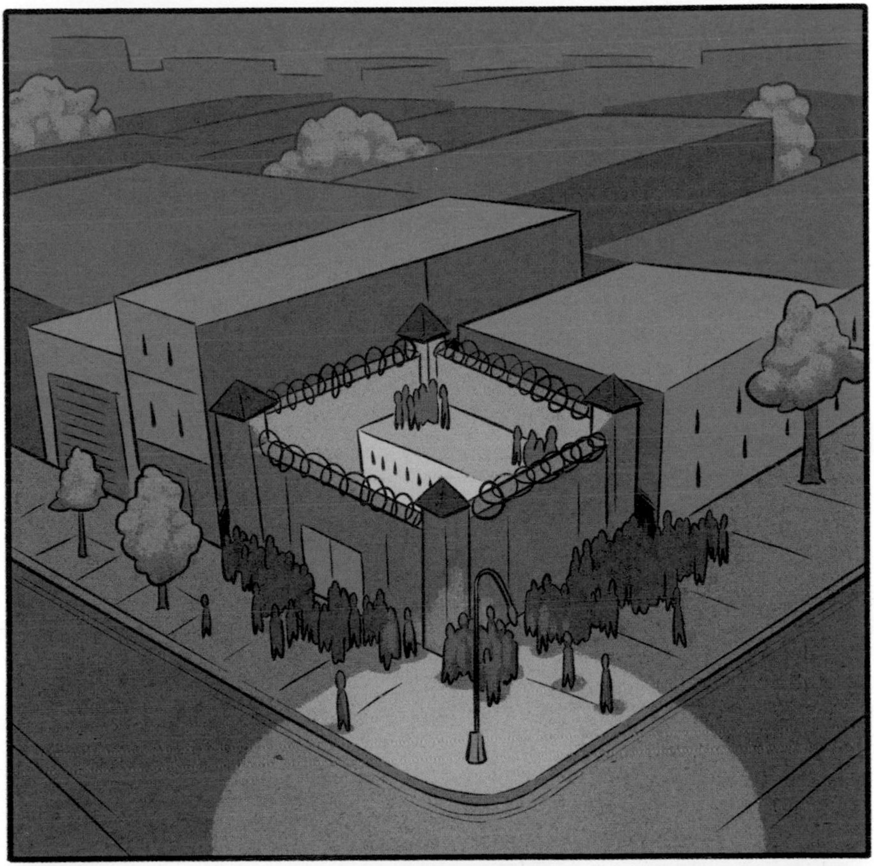

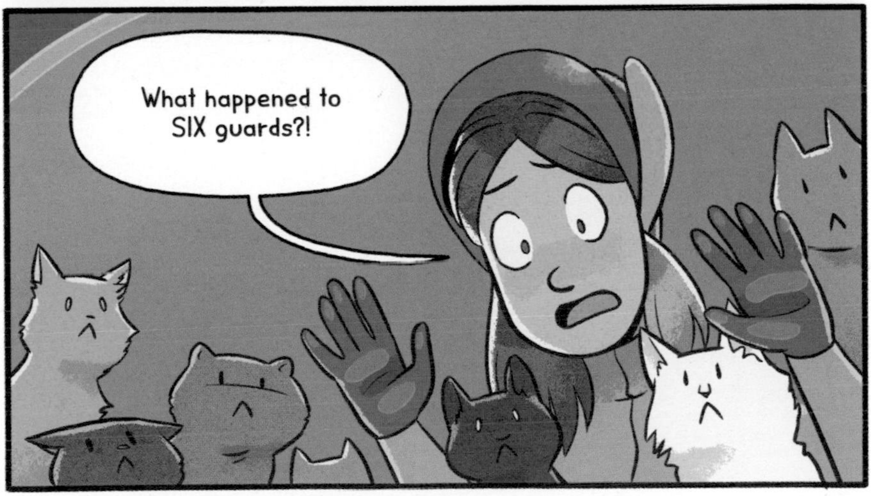
What happened to SIX guards?!

TAP TAP TAPPITY TAP

TAPPITY TAP TAP

TAP TAP TAP

I can't believe he's here!

I know! It's my day off, but I came in! Does my hair look okay?

CLICK

I became a prison guard just so I could meet him one day!

Ha! So I guess you're quitting tomorrow.

Whoa.

Yes.

What?

I don't know. It's like Owl Guy didn't trust us to watch the Mousetress. I find it kind of insulting.

Did you just call him OWL GUY?!

Hold me back! Hold me back!

Seriously. Someone hold me.

Seamus, how many are there?

~~6 GUARDS~~
44 + 1
OWL DUDE

Where's Owl Guy?

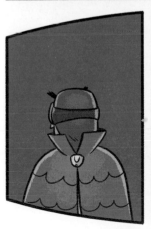

AH!

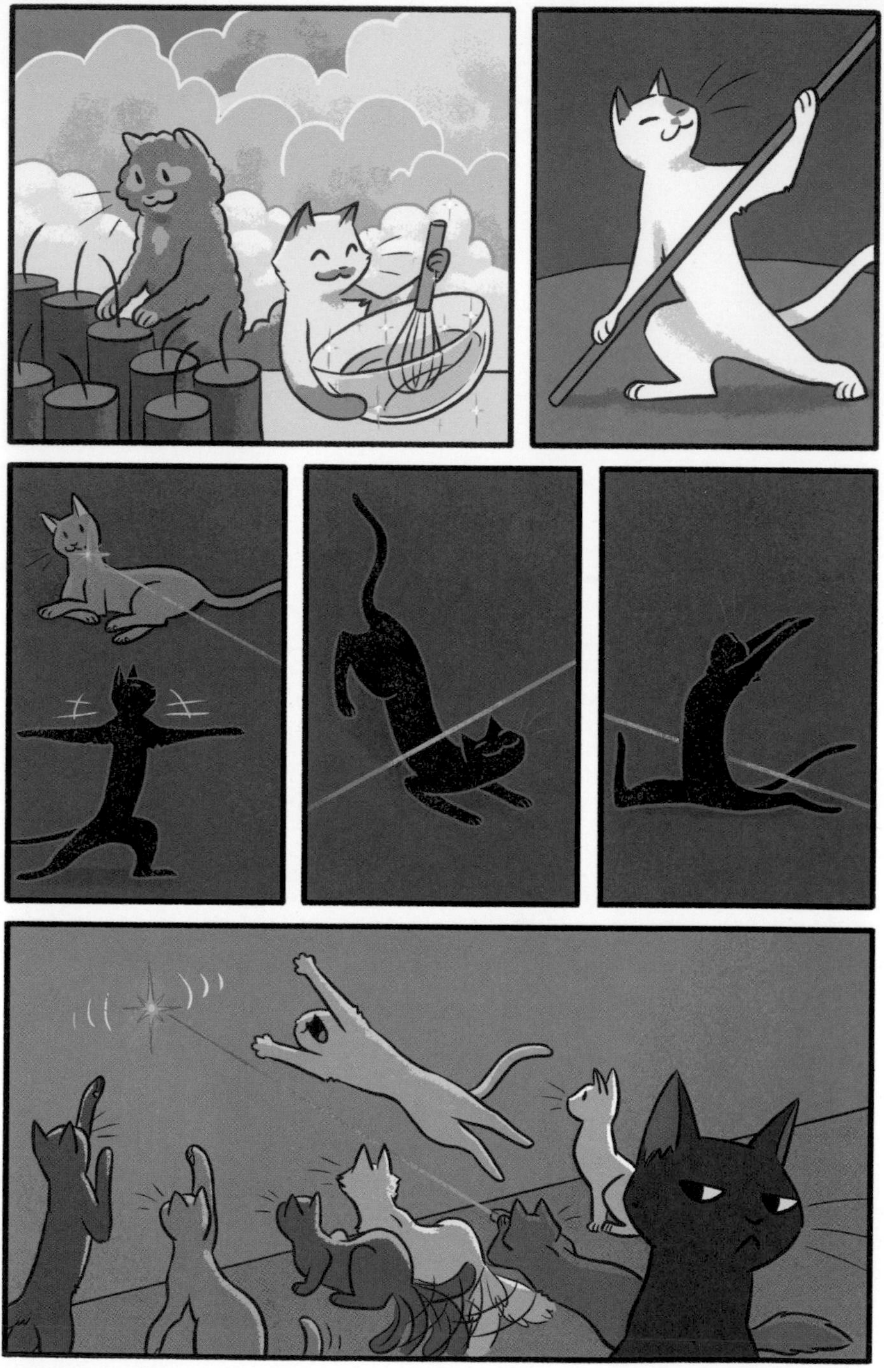

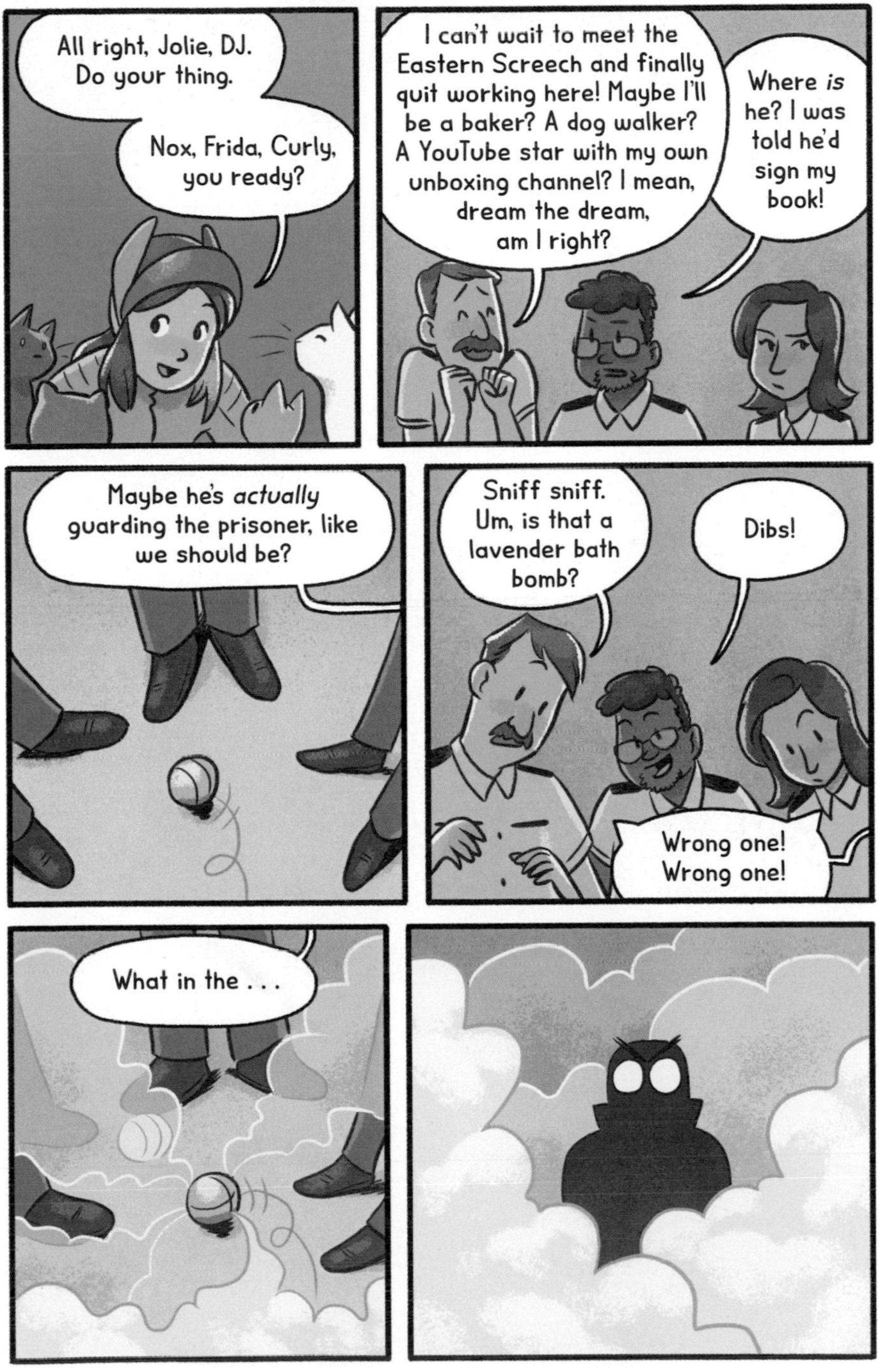
All right, Jolie, DJ. Do your thing.
Nox, Frida, Curly, you ready?
I can't wait to meet the Eastern Screech and finally quit working here! Maybe I'll be a baker? A dog walker? A YouTube star with my own unboxing channel? I mean, dream the dream, am I right?
Where *is* he? I was told he'd sign my book!
Maybe he's *actually* guarding the prisoner, like we should be?
Sniff sniff. Um, is that a lavender bath bomb?
Dibs!
Wrong one! Wrong one!
What in the . . .

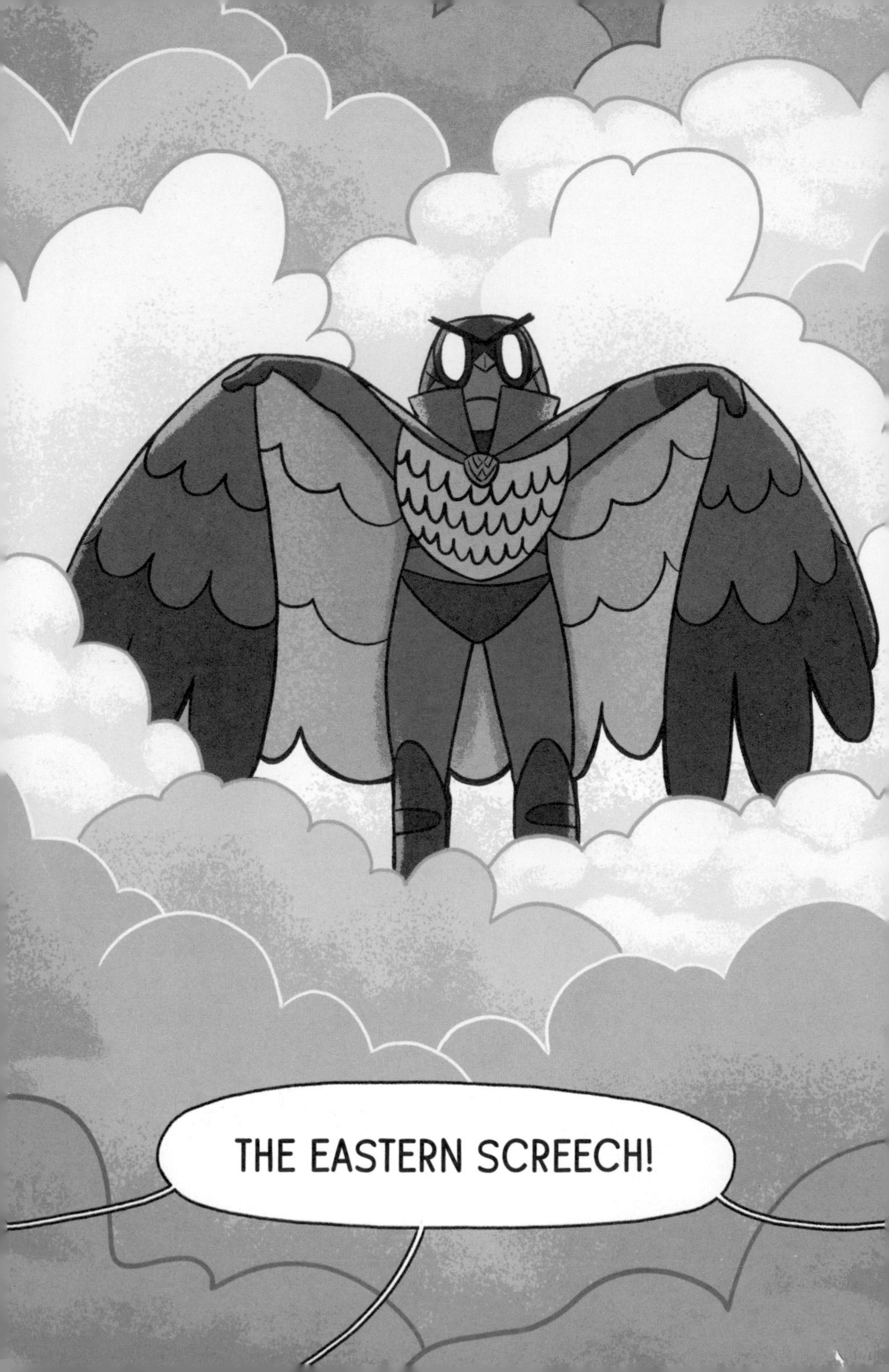
THE EASTERN SCREECH!

He's here!

What an entrance!

YES, IT IS I. EASTERN SCREECH. HELLO, CITIZENS. LOOKING GOOD. I LIKE UNIFORMS.

WHAT WEATHER! WHO WANT AUTOGRAPH?

SEW SEW SEW SEW

Me! Me! I have your book!

I have your *New York Times* article!

I have your limited-edition action figure with 270-degree head rotation and action punch arm!

I have a strand of your hair!!!

CLIK

What?

PHTOOOO

185

CHAPTER FOURTEEN

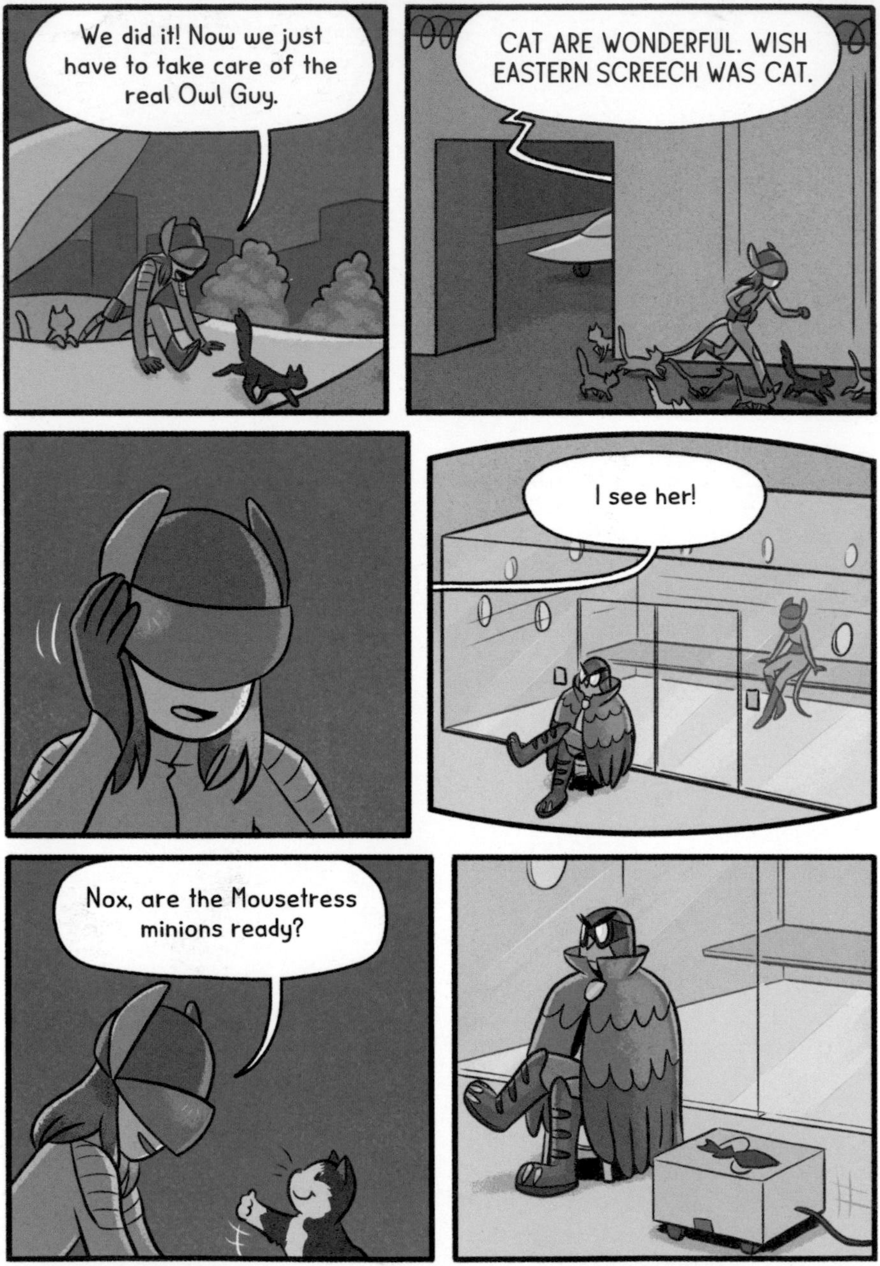

We did it! Now we just have to take care of the real Owl Guy.
CAT ARE WONDERFUL. WISH EASTERN SCREECH WAS CAT.
I see her!
Nox, are the Mousetress minions ready?

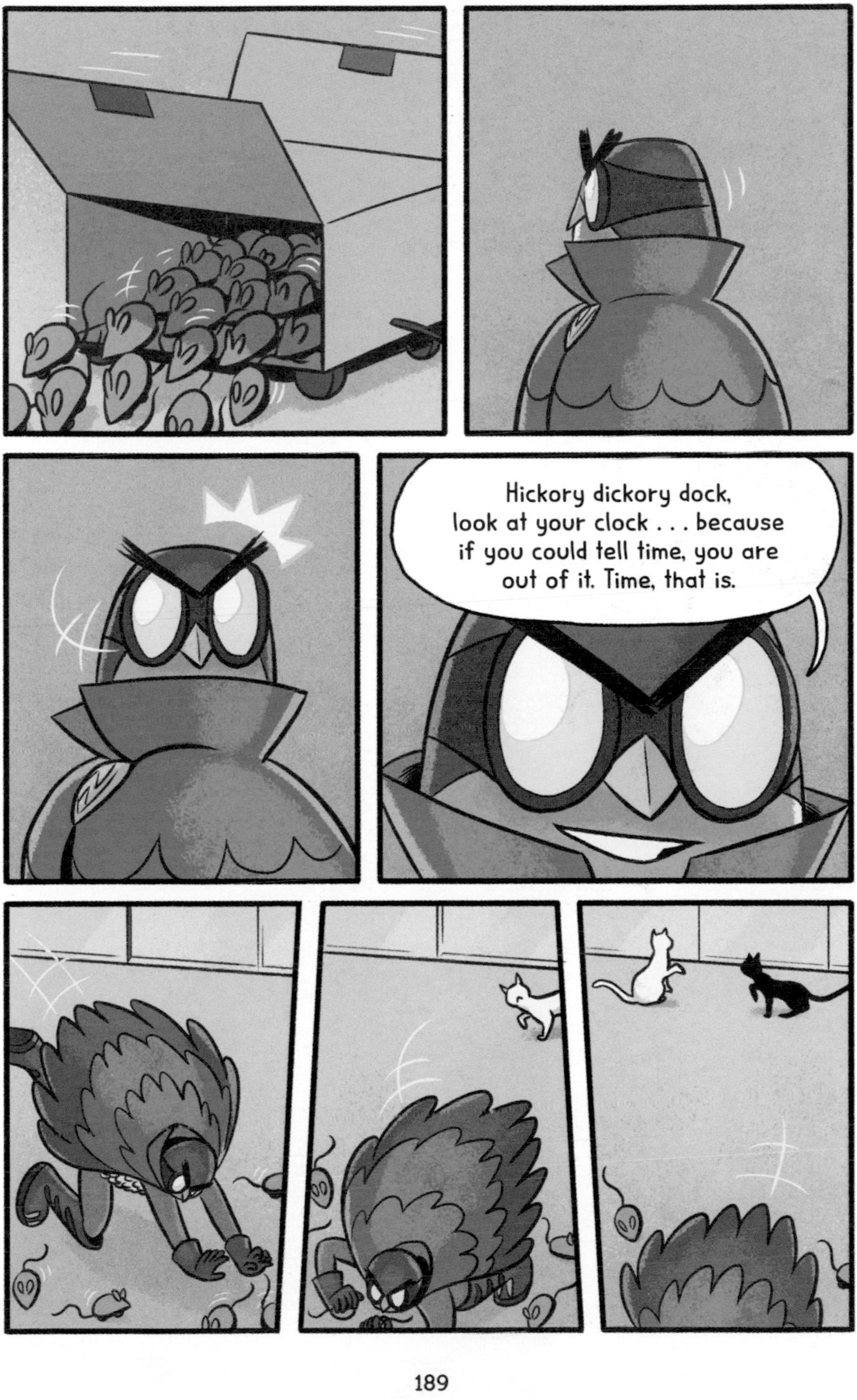
Hickory dickory dock, look at your clock . . . because if you could tell time, you are out of it. Time, that is.

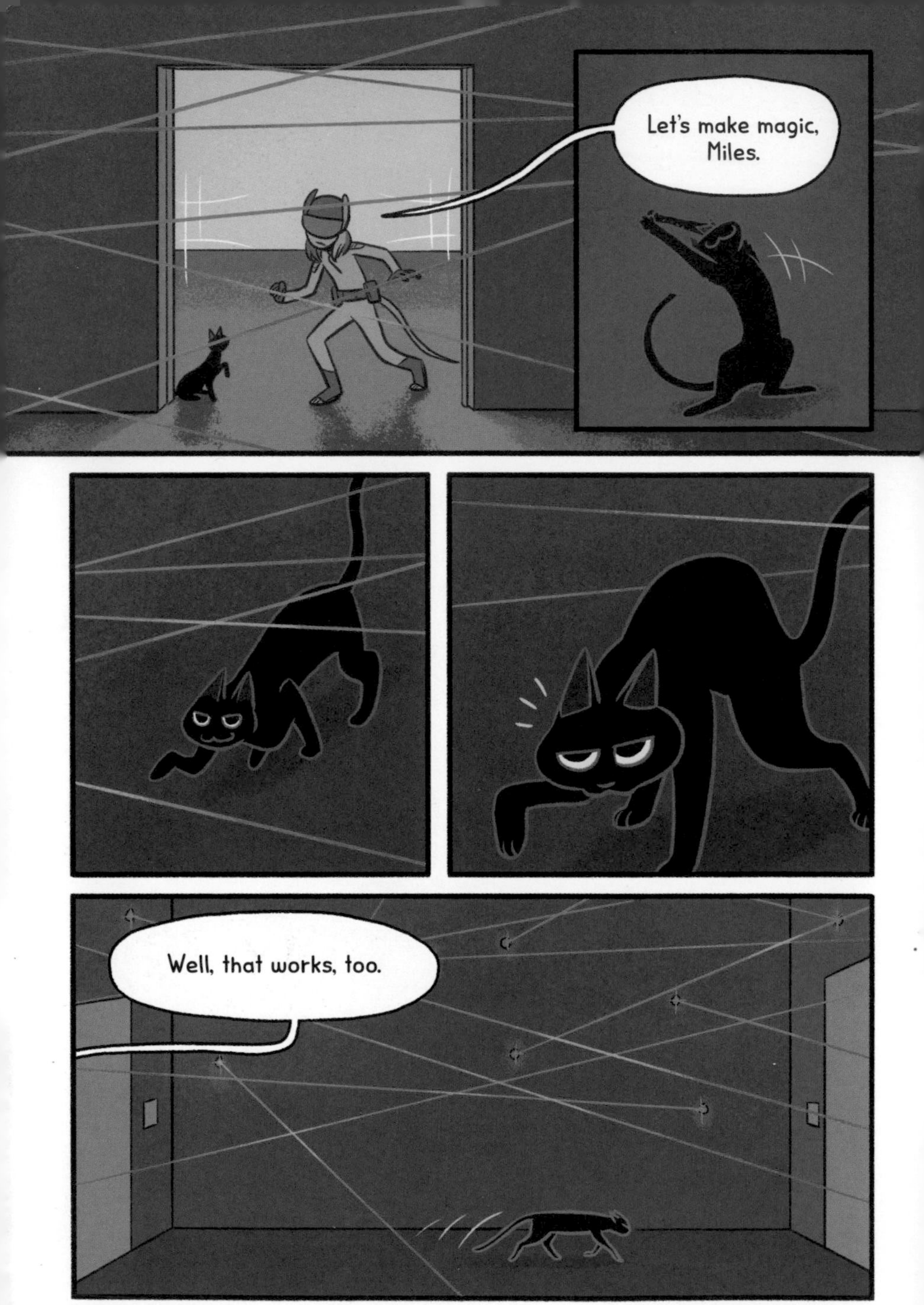
Let's make magic, Miles.
Well, that works, too.

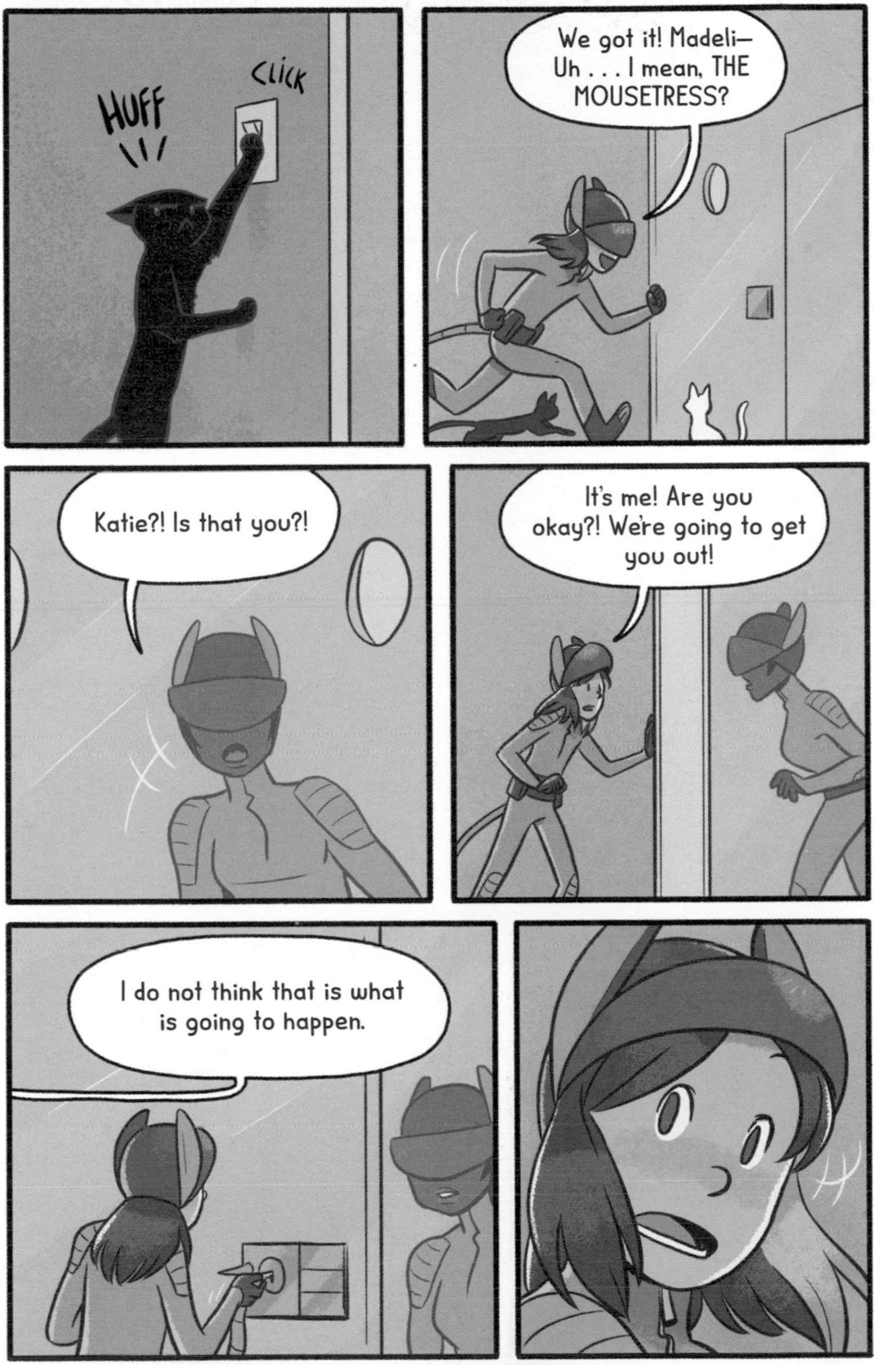
HUFF
CLICK
We got it! Madeli— Uh . . . I mean, THE MOUSETRESS?
Katie?! Is that you?!
It's me! Are you okay?! We're going to get you out!
I do not think that is what is going to happen.

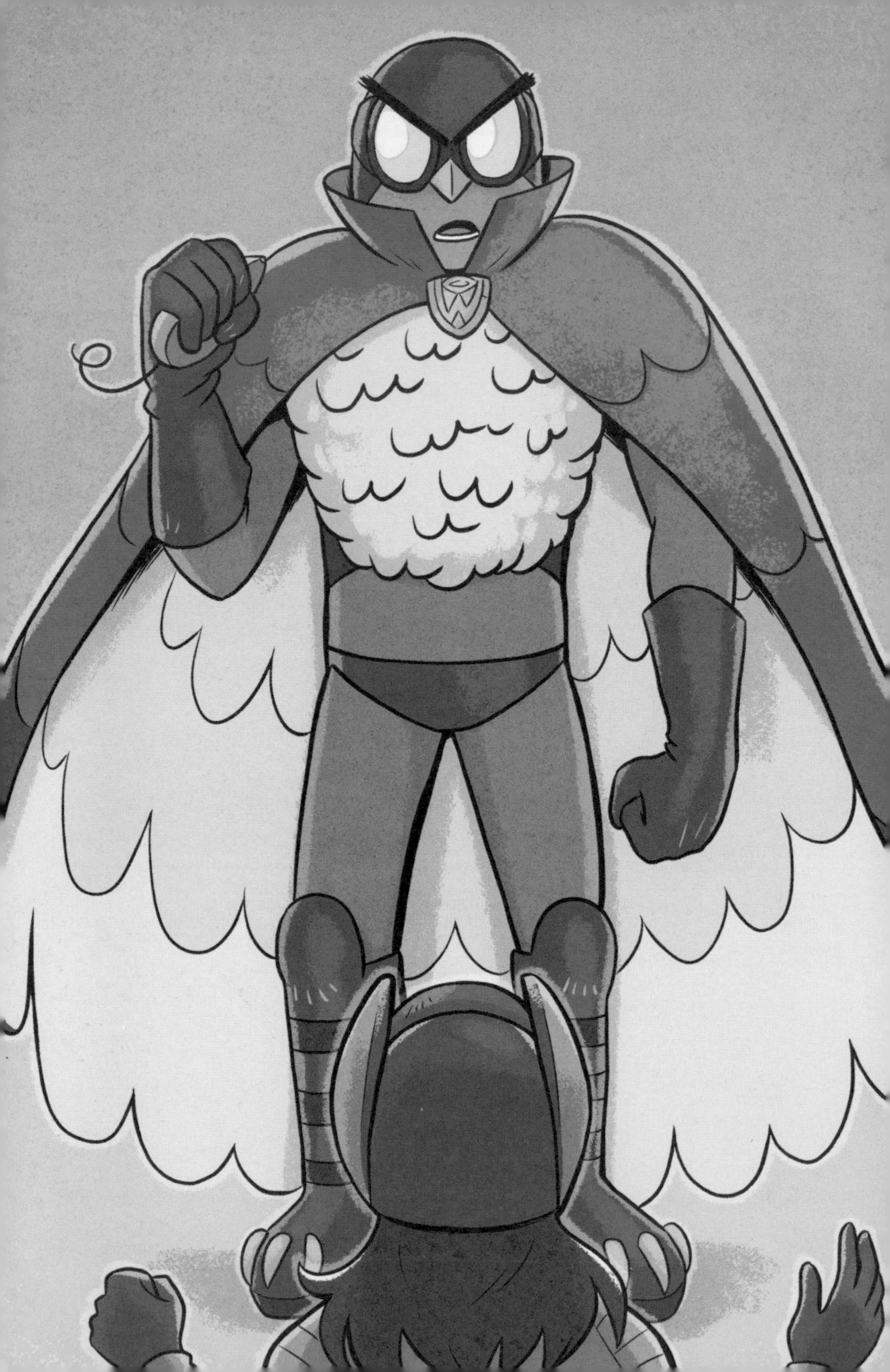

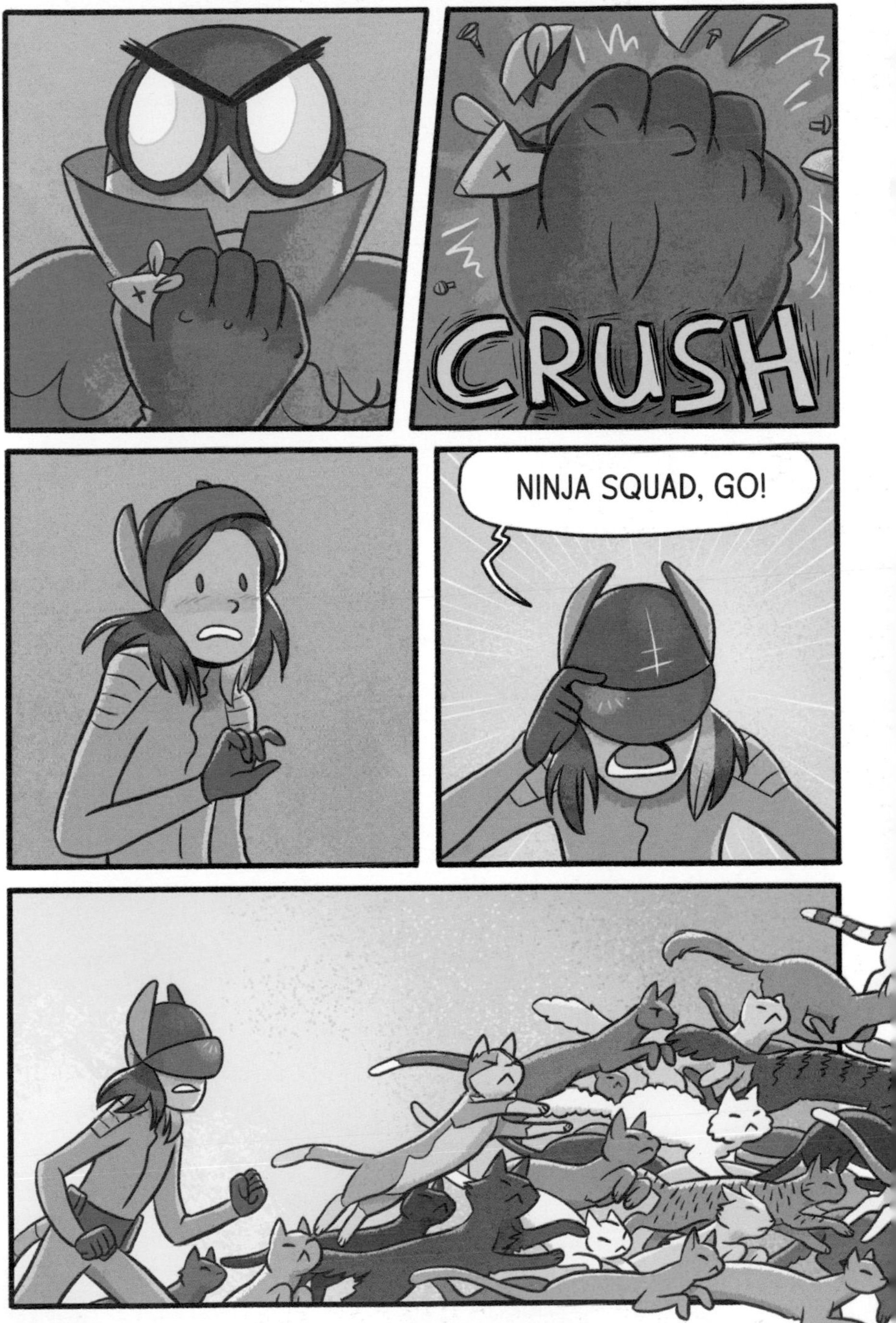
CRUSH
NINJA SQUAD, GO!

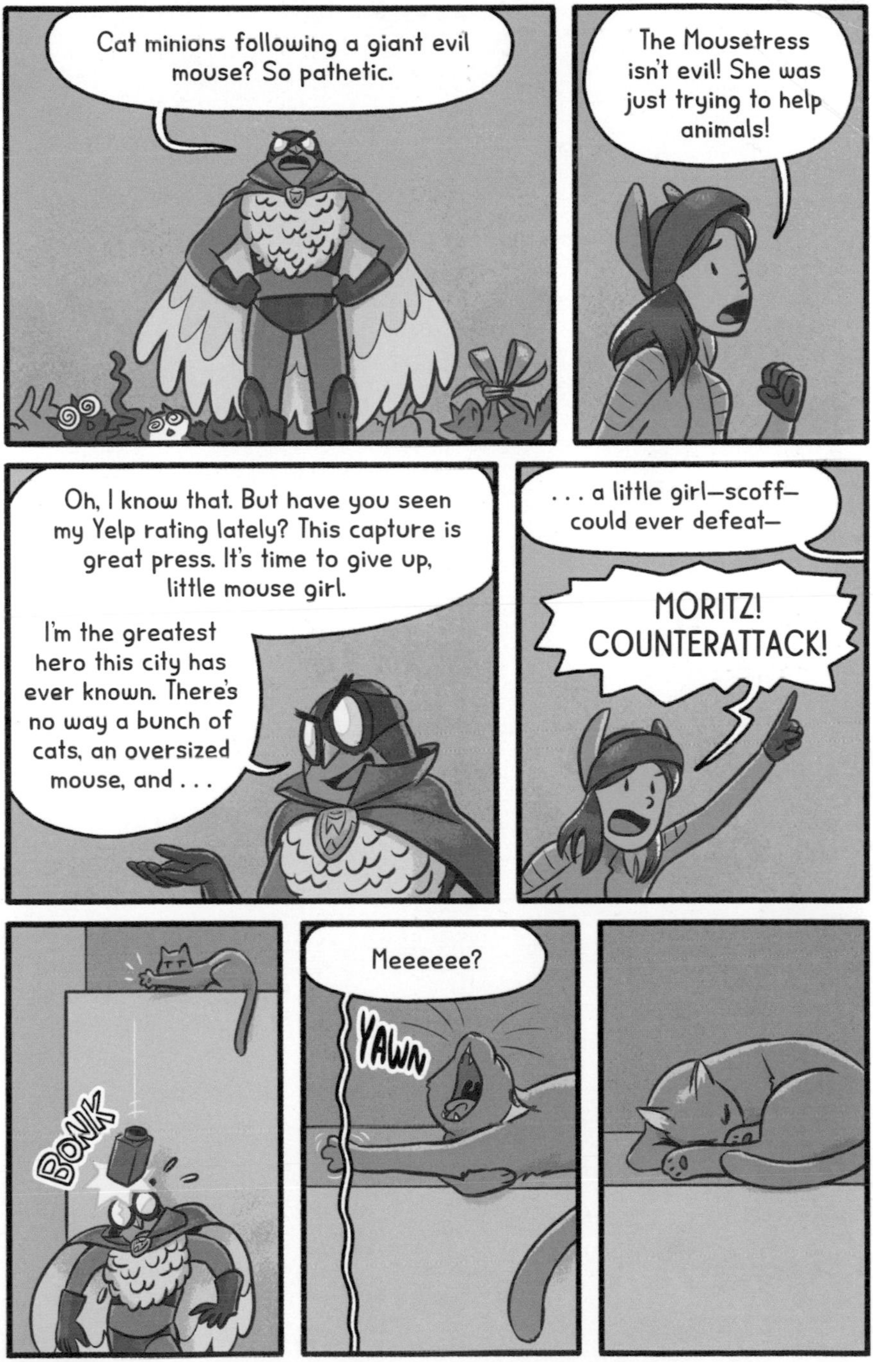

Cat minions following a giant evil mouse? So pathetic.
The Mousetress isn't evil! She was just trying to help animals!
Oh, I know that. But have you seen my Yelp rating lately? This capture is great press. It's time to give up, little mouse girl.
I'm the greatest hero this city has ever known. There's no way a bunch of cats, an oversized mouse, and . . .
. . . a little girl—scoff—could ever defeat—
MORITZ! COUNTERATTACK!
BONK
Meeeeee?
YAWN

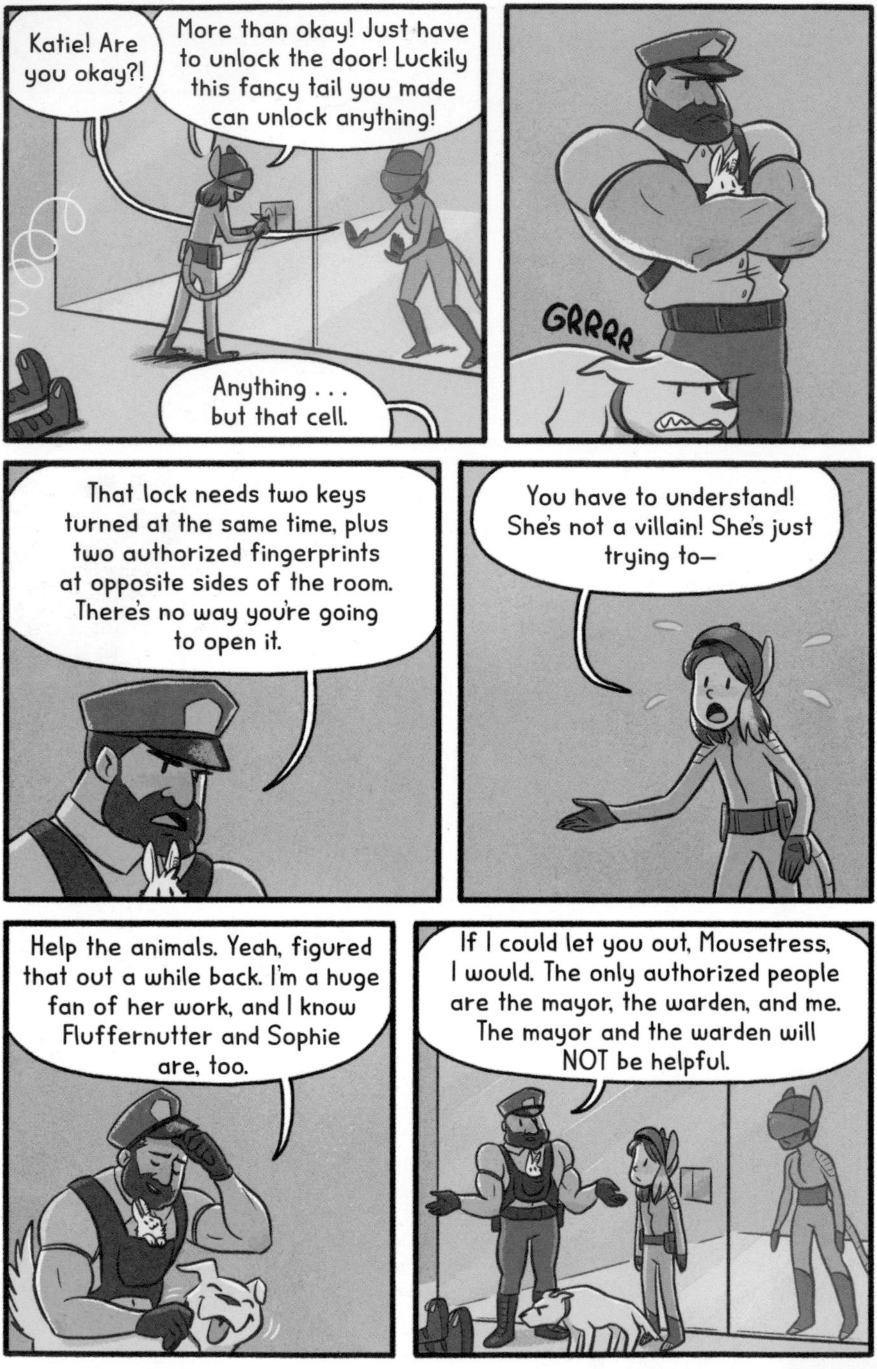
Katie! Are you okay?!
More than okay! Just have to unlock the door! Luckily this fancy tail you made can unlock anything!
Anything . . . but that cell.
GRRRR
That lock needs two keys turned at the same time, plus two authorized fingerprints at opposite sides of the room. There's no way you're going to open it.
You have to understand! She's not a villain! She's just trying to—
Help the animals. Yeah, figured that out a while back. I'm a huge fan of her work, and I know Fluffernutter and Sophie are, too.
If I could let you out, Mousetress, I would. The only authorized people are the mayor, the warden, and me. The mayor and the warden will NOT be helpful.

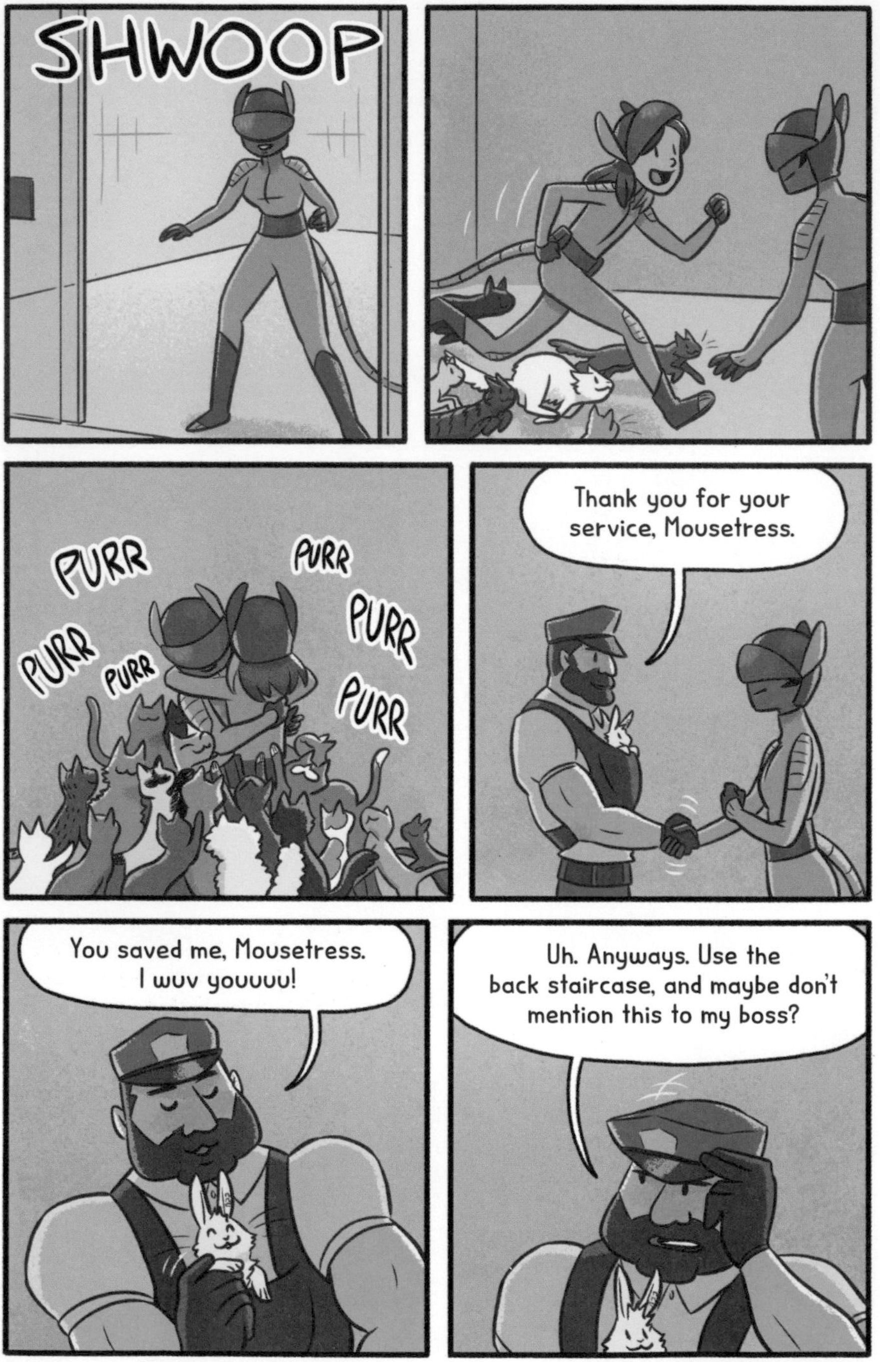
SHWOOP
PURR
PURR
PURR
PURR
PURR
PURR
Thank you for your service, Mousetress.
You saved me, Mousetress. I wuv youuuuu!
Uh. Anyways. Use the back staircase, and maybe don't mention this to my boss?

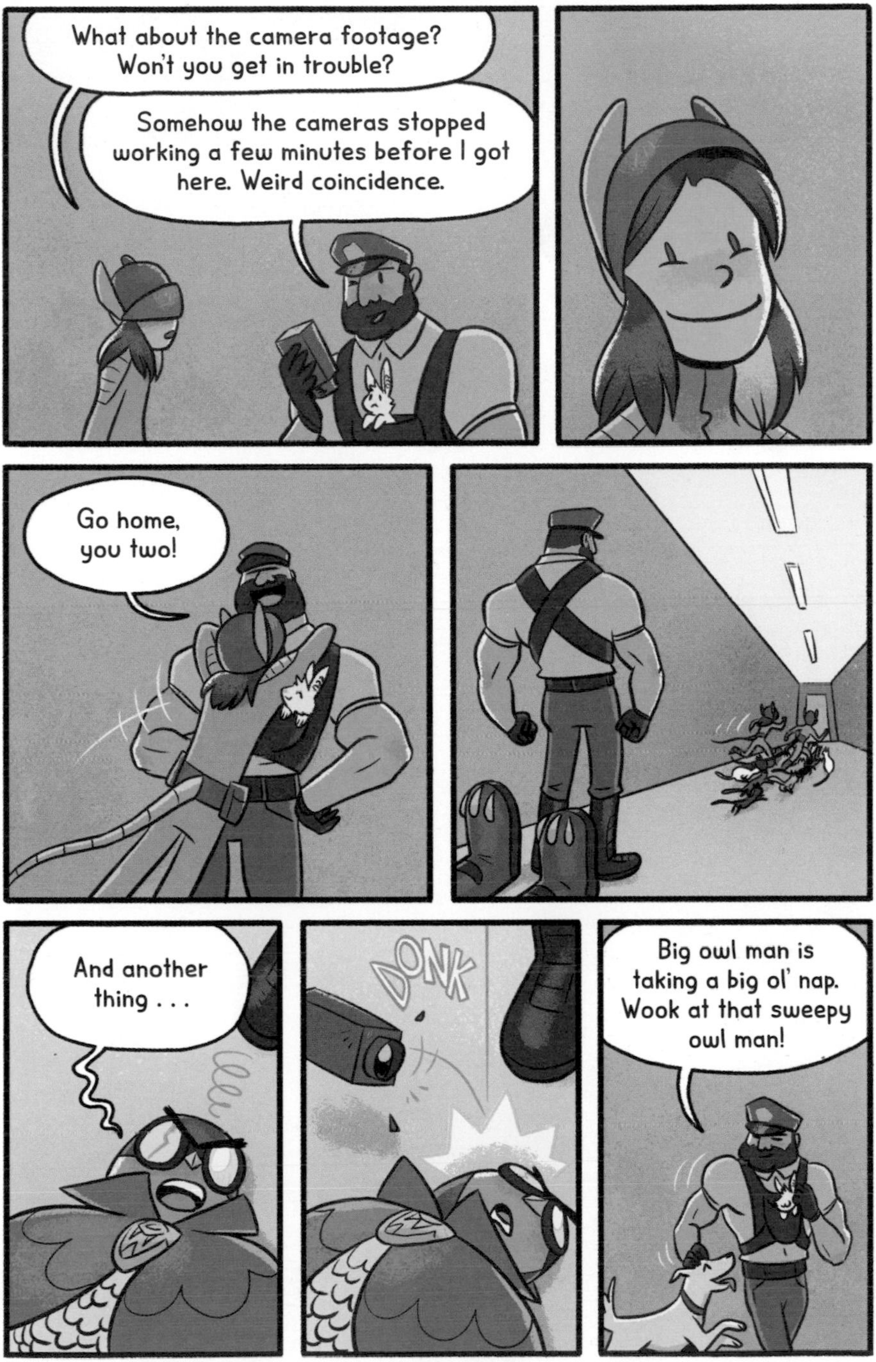
What about the camera footage? Won't you get in trouble?
Somehow the cameras stopped working a few minutes before I got here. Weird coincidence.
Go home, you two!
And another thing . . .
DONK
Big owl man is taking a big ol' nap. Wook at that sweepy owl man!

CHAPTER FIFTEEN

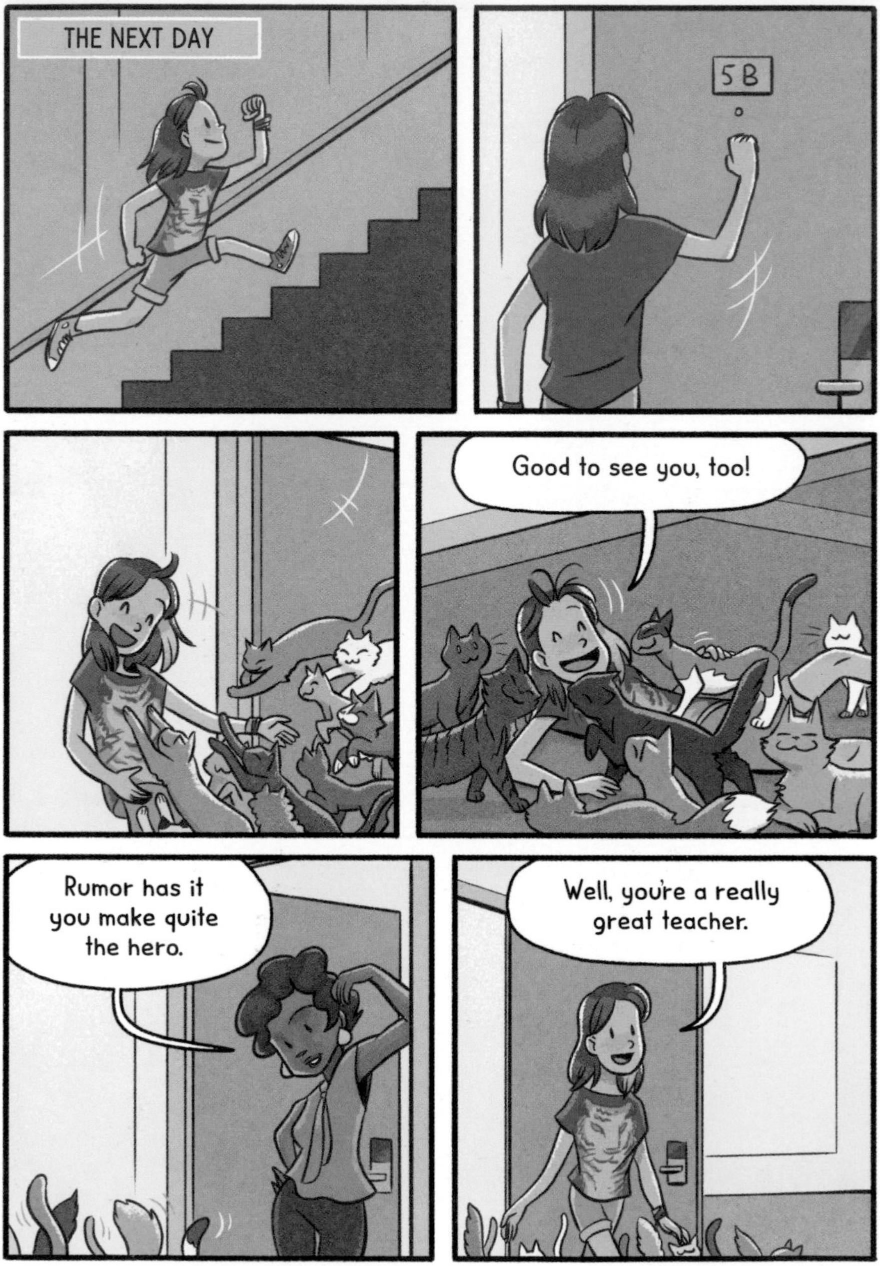
THE NEXT DAY
5B
Good to see you, too!
Rumor has it you make quite the hero.
Well, you're a really great teacher.

I'm going to take a break from my night shift for a while. Focus on ways I can fight injustice during the day.

Here, you earned this. It's the rest of the money for camp, and a few extra things I thought you might like.

My own Mousetress goggles?!

And this. Have you ever been to a Straight from the Farm?

You mean that super-fancy vegan place I definitely can't afford? Haha. Nope.

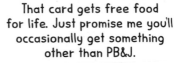

That card gets free food for life. Just promise me you'll occasionally get something other than PB&J.

How did . . . ?

I own them. All of them. And you now own part of them, too. Or at least you will when you turn eighteen.

New York City is lucky to have a hero like you, Katie. Have an amazing time at camp.

A FEW DAYS LATER

Are you SURE you packed everything?

Yes, I'm sure. Don't worry, Mom. I'll be fine!

I know, it's just this is all new for me!

Promise me you'll text.

Every hour.

You ready?

Oh! I almost forgot, a postcard from Bethany arrived earlier.

I'll read it later. Love you, Mom!

I'm gonna get you, Mousetress! Climb up MY building. I don't think so.

SNATCH!

Haunted! This building is haunted!

CAMP FUND

VET SCHOOL ~~CAMP~~ FUND

Katie! We had a superhero day, and the Eastern Screech showed up. He's really not that bad! Kinda cute, almost. AND he was with Stainless Steel! She was so cool, and I feel like I really knew her right away! I can't believe you aren't coming to camp this year. But next year for sure, right? Hope you aren't too bored!

Love ya —Beth

Katie Spera

5965 Ave D, Apt 3B

New York, NY 10009

The ~~End~~ Beginning

Don't miss the next
Katie the Catsitter,
Best Friends for Never—
coming in 2022!

MEET COLLEEN!

© Amber Harrison

COLLEEN AF (ANN FELICITY) VENABLE

grew up in Walden, New York. She's a lifelong comic book fan, maker, and roller-skater, and was the designer for multiple award-winning graphic novels at First Second Books. She is also the author of the Guinea Pig Pet Shop Private Eye series and numerous acclaimed picture books, and was longlisted for a National Book Award for her YA graphic novel debut, *Kiss Number 8*. Colleen's making her middle-grade debut with *Katie the Catsitter*. She lives in Brooklyn, New York, with her pet bunnies, Tuck and Cher, and occasionally starts national holidays. (True story!) Visit Colleen online at colleenaf.com and @colleenaf.

I would never have 217 cats. That's just silly. I'd keep it to under 50. Maybe 75. Plus 42 dogs, 77 rabbits, 91 fish, 86 guinea pigs, 33 sugar gliders, and a single capybara. (They're big. It would be ridiculous to have more than one!) I live in a tiny apartment in New York City with a fish that is 17 years old and two amazing bunnies—one is convinced he's a dog, and the other is convinced she's a cat. They come when I call their names and can open puzzle boxes to get treats. They're well on their way to genius minion status.

TUCK   CHER

The only thing I love more than comic books is helping animals. I'm an adoption counselor for a local animal rescue, and it's my dream to help animals all around the world by volunteering with scientists and animal hospitals.

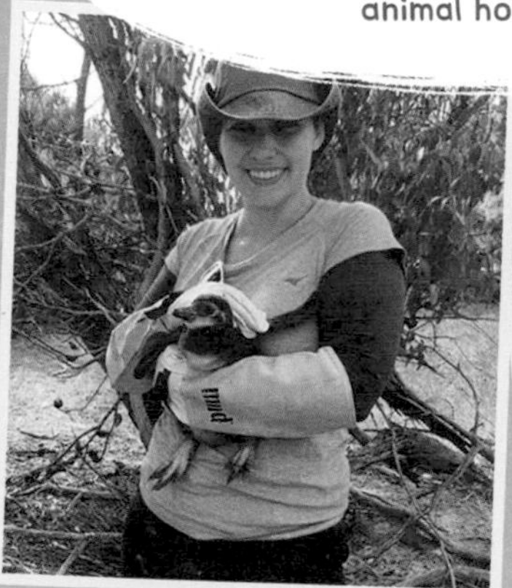

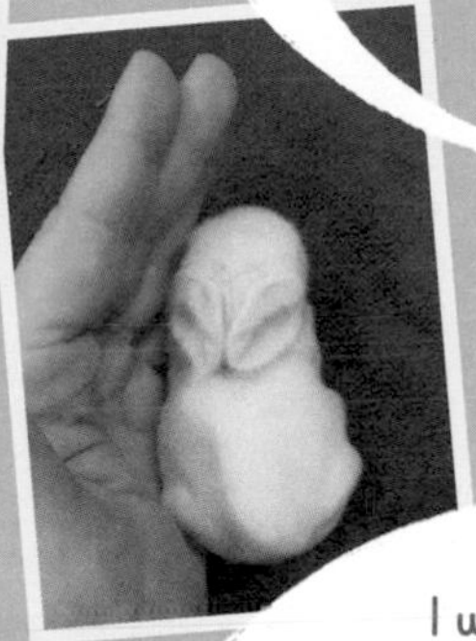

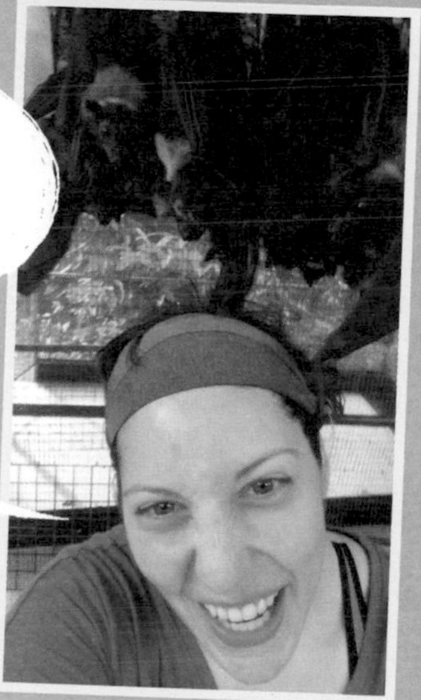

COLLEEN AT 12!

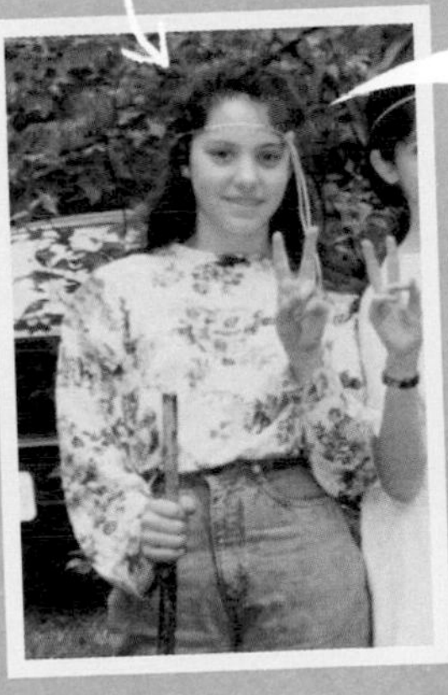

I wrote this book because I love animals, and because I wanted there to be more cool female superheroes, but I also wanted to tell a story about how hard it is when you and your best friend start to grow apart. Bethany (BETH?!) and Katie's friendship was inspired by my own childhood friendship breakups. Just remember, for every friend you drift away from, there are so many more out there who would be honored to have you in their life.

And who knows? Maybe those friends will even help you accidentally co-create a national holiday like mine did. Happy Pancake Day/Lumberjack Day (every September 26)!

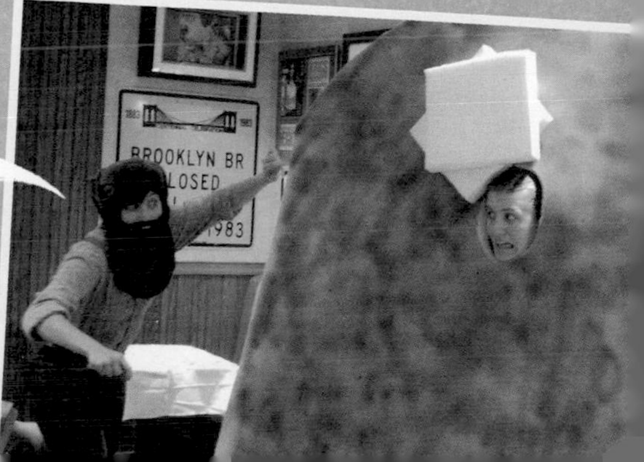
BROOKLYN BR
LOSED
1983

© Timothy Wade Jr.

MEET STEPH!

STEPHANIE YUE grew up in Atlanta, Beijing, and Hong Kong. She's a lifetime comics fan and martial artist (with a black belt in kung fu) and travels the world by motorbike. Stephanie is the illustrator of the Guinea Pig Pet Shop Private Eye series and several picture books and chapter books, and was the colorist of *Smile* by Raina Telgemeier. She is making her debut as a middle-grade graphic novel illustrator with *Katie the Catsitter*. Stephanie currently divides her time between Hong Kong, San Francisco, Lisbon, and Boston, where she's working on the second *Katie the Catsitter* graphic novel. Visit her online at stephanieyue.com and on Twitter at @quezzie.

I definitely wanted to be a superhero when I grew up. It's probably why I got into kung fu, and then Muay Thai, and now Brazilian jiujitsu. I still have time, right?

DEOSAI PLAINS, PAKISTAN

©Anita Munneke

CHICKEN, ALASKA

I love adventure and travel. When I learned to ride a motorcycle it opened up a whole new way to explore the world. I love riding and I want to ride the world! Can you tell the Mousetress's costume was inspired by motorcycle gear?

Katie the Catsitter was illustrated from Hong Kong, Chiang Mai, Boston, Barcelona, and Lisbon, among other places. My portable studio is small enough to fit into a backpack and set up almost anywhere. I even take it on the bike with me!

xpert

Lwax: Candlemaking

Lucy: Jet Pilot

Lyapa: Weapons Expert

Mackerel:
Semaphore Expert

Maxi:
Art Curator

Foot

Mariposa:
Photographic Memory

Marla: Karaoke

Marley:
Murder Podcast Expert

arlowe: Architect

Marmalade: Beekeeper

urka: Teacher

Me
Throw

Max: Charisma

Melrose:
Aircraft Engineer

Meowth von L
Fourth : Fitn

topheles:
anomer

Merlin: Fashion Designer

Mew Mew: Costumes

Miles: Laser Expert

Minnie: Public

les:
or

Miss Moon:
Video Game Expert

Moe: Crafts and Glue Guns

Moogle: Construction

Moritz: Counteratta

Mr. Aaron Purr Sir: Duels

Mr. Pickles: Jiujitsu

Mr. Smackers:
Legume Farmer

Mrs. Kensington:
Botanist

Neko:
Fire Safety Technician

Ness: Hand

Nick Furry: Comic Book Historian

Niko: Ankle Attacks

Niles: Podcaster

Noodle: Advertising

...n: ...anic

...tics Expert

Nugget: Astrophysicist

Obediah: Marine Biologist

Olav: Ceramics Master

Olive Loaf: Animato...

Movie Expert

P Jammies: Prototyping

Partly Cloudy: Meteorologist

Pavement: Physics Expert

Paw Simon: Splitting Up Tea...

Peake: ...cation Specialist

Pearl Mae: Biomedical Engineer

Peeve: Military Strategist

Penny: Movie Director

Pepper: Electrical Re...

...esco: Financial Analyst

Phil: Rock Climber

Pierogi: Textiles Expert

Pigeon: Baseball Expert

Pika... Muay T...

Pippen: Ergonomics Expert

Pixel: Organizing Groups

Poe: Lock Picking

Polly Jean: Cryptologist

Pop... Endod...

Potato: Yoga Instructor

Precious: Super Gas

Prince Namor: Librarian

Prince of Space: Helicopter Repair

Princ... For...

Professor Briar Rose:

Prune Juice: Choreographer

Puff: Smoke Bombs

Puss N Cahoots: Lawyer

Gl...

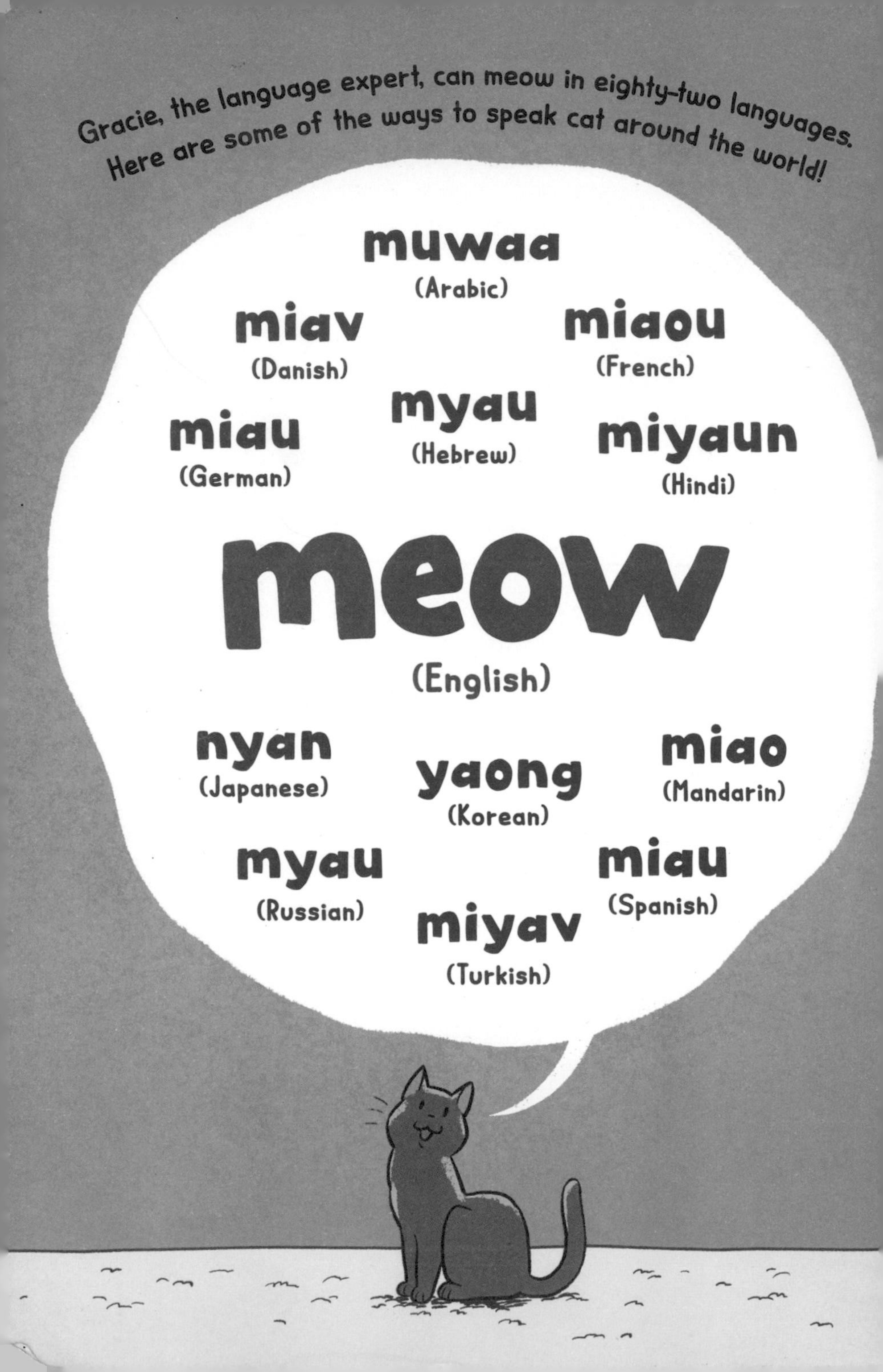
Gracie, the language expert, can meow in eighty-two languages.
Here are some of the ways to speak cat around the world!
muwaa
(Arabic)
miav
(Danish)
miaou
(French)
miau
(German)
myau
(Hebrew)
miyaun
(Hindi)
meow
(English)
nyan
(Japanese)
yaong
(Korean)
miao
(Mandarin)
myau
(Russian)
miyav
(Turkish)
miau
(Spanish)